NOV 1 5 2013

W9-CKH-292

Peak Season for Murder

A LEIGH GIRARD MYSTERY

PEAK SEASON FOR MURDER

GAIL LUKASIK

FIVE STAR
A part of Gale, Cengage Learning

GALE
CENGAGE Learning

Detroit • New York • San Francisco • New Haven, Conn • Waterville, Maine • London

LIBRARY OF CONGRESS CATALOGING-IN-PUBLICATION DATA

Lukasik, Gail.
   Peak season for murder : a Leigh Girard mystery / Gail Lukasik.
— First Edition.
      pages cm
      ISBN-13: 978-1-4328-2729-8 (hardcover)
      ISBN-10: 1-4328-2729-4 (hardcover)
   1. Actresses—Fiction. 2. Murder—Investigation—Fiction. I.
Title.
PS3612.U385P43 2013
813'.6—dc23   2013014019

First Edition. First Printing: September 2013
Find us on Facebook– https://www.facebook.com/FiveStarCengage
Visit our website– http://www.gale.cengage.com/fivestar/
Contact Five Star™ Publishing at FiveStar@cengage.com

Printed in Mexico
1 2 3 4 5 6 7 17 16 15 14 13

To Jerry for his unwavering encouragement

ACKNOWLEDGMENTS

Thanks to Scott Gimboe, author, crime scene investigator and traffic reconstructionist. A special thanks to Jean Weeg for being the best reader a writer could ask for.

PROLOGUE:
TWENTY-FOUR YEARS EARLIER

The woman stood over her sleeping lover, watching the gentle rise and fall of his naked chest, listening to his breathing. In her right hand, she held the pistol, the one he'd given her for protection.

"Mostly from me," he'd joked.

Small, compact with an ivory handle, she could cradle it in the palm of her hand, carry it in her jacket pocket, hide it in her purse, and no one would see it.

She raised her right hand and aimed the gun at his temple.

How easy it would be to kill him, she thought. *And no one could blame me.*

As if he sensed her, he took a deep breath and let out a soft snore, then settled back to sleep.

On his left hand she could see the glint of his gold wedding band.

"You knew what we were about. I never lied to you," had been his explanation.

Was I that weak, she wondered? *No, he was that strong.*

Suddenly, lightning flashed against the window, lighting up the room for a second as if illuminating her weakness—his perfect face.

She pulled back on the trigger thinking how easily she could destroy it.

A clap of thunder crashed overhead.

Had his eyes flickered open for a brief second? she thought, holding her breath. But it was just an illusion; he went on softly snoring, oblivious as always, wrapped up in his own dreams.

No, she told herself as she eased up on the trigger.

She took one more look at him before she crept out of the bedroom.

As she stood in the living room, she was tempted to take something, some reminder of this time. But she knew she had to make it look right.

She put the pistol back in the desk drawer.

Quietly, she opened the front door, locking it behind her, as if she had never been there, as if she had never let him into her life.

Her car was parked in front of the apartment building. But she walked past it into the dark, wet night, the rain soaking through her t-shirt and jeans. She congratulated herself on two things: her cleverness in staging her own disappearance and her restraint in not killing him—the man who had ruined her.

After all, she thought to herself, as she headed toward the highway, *murder was never part of the plan. I simply want to disappear forever.*

CHAPTER ONE:
PRESENT DAY, SUNDAY, JULY 9

"Didn't mean to scare you, Leigh," Ken Albright said, his eyes scanning the woods. "But I can't be too careful, now."

The *now* hung in the air like the blistering heat and humidity. Ken lowered the aluminum bat, and with it his powerful shoulders sagged. He seemed to shrink into himself as if something were eating him from the inside.

"Next time say something, before you jump out at me with that bat." I bent over and gathered up the spilled contents of my shoulder bag, my hands shaking.

He'd left me a cryptic voice message around six this morning that had propelled me to Marshalls Point, where he and Brownie Lawrence lived in a dilapidated shack off North Bay.

"Brownie's dead. I gotta show you where I found him. It isn't right. You come today." Ken's words were clipped with rage, and I was afraid for him. Only one person could keep Ken's anger in check, and that person was dead.

"Yeah, well, c'mon," Ken demanded. That was the closest to an apology I was going to get.

He walked past me, and I caught a peculiar odor of sweat and sweetness like musky rotting fruit. I knew hygiene was a problem for the men and that on warm days they bathed in the bay. Winters they hitchhiked to the YMCA in Fish Creek.

I dusted the sandy soil off my bag, slung it over my shoulder and hurried behind him. I'd been blundering down the path looking for the three stones that marked the hidden entrance to the men's shack when he'd jumped out at me holding the bat like a weapon.

As I walked, I studied his clothes: cut-off jeans and a white muscle shirt. White strings hung from the jeans, and his t-shirt was yellow around the armpits. The gnats and black flies, which kept circling me, didn't seem to bother him. A black fly was perched atop his shaved head.

When we came to the scarred pine, Ken moved left, pushed back a tangle of dense shrubs and then disappeared into the forest. He must have removed the three stones. No wonder I couldn't find the entrance.

I scurried after him, stumbling through the heavy green undergrowth and tall, ancient trees, wondering if it was fear or anger that had made him remove the stone markers.

We walked in silence until the woods opened into a clearing. There stood the ramshackle house the two formerly homeless men had built a few feet from the bay. Like their lives, the house had been pieced together from what was at hand— plywood, tarp and tin. How they lived there in the winter was beyond me. But I knew it was better than living on the streets.

"We got windows now." Ken pointed toward two windows on the front of the house, which caught the sun in a shimmering blaze. "Salvaged them from an abandoned barn down the road."

"How did you get them here?" I knew he was slowly leading up to what he wanted to show me, Brownie's last resting place, and I wasn't going to push him. Always touchy, Ken now gave off the vibe of a wounded animal.

"Carried them." Ken walked away abruptly, still toting the bat. When he came to a gnarled cherry tree beside the house, he stopped. "That's it. That's where I found him when I got back from my sister's yesterday."

I stared at the indentation in the grassy weeds—a yellowed outline where Brownie's body had lain exposed to the elements.

Dark pellets of dry and rotting fruit were scattered under the tree and crushed where Brownie's body had been. I took a step closer and was assaulted with the rank odor of decay. I put my hand over my nose. There was a clumped stain that looked like dried blood. Though it could be crushed fruit. It was hard to tell. And I wasn't about to poke around in it.

"I should have never gone to see my sister in Green Bay." Ken scratched the back of his neck. "I coulda gotten him to a doctor. Maybe saved him. He didn't deserve to lie out here like a dog for days, rotting. The damn insects had already gotten to him."

"Do you know how he died?" I asked, still staring at the clumped stain. "That looks like blood."

"How would I know? I wasn't here. Maybe Brownie hit his head or something. Maybe you could find out." It wasn't a question. "The police kept asking me stuff like were we getting along, where was I, that kind of thing. I wanted to bust them one. But I kept looking at Brownie lying there on his back with his eyes open, and I could hear him saying to me, 'Take it easy, Kenny. Just let it go. You know what happens when you get mad.' So I held my temper."

The last time I'd seen Brownie, he was strumming his beat-up guitar and singing, "Take It Easy," at the beach party celebrating the bequeath of land to him and Ken by the Door Conservancy. That was two weeks ago.

"I'll give Deputy Jorgensen a call and see what I can find out for you." I wondered if the police suspected foul play or were just being thorough.

Ken looked off toward the water. I could see the glisten of tears in his eyes. "But I fixed them cops all right."

I waited for him to tell me why he'd really called me from the marina in Sister Bay this morning.

"I cleaned things up before the cops got here. I didn't touch

Brownie's body, but I got rid of the empty wine bottles. I didn't want them to think that of Brownie."

"You found wine bottles?" Brownie had been a frail man, thin and lean-boned, who, until meeting Ken, had been a hopeless alcoholic living in shelters and on the streets of Green Bay. Ken's fall from grace had been sudden: a job loss, divorce, alcohol, drugs and a monumental temper that kept him from holding a job.

"Yeah, right next to him in the grass."

"Where are they? Did the police take them?"

He smiled slyly. "Nope. I busted those bottles up." He lifted the bat overhead and slammed it on the ground twice. "Then I pitched the damn pieces in the bay. I was so mad."

"You should have left the bottles, Ken," I reprimanded him, my eyes focused on the bat. His erratic behavior had me on edge.

"Those weren't Brownie's. He wouldn't have bought bottles of wine. Someone gave them to him."

It was obvious Ken was in complete denial about Brownie falling off the wagon. "That wasn't up to you to decide. Did you tell the police about them?"

"What did I just say? I don't want them thinking that about Brownie. Someone gave him that wine."

I wasn't about to point out that even if someone gave him the wine, no one made him drink it. But I was curious why he believed Brownie wouldn't have bought wine. "Why are you so sure he didn't buy the wine?"

He ran his hand back and forth over his shaved head. "You have to know alcoholics. They always favor one type of drink. If Brownie had started drinking again, it woulda been bourbon, Old Kentucky bourbon. That's what he liked to drink. And before I smashed the bottles up, I looked at the label. It was that sweet cherry wine they sell all over the peninsula."

"But maybe he bought the cherry wine because it was cheap and easy to get?" I countered.

He stepped close to me, forcing me to step back. "I'm telling you. I know Brownie. He'd a never bought them. We used to talk sometime about if we started drinking again what we'd buy. And he always said bourbon. There's no way he'd drink sweet cherry wine, I'm telling you."

I stepped around him and knelt down near the spot where Brownie had died, holding one hand over my nose to block the stench.

Carefully I ran my hands through the tall grass, making wider and wider circles. Just behind the tree something sharp pricked my finger. I drew back my hand. A small bead of blood swelled on my index finger. I sucked at the blood and leaned in closer to see what pricked my finger. Something red glinted in the grass. I picked it up. It was a dark red shard of glass.

"Were the bottles this color?" I held the shard out to him.

"Yeah, that looks like it." He reached for it but I pulled my hand back.

"Mind if I hang on to it?"

"Just get it outta here. I don't need reminders."

I turned over the shard, looking for any kind of mark. But there was none. "Do you remember the name on the label?" I asked, standing up.

He tugged at his shirt as if it were constricting him. "Bunch of cherries. That's all I remember. What's it matter now, any-way?"

"Probably doesn't," I slipped the shard into my pants' pocket.

"Forget about those damn wine bottles. You gotta do something for me and Brownie. You gotta find Brownie's family. 'Cause I want them to know how he turned his life around. There ought to be an article in it for you."

"Okay, what can you tell me about them?" Even as I asked

the question, I knew I was stepping into forbidden territory. While Jake Stevens, the *Door County Gazette* editor, and I had been bedmates, he'd indulged my forays into investigative reporting, finding them oddly stimulating. Now he found them irritating and counterproductive, or maybe it was me he found irritating and counterproductive.

"Get the story, that's it," he'd barked at me last week. Of course, that was like waving a red flag in front of a bull as far as I was concerned.

"He never talked about them except to say that they were dead to him. And now he's dead." He moved the bat off his shoulder and let it hang by his side.

"And he never said anything else?"

Ken hunched his broad shoulders and looked away. He was holding something back. "C'mon, Ken. I'll need something to go on if you want me to find his family."

He turned away and walked toward the house. I followed him.

The house smelled of dampness and old fires from the Franklin stove in the corner of the one-room dwelling. There were two sleeping bags on either side of the room, one table and two mismatched chairs in the middle. Along the walls were shelves with dishes, books and clothes on them. And leaning against one of the cots was Brownie's guitar.

An image of Brownie putting his hand over his mouth when he smiled, as if he were protecting you from his toothless state, sprung to mind.

"In that article about us getting the land, you make sure you say we're addressless, not homeless," Brownie had insisted.

I shook my head, not wanting to feel the sadness rushing in. Of the two men, Brownie was the more likeable, even putting Ken's erratic rage aside. From the beginning, I'd felt a kinship with Brownie, nothing I could put my finger on, just that feeling you get when you click with someone. Under different circumstances we might have been friends.

"Sit down," Ken demanded, resting the bat against his chair. Then he retrieved a metal box from a high shelf, put it on the table and opened it.

"Here, these were Brownie's." He handed me two silver dog tags. There was something sticky on the edges of both tags. "Since now you got his name, you can find his people."

I looked down at the beat-up tags. "Browning, Lawrence, M., social security number, AB positive, Roman Catholic." It was a start.

All Brownie would tell me was his age, 66, that he'd been on the streets a long time, and that he was a vet. Doing the math, I figured out he was a Vietnam vet. Probably the war had shattered his life. Now the dented dog tags proved I'd been right on all counts.

"Lawrence Browning," I repeated. "Why'd he switch his first and last name?"

"What difference does it make?" Ken said angrily, his face a nasty shade of red. Up close I noticed his brown goatee was shaggy and a faint outline of hair had sprouted on his normally shaved head.

"Anything else?" I coaxed, keeping my irritation in check. Ken's street wariness was like a wall that kept him safe, but from good intentions as well as bad. He'd lost all ability to detect the difference.

He shook his head no, but I sensed he was lying.

"Okay," I said, getting up to leave. "I'll see what I can find out." I shoved the dog tags in my bag and walked outside, pausing to look at the water glittering in the morning sun, alive with so much life.

"I guess I'm going to have to finish it myself." Ken gestured toward the half-finished pier.

"You can do it," I said, hoping he caught my meaning.

"Do you think them rich people are going to kick me off the land, now that Brownie's gone? I got nowhere else to go."

"The homeowners' association doesn't own your land, the conservancy does. But it couldn't hurt to call Mike Roberts at the conservancy and make sure."

Ken might have reason to be worried. The land had been bequeathed to both Brownie and him by the Door County Conservancy in perpetuity. With Brownie's death, maybe the homeowners' association could force Ken off the land. But why would they? They hadn't objected to the original bequest. The majority of the pricey exclusive homes were vacant most of the year, except for the occasional week or two in July, peak season in Door County.

"If only Brownie hadn't died." Ken shook his head sadly. "Everything was going so good."

Back at the truck, I sat for a moment, looking at the shard of red glass, wondering if Ken was right. Had someone bought Brownie the wine? Highly unlikely, I concluded. Finally, I put the glass shard in the cup holder.

As I was turning the truck around, I heard Ken shout at me to stop.

He came up to my window and stood there with his burly arms crossed over his chest, "I guess it's okay since he's dead." He was breathing hard from running. "Brownie once told me his family was from around here."

"Door County?" I asked.

"I don't know," he snapped at me. " 'Around here,' that's all he said."

"Nothing else?" I bit my lower lip in frustration.

"What did I just say?"

Just then an expensive metallic blue foreign sports car approached the gated entry to the Marshalls Point Estates. The driver, a silver-haired woman with a heavily made-up face and disapproving scowl, stopped and stared at us.

When she didn't key in her entry code and continued to stare, Ken shouted, "Why don't you take a picture, it'll last longer, you old hag."

She huffed, keyed in her code and drove through the gate, sending up an angry cloud of gravel and dirt.

"You have to control yourself, Ken," I said calmly, though I wanted to scream at him. "That woman could report you to the homeowners' association."

He stepped back from the truck, putting his hands on his hips. "Let her report me."

"Didn't you say you're worried they might kick you off your land?"

"She was giving me a dirty look. And I don't like that."

"Listen, if you want me to find Brownie's family, you're going to have to do something for me." It was the only bargaining chip I had.

"Like what?"

"Like get control of your temper."

"You just find Brownie's family. I'm not promising anything."

Driving west on Route ZZ toward Highway 42, I scanned the burnt fields. Corn drooped, wild grass yellowed and dust devils swirled in the vacant breeze. The land looked as spent as I felt. My meeting with Ken had drained me, and the day had just begun.

I pondered Ken's revelation that Brownie's family was from around here. What did *around here* mean? Door County? Green Bay? Northern Wisconsin? And were his family all dead as Brownie claimed, or was he saying as far as he was concerned they were dead? If some of his family were still "around here," wouldn't they have tried to find him, especially if they'd seen the human-interest article in the *Gazette* I'd written about the men's bequest from the conservancy?

His dog tags gave his name as Lawrence Browning. Why did he flip his first and last name? If I were going to erase my identity, I'd totally change my name, not flip the first and last name. Was that his way of staying in touch with his former self? Maybe his appearance after years of alcohol abuse made him unrecognizable and flipping his name had scrambled his identity enough to keep him hidden. Or maybe he was dead to them as well.

The rocky shoals of family, I mused bitterly, thinking about my father and our estrangement. How after my mother's death and my moving to Door County, he'd cut me out of his life. Another female who'd let him down.

I picked up the red shard, disappointment rising in me again. Brownie Lawrence had fallen off the wagon and his years of chronic substance abuse had finally caught up with him, more than likely causing or contributing to his death. Ken's staunch conviction that someone had bought that wine for him was sad and pathetic. He couldn't allow himself to believe that Brownie had started drinking again. Because if he did, then what hope was there for him?

Ken's words of protest echoed in my mind. "If Brownie had started drinking again, it woulda been bourbon."

Okay, enough, I cautioned myself, putting the shard back in the cup holder.

As I neared Highway 42, I groaned aloud. Cars were lined up as far back as Dara's Upscale Resale Shop. Peak season was in full bloom, and with it came crowded roads, long waits at restaurants and hordes of tourists.

My fingers tapping the steering wheel, I pulled up behind a massive black SUV with four mountain bikes strapped to the roof like deer carcasses. It was 10:20 and I had forty minutes to drive to the Bayside Theater in Fish Creek. My heart fluttered, thinking about my eleven o'clock interview with Nate Ryan, Hollywood's infamous bad boy.

Rather than fret, I flipped open my notebook and started going over my interview questions. Should I start with his drug abuse, or the downward spiral of his film career, or his reputation with women? I figured he'd appreciate my gonzo approach. He'd probably had his share of journalists kissing up to him. Besides, I stank at kissing up.

The only caveat his publicist Nicki Baker had given me was no questions about his ex-wife Nina Cass, the theater's current owner/actress. I could live with that. Though their marriage had ended years ago, I guess he was still sensitive about the rumors he'd physically abused her.

The Nate Ryan interview would give my feature article on the Bayside Theater—America's oldest professional residential summer theater—the cache it needed. Jake felt the article had legs, and he'd suggested I pitch it to the *Chicago Reporter* on spec.

Suddenly a horn blast startled me. I looked up, glaring at the impatient out-of-state driver behind me. I waited a minute or two before inching ever so slowly forward, letting him know he couldn't intimidate me. Tourists. Can't live with them, can't live without them.

Once on 42, I took the first left at the top of the hill onto Highway 57, avoiding the heavy tourist traffic. As I pushed down on the gas pedal, the wine shard started to rattle in the cup holder like a nagging thought. I grabbed it and shoved it in my bag.

CHAPTER TWO

I stood outside Nate Ryan's upstairs apartment door fuming. It was 11:35 a.m. and Nate wasn't here. Beads of sweat like little bubbles of anger made their slow tedious way down my face, legs and arms, snaking beneath my clothes. And a headache was building behind my eyes like an approaching storm.

Out of frustration, I stabbed at the doorbell again, listened to it echo through the apartment, then knocked on the red wooden door, this time with the force of my anger. Nothing. Where was he? Had he forgotten about the interview? *Well, he is* Nate Ryan, I told myself. Then countered with, *so what?*

I dug out my cell phone and called his publicist Nicki Baker, not sure if I could keep my temper in check. After my unsettling encounter with Ken, I was looking to lash out at someone—not my best trait, I admit. But very satisfying sometimes.

As I listened to Nicki's phone ring and ring, I thought, at least I'd had the forethought to schedule my interview with ballerina-turned-actress Gwen Shaw at one p.m. But there'd be no time to dash home, let Salinger, my Shetland sheepdog, out and grab a quick bite to eat.

The call went to voice mail and Nicki's perky voice said, "Nicki Baker. Leave a message." I closed the phone and debated whether to take off. After all, I'd waited thirty-five minutes. But then again, this interview was too important. So what if my head was pounding and my stomach grumbling. He had until noon, and then I was outta here.

22

My phone jangled and without looking I answered, thinking it was Nicki.

"I thought you were going to call me back." Tom's familiar accusatory tone brought me up short.

"I'm in the middle of something right now." My estranged husband, Tom Girard, was the last person I wanted to talk to right now.

"Did you get me a ticket or not, Leigh?"

After over a year of no communication, Tom had phoned me last night from Sturgeon Bay, saying he needed to see me in person, today.

I'd asked him if anyone had died.

When he'd said no rather brusquely, I told him I was busy. Though I was curious to know why he was here, I didn't want to give him the satisfaction of my interest.

"Look, I came all this way." His annoyed impatience with me was all too familiar.

He wasn't getting off that easily. "I've got interviews all afternoon and then I'm seeing a play at the Bayside Theater. How about tomorrow morning?"

"I've been calling you all week and you've ignored my calls."

I had been ignoring his calls. I was going to call him back when I was good and ready. Whenever that was.

He'd insisted on my getting him a ticket. In the sixteen years of our marriage, I could count on one hand the plays we'd attended together and all of them under duress.

"Yes, I got you a ticket," I answered petulantly. "Be at the box office around seven forty-five."

"I don't know why you have to make everything so difficult," he chided.

Without replying, I shut the phone. His remark hit me hard, reminding me why I'd left him. My getting cancer had made things so difficult for him.

Feeling reckless, I walked back to Nate Ryan's door and tried the doorknob, expecting resistance. To my surprise, it turned. I kept my hand on the doorknob and looked around. The four-unit apartment was secluded in a grouping of tall pine trees. No one would see me. I inched the door open and was instantly hit with a familiar scent, the sweet odor of marijuana.

All the blinds were shut, but in the gloom I saw a large sofa, two side chairs, a coffee table holding two goblets and a wine bottle. Clothes were strewn about the place. Was that a bra flung over a chair?

Wow, I thought, sniffing to make sure of what I smelled. Yup, that was marijuana. So much for Nate's rehab. Just as I was about to step inside, I heard footsteps coming up the bark chip path. Quickly I shut the door and jumped back onto the wooden walkway, colliding with a pitchfork. As I grabbed for it, it went tumbling over the railing.

"Hey," someone shouted from below. I peered over the railing and saw Nate Ryan rubbing the side of his head and looking up at me.

"Sorry," I managed to say without laughing. *Good start,* Leigh, *injure the famous movie star.*

He picked up the pitchfork and bounded up the stairs. He was dressed in a black V-neck t-shirt, faded blue jeans and black sneakers, no socks. As he walked toward me, I was struck by his rugged handsomeness and his lack of height. The handsomeness wasn't a surprise; his shortness was.

"Hope you're not a critic," he smiled, placing the pitchfork next to the door.

"Leigh Girard, I'm the reporter for the *Door County Gazette.* Nicki Baker set up our interview for eleven." My words came out too harshly in my effort not to appear star struck, which I clearly was. "I didn't hurt you, did I?" I added by way of an apology.

"Just a flesh wound," he joked. "Usually women wait until after they get to know me before they hurl things at me."

He pushed open the door and gestured me inside. "Your photo doesn't do you justice."

I could feel his eyes roving over my body as I walked past him into the living room, my nose prickling with that sweet marijuana scent. "Thank you. Nor does yours." I felt like I was in high school flirting with the popular boy. *Get a grip, Leigh,* I told myself, heading for the sofa, a tweedy blend of blues and browns that would hide all sweat stains I might leave behind.

He shut the door and started opening windows. "Stuffy in here."

"Yeah, I noticed that." I said, taking in the motel-like atmosphere of the messy room. Beside the tweedy sofa, there were two blue club chairs draped with clothes, an oval coffee table with a glass top, wall-to-wall brown looped carpet, a small, dated TV, and several small side tables, also glass-topped. On the wall opposite the sofa was a Door County painting of a barn lost in soft shades of grays and greens, a bluebird in the foreground. If it wasn't titled *Summer's End,* it should have been.

"Want something to drink?" He picked up the two dirty goblets and the wine bottle from the table. I could see red wine dregs on the bottom of both goblets.

"Water's fine," I said.

He walked around the breakfast bar into the small kitchen, put the two goblets in the sink, and returned with two glasses of tap water. "I'm out of bottled water," he apologized, handing me a glass. He eased himself down next to me, a little too close for my comfort.

"So let's get to it," he said, leaning toward me.

This close, I noticed crinkling around the corners of his mouth and eyes, a slight looseness of his skin, some gray hairs near his temples. At forty-nine and after years of drug abuse, he teetered on the edge of his handsomeness—still there in the symmetry of his face, his bone structure, his charisma; but I could see in a few more years where the lines would set and deepen, the skin sag, the hair lose its blondish luster, and he'd be just another washed-up, over-the-hill actor paying character parts. Even plastic surgery could only do so much; and then there were the younger actors waiting in the wings for their chance at stardom.

I opened my notebook, clicked my pen and leaned away from him, determined not to be swayed. That seemed to amuse him. He tilted his head and focused *that* smile on me, the one he used in his much-publicized mug shot. I remember thinking when I saw it, "Does this guy ever take a bad photo?"

"Aren't you going to ask about the drugs?" He brushed his reddish blond hair off his forehead, a boyish gesture, rampant with vulnerability.

"The drugs?" For a moment, I thought he meant the marijuana I'd smelled. "Oh, I was saving that for last." I smiled back. Though the drugs were one of the opening questions, I didn't want him to know that.

"When all my defenses are down?"

"Does that ever happen?"

He stared at me with those lake blue eyes, that when I'd seen him in his first film, *Tiger Mountain,* I thought were like an early-morning summer sky full of promise.

"More than you think." His legs were crossed and his one foot began bouncing up and down.

"Okay, tell me about the drugs." That he wanted to talk about the drugs first meant he had an agenda. I was curious to see what that agenda was.

"Let's put it this way. Success, money, it all happened too fast, and I couldn't handle it. Look, I went from doing summer stock like the Bayside Theater, a few TV commercials, and suddenly I'm box office. I was young and stupid. But I paid for my sins, literally. What I spent on cocaine . . ." He shook his head. "I don't even know what I spent on cocaine, Vicodin, heroin. I was an equal opportunity user. But I'm a changed man." He clinked his glass against mine, lifted it in a toast and took a sip. "Live fast and die young was my motto."

Ryan wasn't telling me anything I didn't already know. I'd read a recent interview he did for some obscure magazine in which he'd said the exact same thing. Ryan was trying to make a comeback, and the Bayside Theater was his first step on his road back.

"You know, in my bad-boy days, right now I'd be thinking of ways to seduce you. You're my type: pretty, smart and resistant. If you lean much farther away you'll fall off the couch."

A flash of heat shot up my spine to my face as I glanced away, my eyes falling on the black lacy bra thrown over the chair.

"Sorry, that was rude. See? I am trying to reform." He took another sip of water. "No matter what glass I put it in, this stuff tastes like shit."

I could feel myself curve toward him as if he were a magnetic field and I were the magnet. He wore his beauty like a handicap, something to be overcome. Beauty and vulnerability were a dangerous combination. The beauty I could resist; his vulnerability was proving difficult. I kept wanting to soothe him—for what, I couldn't imagine.

He put the glass down. "So what other dirty little secrets can we talk about?"

"Well, actually I wanted to know how you feel about coming back to the Bayside Theater, where you got your start."

"Purely selfish on my part. I need to prove that I can work again, that I'm bankable, as Nicki would say when she's delivering one of her lectures about behaving myself. So when Nina contacted me about coming back for the sixty-fifth anniversary celebration, I decided what the hell. I told her, I'd come back if they did *The Merchant of Venice* and I played Shylock."

That was the first I'd heard that Ryan had selected the play. Usually the artistic director and the executive producer selected the plays. Alex Webber was the theater's artistic director and co-owner. The other co-owner was Nina Cass, Ryan's ex-wife.

"Were they planning on performing *The Merchant of Venice*?"

"What do you think? Nothing like a pound of flesh to inspire summer theater-goers." Again *that* smile. "But I also came back because of Nina. You know about the campaign to raise money to rebuild the theater."

I shook my head yes. The theater had launched a major funding campaign in May.

"Well, she's desperate to raise money for the rebuilding. She told me they're charging some ridiculous amount for my opening night performance. It's the least I could do after what I put her through in our marriage. But I never hit her. I don't care what you read. I don't hit women."

He was suddenly agitated, slightly flushed. He was so adamant, I doubted him.

"I saw that you performed with another Bayside Theater alumni, Julian Finch, who's cast as Antonio in *The Merchant of Venice*." I'd combed through the fifthieth anniversary program for background information about the theater. The program gave a listing of plays and cast members spanning those first fifty years. Ryan and Finch's paths crossed twenty-five years ago in two BT productions, *Twelfth Night* and *A Streetcar Named Desire*.

"Great guy, great stage actor. I learned a lot from him."

That was amazingly uninformative.

"Like what?" I pursued, sensing his reticence.

He paused for a moment. "I learned how not to act. Sometimes you have to just read the lines, no motivation, no killing your parents to feel something. Just say the damn lines and they'll take over for you. For example, 'If you cut me, do I not bleed?' See how the words do the job. I don't have to shout. It's all there in the words. And if I use the same tone and intonation and say, 'Leigh, you're the most fascinating woman I've met in a long while.' You see how I didn't have to act?"

He was right; the words had taken over. I shifted in my seat, trying not to lean back and show how his words did affect me.

"So how's it been working with Nina after all your past history?" I'd asked the taboo question, but Ryan had opened the door.

He picked up his water glass and drank deeply, then made a face. "I can't drink this." He jumped up from the sofa and went to the kitchen. I heard the refrigerator door open, and then a startled "Shit!"

"Everything okay?" I called from the living room.

"That sick perv," Ryan answered, laughing nervously.

Curious, I got up and walked around the sofa to the kitchen area. Nate was staring into the refrigerator, shaking his head, one hand on his hip.

Peering over his shoulder, I saw what looked like a dead chicken resting on a silver platter splattered with thick red blood.

Before I could say anything, he picked it up by its head and held it in front of my face. It was a fake. I could smell the ketchup dripping from its rubbery chicken body.

"I gotta start locking my door." He tossed the chicken into the trash. A spray of ketchup hit the wall before it thudded into the can.

"Who's the sick perv?"

"Finch, who else?" he blurted out.

"Why would he do that?"

"Another of his sick practical jokes," Nate explained.

I didn't see the humor in it, especially the faux blood. "Why a bloody chicken? Seems like a weird choice for a practical joke."

"He probably found it in the prop box. Thought it would be funny. When we did *Streetcar Named Desire* we used to pull stupid pranks on each other all the time." He laughed. "Listen, I gotta grab something to eat before rehearsal."

"I still have some questions," I protested. I was planning on confronting him about the marijuana and the empty wine glasses. I didn't expect him to admit to falling off the wagon, but I wanted to hear what story he'd concoct. "How about we talk after rehearsal tomorrow? I'll be sitting in."

He didn't seem to hear me as he walked toward the door, his mind clearly somewhere else.

"Mind if I take some photos for the article?"

"Sure, but make it quick."

I snapped several digital photos, thinking about how Ryan didn't have a bad angle and how he knew it.

"Then we can finish the interview after rehearsal tomorrow?" I pushed, repeating my request.

"Okay," he said, his face shifting from relaxed to distracted. He escorted me to the door and shook my hand. "Do you know someplace I can get a massage?" he asked. "My back's been giving me problems again. But it has to be someone discreet who isn't going to get all stupid about this." He stretched from side to side to emphasize his request.

"Lydia Crane just opened The Crystal Door Spa. She's a friend of mine." Over the winter Lydia had expanded her New Age shop in Fish Creek to include yoga classes and massages. I wasn't even aware she'd become a masseuse until I saw her ad in the *Door County Gazette*. When I questioned why she hadn't told me she was training to be a masseuse, she'd said, "I thought

I had." That was so Lydia. She probably didn't want to say anything in case she didn't finish her training.

She'd be starstruck but too self-possessed to show it. I wrote down Lydia's name, the spa's address and phone number and tore the page out of my notebook. "Tell her I sent you."

"Thanks, I'll give this to Nicki to handle."

"See you at rehearsal tomorrow then," I said as a reminder. He was so agitated and distracted, he didn't even pose when I took a last photo of him standing outside next to the pitchfork, a vacant look on his near perfect face. Why was I feeling the interview wasn't going to happen?

"Nate, one more thing." I decided it was now or never. "Have you relapsed?"

He feigned shock, so I pushed it. "That was marijuana I smelled in your apartment, right? And the empty glasses; looked like red wine."

Now his eyes were back on me with the full force of that famous blue focus. "Like I said, I gotta start locking my door."

As I walked away from the building, I glanced back at Ryan's apartment. The devil's pitchfork tilted precariously beside the door like an omen.

CHAPTER THREE

Gwen Shaw, ballerina turned actress, leaned forward into that dancer posture that seemed to define her—precise, beautiful, flexible yet strong. "One surprising thing about me?" she mused. "I don't think I've ever been asked that question."

We were seated on the patio deck behind the Blue Stone Bistro in Fish Creek where she'd insisted we meet. "I need a break from communal living," she'd explained when she'd phoned me at the *Gazette* to change the meeting place for our interview.

Though it was hot as Hades on the patio deck, it was worth the sweltering inconvenience. The view of Fish Creek's harbor, awash in sailboats and endless blue, was a stunner.

Gwen laughed nervously. "I'm deathly afraid of bats. Have been since I was a kid. Totally irrational, I know, but there it is."

"And you took the acting job with the Bayside Theater anyway?" I joked.

"When Nate invited me to audition for the BT, he conveniently left out the part about bats buzzing around on stage during performances." She circled her hand around her head several times. "I'm terrified one of those beady-eyed monsters is going to land on me. I swear every night there's more of them. Probably just my actor's vivid imagination." She forked the last remnants of her lemon cheesecake and slid it into her mouth. "This cheesecake is to die for."

"The bats go with the territory," I said. Because the theater was a large tented pavilion open to the night, bats were a part of performing there.

"I know that now. My first performance one dive-bombed me. I thought I was going to have a frickin' heart attack. It's not easy staying in character when you have bats dive-bombing you."

I wasn't sure if she was exaggerating the bat problem. But talking about them had raised her blood pressure. Her neck and face were flushed; or maybe it was the unrelenting heat.

"Are you coming to tonight's performance?" Gwen asked.

"As a matter of fact, I am." Tonight would be my first time attending a BT performance.

"You'll see that I wear a hat the entire time I'm on stage. Guess whose idea that was? I'm not taking any chances one of those gross things gets tangled in my hair." She tousled her auburn hair vigorously, as if a bat were lodged in it.

"As far as I know, and I've done a lot of research on the Bay-side Theater, a bat has never attacked an actor." I, too, was deathly afraid of bats, and Gwen's fear was pumping up my own. Maybe I'd wear a hat tonight as well.

"There's always a first time." She patted my hand as if we were best friends. "Any other questions for me before I take off?"

Gwen had been the perfect interviewee: open, friendly and honest. I had a slew of good quotes for the article, so I should have said no. But Nate's reaction to the fake chicken prank was still on my mind. "Just one more. It's about Nate Ryan."

"Isn't it always about Nate?" She smiled, but it didn't reach her eyes. "Go ahead. I should be used to it by now. But in case it's about our relationship, it's strictly professional. We share the same publicist and that's all. I'm a happily married woman with a five-year-old little girl who I'm missing terribly." She held up her left hand, wiggling her fingers to show me her gold wedding band and stunningly large diamond engagement ring.

Why was she being defensive? Did the lady protest too much? "Actually I should have said it's about Nate and Julian. Have they been pulling pranks on each other?"

She visibly relaxed. "Pranks? Are you serious?"

Now I felt foolish for asking. "Well, during my interview with Nate he found this fake chicken covered in ketchup in his fridge. He claimed Julian put it there as a prank. I just thought it was odd."

Gwen pushed her drink away as if it offended her, and then gave me an appraising stare before answering. "I haven't seen any pranks. But there's been a weird vibe since Nate arrived. I can't put my finger on it." She took in a deep breath, then let it out. "Or maybe I'm just freaked out by the bats. So are we done?" She'd said it nicely, but her tone had changed from friendly to wary.

"If I have any follow-up questions, how can I contact you? Barbara Henry wouldn't give me any of the actors' cell numbers." Barbara Henry, the BT's overly protective public relations director, had arranged all the cast member interviews except Nate Ryan's, claiming she was being helpful.

Gwen turned my notebook toward her, took my pen and wrote something down. "My cell number. Feel free to call me."

"Thanks," I said.

"By the way, am I your last interview?" she asked.

The question was freighted with some hidden meaning. I wasn't sure what she really was asking. Was this interview going to end strangely, like Nate's? Did she think being last reflected a pecking order? Was I dealing with an especially insecure actor? With her acting pedigree, which included touring nationally with the revival of *West Side Story*, I'd be surprised.

"Next to the last. But I had nothing to do with the scheduling. That was all Barbara Henry." I jiggled my pen between my two fingers.

"Who's the last one?" Though she was smiling, her green eyes were sharp.

"Harper Kennedy, Tuesday morning." Harper Kennedy was the new kid on the block. Bayside Theater was her first professional acting gig, except for a few minor roles in Chicago theater productions.

"Interesting," she said, considering that for a moment. Then she grabbed her oversized tooled leather handbag and started to get up before changing her mind, and plopped back down. "I know Alex said we have to play nice. But I should warn you, don't be taken in by Harper Kennedy's innocent act. Underneath all that fluffy blond hair, she's a barracuda. And I should know. I used to be her before I became rich and famous." The last part was meant to be funny but came out bitter.

"According to Barbara Henry, you're all one big, happy family," I countered. When I asked Barbara how actors living and working together all summer got along, she'd replied in a monotone, "We're one big, happy family. Everyone gets along." I'd put two exes by her quote, my shorthand for bullshit. So I wasn't surprised by Gwen's remarks about Harper.

"What do you expect her to say? She's the PR director. C'mon, a bunch of actors living together, there's bound to be tension."

Where was this sudden vitriol coming from? The other cast members I interviewed had nothing but good things to say about their experience with the BT. Gwen was the first one to break ranks and admit that the BT's residential living wasn't perfect.

"Is there something else going on I should know about?"

She hugged her handbag to her chest as if it were a shield. "No, nothing. Forget I said that about Harper. It was unkind. Rehearsals aren't going well. And it doesn't help that Harper's breathing down my neck. She's my understudy for *The Merchant of Venice.* You know, I'm playing Portia. Just forget I said anything at all, okay?" This time she stood and slung her large bag over her shoulder.

I got up and extended my hand. "Thanks for the interview. And break a leg tonight."

We shook hands and she said, "You know, I never did like that saying."

As I sat back down, I stared out at the harbor, watching a motorboat skim the water under the faded blue sky, I wondered what Gwen Shaw was afraid to tell me and why she'd blurted out that warning about Harper Kennedy. In my limited experience, most actors chose their words carefully, always conscious of appearances. After all, words were part of their craft. From the interviews I'd done, I realized that most of the time I didn't know if they were acting or being genuine. Gwen seemed honest. What was really behind her outburst? Bad rehearsals? Harper Kennedy, the ingénue upstart, breathing down her neck? Bats? Or all of the above?

The interview had turned sour when I asked about Nate Ryan and the bizarre prank. "There's been a weird vibe since Nate arrived," Gwen had said, and then blamed the weird vibe on her fear of bats. I flashed on that chicken slathered in ketchup. Was it a prank or a message? A chicken stood for many things—a coward being foremost. Was someone accusing Nate of being a coward?

CHAPTER FOUR

More bats on stage than actors, I jotted on the BT's playbill. Then added a question, *Bats acting weirdly?*

I counted five bats banging around the overhead stage lights; two others flapping against the stage right curtains, making a beating sound much like my accelerated heart rate; and bat number eight, the one I'd named Fang, hovering above the sheeted corpse as if he were a part of the play. Sitting front row center, I saw in vivid detail Fang's glossy brown fur, pointed ears and hairy toes. Gross.

Just then one of the overhead bats dropped down onto the stage as if shot. I held my breath and sank lower in my canvas theater chair as the bat fluttered around for a few moments, and then careened back up toward the lights. It took all my willpower not to don the floppy straw hat I'd brought as protection.

Gwen Shaw was right. There were a lot of bats on stage, but since I'd never attended a BT performance, maybe this was show business as usual.

"They're not going to hurt you," Tom whispered in my ear, his warm breath intoxicating.

If the bats weren't terrifying enough, Tom was seated next to me, wearing an expression of amusement. The lower I sank in my canvas theater seat, the broader his grin.

I caught another whiff of his musky cologne, probably something called Victor or Assert. Something new and expensive, like his beige linen shirt with the hidden buttons, his stylishly faded blue jeans, and his casual haircut. Even his nails were buffed, the half-moons of his cuticles pearly and white. He smelled good and looked even better. My hackles were up.

Tom nudged my arm and pointed to the overhead stage lights, where clots of moths and other insects circled. "They're feeding on the moths."

"Maybe the bats are looking for the playwright," I whispered back.

Though the actors were quite good, the play, *The Red Fish*, wasn't equal to their talents. Billed as a film-noir spoof, it involved the FBI, a Soviet spy and Joe McCarthy's daughter.

Harper Kennedy, who was playing McCarthy's daughter, was intriguing with her lithe body and voluminous wavy hair, which seemed to have the consistency of cotton candy. If she was a barracuda, as Gwen claimed, on stage she was all lightness and fun.

A communal gasp from the audience made me turn around in my seat just as another bat swooped low as it flew toward the stage. For a few moments it circled over the four actors' heads, and then disappeared backstage. The actors didn't miss a beat, but I could see from their body language that they were shaken. Gwen, who was playing Maggie, one of the FBI agents, instinctively pulled down on her hat and hunched her shoulders. Though she stayed in character, I knew she was terrified.

Suddenly, Fang dropped down onto the sheet, causing Gwen, who was holding up one corner, to gasp.

I had to give her credit; she didn't drop the sheet, but let go of it gradually, her hand visibly shaking as she stepped back. Then she exited stage right, practically running, as if the bat were pursing her.

The bat flapped its wings slowly up and down as it crawled toward the corpse's head. I could see Fang's sharp white teeth, evoking in me images of bared necks and blood-sucking vampires. Then the bat rose from the corpse and flew backstage.

Julian Finch, the actor who was pretending to be mute, started gesturing, flapping his arms and stomping his feet—a long drawn-out series of movements interpreted by Nina Cass, who was playing the female spy, to mean, "I don't know that name."

Just as the audience laughter died down, a loud crash echoed through the theater tent, followed by someone shouting, "Oh, no! Oh, no!"

The theater went silent. Only the water lapping Green Bay's stony shore could be heard.

The actors exchanged glances, then the mute actor started gesturing again.

From the right side of the tent, I watched Barbara Henry, a plump woman festooned in a white ruffled blouse and a flowery midi-skirt, disappear through the tent flap.

As the actors exited at the conclusion of the scene, the stage went black. A few minutes later, a voice came over the loud-speaker.

"The part of Maggie will be played by Rebecca Hanson, who will be reading her lines from the playbook," the voice explained. "We appreciate your understanding."

Twenty minutes later, ambulance lights swirled the night red and blue.

"You know, it wasn't the bat's fault," Tom said, sipping his expensive Scotch whiskey with a twist. He was already down to the ice, which he was chewing on nervously. With every crunch, my tension level ratcheted up.

"Tell that to poor Gwen Shaw." I'd cornered the understudy, Rebecca Hanson, backstage. She'd told me that Gwen had broken her arm when she tripped over rigging ropes running from a bat. Rebecca had said, "What the ropes were doing there, I don't know. Usually they're stowed away."

I curled the edges of the napkin under my wine glass.

"So why are you here, Tom?" From the moment he called, insisting on meeting, I suspected the reason, but I wanted him to say it. Either he wanted us to get back together or he wanted a divorce. My money was on divorce.

We were seated in the Isle View bar, a converted cottage in Gills Rock at the tip of the peninsula. Whatever Tom had to talk to me about, I wanted as much distance as possible between the Door County grapevine and me. At least up here, it would take a little longer for the news to travel down the peninsula. And I definitely didn't want him at my house, a Silver Stream mobile home I was renting near Baileys Harbor.

In the year and a half since I'd heard from Tom, I'd made no move to contact him. When I'd come to Door County to heal from my mastectomy, I'd wanted to erase the part of my life Tom represented. The breast cancer had been too much for him to handle, and every day I stayed with him was like another day I had to see how I had let him down.

He reached for his jacket that he'd hung on the booth's edge and pulled out a packet of papers from an inner pocket. Though I knew what was coming, my stomach did a flip-flop.

"Leigh, it's been over a year since you left. I haven't heard from you. Nothing."

"Could we skip the recriminations and cut to the chase. You could have called. You could have come up here." I wasn't going to let him put this all on me. Though, in truth, I probably bore the majority of the blame. My year and a half of silence had been my way of punishing him.

"I did call, and you didn't call back. What would be the point of my coming up here?"

To woo me back, I wanted to say. *To convince me that the cancer made no difference. To see me, just to see me. To show me that love conquers all—even disease.*

"So I moved on."

"Uh-huh," I said, taking a big swallow of my chardonnay. Its dry tartness felt good in my mouth. I looked over his head as the door opened and a man and a woman came in. I couldn't see them clearly, but something about them seemed familiar.

"Leigh," Tom said. "Are you listening to me?"

He had pushed the papers toward me, and I read the words "Decree of Divorce" on the top page.

"You can get a lawyer if you want. But it's all pretty straightforward. The assets are split fifty-fifty. I'll buy out your share of the house. It's more than fair."

The couple sat down on the wooden bar stools. As they turned toward each other, I recognized them from the Bayside Theater—Harper Kennedy, the upstart ingénue, and Alex Webber, BT's artistic director and co-owner. They were sitting very close and whispering back and forth.

I picked up the papers and leafed through them quickly. "Anyone I know?"

He sat back in the booth and crossed his arms. "Look, Leigh. What did you expect me to do? I'd like to have a family."

I shook my head. That hurt. The chemotherapy had wiped out my chances of ever having a family. Maybe he had forgotten that, though I doubted it. Underneath his stylish exterior still resided that cruel streak as sharp as a whip, and as certain. What had I ever seen in him?

"Sorry," he said. "You don't know her. Someone I met at work. We're getting married as soon as the divorce is final."

I dug in my purse, pulled out a pen and signed my name in big, bold black ink by all the Xs. And just like that, it was over.

"You want another drink?" Tom asked.

"To celebrate?" I lifted my glass, clinked his and gulped down the rest of my wine.

"Leigh, c'mon."

"Sure, why not." I blinked back the tears that were building behind my eyes.

Tom got up from the booth and went to the bar to order another round.

Sixteen years of marriage over with the flourish of a pen. It was like taking a long, deep breath and exhaling till there was no air left—the exhalation not visible to anyone, but out there floating somewhere, waiting to be inhaled again, by some unlucky bastard.

I glanced over to where Tom was standing at the bar next to Harper Kennedy and Alex Webber. Their shoulders were touching, and they were whispering into each other's ears. I noticed they were holding hands.

Now isn't that interesting? I thought. *Considering Alex and Nina Cass, Nate Ryan's ex, were an item.* Why wasn't Alex with Nina instead of holding hands with Harper in a bar? Alex had to be twice Harper's age. But if I'd learned anything from interviewing actors, it was that their emotions and relationships were as reliable as Door County's weather.

Tom placed the drinks on the table and slid into the booth.

"Isn't that woman one of the actors from the play?"

"Yup."

"Who's the guy?"

"Alex Webber, artistic director and co-owner."

"You know them?"

"Apparently not," I said as I watched Alex raise his hand, still holding on to Harper's hand. Then he slowly kissed the back of it.

Tom had been watching too. "Actors," he said, folding the

papers and slipping them into his jacket pocket.

"One big, happy family."

I was glad I had brought my own transportation, but not so glad that I'd stayed after Tom left, downing three more glasses of chardonnay. My head felt stuffy, and whatever surge the alcohol had given me was turning into a low-grade headache.

"Sweetie, you should have just ordered a bottle," the blond middle-aged waitress said, as if in apology as she put down the bill. "It'd been cheaper for ya."

It was after one in the morning, and she wanted to close up. I was the only one left in the bar. Harper and Alex had left shortly after Tom. Neither one had even noticed me sitting in the dark booth.

I left her a big tip.

"You sure you're all right to drive?" she asked as she flipped off the lights.

"I don't have far to go," I lied.

The night air felt heavy. The persistent heat wave that had descended on the peninsula in mid June didn't show any signs of leaving.

It took me two tries to get my keys into the truck door lock. I pulled out onto Isle View Road and headed toward Highway 42. There were no streetlights, and I was having a hard time seeing. Everything had a kind of blurry glow to it. I put on my bright lights and that just made the blurry glow more pronounced.

I pulled over and sat in the idling truck. Joe Stillwater lived off Isle View on Timberline. Joe and I had become friends after some horrible murders last year. But that was the extent of it. We'd decided to take things slow, after a very fast start.

I eased the truck back onto Isle View. Joe deserved better than me showing up at one in the morning, drunk and divorced on his doorstep.

By the time I'd made it home, it was 1:45. I'd driven under thirty miles per hour the whole way. Salinger, my faithful Shetland sheepdog, was howling and scratching at the door when I pulled into the gravel drive.

When I opened the door, she immediately sensed something was wrong and instead of running out into the woods, jumped up at me.

I knelt down and held her to me, inhaling her musty dog scent.

"He didn't even ask how you were," I told her. "Who needs him?"

I couldn't sleep, so I read an essay on bats from Linda Hogan's book, *Dwellings*. Better to think of bats than a failed marriage.

The windows were open, and I could hear the faint rush of Lake Michigan against the shore. Like the bats, if I really listened. What else could I hear? What undercurrents were moving through the warm July night? Alex and Harper: what game were they playing? Were they like the bats living between worlds, at the edges of their lives? And right now, can the bats hear the silent rush of emptiness inside me?

In the blue dusk, a bat is flying toward me, and there's nowhere I can hide. I duck, but it flies right into my hair. I beat at it with my fingers, but it just keeps flapping and flapping, pulling on my hair. I feel its breath and can smell its ammonia scent. I'm terrified; my heart is pounding. Then Tom is standing before me telling me to calm down, to hold still. He raises a pair of large scissors and begins cutting my long, beautiful hair.

I woke in a sweat with Salinger sleeping on my hair. Slowly I pulled my hair from under her, trying not to wake her. A thin trickle of dawn seeped into the mobile home, making everything appear both light and dark. I got up and stumbled to the bathroom, opened the medicine cabinet and reached for my migraine tablets. My head felt like a building was being erected inside it.

"Don't take with alcohol," the label read.

I tossed the pills in my mouth, put my mouth under the faucet and drank enough water to swallow the pills.

Don't do the crime, if you can't do the time, I told myself as I crawled back into bed.

CHAPTER FIVE:
MONDAY, JULY 10

As I punched in the numbers for my cell phone voice mail, I rubbed at my throbbing forehead. The heat was already rising in the mobile home. Everything was damp and sweaty. Even the walls were slick with humidity.

"Message one. 'Leigh, it's Sarah Peck. I'm leaving Chicago in a few weeks and need my place back. I'm sure you can find a rental. If not, you can stay on with me until you do. Sorry.'"

Thanks, Sarah, for the short notice, I grumbled to myself. Add looking for another place to live to my to-do list.

I pressed seven, erasing her message.

Too bad Tom hadn't moved faster on the divorce, I thought bitterly, sipping at my coffee. At least then I could maybe buy a place. With the depressed real estate market, there were plenty of homes to choose from at reduced prices.

Message two snapped me out of my self-pity. "Why the hell aren't you answering your phone? And if you haven't heard, Brownie Lawrence is dead. I want you to write an obit article STAT. Where are you? You were supposed to be here this morning."

"It's still morning, and I know about Brownie already," I shouted into the phone, causing Salinger to let out a sharp bark.

Jake's bossy tone sent an angry spark up my spine. Ever since we'd ended our relationship last summer, he'd turned into the Editor-in-Chief from hell.

That's what you get for sleeping with the boss, I reminded myself. I punched seven and took another gulp of coffee.

"Message three. 'You find anything out yet about Brownie? Police came by again yesterday hassling me. I told 'em you were looking into Brownie's past and that they should talk to you.'"

I pressed nine and closed the phone. "Great," I moaned. Ken Albright had sicced the police on me. It would only be a matter of time before I got a warning from Chief Burnson to butt out.

Quickly, I showered, threw on khakis, a mauve tank top, my hematite necklace and red wedged sandals. It was going to be a long day. First stop, the *Door County Gazette,* soothe Jake's ruffled feathers, then grab some lunch before heading over to the Bayside Theater's rehearsal at one p.m. After that I could start looking for a new place to live—without doubt, a rental.

As I pulled away from the mobile home, Salinger was standing at the kitchen window, howling as if she knew we were homeless yet again.

"How's the Bayside Theater's article coming?" Jake asked, shuffling through the stacks of papers, books and magazines piled pell-mell on his battered antique desk. Even after a year, I still couldn't get used to his short, trim haircut, which I considered a symbol of our breakup. Not that I wanted the return of the long gray ponytail, just the man who'd once sported it.

"Okay," I answered, massaging my aching forehead. A part of me wanted to tell him about my divorce. My refusal to end things with Tom had been a contributing factor to our breakup, as had Jake's disappearing a year ago last May for a month and not telling me where he was. But I hesitated, afraid I'd dissolve into a weepy mess. The last thing I wanted from him was pity.

"You get the interview with Nate Ryan?" He stopped shuffling and stared at me, leaning back in his chair with his hands behind his head. He must have calmed down since leaving his curt message on my cell phone.

"Short and perplexing, but probably enough for the article. I'm going to try him again at today's rehearsal. He was all charming and cooperative until he discovered a dead bird in his fridge. Not a real one, as it turned out. But after that, he couldn't get me out the door fast enough."

"You yanking my chain, Girard?" Jake plopped his big feet on his desk.

"Nope. According to Ryan, he and Julian Finch like to play pranks on each other. Though how a fake dead chicken is funny is beyond me. Then last night in the middle of the performance, Gwen Shaw fell over some rigging backstage and broke her arm, apparently distracted by a berserk bat. Speaking of which, you should have seen how many bats were on stage. It was like the stage was a bat magnet. It was weird."

"Don't get sidetracked. You need to get that article done before the end of the month. Wallace Bernard stuck his neck out for you at the *Chicago Reporter.*"

Wallace Bernard, a retired journalist and Jake's mentor, had been instrumental in helping me solve a series of murders last year. Now he'd greased the wheels at the *Reporter* for my article on the BT.

"Don't you have any faith in me?" It was a question that had little to do with the article.

"That's the problem, Leigh. I have too much."

If only, I thought.

"You heard about Brownie?" he asked.

"Yeah. Ken Albright called me early Sunday morning, and I went out there to talk to him. He's in bad shape. I'm afraid he's going to relapse without Brownie. And he left me another message this morning about the police hassling him. I wish there was something I could do."

"I know you have a soft spot for these guys. Why, I don't

know. But stay out of it. I need you to write Brownie Lawrence's obit article and have it on the computer before deadline on Thursday."

"You mean Lawrence Browning." I retrieved the dog tags from my bag and put them on Jake's desk.

He took his feet off his desk and picked up the tags.

"How'd you get these?" he asked, studying the tags.

"Ken Albright. He's feeling guilty about not being there when Brownie died. He also told me Brownie's from around here. I promised him I'd find his family."

Jake was still holding the tags running his long fingers over the raised letters and numbers. I waited, watching his fingers, studying the breadth of his broad shoulders. I could almost smell the fabric softener in his blue shirt mingled with his musky scent. *Stop it,* I cautioned myself. *You're hurting right now, and it's making you vulnerable.*

He looked up as if he could read my thoughts, his eyes full of questions. "We'll run a short obit instead of a longer piece. Once you're through with the BT article, follow up on this. If he's from around here, it'll make a good human-interest story. But only after you're done with the BT." He pushed the dog tags toward me, but I didn't take them.

"Okay, I know that look. What aren't you telling me?"

He knew me too well. "It's probably nothing. But Ken found wine bottles near Brownie's body. Cherry wine. Of course instead of leaving them for the police, he threw them in the bay. He didn't want the police to think Brownie had started drinking again. But he was adamant that Brownie would never drink cherry wine even if he fell off the wagon."

"Ken's whacked from all the drugs and booze, and you know it. Let the police handle it."

Rather than show him the red shard I'd found near where Brownie died, I stood up and reached for the dog tags, not wanting another lecture about staying out of police investigations.

"Everything else okay? You seem . . ." He struggled for the right word.

"What?" I challenged him.

"Tired."

"Sarah Peck's reclaiming her mobile home, and I need a place to live ASAP. Any ideas?" *Coward,* I thought.

"You can always crash at my place." He raised his eyebrows and tilted his head. What was he really saying?

I was holding the dog tags so tightly in my hand, the jagged edge pierced my skin. "You think that's a good idea? Considering everything."

He shrugged his shoulders and looked away. "Yeah, you're probably right. But if you get desperate."

"I'll know who to call," I finished.

"Yeah, something like that."

I stood outside his door for a few minutes, trying to still my racing heart by taking in long, slow breaths through my nose and letting the air out through my mouth. That was always the problem between us. Neither one of us had the courage to put our feelings on the line.

"You all right, honey?" Marge, the *Gazette*'s office manager, called from her desk near the door. She must have spotted me leaning against the wall. I pushed away and strode into the room as if I didn't have a worry in the world.

"Could you do me a favor?" I put the dog tags on her desk.

"Depends. You gonna introduce me to that hunk Nate Ryan after the play?" I'd made sure Marge had an invitation to the invitation-only party after the opening performance of *The Merchant of Venice.*

"What would your husband say?" I teased.

She swatted her hand at me. "He'd be happy to have the

house to himself. Anyway, what's the favor?"

"I need you to run Brownie Lawrence's Social Security number." Jake hadn't said anything about someone else following up on Brownie.

"So his real name was Lawrence Browning," she said, holding the tags in her hand. "So sad about him dying like that."

"Yeah," I said. The yellowed grass outline of Brownie's body flashed into my mind. "See what you can find out. Anything would be helpful."

"Okay if I get to it tomorrow? I'm swamped today with work, then I gotta run home and change before the meeting."

"Which meeting's that?" Marge was a notorious joiner, from knitting groups to animal rescue organizations. Pretty soon she'd have to arrange her job around her volunteer duties.

"Door County Historical Society. I'm helping put everything on computer. You wouldn't believe what a mess the records are in."

"When do you sleep?"

"Plenty of time for that when I'm dead. Anything else I can do for you?"

"You know of anyone on the peninsula looking for a renter? Someone who doesn't mind pets and is in my price range?"

"When's Sarah coming back?"

"Too soon."

"I'll ask around," Marge offered.

I went over to the communal desk and phoned Deputy Chief Chet Jorgensen, a personal friend and contact with the police department.

"I wondered when you'd get around to pestering me," Chet said. "And before you ask, Brownie's cause of death has not been determined."

"How do you know that's why I'm calling?" I said indignantly.

"Well, isn't it?"

It was one of my reasons, but I wasn't going to give him the satisfaction of being right. "Actually, I wanted to know if Ken Albright is a suspect."

"What do you think?"

"Ken would never hurt Brownie."

"Let's just say that the crime scene says otherwise. That's all I can tell you. So don't work too hard there, Leigh."

He hung up before I could ask him to elaborate. What hadn't Ken told me? Why were the police calling it a crime scene?

I glanced up at the office clock. It was almost eleven-thirty, and I still had to finish my piece on the Village of Egg Harbor's unique distinction of having the most liquor licenses per capita in Wisconsin. I needed a quote from Jerry Lucas, the spokesperson for the Door County Visitor's Bureau. Then I'd grab something to eat before heading to the BT's one o'clock rehearsal. Driving to Marshalls Point to see Ken would have to wait.

Before dialing the Visitor's Bureau, I scanned my notes. *Egg Harbor, population 201. Number of liquor licenses, 21. Comes to one license for every 21 residents.*

You can't make this stuff up, I thought as I waited for Jerry to answer his phone.

"Hi Jerry, it's Leigh Girard. Do you have a minute?"

"Sure, Leigh. What's up?"

"I'm writing an article for Friday's paper on Egg Harbor having the most liquor licenses per capita in Wisconsin. What's your take on it?"

He chuckled. "No secret there. It's tourism. We serve an estimated two million tourists a year. As for Egg Harbor, a lot happens in that village for only two hundred one people living there."

"You could say the same thing about the whole peninsula," I answered.

"You ought to know."

CHAPTER SIX

After three hours in the stifling room watching the final run-through of *The Merchant of Venice* before tonight's dress rehearsal, I was back to worrying about Ken Albright and why the police were treating Brownie's death as a crime. Anything to distract myself from the tortuous rehearsal.

Out of sheer boredom, I'd learned each actor by their scents, sometimes closing my eyes as they passed in front of me to test my olfactory acumen.

Nina Cass, Ryan's ex-wife, who was playing Nerissa, smelled like cigarettes and coffee, which probably accounted for her nervous, angular body and tightly curled black hair. She stood near me, tapping her foot, clearly annoyed as Julian Finch, the play's Antonio—sandalwood soap, anise and faint BO—went up on his lines again.

With a two-and-a-half week turnaround between plays, the actors were always rehearsing one play during the day and performing a completely different play at night. Though a mentally grueling schedule, I was still surprised that Finch was having problems remembering his lines. Not only was Finch a noted Shakespearean actor, who'd surely played this role before, but also, this was the final rehearsal before dress rehearsal, Monday being the only dark night for the BT. The play opened tomorrow.

Earlier, when I'd asked Nina Cass how she kept the plays straight and remembered her lines, she said, "It's like a muscle.

The more you use it, the better it becomes."

Obviously, that muscle wasn't working for Julian. And from the expressions on the other actors' faces, they were as annoyed with him as Nina was. Secretly, I wished Shylock, aka Nate Ryan, would get his pound of flesh so the play would end and put everyone out of their misery.

"For if the Jew doth cut deep enough," Julian repeated, looking up into the rafters as if the lines were floating above him. "Line," he said.

I sighed inwardly. Marooned between Alex Webber, the play's director, and Barbara Henry in an island of chairs beneath a bank of windows, I felt sweat running down the backs of my legs, under my arms and in my crotch. Every time I moved, my damp clothes clung to me. I knew I had a big wet stain on my bottom. I only hoped I didn't smell.

I looked with annoyance and envy at the three crewmembers who were huddled in front of the one wall air conditioner. Humming gently like background music for the play, it did little to relieve the vaporous heat that filled the large room. I felt like I was inhaling everyone's exhale.

Alex, who was following the lines with a small ruler, called out, "I'll pay for it instantly with all my heart." His garlicky breath was muted by the starchy scent of his shirt. He ran his hand through his wavy and thinning dun-colored hair—a gesture that seemed to calm him.

"I'll pay it instantly with all my heart," Julian repeated.

Julian was bound to a chair stage center, his bony chest thrust out, ready for a pound of flesh to be cut from him—nearest his heart. Beside him stood Bassanio, played by Matt Burke—spicy deodorant and spearmint. He had a commanding presence. At around six feet, four inches, he seemed out of proportion to the other actors. Matt was the only actor there, besides Nate Ryan, who'd done TV. He'd been the TV spokesperson for a national cell phone company a few years ago in which he was dressed as an urban cowboy and flipped his phone open as if it were a gun. He'd also done a stint as a murderous villain on a daytime soap titled *Days of Our Children*. He was good-looking in an average, nonthreatening kind of way.

As Portia, played by Harper Kennedy—lavender and hair spray—drew Shylock into her clever web of words, I studied again the soft-looking Julian. I wondered how the audience would react not only to the liberal cuts Webber had taken with the play, eliminating Act V, but also to the blatant homosexuality that he'd infused into the play, having Bassanio kiss Antonio in early scenes on the mouth and for a little too long. As well as the less blatant homosexual overtones between Portia and Nerissa, once they'd donned men's clothes.

I wasn't sure what Webber was trying to prove, but whatever it was, he certainly was going to prove something. With so many interpretations of the play over the years, I doubt if Shakespeare was rolling over in his grave, but he probably was scratching his head.

"Most rightful judge!" Shylock brandished the long-bladed knife in front of Antonio, releasing his sweet scent that smelled like plums. In what could only be called anti-casting, Nate Ryan was playing Shylock to the hilt. His blond good looks were at odds with the part of the Jewish merchant. He'd barely acknowledged me when he'd entered the rehearsal room, looking briefly in my direction, smiling, and then joining the other actors.

Maybe I was too much of a distraction? Yeah, right. More likely my questioning his sobriety was the distraction.

Then there were Alex and Harper. I couldn't dislodge the image of him kissing Harper's hand last night at the bar and their raw, lustful looks. Throughout the rehearsal they'd been distant and professional, by far her best performance of the day.

Portia answered. "And you must cut this flesh from off his breast. The law allows it, and the court awards."

"Most learned judge! A sentence! Come prepare!" Shylock flourished the knife once in the air, and then pressed its tip against Antonio's chest. A single drop of blood appeared.

"What the hell," shouted Julian as he looked down at the blood on his chest.

It took me a moment to realize that the blood was real and not some trick of the knife to give authenticity to the scene's horror.

Julian wrested his hands free of the ropes, jumped up from his chair and swiped at the blood drop.

Nate held the knife out away from him as if he had no idea how it had gotten into his hand, let alone drawn blood.

"This is too much, Ryan, even for you," hissed Julian. "Maybe this play is a big joke to you, but the rest of us take the BT and our profession seriously."

Nate shrugged his shoulders at Julian. "The rest of us know our lines."

For a second the two men stared at each other as if deciding their next move. Julian's right hand fisted and Nate's chin thrust forward as if to say: go ahead and hit me. Then Julian stormed past Nate and went outside, slamming the door behind him. If Nate was getting even for the fake chicken in his fridge, again I didn't see the humor. A bloody chicken was harmless; drawing blood wasn't.

"Everybody calm down," Alex said, getting up and taking the knife from Nate's hand. He ran his finger over the blade. "Bob, how did this knife get here? Where's the one with the blunt end?"

Bob, a doughy-looking college student who was in charge of props, moved away from the air conditioner, red-faced.

"Did you check the knife before rehearsal?" Alex demanded.

"It wasn't that knife," Bob protested.

"Okay, who's the jokester?" Alex said, smiling at me as if I were in on the joke. Why wasn't he asking Nate about the switched knife? I wondered, since Julian had accused him of planting a real knife.

Barbara Henry, who was sitting on my right, leaned toward me. "Stage jitters," she whispered. Again she was clad in a ruffled blouse and a florid midi-skirt. Did she buy them in bulk? I wondered.

"Understandable," I said. Not adding, "Especially considering he'd just been pricked with a real knife."

Since the start of rehearsal three hours ago, this was my first opportunity to ask her about the play. "Is Alex at all concerned about the audience's reaction?"

Barbara looked at me as if I were speaking in a foreign tongue.

"The homosexuality?" I added.

"You'll have to ask Alex about that." Barbara got up abruptly and went outside.

"I want you to double-check all the props before you set them up—all of them. Got it?" Alex handed the knife to Bob.

"I did check it. Honest," he answered, his head down, the tips of his ears a fiery red.

"Just make sure it doesn't happen again." Alex looked at his watch. "Okay, fifteen minutes, and then we'll take the scene from the top."

The actors quickly made for the door. Nina already had a cigarette in her mouth. Harper and Matt were arm and arm, laughing. And Nate was chatting with Alex. I heard him say as they passed, "Maybe now he'll remember his lines."

I got up and pulled at my damp khakis, standing for a moment until the circulation returned to my legs and feet. Bob was in the corner, rummaging around in the prop box. I walked over to him. The suspect knife was on the floor beside the box.

It was a long-bladed kitchen knife, the kind you use to cut meat.

"Hi. I'm Leigh Girard from the *Door County Gazette*." Bending down, I held out my hand to him.

He looked up at me, wiped his hand on his rumpled cargo shorts and then shook my hand. His cheeks were still flame red. "You're not going to put this in the paper, are you?"

"Why would I?" I sat down on the floor beside him. "Alex was kind of hard on you."

"He's always like that the night before opening. Who he really wants to yell at is Finch. But he can't. Finch being such a famous actor and all. So he takes it out on the intern."

"How did a real knife get in with the props?"

He tilted his head at me. "Damned if I know."

I was being shut out again. "Cross my heart," I said, making an imaginary cross on my chest. "Nothing you tell me is going in my article. I'm just curious. It's an occupational hazard."

He looked around to see if anyone else was in the room. "This is my second season with the BT, you know. It's not like I don't know what I'm doing. And I'm real careful with the props, because if I screw up I don't get credit for my internship. And I need the credit or I don't graduate next spring. So do you think I wouldn't check that knife before rehearsal? I checked it. Someone else switched knives."

"Do you remember what time you checked it?"

"Right after lunch. Around noon. Then I put the box in here, where I always put it."

"So anyone could have come in here and switched knives."

We sat for a moment and listened to the rattling hum of the air conditioner. I could sense that Bob had something else he wanted to tell me, but he wasn't sure yet if he could trust me.

"That's not the first time something's gone wrong," he began, "that Alex's tried to pin on me."

He looked sideways at me. "The other day there was a dead rat in one of the caskets. You know the scene where Bassanio has to guess which casket is the right one: gold, silver or lead? You should have seen Burke, Mr. Cell Phone Cowboy, jump when he opened the lead one and a dead rat was in there. Then last night, you have to admit there were a lot of bats on stage. I mean I've never seen that many before. Then when Gwen tripped over those rigging ropes and broke her arm, guess who Alex blamed? Me. I didn't leave those ropes out, honest. I don't blame Gwen for leaving."

I didn't blame her either. When I'd asked Alex how Gwen was doing, he'd told me she'd left last night for Chicago.

"Bob, any idea who's behind the practical jokes?" Why hadn't Gwen told me about the dead rat in the casket? As Portia, she was present for that scene in the play. Weird vibe, indeed.

"If I knew, don't you think I'd tell Alex, so he'd get off my back?"

"How about a guess?"

"Nate Ryan, just like Finch said. It's obvious he's not into the play or the BT."

"What do you mean, not into the play or the BT?"

"Half the time he looks bored. Like he wants to be someplace else. Other times he seems all agitated and hyped up. He's just killing time here until Hollywood offers him another movie." He put his hand over his mouth. "Don't say I said that, okay? Or I'll really be in trouble."

"This is strictly between us," I reassured him.

"You gonna put anything in your article about the curse?"

"What curse?" This was the first I'd heard about a curse.

"Well, I'm staying in the boathouse over on the bay with the rest of the techs. And one of them told me about the last time BT did *MOV*."

"*MOV*? You mean *The Merchant of Venice*?"

"Yeah. Well, anyway the last time they did that play, it was way back in the nineteen eighties sometime, you know when the Moyer family ran the BT. They're the people who saved the theater when it was in financial trouble."

That I did know. The Moyers rescued the theater group from bankruptcy and built the present tented pavilion, replacing the huge canvas top that once draped over the audience and was a menace on stormy nights.

"Anyway, opening night Danielle Moyer, who played Portia, disappeared after the play and was never seen again. She was the daughter. You been to the old cabin where they lived?"

I shook my head no. I didn't even know there was an old cabin.

"Well, if you want, after rehearsal I can take you there. It's all locked up. But you can look in the windows. It's creepy."

Obviously, I'd been talking to the wrong people. Bob, the intern, was a fountain of information. Though how much was accurate, I wasn't sure.

"Okay, where should we meet?"

"By the beer garden." He smiled for the first time.

Where else would a college student want to meet?

With ten minutes left before rehearsal resumed, I walked over to the ticket office, wanting to talk to Alex and get his reaction to the knife incident. Barbara told me he was on a conference call and I could wait in the garden.

I followed the stone path around the ticket office to the garden. It was empty except for Julian and Harper, who were seated on a wooden bench near the garden's edge lost in conversation. As Harper stood, she patted Julian on the shoulder, then leaned over and kissed his cheek. After Harper left, I waited a moment before walking to the bench.

"Mind if I join you?" I asked.

"Come to see how the mighty have fallen?"

I took that as a yes and sat down next to him. An open play-book was in his lap. His shirt was unbuttoned, and I could see the cut on his hairless chest. He pulled his shirt closed and crossed his long legs at his ankles.

He had an imperial face, a profile fit for a coin—patrician nose, high forehead and graying hair that seemed unusually thick for a man in his fifties. His strong features were suited to a stage actor, easily seen from the back of the theater.

"I'm a great admirer of yours," I began. "I saw your Lear at the Chicago Shakespeare Theater a few years ago."

"Ah, yes. Lear, a man who loses everything because of his hubris. 'We will be like two birds in a cage.' Always loved that line. But then it's already too late, isn't it? Cordelia soon dies, and all hope is lost."

I was enthralled with his deep voice, like rich coffee.

He picked up the playbook and leafed through it. "Do you know how many times I've done this play? Six. And one of those times was at the Globe Theater in London. I've played Antonio twice, Shylock three times."

Besides being a Shakespearean actor who'd played London and Chicago, Finch had made an independent film when he was in his twenties that had garnered him an Academy Award nomination. That had been the highlight of his acting career. Now it seemed as if he was on a slow downward slide. I felt sorry for him. Not only because he'd forgotten his lines, which was humiliating enough, but also because he'd been the victim of a cruel prank.

He thrust the book at me. "Read a line from the trial scene."

"What?"

"Anywhere in the scene. Read a line before Antonio's."

I opened the book to Act IV. "You, merchant, have you anything to say?"

"But little. I am armed and well prepared." He continued, not missing a word, imbuing the speech with the pathos it merited. When he'd finished, he took the playbook from me.

"So why were you going up on your lines in rehearsal?" I asked.

"That's what I've been sitting here asking myself. There's a saying in the theater, 'The worse the rehearsal, the better the opening night.' But, of course, that refers to the dress rehearsal."

He put the playbook down, but I'd seen the tremor in his hand. And he'd seen that I'd seen it.

"That would make a good quote for your article, don't you think?" He raised his eyebrows and stared at me with his bluish-gray eyes.

"Does a bad rehearsal include a switched knife?"

"Not usually. But these things sometimes do happen, you know. Mistakes are made. People fall short."

His sudden mood change from frustration to calm was peculiar. Again I chalked it up to actors' mercurial personalities. Their emotions must course so close to the surface that the slightest touch ignites them.

"Maybe Nate was getting even with you for putting a fake chicken in his fridge."

"What are you talking about?" He stared at me as if I'd just sprouted a second head.

"Nate told me you two have a history of practical jokes. He found a fake chicken in his fridge when I was there interviewing him yesterday."

"Is that what he said?"

I nodded my head yes.

"No, I didn't put it there. Not my style."

"But you two like playing jokes on each other?"

He let out a deep breath. "I made the mistake once of sinking to his level. You've probably noticed he's a bit of a child."

He got up and straightened his crisp white trousers. He was a meticulous man, who chose his words as carefully as his clothes. "Well, no rest for the wicked. You coming?"

"I wouldn't miss it."

The next hour flew by in a dramatic haze. Finch was flawless, and everyone else had to rise to this performance. Even Ryan lagged behind.

After the run-through, I asked Barbara Henry what time dress rehearsal was that evening.

"You'd better check with Alex first and ask if he wants you there." She twisted her thin ponytail around her finger, her one eyebrow raised defiantly.

That was a change. Only yesterday I was told that I had *carte blanche* for my article.

Since the knife incident, Alex had been avoiding me, not even looking in my direction, even though I sat next to him for the remainder of the rehearsal. I had to literally block the door to talk to him.

"Barbara said I had to check with you about dress rehearsal tonight."

"I can't let you backstage. It's too distracting to the actors."

"No problem. I'll just sit in the audience. What time should I be here?"

He glanced over my head as if someone was behind me. "Look, I'm running a closed dress tonight."

"I'm almost finished with the interviews. And the dress rehearsal will really add another dimension to the piece," I protested. "What happened to *carte blanche*?"

He let out a deep sigh. "My first obligation is to the actors and the play. And frankly, some of them have told me they find your presence a distraction."

Now I was miffed. "Distraction? Which actors?" I had my

suspicions that Nate Ryan was behind this.

He pursed his thin lips. "Sorry, but that's the way it is."

CHAPTER SEVEN

Bob was waiting for me by the beer garden, a plastic cup in his hand. *That explains a lot*, I thought. Maybe Alex was right to blame him for the switched knives. It was just after four o'clock, and he was drinking.

"Want one?" he asked, holding up the cup. "Free for you."

The yeasty beer smell was tempting, but I passed. I'd finally shaken my headache, and I wasn't going back there.

"Sometimes Rich comps me one."

Rich Koch was the groundskeeper and bartender at the beer garden. I could see him in the back, stacking up cases of beer, his Irish setter pup, Dixie, hanging on his every movement.

"Perks of being an intern?" I asked. Bob grinned as if he'd been given the keys to a Milwaukee brewery. I was still miffed about being shut out of tonight's dress rehearsal. But Bob's youthful enthusiasm over a free beer was infectious.

"The least they can do, all the crap I take. So, the quickest way to the old Moyer cabin is the path that runs along the bay, unless you want to see where the actors live." He pointed up the hill. "You can't see them from here, what with the trees, but it's a bunch of six packs."

"Already saw them yesterday, thanks to Nate Ryan."

"Then you know how good the actors have it. Unlike us interns and techs, who have to share one bathroom. But, hey, you can't beat our view."

Bob wasn't handsome, but his openness made up for what he

lacked in the looks department. His hair was a corn yellow and longish, his wire-rimmed glasses thick, and he had a slight overbite that made him seem a bit dopey. His short, soft, pudgy body reminded me of that Doughboy character in those TV commercials, minus the chef's hat.

"If you're showing her the Moyer cabin, you'd better finish that beer first." Rich emerged from behind the bar. "I don't want anybody to see ya walking around with it." He was a tall, gangly guy with a pronounced slouch and a lush dark mustache, which was in contrast to his balding head. He was probably in his early fifties but moved like a much older man.

Bob chugged the beer and threw the cup in the open garbage bin. "I'm legal."

"You know what I'm talking about. You're not supposed to be drinking during work hours."

"Got you covered, Rich. Don't sweat it."

"Now I know I'm in trouble," Rich joked, winking at me. "You just holler, Leigh, if he gets out of hand. And hey, when you gonna let me show you around the gardens?"

Last week he'd stopped me in the parking lot, introduced himself and asked me when I was going to tour the gardens. There was a feverishness about his request. I suspected he never felt appreciated and wanted some recognition. "How's Wednesday morning around nine?" Better to get it over with than have him dogging me.

"It's a date, Leigh." He grinned at me as if it *were* a date.

As Bob and I walked the shoreline, I caught glimpses of the bay through the tall cedars lining the shore. The water was flat as glass, not a whisper of a breeze ruffling it, which kept the mosquitoes and black flies in front of my face like a veil.

"So, besides props, what else do you do around here?" I asked.

"Lighting, work on sets. Whatever Alex the boss wants me to do." That note of anger was back. "He's always ragging on me.

Thinks I'm lazy and stupid."

"I'm sure he wouldn't have you back for a second year if he thought that."

"Maybe he gets off on torturing me."

As the trail curved, I saw a bench up ahead near the water. Bob went to it, picked up a rock and threw it into the bay. We stood for a moment and watched the water ripple out. "C'mon," he said, turning away from the water and crossing the trail. "It's this way." He walked off into the woods.

"Where you going?" I called to his retreating back. My nifty red wedge sandals weren't made for hiking through dense woods.

"The Moyer cabin. Where else?"

"I don't see a path."

He pointed back from where we'd come. "Yeah, that's what's so cool. The path is right across from the bench."

If you didn't know it was there, you wouldn't see the path. It was narrow and rocky, and at times seemed to disappear then a few steps later appear again. I stepped carefully over the rocks jutting up through the ground, planting my wedges tentatively.

"How much farther?" I protested. We'd been walking for what seemed like forever, but was probably only about ten minutes. My calf muscles were aching from the strain of walking this tightrope path.

Bob stopped and turned toward me, a stupid grin on his chubby face. "We're here."

I glanced around and didn't see anything except trees and more trees. "Where is it?"

He was grinning so broadly, I thought he was playing a joke on me. "It's right there, behind that stand of trees." He took my arm and pulled me forward a few steps.

Buried deep in the woods, surrounded by tall trees, was a green hodgepodge of a cabin. It seemed sad and dilapidated.

Tall grass and scattered rocks surrounded the entire structure as if nature was reclaiming it. Trees precariously overhung the moss-carpeted roof.

"C'mon," Bob beckoned. "You have to see this thing up close. It blows my mind that a whole family lived in that dump. Though it probably wasn't a dump back then."

When we reached the cabin, I noticed that all the windows along the back were boarded up with plywood. I ran my hand over the weathered wooden slats, which crumbled between my fingers.

"Check this out," Bob called out excitedly from the other side of the cabin.

As I walked around the back of the house, I noticed that one of the windows wasn't covered in plywood and stopped to glance inside. The dusky room was a kitchen.

"Leigh, you gotta see this," Bob called again.

Bob was standing next to a sign that read Shown By Appointment Only.

"Rich and I put that sign there," Bob boasted. "Pretty funny, huh?"

"Hilarious," I said sardonically.

I was beginning to think Bob was the prankster. Maybe the pranks were his way of getting even for all the blame Alex heaped on his doughy shoulders.

"Did you and Rich take the plywood off that window over there by the back door?"

"I didn't touch any windows," Bob said petulantly, obviously hurt over my less than enthusiastic response to his joke.

Bob trailed behind me as I walked back to the window. "Was it like that when you were here last?" The glass was amazingly clean, considering the filthy state of the rest of the cabin.

Bob looked down at his sneakers, then up at me. "I don't think so. But I really wasn't paying attention."

I cupped my hands to the glass and peered inside. There was a small round table and four chairs in the middle of the room. Shoved in a corner against the back wall stood a tall cabinet. On the other side of the room were a sink and a counter top. Beside the back door was a wood-burning stove. Everything was covered with a thick layer of dust, except for one of the chair seats and part of the table. On the table were a partially burnt candle and a book of matches.

"It looks like someone's been here recently," I surmised.

"No way." Bob came up behind me and peeked over my shoulder.

"See how there's no dust on that chair and part of the table? And look at the candle."

"I'd like to know how they got in." He pointed to the piece of wood hammered across the door. "The front door's the same way."

"Well, someone's been here."

"Maybe it's Danielle Moyer's ghost," Bob whispered eerily.

"Right," I said sarcastically. Before leaving, I jotted down a few notes, then snapped some photos. If this was where the Moyer family once lived, it might make a good side story to the article.

"You're sure the Moyer family lived here?" I asked Bob as I shoved my notebook and camera into my shoulder bag.

"If you don't believe me, ask Rich. He's the one who told me about it. You know he's been with the BT for, like, forever. He should know."

When I interviewed Rich Wednesday morning, I'd ask him about the Moyer cabin.

Before we left, I gave Bob one of my business cards. "If you find out who's behind the practical jokes, let me know. Okay?"

He took the card and examined it. "You got it, Leigh."

When I got back to my truck, I pulled out the Bayside

Theater's fiftieth anniversary booklet with the list of past plays and flipped to the nineteen eighties section. I read through the list twice. Then I went through all the past plays. Bob was wrong. The BT had never performed *MOV* in the nineteen eighties or any other time. However, on page thirty-five, there was a photo of Danielle Moyer from the 1988 production of *Twelfth Night*. Danielle was Viola, dressed as a boy in period costume. And standing behind her with his arms around her was a very young Julian Finch. He was Orsino, the Duke that Viola falls in love with. They made a very handsome couple. Nate had a minor role as Sebastian, Viola's brother.

Curiously, there was no photo of Nate Ryan from his performance as Stanley Kowalski in *A Streetcar Named Desire* or, for that matter, anyone else from the cast. But Julian Finch and Danielle Moyer had appeared in the play—Julian as the gentleman caller and Danielle as Blanche DuBois. I read through the succeeding cast lists for the next few seasons, and Danielle Moyer's name never appeared again. Had she disappeared after the production of *Streetcar*?

I flipped back to the four-page introductory history of the BT and reread it. The intro briefly mentioned the Moyers saving the theater from bankruptcy, building the present pavilion, and then, because of personal and financial reasons, selling the property in 1992. That's when the theater became a nonprofit organization. Since then, ownership had passed through several hands. From my interview with Alex Webber, I knew that he and Nina Cass were the present owners and had acquired the theater five years ago. Now they were in the midst of a major fundraising venture coinciding with the sixty-fifth anniversary year of the BT. The funds were to be used to build a new theater.

Based on the scanty facts about the Moyers, Danielle had probably disappeared after *Streetcar* and then her parents, Constance and Alfred, stuck it out another four years before selling for personal and financial reasons. The question remained: What happened to Danielle Moyer?

CHAPTER EIGHT:
TUESDAY, JULY 11

Already fifteen minutes late, I hurried down the stone path with Salinger in tow toward the BT garden where Harper Kennedy was waiting for me, sitting on the same bench she and Finch had occupied yesterday.

She'd confirmed our interview last night, leaving a voice message on my cell.

"Do you mind if we meet in the BT garden, then take a walk along the shore?" Her voice matched her ethereal body, wispy and fragile.

Usually chronically early for interviews, I'd run into bumper-to-bumper traffic in Sister Bay. Before Harper's interview, I'd driven up to Marshalls Point to see if Ken knew why the police were treating Brownie's death as a crime. I also wanted to offer him my support. But the place was deserted.

He's probably out on a job, I'd reassured myself. A twinge of sadness overtook me as I looked at the forlorn shed that had been the men's refuge and home.

It was taking all my strength to restrain Salinger, who pulled on her leash as she bounded toward the bench where an errant squirrel was frolicking. "Easy, girl," I cautioned her, holding the leash with two hands.

When we reached the bench, the squirrel had skittered up a tree, to Salinger's chagrin.

"Who's this cute doggy?" Harper asked.

"Salinger," I answered, sitting down beside her. Salinger gave her a good sniffing and then settled down as well, sitting between us, one paw crossed over the other. I'd decided to bring her with me today. She deserved to be out and about on this crystal clear morning of puffy white clouds and high temps.

"As in J.D.?"

"Right. Sorry I'm late. Got tied up in tourist traffic."

"No problem," Harper responded. She slid off the bench and knelt beside Salinger. "What a beautiful doggy you are."

As she ran her fingers through Salinger's fur, a rich blend of what smelled like jasmine, lemon, and geranium rose from her skin. She wore jean shorts, a white peasant blouse, sandals, a black-corded necklace tight around her throat, and huge silver hoops. On her wrist was a silver mesh cuff. With the rising humidity, her fluffy blond hair haloed her delicate face. She looked more like a poet than an actor. Or maybe a poet's muse.

She stood up and pulled on her tight shorts. Her legs were like two twigs. "You up for a walk? I have to nap before my performance. It's one of my rituals. And a walk helps me sleep." Though she was twenty-four, she could have passed for sixteen.

We headed toward the shoreline trail. The same path I'd walked yesterday with Bob. Once we were out of sight of the theater grounds, I let Salinger off her leash. She ran ahead of us, stopping and turning every so often, ever watchful, one of her most endearing traits.

I glanced down at my paltry research notes. Harper Kennedy had the shortest bio of all the cast members. She'd grown up in a small central Illinois town, studied acting at the University of Illinois and appeared in a few Chicago-area productions, playing minor roles. This was her first summer with the BT.

"So why acting?" I sensed I didn't need to ease into her interview. There was an openness about her, probably more to do with her age than her personality. So I skipped the small talk, which I was usually bad at, and began with the "real"

74

questions. If she was a barracuda as Gwen had warned me, I'd had yet to see it. But then, she was an actress.

Since this was my last cast interview, I already knew how I was going to focus the section on the actors: what drew them to acting; where they were in their careers; and one unexpected thing about them.

She took in a deep breath. "This is so lame I'm embarrassed to tell you. I guess when I make it big, I'll have to make up something better. Well, here goes. When I was eleven, I tried out for our junior high Christmas play. Why I got the lead, search me. I know it sounds ridiculous, but I was hooked from then on. Lame, right?"

"No, it's charming." She's not the only one who could stretch the truth. Why did that story seem disingenuous, meant to cast her in a naive, sweet light?

I let it go, wanting to test Gwen's theory about Harper's competitiveness. "Were you surprised when you got the role of Portia after Gwen left?" Though Harper was the right age for Portia, Nina had the better acting chops for the role.

She stopped for a moment and gazed at the bay where two sailboats were crossing, their sails billowing out. "Wow!" she gasped. "I just can't get over how beautiful it is up here. Kinda like a dream of summer."

She seemed so lost in the moment, I didn't break into her reverie. Once the sailboats had crossed, she turned toward me. "You were asking about my getting the part of Portia? Yeah, I was surprised I got any part. There were a lot of actors audition-ing in Chicago. I almost turned around and walked out of the theater. But you know, when you're a nobody, what do you have to lose?"

She'd skillfully sidestepped my question. "What's it like act-ing with Nate Ryan?"

She laughed and started walking. "It always comes back to

the famous Nate Ryan. He's a total dog, apologies to Salinger. First rehearsal he made a pass at me. Put his arm around my shoulder and whispered something disgusting in my ear about his pound of flesh. Then he showed up on my doorstep that night with a bottle of wine and two glasses. I politely told him no. But he keeps trying."

The empty bottle of wine and two glasses I'd seen in Nate's apartment flashed into my brain and with them, the lacy bra. Surreptitiously, I glanced at her body. The lacy bra might fit her. Was she telling me the truth? After all, there was that intimate moment between Alex and her at the Isle View Bar that I'd witnessed. Was Harper a serial flirt? I didn't know. So I pushed her. "Not even a little bit tempted? After all, he knows a lot of people in the biz."

"More like he *knew* a lot of people. I'm going to make it on my talent, not on my back. What did Nate do for Nina? Nothing, and she was married to him. Can we talk about something else besides Nate Ryan?" She said it kindly, but I sensed her annoyance. Her pace had increased, and I was having trouble taking notes and keeping up with her.

"Sure. Tell me one surprising thing about you."

She lifted her voluminous hair off her neck, held it atop her head for a second, and then let it fall. "I'm very superstitious."

"Aren't all actors superstitious?" I countered.

"Well, yeah. But I have this one thing I do that other actors who are superstitious would never do. You know about it being unlucky to wear real jewelry on stage?"

"No, I hadn't heard that one."

"Okay, well, it is unlucky to do that. Anyway, I always have this teeny, tiny gold key somewhere on me when I perform. When I tried out for that junior high play, I was wearing it on a chain around my neck. Then after that I just kept wearing it."

She stopped and grabbed my arm. For someone so petite

and thin, her grip was surprisingly strong. "Oh, I shouldn't have told you that. Please don't put it in your article."

I was planning on doing just that. "C'mon, Harper, what difference does it make if I put it in the article?"

"Because if the other actors find out, they'll freak." She sounded truly panicked. "Julian Finch is one of the most superstitious actors I've ever seen. Not that I've seen that many. He has all these rituals, like pulling on his tongue with a paper towel, hitting his chest repeatedly, jumping up and down twenty times."

"He really does those things?" I'd have to ask Julian about his rituals. He'd told me the most surprising thing about him was his fear of spiders, which he'd had to confront when he starred in a B-movie about killer spiders.

"Then tell me something else surprising about you." Why did she tell me it in the first place if she didn't want me to use it? I was beginning to think that Harper was purposely misleading me. For what reason, I didn't know.

She thought for a moment and then said, "I once was arrested. Before you get too excited. I was part of a group protesting the tearing down of a historic building in our town to build an incinerator. We tried to block the demolition of the building. I spent a few hours in jail with the other protesters, and they built the incinerator anyway."

I would have never figured Harper for an environmentalist. She seemed too self-absorbed.

We reached the bench that marked the path to the Moyers' cabin, and Harper stopped and looked off into the woods. "You want to see the Moyer cabin? You know about Danielle Moyer, right? That would be so interesting for your article."

So Harper knew about the cabin and Danielle Moyer. "Yeah, Bob the intern told me that she disappeared after the performance of *The Merchant of Venice,* only he was wrong about the play, it was *A Streetcar Named Desire.*"

"So sad," Harper mused. "Have you seen pictures of her? She was so beautiful. Then to take her life like that."

"She committed suicide? That was never reported." After my conversation with Bob and rereading the fiftieth anniversary booklet, I researched the *Gazette*'s archives for information about the Moyer family. Danielle Moyer had disappeared after *Streetcar,* as I surmised, and was never seen again, just as Bob said. There was no mention of suicide.

"Well, what else could have happened?" She looked at me with those limpid hazel eyes that seemed too big for her face.

"She could have just run away. Three years after Danielle disappeared, her parents, Constance and Alfred, sold the BT, lock, stock and barrel."

"What happened to them?" Harper asked.

"No one knows."

"Kinda like their daughter, huh?"

"Yeah, like that."

"The cabin's so spooky. I just love it." She shivered dramatically. "Let's go see it."

Before I could object, she'd disappeared down the rocky path. I had no choice but to follow her. Why did I feel like Harper was manipulating me? That the entire interview had been rehearsed? And I'd yet to see the real Harper Kennedy.

In the shadowy afternoon light, the cabin appeared even more dilapidated and abandoned. "Oh, look," said Harper, "someone's taken the plywood off the windows."

All the windows on this side of the house were unboarded. I looked around for the plywood. It was neatly piled against a tree. *What is going on here?* I wondered.

Harper went to the back of the cabin and peered through one of the windows. "Look at this. Two plates and two glasses are on the table. Oh, and knives and forks."

"What?" I came around behind Harper and looked over her shoulder. "That wasn't here yesterday," I blurted out.

"Well, it is now. Do you think someone's staying here? Like a homeless person, or maybe grifters," Harper speculated. "That's kinda scary. What if they break into one of our apartments and steal something?"

Where was she going with this? Her imagination seemed to be on overdrive, and it was making me nervous. Even Salinger seemed wary, her tail between her legs as she nosed around the house, taking sidelong glances at Harper.

"Have you seen someone suspicious around the apartments?" I questioned.

"No, not really. But you never know." She tugged on her peasant blouse as if it were too tight.

I walked around to the other side of the cabin with Harper following. The Shown By Appointment Only sign was still there, but those windows were unboarded as well. The low-slung front door's doorknob was still missing, the wood slat still hammered across the door.

I tried opening the windows and found a loose one at the rear of the house. I pushed on it and it creaked open. Below the window the grass was tamped down. I was about to climb through the window when Harper said, "Listen, if you don't have any more questions for me, I'd like to head back to my apartment."

"Just a few more, but I can ask them as we walk back." I could always nose around the old house later.

When we reached the garden, I shook hands with Harper and told her to break a leg.

"If you need anything else, just call me," she offered. "Are you attending the after-party tonight?"

"Wouldn't miss it."

After her lithe figure disappeared down the flagstone path, I doubled back to the Moyer house, with Salinger leading the way. When I reached the house, I told Salinger to sit while I pushed open the window and climbed into the kitchen. The air was damp, but the place didn't have that stale smell houses have when they'd been shut up for long periods of time. And the floor was free of dust, as if it'd just been mopped.

I picked up one of the white stoneware plates, then a glass. No mystery here. These were from the BT's cafeteria. I recognized the ringed glasses and the fluted-edged plates as well as the knives and forks. Unless a homeless person or grifter had stolen these items from the cafeteria, which was possible but highly unlikely, the culprit was part of the BT's cast or crew. Though both glasses were empty, I sniffed them anyway. Nothing. Then I checked out the two small bedrooms and the one bathroom. Empty. No furniture, no footprints marring the dusty floors. The kitchen was the only room with furniture: table, four chairs, a cupboard and a spotless floor.

There was only one more thing to check before I left: the pine cupboard.

I yanked the door open and jumped back, knocking over a chair and causing Salinger to start barking outside.

Hanging inside the cupboard was a white nightgown, a pair of white satin slippers beneath it, giving the impression of a headless ghost. The gown was frayed and worn and had a brownish stain on the bodice. Was that dried blood?

Barking and jumping at the window, Salinger was frantic to get inside. Her outburst had sent animals scurrying back and forth over the roof, inciting her even more.

I shouted at her to be quiet. Finally, she whimpered into silence.

What's going on here? I took a deep breath. Who had placed these items here and why? The room resembled a stage set. The nightgown was something out of a horror movie. Could Bob be the prankster? After all, he and Rich had put up the realty sign.

But then there were Julian and Ryan and their history of pranks—that Julian denied. Stepping closer, I touched the lifeless nightgown; it felt cold and damp. This close, I saw the brown stain wasn't blood. It was too watery looking. If either Ryan or Julian had done this, I didn't see the humor. No, this felt like some kind of message. But to whom and for what purpose?

Slowly I closed the cupboard door, listening to what sounded as though the animals that had scampered overhead were now inside the house. Without waiting to find out, I crawled back through the window, ripping my cotton camp shirt in the process. Once outside, I walked around the cabin, my eyes searching the roof, but didn't see any holes. Maybe the scurrying had been on the roof and not inside the house.

On my way back to the parking lot, I stopped at the box office and asked a spritely older woman with the reddest lipstick I'd ever seen if Barbara Henry was around. Salinger was resting under one of the big cedars nearby, clearly spent from her antics at the cabin.

"Barbara," the woman called to the adjoining office. "That reporter wants to see you."

Barbara had a pasted-on smile, and her ponytail drooped off the back of her head. Surprisingly, she was wearing a flowing white and black sundress. "Yes. Something I can do for you?" she asked.

"The Moyer house," I began. "What can you tell me about it?" I decided to ask a vague question so as not to alert the overly protective PR director.

She looked genuinely perplexed. "It's where the Moyers lived. It's been shut up for years."

"Do you plan on demolishing it? Using it as a museum? It's in pretty good shape."

Her chin jutted out. "What were you doing there?"

How much should I tell her? Especially with the other woman glued to my every word. Contrary to my best interests, I decided on the truth. "The Moyers are part of the BT's story. I wanted to see where they lived."

"The board hasn't decided yet what to do with it. There's been some discussion about moving it once the new theater is built, maybe using it as a museum. But nothing's definite, so don't mention it in the article. Okay?"

"You should have someone board it up until you decide," I advised her. "Because someone's been inside."

Uncharacteristically, Barbara started chuckling. "Oh that's probably Bob. He and Rich put up a realty sign."

"Have you been inside?"

"That creepy place? I don't think so."

"Well, someone has been, and recently. The table's set for two, and there's a nightgown and slippers in the cupboard."

If Barbara was surprised, she hid it well. "I'll make sure it's boarded up. And I'll have Alex talk to Bob about it."

My intention hadn't been to get Bob in trouble. I wasn't even sure Bob was the culprit. "It might not have been Bob. It could have been anyone."

"We'll take care of it. Thanks for telling me about it."

Now I was sorry I'd told her. She'd made up her mind it was Bob. He might even lose his internship and not graduate.

I walked over to the beer garden with Salinger trotting alongside and asked Rich if he knew where Bob was.

"What's he done now?"

I told Rich about the Moyer house and the staged room with the creepy hanging nightgown and how Barbara Henry was convinced Bob had been the culprit.

"Don't worry. I'll take care of it."

"How?"

"I'll say it was me. They'd never fire me. I know where all the bodies are buried." He grinned and then squeezed my shoulder. "Good thing you told me. Don't forget our date tomorrow morning."

I smiled weakly. "Interview," I corrected him. "Tomorrow around nine."

"Sounds like a plan."

Before heading home, I checked out a rental house off Route A in Fish Creek: a squat modular house that listed ever so slightly sideways and looked like it'd been dropped in the middle of the weedy field by a tornado. I didn't even bother getting out of the truck. Finding a place to live by the end of the month might prove more difficult than I thought, especially considering my limited budget. Who knew when I'd get the divorce money?

Damn you, Tom, I fumed. Divorced and homeless really sucked.

CHAPTER NINE

A flutter of bats rose toward the lights in the crescendo of applause and bravos. The audience *en masse* was on its feet as the cast took their fourth curtain call: Nate Ryan front and center, Harper Kennedy on his right, and Julian Finch on his left—all holding hands, all looking like the best of friends.

As the cast took another bow, the audience began to chant, "Shylock, Shylock, Shylock." Nate shrugged his shoulders modestly and then stepped forward to take a solo bow. When he stood up, he turned and gestured to Harper. For a moment she hesitated, then she joined him and together they bowed.

Just as they finished, Ryan reached out and pulled off Harper's hat, releasing her glorious hair, then grabbed her in his arms and bent her backward, kissing her passionately. When he released her, he straightened up awkwardly. The audience roared with laughter, and though she was smiling, it was an uncomfortable smile. To cover her embarrassment over the kiss, Harper turned abruptly and gestured the rest of the cast forward for one last bow.

"Wow," Lydia Crane gushed into my ear. "That was spectacular. I can't wait to meet him at the party."

I didn't need to ask who *him* was. Lydia had been salivating over Ryan since we'd had a drink in the garden before curtain. And I'm sure kissing Harper only added to his allure.

The performance had been flawless, and the audience didn't seem to mind the homosexual overtones, merely gasping when

Bassanio and Antonio kissed, hard and on the lips. I couldn't help but wonder where Harper had hidden her golden key. Probably inside her bra, or maybe inside her voluminous hair.

Once the applause died out, the cast exited the stage, and the audience slowly moved toward the open tent flaps. Some were dressed casually and others were dressed in suits and gowns. My guess was that the suits and gowns had paid the exorbitant ticket price of $500, entitling them to attend the after-party at Serenity House—a mansion adjacent to the BT's grounds. Lydia, who was dressed in a short, ruffled magenta cocktail dress with a low decoupage, was attending, as was I, courtesy of my article.

As Lydia and I walked through the fragrant garden under a full moon, my cell phone began to vibrate again in the pocket of my black linen trousers. No gown for me. Black linen pantsuit with a pale blue silk blouse underneath. Black and blue. The colors matched my bruised psyche. Tom had ended our marriage so abruptly; I was still trying to deal with my hurt feelings and my new status as a divorcée. I hadn't even told Lydia about it. Was I afraid that if I spoke the words aloud, they would make it real?

I took the phone from my pocket and looked at the number. Sturgeon Bay Police Department. Why would the police department be calling me? I flipped the phone open and listened to the message.

"You gotta come get me out," slurred Ken Albright. "That guy had it coming. I'm at the police station. I didn't have no one else to call. They said somebody has to come get me if I'm to get out of here."

I closed the phone, debating what to do. Apparently Ken, under the influence of some substance, got into a fight and had been thrown in jail. Maybe I should let him stay the night to teach him a lesson. Besides, it was important I attend the after-party where I could chat up the actors fresh from their performances with their defenses down, maybe get some unexpected quotes. Then tomorrow I could finish up the article, which would free me to concentrate on looking for a place to live.

"What's up?" Lydia asked. "Bad news?"

"That was Ken Albright. You know, the formerly homeless guy I did the article on, whose friend just died."

Lydia looked bored, her eyes roving the garden impatiently. "What about him?"

"He's been arrested."

She let out an impatient sigh. "Leigh, no."

"Why don't you go on ahead to the party? I'll catch up later."

"C'mon, you're supposed to introduce me to Nate Ryan. How else am I going to get him into my studio for a private yoga lesson? That publicist never called to set it up. When I think of all the positions I could put him in." She moved her eyebrows up and down suggestively.

"That's wrong on so many levels." I laughed. "Didn't you tell me your father had the rich and famous to your house on a regular basis? I'm sure you can handle an actor." Lydia was from money, and her family owned a mansion on Lake Michigan in Lake Forest, Illinois. In college she'd rejected their lifestyle and become a nurse, New Age shop owner, and now yoga master/masseuse/psychic healer. I had serious doubts about Lydia as a psychic healer. She seemed too bound to the physical plane.

"Fine," she huffed. "But one of these days, you have to stop rescuing all these strays who seem to gravitate to you." She'd done a psychic reading on me a few weeks ago, in which my guides showed up and said I needed to shift my direction in life. Too bad none of them mentioned Tom turning up with divorce papers and shifting my direction without me even trying.

86

She stomped away down the slate path to the parking lot. Her stilettos made sharp pings of protest on the stone.

For a moment, I stood there, letting the intoxicating scent of the flowers fill my senses. Their fragrance was as illusive as the moon slipping in and out of cloud banks, as if it too couldn't make up its mind. Maybe I should attend the after-party and let Ken fend for himself.

I opened my phone. "This is Leigh Girard from the *Gazette*. I understand you've arrested Kenneth Albright."

After filling out some paperwork, Deputy Chief Chet Jorgensen gestured me into one of the interview rooms—a windowless, gun-metal gray room as cold and stark as a fallout shelter.

"What's up?" I asked Chet as he pulled out a chair for me before sitting down. Chet was a throwback to a time when men held seats out for women. Luckily, his chivalrous nature didn't indicate a belief that women were helpless.

"You sure you want to do this?" he asked, crossing his large arms on the table.

A massively built Nordic type, Chet took in a deep breath, which seemed to suck up most of the air in the room. He and I had our differences in the past, but deep down we liked and respected each other.

His question was one I'd asked myself on the drive to Sturgeon Bay. Was I letting my sympathy for those two men wipe out my common sense? Was I falling for my own story about them, not wanting it to be proven false?

"Look," I began, placing my hands flat on the shiny steel table. "Ken feels guilty about leaving Brownie and not being there when he died. Yeah, he's had a setback. But he only needs someone to show a little faith in him."

Chet straightened. "Maybe he should feel guilty. Guys like him never change. I've seen it time and again. Eventually they go back to their scumbag ways. You want to mess with that?"

"Is there something you're not telling me about Ken? And why are you treating Brownie's death as a crime?"

"Best stay outta this one." Chet stood up and went for the door.

"Why'd you arrest him?" I asked, still not satisfied with Chet's answers.

"Never arrested him. He and the other drunk got into a fight. Bar owner didn't press charges, just wanted them gone. We only hauled them in to sober 'em up. He just needs a ride back to his . . ." Chet hesitated. "Shack."

I stood up and said, "Okay, I'll take him *home*." I stressed the word *home*.

Chet opened the door. "You wait out in the lobby. I'll get him." He started to walk away and then turned back. "Just be careful, okay? Guys like Albright always have one agenda, and that's getting wasted."

"Where'd you get the money to drink?" I asked Ken as we neared Sister Bay. He'd been slumped against the truck's door for most of the trip, only stirring now.

He reeked of booze. I didn't need to ask him what his drink of choice was. I could smell it: beer. The yeasty smell was making me feel sick.

"My paycheck from the Orchard," he snapped at me. I was expecting a contrite Ken, but he didn't do contrite. He was angry and belligerent.

"Why?" I asked as I turned east and headed down Route ZZ.

"That guy had it comin'. Callin' me a cheat. I almost hit him with the pool cue. Slugged him instead."

"You want to end up dead like Brownie?" I wanted to get through to him.

He punched his fist so hard against my dashboard, I jumped.

"Shut up. Just shut up about Brownie."

I slammed on the brakes and pulled off onto the shoulder.

"Whatta you doin'?" he asked.

"Get outta my truck," I said in a low voice.

"What?" It was as if I'd thrown cold water in his face.

"You heard me. Out!"

He looked around as if he'd suddenly realized where he was. I saw his hand reach for the door handle, then stop. On the dark road surrounded by open fields, I heard the wind whispering, an owl hoot, and then Ken's ugly sobs. I kept my eyes straight ahead, not looking at him, waiting for him to stop. Finally, he swiped his arm across his eyes and said, "I'm not gonna make it."

"You need to get some help. The YMCA has a twelve-step program."

"No, you don't get it. Them cops busted my alibi."

Now I turned and looked at him. His shoulders were slumped forward; he seemed to have lost some part of himself. "Weren't you at your sister's in Green Bay?"

He chewed on his lower lip and shook his head. "Me and Brownie got into it Thursday. I took off, looking to score. Hitchhiked to Green Bay an' caught up with some of my old buddies and got high. Never made it to my sister's. When I got back Saturday, I found Brownie dead. So it's my fault. I should have never left him."

"What did you fight about?" Now his self-destructive behavior was making sense.

"He didn't want to stay on there anymore. He wanted to pack it in. He wouldn't tell me why. And I just lost it. Told him he was weak and stupid, that kind of stuff. Then I took off."

"It's not your fault." Even as I said it, I felt the doubt in my own words.

"It is my fault. Because of me, he started drinking again and it killed him. I might as well have put a gun to his head and pulled the trigger." He opened the door and stumbled out. "I need to walk. Thanks for getting me out of jail."

I watched him disappear into the night, wondering if some things really couldn't be fixed and if Ken's life was one of those things.

Chapter Ten:
WEDNESDAY, JULY 12

"I'm almost going to miss the old theater," Rich said as he directed me along the slate walkway toward the tiered gardens.

I stifled a yawn. Last night I'd tossed and turned, wondering if Ken had made it home. Finally, I gave in to my insomnia, got up and read *The Importance of Being Earnest,* the BT's next production after *MOV.* I'd gotten maybe three hours of sleep and a few good laughs.

"It just won't be the same. No more bats, no more sharing washrooms with the audience. Though you have to admit, the bats do add a bit of fun," he winked at me. "Can't imagine what's going to happen to them when they tear down the old theater. All them bats will have to find another home. Must be five hundred of them living around the theater."

Rich was wearing a black t-shirt that read "Celebrate Diversity," with at least twenty-five different handguns depicted in white. The blue bandana that covered his balding head and his dark mustache made him look like a pirate. He seemed to be moving even slower than usual, probably because of the unrelenting heat. The humidity and high temps made me feel like I was running a low-grade fever. I'd even taken my temp this morning, thinking I might be sick.

"You seem pretty sure that there'll be a new theater." I didn't want to think about five hundred bats nesting somewhere nearby.

"Oh, it's going to happen. Not only did last night's opening break box office records for a single performance, but Nate Ryan pledged a half million dollars. Right before the performance he told the cast and crew. It'll happen."

Ryan pledged a half million dollars? Why hadn't he told me about the donation when I'd interviewed him? It would have been great PR for him, putting him in a very favorable light. Could he have developed a conscience in rehab? Atoning for all the hell he put Nina through? Or was it his very generous attempt to remake his image? My mind was spinning with questions.

"How was the after-party?" I'd left Lydia two voice messages this morning asking about the party. She still hadn't returned my calls. Which wasn't like her. Unless her plan to corral Nate into her lair hadn't worked and she didn't want to talk about her failed seduction plan.

"Oh, that," he laughed. "I didn't go. I've been to so many of those through the years. They're pretty much all the same. Lots of drinking and people doing and saying things they regret in the morning, if they remember. Rather stay home with Dixie. Well, here it is. Hope you're gonna take some pictures."

We'd stopped on the middle tier of the limestone steps. On either side were banks of flowers so vibrant in color, they looked unreal.

"Sure thing," I answered. Though it was unlikely I'd use the photos, I didn't want to dampen Rich's enthusiasm. He was visibly proud of the gardens. Later if he asked about the photos, I'd blame Jake for their not being published. That's what editors were for.

"Over there where it's shady, I planted mostly ground cover. Then you can see where there's full sun, I put in daylilies, sunflowers, purple coneflowers. There's even a Shakespearean garden. Over there by the bench."

I looked to where he was pointing. Sure enough, I recognized roses, columbine, pansies, rosemary and violets. *A rose by any other name,* I mused lamely.

"Don't ask me which flowers are from which play. You'll have to talk to Nina about that. The garden was her idea. Something new we put in this year."

I couldn't remember if there were any flower references in MOV. "So the garden is new this year?" I coaxed.

"Yeah, and the moon garden too."

"Where's that?" I'd never heard of a moon garden.

He chuckled. "You walked right past it, all along the edges of the path."

I didn't see anything but snarls of green. "I'm guessing the flowers only bloom at night?"

"Right. Evening primrose, moonflower, night phlox, jasmine. Once they open, they have a real strong scent meant to attract moths."

So that was the illusive fragrance I smelled last night. "Your idea?"

"Nah. Nina again. She's really into the flowers, says they add ambiance. Of course, I'm the one who has to do all the work."

"So how much time do you spend a week tending the gardens?"

We started back down the steps toward the theater. He offered me his hand, which I politely waved off. "Depends, but I'd say anywhere from twenty to twenty-five hours a week. But that's after everything's in. Because of the Shakespeare garden, I had to hire some guys to help out with the plantings and such."

He wasn't an actor, and I probably wouldn't use most of what he told me, but I asked anyway. "Tell me one surprising thing about yourself."

He scratched his neck and tightened his mouth. "I have an engineering degree from Purdue University."

I looked down at my notes to cover my shock. "What happened?"

"That's why I never tell anyone. They always ask that question. Nothing happened. It wasn't for me."

I didn't believe him, and I wanted to challenge his answer. But Rich was a minor character in this piece that I still had to write. "Well, thanks for the tour." I started to walk away.

"Thought you were going to take pictures." He sounded hurt.

"Right." I took my digital camera from my bag and snapped a few photos, not really aiming at anything in particular.

"I'll be looking for those photos. And here's my cell number in case you have more questions for me."

He handed me a piece of paper with his name and number written on it. "By the way, just so you know, I told Barbara I'd been messing around the cabin. Bob's in the clear."

"Thanks." I shoved the paper in my pocket. "Any guesses who unboarded the windows and put those things in the kitchen?"

He shook his head no. "Don't worry about it. Soon as I get a minute, I'm going to board everything up again, and this time it'll be permanent."

He held out his hand for me to shake. "Been a pleasure, Leigh." He put his other hand on top of mine and held my hand just a second too long before he let go. Then he listlessly ambled down the stone steps. His hand had felt rough and feverish.

As I watched Rich walk away, a line from *Julius Caesar* came to mind, something about a character having a lean and hungry look. There was something rapacious about Rich that went counter to his laidback lifestyle as the BT's groundskeeper and bartender.

On my way to the parking lot, I took a detour to Ryan's

condo, wanting more information about his generous gift to the BT.

I hustled up the steps to the second floor and knocked on his door, noticing that the pitchfork was gone. No answer. I knocked again. It was nearly eleven o'clock; he had to be up by now. If he'd slept in his own bed.

Was this a good idea? I asked myself as I knocked a third time. What if he is sleeping and I wake him? So what? I wanted to know why he'd neglected to tell me he was donating half a million dollars to the BT.

Silence. I put my ear to the door and heard the hum of the refrigerator.

Just then my cell phone trilled, startling me. It was Lydia, finally.

"Where have you been, or should I say who have you been with?" I teased.

"Leigh, you've got to come now. He's dead. The police are here. But I need you."

"Who's dead?"

"Nate Ryan. He's dead. I tried to resuscitate him." She sobbed. "But it was too late."

"Where are you?"

"The studio. Come to my studio. I don't know what happened."

"Okay, sit tight. I'll be there in a few. I'm leaving the BT now."

I ran to my truck, jumped in and spat up gravel as I sped out of the parking lot, my mind whirling. Nate Ryan was dead. Lydia had tried to save him. But her effort had been too late.

An ambulance and two police cars were parked in the lot behind Founder's Square in Fish Creek. Gawking tourists milled around near the back entrance of Lydia's studio. Before exiting my truck, I considered how I was going to get past the ever-diligent Deputy Ferry, who was guarding the door, directing tourists to move on.

From my other encounters with Ferry, I decided that charm wouldn't work. Like most of the Door County police force, he considered me a nuisance. So charm would be like bullets to Superman. My only other option was the professional approach. Failing that, I'd plead friendship. My friend was in trouble and had asked for my help. You have to let me in.

Notepad in hand, pen tucked in my shirtfront, I slammed the truck door and headed for the studio. When I reached Ferry, I said hello and moved to go inside.

But he blocked my entrance with his body. "You can't go in, Leigh, press or no press." Ferry was a short man with dark hair and a sharp nose, who had a habit of putting his thumbs in his belt loops and bouncing on his heels when he asserted his authority, like a boxer about to deliver a punch.

"Lydia called me and asked me to come," I pleaded. "Could you at least tell her I'm here?"

He looked around the parking lot and said, "Move along," to a group of teens. "Nothing to see here," then turned his attention back to me. "You know I can't let you in there."

"But Lydia needs me." I tucked my notepad in my pocket.

"That so? I'll tell you what. Soon as Chet is done interviewing her, I'll let him know you're here. Then we'll see how that goes. Now I'm going to watch as you walk back to that truck of yours." He gestured at my truck.

I let out an exasperated sigh. Because of my interference in a murder investigation last year, I'd been responsible for Chet being suspended. Ferry wasn't going to let me anywhere near Lydia.

Cell phone at the ready, I sat down under a honey locust tree adjacent to the ambulance and texted Lydia, "I'm here." Ferry wasn't going to tell me where I could or couldn't sit. I stared right at him as I finished my text, daring him to make me move. He bounced a few more times on his heels then looked away.

In about fifteen minutes, Chet emerged from the studio, glanced my way, and then motioned to me. When I reached him, his finger was already pointed at my face. "Here's how it's going to work. You're here as Lydia's friend. That's it. No quotes for that paper there." As his finger jabbed at me, I studied the jagged, bitten edge of his fingernail, rather than the red glare of his face. "She's in bad shape. That's the only reason I'm letting you anywhere near her. Got it?"

"Okay," I answered. "You don't have to go all commando on me."

"Don't I?" He leaned in so close to me, I wanted to take a step back, but I didn't. He wasn't going to intimidate me. For about a minute we faced each other down. Then he turned and walked into the studio and I followed.

The studio's burnt-incense smell was in stark contrast to the blare of the overhead lights. I only caught a glimpse of Nate Ryan's body, splayed on his back, as if he'd lain down to take a nap from which he fully expected to wake from. On the floor scattered around him were an assortment of items: crumpled eye pillow, jacket, overturned metal water bottle and a yoga bag lying on its side.

Beside the mat was what looked like vomit. I took in a deep breath. Yep, it was vomit. Kneeling over the body was Sonny Chambers, the undertaker at the Chambers Funeral Home. Before I could get a better look, Chet grabbed me by my upper arm and steered me toward Lydia's office to the right of the door and off the main studio.

"Leigh," Lydia cried as I walked into the room. She sat on a futon hugging her knees to her chest, shivering. "It all happened so fast. There was nothing I could do."

I'd never heard Lydia sound so helpless and vulnerable. Chet stood in the room against the wall, his arms folded across his chest.

"It's okay," I said. "We know you did everything you could." I turned toward Chet. "Right, Chet?"

He didn't answer, just stood there like he was guarding Hannibal Lector.

"What was Ryan doing here?" I whispered as I sat down next to her and put my arms around her.

"Like I told Chet." Lydia seemed oblivious to Chet's presence. "We hit it off last night at the party. I gave him my card, and he asked if he could come by this morning for a massage and a yoga class. So we arranged for him to come around eight a.m., before the shops opened. He wanted to avoid the tourists." She took in a deep, shuddering breath.

"I gave him a restorative class because he said his back was bothering him. Then, like always, I ended with Savasana. You know, corpse pose. Where you lie on your back, arms at your side, eyes closed. He hadn't brought an eye pillow, so I placed one over his eyes once he was in the pose. And—"

Chet interrupted, "That's enough, Lydia. You know what I told you."

"I was only going to say, and he suddenly sat up, vomited and grabbed his chest, then fell backward. That's all. Can I go upstairs now and change?" Lydia's living quarters were above her shop.

"Not a good idea. Leigh, how about you take her to your place? We still have some work to do here."

What was going on with Chet? Why couldn't she go upstairs and change? He was acting like this was a murder investigation, not a natural death, and that Lydia was the prime suspect. "Chet, do you suspect foul play?"

His face went scarlet. "There you go again. How many times do I have to tell you this isn't Chicago here? This Nate Ryan died suddenly. Famous or not famous, this is standard police procedure in a sudden death."

"Okay, okay. Don't bite my head off."

"Can I get a few of my things?" Lydia repeated her request. Again I was struck by how Lydia didn't sound like herself. Normally she'd be flirting with Chet, tousling her hair, smiling and deepening her dimples to get her way. But the circumstances were anything but normal.

She was still dressed in her yoga outfit, tight-fitting black pants, spaghetti-strapped black top, and she was still barefoot.

"Sorry, not yet. I'll let you know when. Leigh, I'm sure you have something she can wear at your place," Chet grumbled.

"C'mon, Lydia. My truck is out back. Can she at least have some shoes?"

Chet pointed to her flip-flops by the door. Lydia was so shaky, I had to slip them on her feet. Something was off with Lydia. As a nurse, she dealt with life and death on a regular basis. Why was she so shaken up?

Lydia kept her eyes down as we walked back into the studio room, not even glancing at Ryan's body. Once outside she put her hands over her eyes, shielding them from the sun's glare and the stares of the tourists. I helped her into the truck's cab and headed south on Highway 42 to avoid Fish Creek with its gaggle of tourists. I'd cut across the peninsula at Route EE, taking the back roads.

"Are you going to tell me what's going on with you?" I coaxed her. She was huddled against the door, hugging her arms.

"A man died in my studio, and I couldn't save him. Isn't that enough?" Then she closed her eyes and pretended to sleep.

There was nowhere for Lydia to hide in the Airstream mobile home. So after she changed into a pair of my sweatpants and a t-shirt, which hung on her petite frame, she went outside and sat in one of the lawn chairs perched on the rise overlooking Lake Michigan.

Salinger, sensing something was up with Lydia, followed her. I decided to give Lydia some space. Besides, I needed to call Jake and tell him about Ryan.

When he didn't answer his cell phone or his office phone, I left a message explaining what had happened and that I would be in the office as soon as I got Lydia settled. Though it wasn't even one o'clock yet, I grabbed two glasses and a bottle of chardonnay, along with a box of crackers and a block of cheese, and joined her.

After I poured two generous glasses of wine, we sat silently gazing out at the lake, its restless surge like the undercurrents I could feel moving inside Lydia.

"What were the odds?" she asked, then paused to take a deep swallow of wine. "If he was going to die, why at my studio? Why not while he was doing drugs or—" She stopped, maybe realizing how selfish that sounded. Lydia's fallback position was always narcissism.

"You know what's going to happen, don't you? The media is going to descend on me like a hoard of locusts. They're going to dig into my life. They're going to imply things. Nasty things. None of which will be true, but does that matter? Maybe I need a lawyer."

Her eyes were brimming with pain. I reached out and put my hand over hers.

"Yes, the next week's going to be tough," I reassured her. "But then some other famous person will die or do something outrageous or criminal, and the media will move on. You'll be nothing but a footnote."

"Maybe." She swirled the wine in her glass, then drank the last of it. "Did I ever tell you why I left my life of money and privilege behind to live here?"

"Something about you being your family's conscience?" When we'd first met after my embarrassing fainting spell at the hospital, she'd joked about being the family's conscience.

"That was only part of it. The other reason was I saw that if I stayed, my life would be a series of shallow moments, one after another. Days filled with choosing the right clothes, the right schools for my children, charity luncheons and business dinners. My father spent his entire life courting fame. He had the money, but that wasn't enough. He wanted to be known."

"You're not him."

"That's where you're wrong, Leigh. I am very much my father's daughter. Why else did I hunt down Nate Ryan last night and literally force myself on him? You know how I can be with men."

"You slept with him?" Her ironic smile said it all. Lydia was attractive, fun, and Ryan was a womanizer. I shouldn't be surprised, but I was. Why? Because I'd resisted? I wasn't like Lydia either in temperament or in body.

"You make it sound so pretty. No, we didn't sleep together. We had sex in the back of my car like two horny teenagers. Quite the aphrodisiac. While everyone was inside at the party, we were having a party of our own, right there not ten feet away from the house. What's worse, I think he felt he owed me the private yoga class and massage. He handed me three hundred dollars before the class. You know, kind of payment for my services."

Lydia had a tendency toward melancholy, which she kept at bay with self-created dramas. Now the drama had become unmanageable. I could feel her spiraling downward.

"You know that's not true. When I interviewed him, he asked about a massage. You've got to give yourself a break. You didn't do anything wrong."

A few seagulls squawked and circled overhead. "Did you tell Chet that you had sex with Ryan?"

"You think I want that out there? Besides the sex had nothing to do with his dying in my studio this morning. Believe me, when we had sex, he was just fine. In fact, more than fine." She smiled, then shook her head. "I didn't mean to say that. See? I can't help myself."

"You're in shock, that's all." I knew that wasn't all. Lydia was feeling guilty about something. But what? I wasn't sure I should pressure her; she seemed so brittle.

She poured herself a second glass of wine and took a long gulp. "Can I stay here until all this blows over? I'll sleep in Sarah's art studio. Too cramped in that tin box of hers."

"Sarah's coming back in two weeks. But until then you can have my bed. I'll take the studio for the time being." Though Sarah hadn't left me a key to the studio, I still hadn't fixed the broken lock from the break-in last year.

"What about your shop and the hospital?" I asked, the lingering question of her guilt still rumbling around in my head.

"Carrie can cover for me at the shop. She needs the extra money. And I'll call in sick at the hospital."

The thought of sharing the living quarters with Lydia was fraught with all kinds of problems, space being the least of them. But she was my friend, and she was in bad shape.

"Just another one of your strays, huh?" Lydia teased lamely.

I smiled and then plunged in. "Lydia, I have to ask you something. Why are you feeling so guilty about Ryan's death? Is there something you're not telling me?"

Her mouth went tight and her jaw rigid. "Maybe this isn't a good idea, my staying with you." She jumped up from her chair, knocking over the bottle of wine. "I'd forgotten how you can be. Nothing stands between you and a good story, not even friends."

I righted the bottle and followed her as she strode toward the mobile home, slamming the door before I could go inside. I heard the click of the lock. "Lydia, c'mon. Open the door."

Through the window I heard her sobbing.

"Lydia, I'm sorry. Please open the door."

Finally I gave up, got in my truck and drove away.

What was Lydia holding back? I wondered. Chet had been quick to cut her off when she'd been relating how Ryan died. What hadn't she told me?

CHAPTER ELEVEN

"Haven't gotten to the dog tags yet," Marge said as I walked into the *Gazette* office. "Jake's got me working on a special project. But it's next on my list. By the way, Jake says you're not to leave until he gets back from Green Bay. How's Lydia doing?"

How did she already know about Lydia and Ryan's death? "You sure you don't want to cover the news beat, Marge?" I teased.

"Honey, I'd much rather talk about it than write about it. You didn't answer my question about Lydia."

At the mention of Lydia's name, Rob Martin's head popped up. He was sitting at our shared desk, the only one with a computer, typing away. He was doing a series on how the inordinately hot summer was affecting Door County's flora and fauna. As the *Gazette*'s environmental editor, nature he was good at, people not so much.

We had a love–hate relationship—more hate than love. Of late, however, we'd come to a truce based on the realization that we were stuck with each other.

"She's in shock, but she'll be okay." I didn't want to elaborate on Lydia's fragile state or my suspicions that she was keeping something from me.

The phone rang. "Not another one." Marge held up one finger. "Just a sec, hon."

"*Door County Gazette,* this is Marge. No, I really don't know.

That I can't say. You'll have to call the police department. Have you tried Mr. Ryan's publicist? Sorry you feel that way." When she hung up, her cheeks were flushed. "Damn rude reporters."

"When did that start?" I asked.

"About a half hour ago."

Martin strolled up to us. "Marge, did you show her?"

"Show me what?" I asked warily. Whatever Martin wanted to show me, I knew I wasn't going to like it. He looked too smug.

"Not now, Rob," Marge said.

"She's going to see it sooner or later."

He leaned over Marge and opened the search engine on her computer. Under the Today's Highlights section was the headline, "Nate Ryan dies suddenly after yoga class." And over the headline was a photo of Lydia being escorted from her shop by me. The story read, "Nate Ryan died today of unknown causes after taking a yoga class. He was performing with a Wisconsin residential theater company owned by his ex-wife Nina Cass."

Martin smiled up at me and his normally ruddy complexion seemed to be glowing. "You want to read the rest?"

I did, but I didn't want to give him the satisfaction of seeing my reaction.

"No, thanks."

"You sure? The article names you and Lydia. You're famous." He smirked.

How was I going to protect Lydia now? It wouldn't take too much digging before reporters figured out where I was living.

"Damn," I said. "I gotta get home. Tell Jake I'll talk to him later."

As I started down the gravel driveway to the mobile home, I spotted only one TV van: Channel Twelve News, Green Bay. Good, I thought. One, I could handle. Then as I neared the mobile home, I realized it was too late.

Alison Foster, the news anchor, was standing outside the home, a microphone in her hand, a cameraman shooting and Lydia talking.

Quickly I parked the truck next to the TV van and strode over to them with Salinger nipping at my heels. "Lydia, what are you doing?" I shouted.

Allison answered, "Here's Leigh Girard, the *Door County Gazette* reporter who's doing an in-depth article on the BT for the *Chicago Reporter*." Gosh, how much had Lydia told her? This was way beyond my ability to do damage control.

The camera swung my way. Instinctively, I put my hand up to shield my face. If I'd had a newspaper, I would be using it to cover my face like a guilty criminal.

"Shut that thing off, right now!" I demanded.

The cameraman kept shooting until Alison said, "Turn it off, Josh."

"Lydia, get inside." I gestured toward the mobile home. She looked unfocused, as if she didn't know where she was. She was still wearing my baggy sweatpants and t-shirt. Her hair was flattened on one side. The other side stood out from her head.

"Leigh, it's okay. I know Alison." She was slurring her words. "She's going to handle this whole thing. So chill." Had she finished the rest of the wine while I was gone? She sounded delayed, like a satellite feed. Had she smoked a joint? I'd never known Lydia to do drugs.

"You're in no condition to be giving an interview," I said, taking her by the arm and dragging her up the wood steps to the door. She didn't resist, letting me guide her inside and into the bedroom where I eased her down and pulled the thin blanket over her. She stared up at me with a stupid grin on her face.

"Thanks, Leigh. You always know what to do."

"Just rest, okay?" I said, and then closed the door. Through the kitchen window, I saw Alison still outside, holding the microphone against her cotton jacket. I wanted to shout at her to leave; instead, I hurried back outside for the inevitable confrontation I was dreading. "You took advantage of her," I accused.

She put up both of her hands as a sign of innocence. "Look, she called me."

That was a surprise. What was Lydia thinking? "Why would she do that?"

"She and I go way back. We're both Mount St. Mary's girls. You know, the private girls' school on the North Shore in Lake Forest. She knew the press was going to hound her, and she asked if I could do an interview and then feed it to the national news outlets, and that's what I did. It'll buy her some time. How about you?" She held the microphone out to me.

"I'm not giving you an interview, if that's what you're asking. You can read what I have to say in the *Gazette*."

"Your choice. Okay, Josh, we're done here."

"Wait." I realized I might have been too quick to dismiss her. "What did she say?"

She looked me up and down, then smiled knowingly. I did the same. Up close she was even prettier and thinner than on TV, with her carefully highlighted blond hair and taut, trim figure. "Guess you'll have to watch the news at five."

After the van left, I went inside the mobile home and checked on Lydia. She was out cold. I carefully inched the door closed, then peered into the kitchen trashcan. There on top was the spent bottle of wine. I didn't think her spacey condition was just the product of too much wine. She was stoned. Where had she gotten the stuff? Had to be Nate Ryan. His place had reeked of marijuana. What had happened this morning between them? More than yoga, that's for sure. Did they continue last night's sexual hijinks? Was that why she was feeling guilty? Did she think she caused his death with the potent combo of sex and drugs?

I walked outside and sat down on the steps. Salinger nestled close to me, resting her head on my leg and looking up at me as if to say, "It's too hot for all this drama."

As I watched the green shadowy leaves rustle in the hot breeze, I considered where to take Lydia so she'd be sequestered from the media. Clearly my place wasn't safe anymore.

Jake had offered to put me up at his place, but how would he feel about Lydia? Then there was Joe Stillwater. Lydia and Joe both worked as nurses at the Bay Hospital. And Joe had no connection to the media or this story.

I took my cell phone from my pocket. When he picked up, I said, "Joe, I have a favor to ask."

Before I could make my request, he cut in, "Hey, Leigh, you get my messages? Thought we might catch some dinner. You know, nothing serious."

"Yeah, dinner sounds good." I'd been avoiding calling him back. Now that my divorce was a done deal, I was a free agent—and all that it implied.

"I hear you're looking for a place. Got just the house for you. Though knowing you, you're probably gonna say no. But hear me out. There's this little cabin. It doesn't look like much, but it's cheap and clean. Guy who owns it, Ray Brill, a professor from Iowa, had a medical emergency, so he had to head back to Iowa. I only know about this because I took care of him in the ER. You interested?"

"Sure, whatever." My mind was elsewhere. "Look, you probably know about Nate Ryan and Lydia. Well, I've got her at the mobile home with me. But she's in bad shape and needs some place to crash until things calm down."

Before I could finish my request, he said, "Bring her here to my place."

"You sure?"

"What are friends for, right, Leigh?" His words were freighted with meanings I didn't want to explore.

"Right. I'll be there in a few."

As I started to get up, I noticed the garbage bin lid was flipped open. I went over to close it and saw an unfamiliar can on top of the pile. I picked it and sniffed. Inside was the tip of a marijuana joint. My hunch had been right.

CHAPTER TWELVE

Surprisingly Lydia hadn't fought me when I told her I was taking her to Joe's. All she said was, "I probably should have called him first anyway. Saved myself the trouble."

"I'll go by your studio later and pick up some of your things," I answered. Chet had left a message on my cell phone that they were done and Lydia could go home. The nap hadn't improved her appearance or her demeanor. There were dark circles under her eyes, her face was puffy, her disposition mean.

"You'll need these." She threw her keys at me. "I don't see why I can't go home now."

"If you hadn't given that interview, maybe you could," I told her. "The media is probably staked out at your place waiting for you."

"You know sometimes, Leigh, you're a real bitch."

I should have just shut up, but I was annoyed with her carelessness and her shutting me out. "You're mad at yourself, not me," I spat back.

"Oh, so now you're a therapist in addition to being a detective, a journalist and an ex-teacher?"

Where was all this anger coming from? "I thought we were friends. What's going on with you?"

"Yeah, I thought so too."

When we pulled up in front of Joe's house, Lydia was out of the truck before I turned the engine off.

As I opened my door, Salinger leapt out of the truck and ran in the direction of the open field beside Joe's house. I didn't call after her. I was tired of fighting difficult females.

Joe's Gills Rock house suited him. It was a single-story, modular, blue-sided house, modest with white shutters and sur-rounded by open fields and savannahs. Next to the house rested several canoes on sawhorses.

By the time I reached the front door, Lydia was already inside. I could hear her apologizing. "Sorry about this. But Leigh and I . . . well, you know how she can be."

I let the screen door slam behind me. "How can I be?"

Joe interrupted. "Got some iced tea in the fridge. Or there's soft drinks, wine, beer?"

"Water's fine," I said, hoping Lydia would follow suit.

"This is only for one night," Lydia explained to Joe. "By tomorrow I'm going back home, no matter what. Mind if we turn on the TV? It's almost five."

Joe looked at me questioningly.

"Lydia gave an interview to Alison Foster from Channel Ten, Green Bay."

Joe turned on the small TV and, instantly, Alison appeared behind the ubiquitous anchor desk. She was still wearing the sky-blue cotton jacket, her hair as polished as before.

"Actor Nate Ryan died suddenly this morning in Fish Creek after a private yoga class at the Crystal Door Spa. Lydia Crane, the instructor, was with him at the time of his death. We have an exclusive interview with Lydia Crane."

Then the screen cut away to the interview. There was the mobile home in the background and Lydia standing outside it addressing the camera.

"Can you tell us what happened?" Alison asked.

"Everything seemed fine. Then at the end of the class when he did the last pose, you know, Savasana, the corpse pose"— Lydia grinned stupidly—"he sat up, grabbed his chest, let out a pained cry, then fell back."

For some reason she'd left out his vomiting.

"I understand you're a nurse. Did you try to revive him?"

Lydia's eyes looked glassy and unfocused. "Yes, but it was too late. I mean, he had no pulse. I could tell he was dead. But I still tried CPR."

The screen cut back to the live news show. "That was Lydia Crane, the woman who tried to save Nate Ryan."

Her male anchor, Ben Santos, wearing a grim expression, said, "Very eerie, what she said about that pose. Don't you think so, Alison?"

"Very."

Joe clicked the remote and the room fell into silence.

"I'll get you a glass of water, Leigh. Lydia, what do you want?"

"I don't care. I really don't care." She sat on the couch, hugging her knees to her chest and rocking back and forth.

As I waited for Joe to return, I considered what I could say to ease Lydia's distress. *You did everything you could to save him. Stop beating yourself up! You have to know that having sex with him last night didn't cause his death.* Before I could say anything, Joe returned with a glass of water and a tumbler of something amber.

"Whiskey," he said, handing the tumbler to Lydia, who sniffed it. "Good for the nerves." Lydia took a long pull then edged herself back, letting go of her legs.

I quickly drank the water while Joe filled the silence with gossip about work and the marina and anything to keep off the topic of Ryan's death. Finally, even he ran out of things to say.

It was past six o'clock. "I'm going to head out," I said. "Let me know if you need anything."

Lydia stared at the tumbler as if I were already gone.

Joe walked me outside.

"What do you think is going on with Lydia?" I asked.

"Shock, that's all."

"I'm not so sure it's just shock."

He rested his hand on my arm. His touch felt warm and soothing, full of strength and reassurance. I'd forgotten how secure he made me feel. Or maybe I didn't want to remember. "Leigh, a man died at her place, and there was nothing she could do. Take my word for it, no matter how many times you deal with it, you never get used to something like that."

Salinger took that moment to come bounding out of the field, weeds tangled around her neck. Joe let go of my arm.

I bent down and disentangled her from the weeds, then opened the truck's door. It took two jumps before Salinger settled herself in the passenger seat. After I climbed in the other side, Joe handed me a torn piece of paper. "Here's the address to that cabin I was telling you about." He was leaning in the window, and I caught his familiar piney-outdoorsy scent.

I glanced down at the address, Timberline Road, down the road from Joe's house. "You gotta be kidding."

"Like I said, it's clean and cheap. What have you got to lose?"

"Nothing, I guess."

Before heading to Fish Creek, I drove south on Timberline Road. What did I have to lose, right? The mailbox was in a culvert, and trees hid the green county address marker, so I missed the house and had to double back. The truck bumped down the winding gravel driveway, low-lying tree branches scraping the top of my truck and causing Salinger to let out menacing growls. The driveway ended in a turnaround in front of the cabin. White cedar logs, if I knew my wood, mortar between the logs, and white lacy curtains on the windows. The cabin had to be at least a hundred years old. Salinger let out a series of barks as a squirrel scurried up one of the tall pine trees surrounding the cabin.

"It's okay, girl," I said, running my fingers through her matted fur. "In fact, it's better than okay."

That sly fox, Joe Stillwater, I thought as I got out of the truck to check out my future home. How did he know I'd fall in love with this charming house? Even before I peered in the windows and saw the stone fireplace and rustic furniture, the walls lined with floor-to-ceiling bookcases, I'd made my mind up.

For once Salinger didn't go tearing off into the woods. Instead, she stood beside me, her nose twitching with the earthy, dark scents of the place.

"I know," I said, crouching beside her, "it's kinda magical."

CHAPTER THIRTEEN

It was after eleven p.m. when I parked the truck on a side street across from Founder's Square. I'd driven by after leaving Joe's house but hadn't stopped, glimpsing a plethora of reporters and camera people on the sidewalk and in the parking lot behind Lydia's studio. Rather than risk the media gauntlet, I'd gone home and waited.

Now only a few tourists were ambling past the shops. And when I walked behind Lydia's studio, the parking lot was empty. The media must have moved on to the next big story.

Even so, I took my time glancing right and left before I unlocked the door and went inside. Immediately the lingering incense scent and the underlying stink of vomit assaulted me. I put my hand over my nose as I entered the studio where Ryan had died. All Ryan's stuff was gone, and his vomit had been cleaned up.

If it wasn't for the smell, the studio was as it was before. I figured the police had done a thorough search of the studio, so there was no need to look around. I hurried up the back steps to Lydia's living quarters. At the top of the stairs was a large carpeted room that served as a combination great room and office. Piled against one wall were large floor pillows that Lydia used for her monthly women's circle, sort of a New Age bull session. There were three doors leading from the room. I took the first door on the right, which led into her bedroom. The bed was made, so if there'd been any further sexual antics this morning, they hadn't happened here.

In the bedroom closet I found her carry-on black suitcase and stuffed it with an assortment of clothes from her closet and dresser drawers. Then I went into her bathroom, took her nightgown from behind the door, rifled through the bathroom medicine cabinet for her toothbrush, hairbrush, and an assortment of other toiletries. I was about to leave her bathroom, when I thought I heard a noise from downstairs. I froze. Had I locked the door behind me? In my hurry I couldn't remember. For a moment I didn't move as I strained to hear any sounds.

Silence. I let out a deep breath, gathered up Lydia's remaining things, threw them into her suitcase and hustled down the stairs into the studio. Then I stopped. The studio was in total darkness. I distinctly remembered switching on the tiny table lamp at the entrance to the studio.

Someone else was in the studio. I could run back upstairs, and then what? There were no locks on any of the doors. If someone were here, I'd be trapped upstairs. Or I could make a run for the hallway, which led to the parking lot door. Not liking either choice, I decided to run.

Awkwardly clutching Lydia's suitcase to my chest, I sprinted toward the hallway. Just as I reached the hallway, I sensed movement behind me, started to turn, then never made it around. The blow struck my head hard and fast. I reached out toward the wall as I fell forward. Just before everything went black, I knew I was in trouble.

When I awoke, I was flat on my back, Lydia's suitcase beside me, all its contents scattered across the hallway as if it'd exploded.

My head was throbbing, banded in pain. Gingerly I felt around the back of my head and grimaced when I touched a marble-sized bump. Ouch! I touched it again, feeling for blood. There wasn't any, just pulsating pain.

Slowly I inched myself up to a seated position, and a wave of nausea washed over me. I eased myself back down, taking in deep breaths to settle my stomach while listening for any sounds. The studio was silent except for the whoosh of the A/C. Whoever had attacked me was gone.

Finally, my stomach quieted and I tried sitting up again. This time there was no nausea. Crawling around the hallway, I gathered up Lydia's stuff and slowly got to my feet, using the wall for support. For a few minutes I leaned against the wall to steady myself.

Looking around the dark space, I chided myself for not making sure the door was locked behind me. Most likely my attacker had sneaked in after me, hid, then hit me over the head as I was leaving with the suitcase. But why not stay hidden and wait for me to leave? He or she thought there was something in Lydia's suitcase, since the attacker had obviously searched the suitcase. What for?

As I moved gingerly down the hallway toward the door, something shiny near the threshold caught my eye. Slowly I reached down and waited as dizziness washed over me before picking it up. A tiny gold key. Was this the good luck charm Harper'd told me about? I turned it in my hand, studying the exposed edges, where the gilt had worn away over time.

Had Harper been my attacker? Or had someone wanted me to think that Harper was my attacker? And if so, why? I slipped the key into my pocket and exited the studio, locking the door and jiggling the knob twice to make sure it was locked.

The warm summer air was sticky with humidity and a breeze blew off the Bay as I walked to my truck. It must be really late because no one was on the street.

As I drove east on Route A toward home, my head was throbbing and my stomach was roiling again. Whether Harper had been my attacker or someone wanted me to think it was Harper, someone had been looking for something in Lydia's studio. What could that have been? Lydia was going to tell me what she was holding back one way or another.

Chapter Fourteen:
THURSDAY, JULY 13

Joe's truck was gone when I pulled up to his house the next morning. I grabbed Lydia's suitcase and strode up the porch steps, determined to wheedle out of Lydia what she wasn't telling me. Someone had attacked me last night, and I wanted to know why.

Without knocking I went inside, following the acrid scent of strong coffee.

Lydia sat at the kitchen table, hugging a mug with her hands and staring out the screen door toward the endless stretch of burnt yellow fields. She didn't even look away when I set her suitcase on the floor and went over to the coffee maker and poured myself a cup.

Without saying a word, I sat across from Lydia, purposely blocking her view. She stared at me as if she needed to get me in focus. Then she looked down at her hands and back up at me.

"Thanks, you know, for getting my stuff." Her voice was barely a whisper.

I shook my head and instantly regretted it as a stab of pain radiated through my skull. Automatically I reached back and fingered the bump.

"You okay?" Lydia asked. "You look kinda green."

"Someone whacked me over the head last night." I'd taken two analgesics when I'd gotten home last night and two more this morning, which had only dulled the pain.

"What? When you went to my place?"

"Yeah." I was about to demand what she was holding back when she jumped up out of her chair and started feeling around the back of my head, making me gasp with pain.

"Ouch! Go easy, will you?" I pushed her hand away.

"Why didn't you call me? Did you ice it?" Before I could answer, she went to the counter top, tore off a strip of paper towels, took out a bunch of ice cubes from the freezer, wrapped the paper towel around the ice cubes, and then pressed the makeshift ice pack to the lump.

"Hold it there for ten minutes," she instructed me, taking my left hand and placing it on the ice pack. Then she sat down again, chewing on her bottom lip.

The ice felt good, and the pain began to lessen. "You're seeing a doctor. I mean it," she sounded like the old, self-confident Lydia. "You could have a concussion. This is nothing to fool around with. You could develop a blood clot."

"Lydia, stop," I demanded. With the old Lydia back, now was the time to probe. "If you want to help me, tell me what you're hiding."

Her gaze bounced around the room, then finally came back to me. "I can't. He swore me to secrecy."

"Who? Nate Ryan?"

She nodded. "I don't think he meant to tell me. But he was so angry when he showed up at the studio. He was like another person. At first I thought he might be on something. He was practically jumping out of his skin, pacing back and forth, flushed and agitated. But no, he wasn't. I could tell." She took in a deep breath, and I readied myself for whatever it was that Ryan had told her, expecting the worst.

"He changed his mind. You know that half mill he was going to donate for the rebuilding of the theater? He wasn't going to do it. Something changed his mind."

"Did you ask him what it was?"

"He wouldn't tell me. All he would say was he almost wished he had hit her. You know, Nina, his ex-wife."

"But he'd already announced his donation to the BT before the play," I reasoned. "How could he withdraw it? I'm sure he signed something before the announcement."

"He said he didn't care what he signed or what people thought about him. They were going to think it anyway. Something about there being worse things in life. When I asked him what he meant by that, he shut down."

"Did you tell Chet about this?"

"I was going to, then I thought, why? Ryan's dead, and the BT needs that new theater. Why start some kind of legal wrangling? I mean, I don't even know if what he told me would hold up in court. And maybe if he hadn't died, he would have left things as they were once he'd calmed down."

"You can't know that," I countered. "You have to tell Chet." Her reasoning was totally skewed.

"Look who's talking." She let out a tight laugh.

She was right. In the past I'd held back my share of info from Chet, but this was different. If the autopsy showed foul play, she'd have to tell Chet.

"I don't see what difference it makes anyway." Lydia shrugged her shoulders dismissively. "I just want this whole thing over with."

"And there's nothing else?"

"Like what?"

"I don't know, Lydia. Someone bonked me on the head so they could search through your stuff. Humor me."

"Maybe it was the paparazzi or someone like that. Thinking there was something in my studio that would make a great story."

"As much as I'd like to blame this on them, I don't think so.

You're sure Nate didn't give you anything that said he was withdrawing his donation?"

"Don't you think I'd give it to the police if he had?"

"You didn't tell Chet about his wanting to withdraw the money," I countered.

"That's different." Her protest sounded half-hearted.

With my free hand, I reached into my pocket, pulled out the gold key charm and put it on the table. "Have you ever seen this before?"

She didn't touch it, just stared at it. "No, why?"

"After I came to, I found it in your hallway. I think whoever attacked me dropped it or left it there on purpose." Until I knew for sure, there was no point in upsetting Lydia more by telling her it might be Harper Kennedy's key charm.

"Left it there on purpose? Dropped it? Stop it, okay?" She held up both hands. "I can't take your probing and leaps of imagination right now." Her eyes filled with tears, which she blinked away. "A man died in my arms and there wasn't a thing I could do to save him. Nothing. So keep whatever crazy thoughts you're having to yourself."

She pushed back on her chair and stood up.

"I'm sorry," I said, really meaning it. I'd never seen Lydia so vulnerable and upset. Still dressed in my oversized sweats and t-shirt, she looked like a little kid. All my protective instincts were in high gear.

"Just have that bump looked at today, okay?" she pleaded, swiping at the tears running down her face. "For me?"

"Sure." I put the ice pack down on the table, got up and moved toward Lydia, not sure what to do to comfort her.

"Leigh, I'm not kidding."

"I said I would," I reassured her, telling her what she wanted to hear.

"You say a lot of things." She smiled, the dimples in her

cheeks a welcome sight.

"Don't we both?" I gave her an awkward hug. "You know none of this is your fault, don't you?"

"Then why does it feel like it is?"

CHAPTER FIFTEEN

When I arrived at the BT grounds, the place was eerily quiet. The ticket office was closed, and the sign in the window read: *Theater Will Reopen Tonight*. Below the message was a number to call for more information.

That's strange, I thought. *Shouldn't the ticket office be open? The show must go on and all that.*

Maybe the cast was in rehearsal and that's why it was so quiet. I walked over to the rehearsal building. The windows were shuttered, so I put my ear to the door. Nothing, not even the rattling of the air conditioner. It was after one p.m. The cast should be in rehearsal. What was going on?

I pulled out my cell phone and called the theater number. A recorded message said that tickets for *The Merchant of Venice* were sold out for the entire run. There was no mention of Nate Ryan's death or who would be playing his part.

For a while I just stood outside the squat brown plank building staring at the pine trees, considering my next move. There were two people I needed to talk to—Harper Kennedy and Nina Cass. Was that Harper's key I'd found? And what had Nina done that had made Ryan so angry he wanted to withdraw his donation?

I jogged up the flagstone path to the first apartment quad and knocked on Harper's door. No answer. I scrolled through my phone log, found Harper's number and waited. On the third ring, she answered.

"Harper, it's Leigh Girard. Any chance I could talk to you today about Nate Ryan? I'm on the BT's grounds right now. Are you around?"

"I just can't believe he's dead. He was such a great guy," she gushed.

That was a switch. The other day he was a dog. "It is a shock," I said.

"Listen, I gotta go. I'll call you later."

Before I could respond, she hung up. Well, she'd be back here for tonight's performance. I'd catch her then.

I tapped the phone against my chin. If only I had Nina Cass's phone number, but Barbara Henry had arranged all the interviews with the cast members, except Ryan's. I could call her, but I doubted I'd get anywhere with her, especially with the fallout from Ryan's death. There was always the off chance that Nina was in her apartment.

Hurrying down the flagstone path and up the limestone stairs toward Nina's apartment quad, I thought about my approach with her. What I wanted to know was if she was aware that Ryan was going to withdraw the donation. That bonk on the head had me in overdrive. Asking her outright wasn't an option. From my interview with her for the article, I'd learned two things: she was cagey, either giving one-sentence answers or changing the subject, and she didn't trust the media. Talking to her was so nerve-wracking, you just wanted the interview to end. I remember leaving with a stiff neck and the suspicion that was her intention.

Just as I reached the second landing, I heard voices coming from the end unit. A door opened and Alex Webber emerged. Quickly I stepped back around the corner out of sight.

"Then you're okay with that?" he asked in a conciliatory tone.

"Do I have a choice?" Nina answered, slamming the door

hard enough to shake the walkway. After Alex's determined-sounding footsteps echoed down the steps, I emerged from hiding and went to Nina's apartment door.

I'd barely rapped on the door when it flew open. Nina must have expected Alex, because her face went from a scowl to surprise in an instant.

"This isn't a good time," she said, edging the door closed.

"I know it isn't," I began. "And I'm really sorry about Nate, but if you could spare a few minutes, I'd like to get a quote from you for the feature article on him I'm writing for the *Gazette*. I'm sure you'd want to say something about him."

She glanced down at my notebook, which I was holding out toward her. I could tell she wanted me to go away, but she was savvy enough to know it was to her advantage to give me a quote.

"All right, whatever," she agreed reluctantly, but she didn't move, her arms crossed over her chest.

"Can I come in? It's blistering out here."

She opened the door and walked inside. I followed. Her apartment was a duplicate of Ryan's, right down to the furniture, but there were no errant undergarments or a wine bottle and glasses; just the smell of cigarette smoke.

She flopped down on the sofa, her yellow silk caftan billowing out around her thin frame. The bright yellow was in stark contrast to her black hair and dark eyes, which gave her an exotic appearance. She leaned over and grabbed the pack of cigarettes from the coffee table, shook one out, and then lit it. After she took a long drag on the cigarette, with her free hand she picked at her short curly hair impatiently, her bare feet tapping in a frenetic rhythm. The tension and heat coming from her was causing my shoulder muscles to bunch into knots. I took in a deep breath, trying to relax. The cigarette smoke was making me feel lightheaded.

"Who's taking Nate's place as Shylock?" I asked, sensing that at any moment she'd jump up from the sofa and demand I leave.

"Julian." She blew smoke up toward the ceiling. "I thought you wanted a quote about Nate?"

"Just curious. Why not the understudy?"

"Look, you should be asking Alex these questions. Not me."

She was right. I'd have to hunt him down.

"Were you surprised by Nate's sudden death?"

She choked on her cigarette smoke. But at least her feet stilled. When she stopped coughing, she said, "When we were married, I lived expecting *that* phone call. You know, the one in the middle of the night saying your husband's died from an overdose or a car accident or whatever addicts die from." She picked up the glass ashtray from the table and balanced it on her thigh, nervously flicking ash into it. "But to answer your question, yes, I was surprised. And as far as I could tell, he was a reformed man. Ironic, huh? He finally slays all his demons. Then he drops dead taking a yoga class. But that's how it works sometimes, doesn't it?"

"What do you mean?" I was surprised by her cold candidness.

She snubbed her cigarette out in the ashtray and placed it back on the table. "You get your act together, then fate steps in and says, 'Sorry, too late.' " She snapped her fingers. " 'You had your chance and you blew it.' "

Wow, that was both angry and bitter. "But he lived long enough to donate money for the rebuilding of the theater," I said. "At least he was able to do that." I was slowly leading up to my real reason for being here.

She adjusted the caftan so it covered her long, bony feet. Then she fiddled with her silver bracelets. "We're dedicating the new theater to Nate."

"Is that what you and Alex were discussing?" She looked at me suspiciously. "I saw him leave as I came up the path."

"That and tonight's performance." She pulled one of her tightly wound curls away from her head and then let it spring back.

"And nothing else? Like the rumor that Nate was withdrawing his donation?"

Her forehead crinkled in confusion. "Where'd you hear that?"

Her tone was even, but she'd suddenly stopped fidgeting. I'd struck a nerve.

"I can't divulge my source. Is it true?"

"I don't know who told you that, but it isn't true." She sounded sincere. I remembered what Nate had said about acting. Just say the words. Don't emote, let the words do the work.

"I had to check it out, you understand," I answered, matching my tone to hers: even, sincere, and false.

"So when's the BT article going to appear?" Right on cue, she changed the topic.

"Not sure. It's up to my editor. But probably after the piece on Nate's death."

She nodded her head, her eyes shifting right. "What did Nate say about me?"

The question seemed to come out of nowhere, and I wasn't sure how to answer. "You mean when I interviewed him?" My face flushed in confusion.

"When else?" She grinned sardonically. "Don't tell me you fell for his shit?"

"No. I mean, he didn't say anything about you." Why was I sounding so guilty?

She was staring at me in perfect stillness. Not a muscle moving, except for the smile playing around her mouth. "Listen, I'm exhausted. So if you don't mind." She got up from the sofa and shook out the caftan, which had faint sweat marks where it had creased.

"Sure thing," I said, rising from the chair. "And what do you want to say about Nate for the article?"

"He was a very generous man, both as an actor and as a friend. I'll miss him."

I wrote down her words, aware of their hollow falseness. Nate Ryan was a lot of things, but generous wasn't one of them, unless you counted sexual favors. And I doubted Nina was going to miss him.

Nina's deep, melodic voice cut into my thoughts. "By the way, you shouldn't be embarrassed to admit being seduced by Nate. It's happened to the best of us."

I started to protest, then realized it would be useless. She'd already decided that I'd fallen for "Nate's shit," as she put it. That must have been the story of their marriage, his constant infidelity and substance abuse. What a nightmare of a marriage.

As I ambled down the steps and started toward the theater office to search for Alex, my face was still hot, and my head was aching painfully where I'd been hit. What had just happened? How had Nina thrown me off like that?

Then it hit me. Nina's nervousness, which I'd initially chalked up to her vulnerability due to a dislike of the media, was a form of control, a way of disarming you. Watching her constant fidgeting, like she was on the verge of falling apart, I'd let my guard down. So when she'd asked about Ryan, implying something sexual had happened between us, I'd been defenseless. Clever, very clever. She was about as vulnerable as a cobra.

The sign in the box office window was gone, and the box office was open. I peered inside and saw Barbara Henry and Alex Webber seated at a desk, deep in conversation.

They must have sensed I was there because they both stopped talking and looked toward the window.

"Leigh," Alex called to me as if I was his long lost friend.

That was a switch. "We need to talk." He scooted back his chair and stood. "Why don't we finish this later," he said to Barbara, who looked miffed by my interruption. Her fleshy face was slightly pink.

Without waiting for her answer, he left the cottage-like building and came outside where I was waiting.

"Let's go sit by the water. Maybe catch a breeze." He strode ahead of me, walking at a quick pace, his muscular legs and arms in contrast to his wiry thin frame. Though he wasn't handsome, his face was compelling. Even his dull brown hair, which stuck out around his head as if he'd just gotten out of bed, didn't deter from his commanding presence.

He waited until we sat down on the bench before he began talking. "I want to discuss with you how to handle Nate's death. Here's the thing, and I know you'll agree. We have to stress Nate's comeback. How the BT was instrumental in giving him a new start. You know he'd donated a sizable amount of money toward the rebuilding project? I'm counting on you as the hometown journalist to skip the trash. No need to rehash that stuff."

As he talked, I kept glancing at the tiny birthmark on his forehead that looked like an ink drop to keep myself from interrupting him. Finally, he seemed to run out of juice and ended his monologue by patting my leg paternally. "So we're good then." It wasn't a question. He stood up.

"Alex, I'm a journalist, not a public relations person." I resisted the urge to stand. "I'm going to write the article the way I see it." I tapped my notepad to make my point.

He remained standing, his legs apart, his hands on his hips as if ready for combat. "No one's telling you to compromise your standards, Leigh. I'm just strongly suggesting that you avoid the trashy stuff you read in those other publications." He said *other* like it was a dirty word.

Now I stood and faced him. I needed to see his eyes when I dropped the bombshell. "Did you know there's a rumor going around that Nate was going to withdraw his donation?"

His right eyebrow arched. "Nonsense. I already have confirmation of the donation. This is what I'm talking about." He pointed a finger at my nose. "Unfounded rumors, speculation. I'd really hoped better from you."

His eyes shifted toward the water. When they came back to me, he said, "You're going to have to submit your article to me before you print it."

"That wasn't the deal," I protested.

"Well, it is now. In fact, I'll have Barbara call your editor—what's his name? Jake, today, to make sure we see it before it goes to print."

"That's not how it works, and you know it," I said, trying to keep a lid on my temper.

"I'm sure I'm not the first person to ask to see an article prior to publication." He reached out and put his hand on my shoulder. "I don't know what you're getting so upset about."

I shook off his hand. "I'm not changing anything, if that's where this is going." *Keep your head, Leigh. Don't lose your temper.*

"Even if it's inaccurate?" He smiled broadly, as if I was a naughty child.

What could I say to that? "I'll e-mail you a copy," I said grudgingly. "If there are any inaccuracies, which there won't be, let me know."

"That's all I want."

He was playing with me, just as Nina had played with me. "Who else have you given interviews to since Nate's death?" I was wondering if that was the issue here: irresponsible journalists.

"Too many to name. You're just another one."

Then he turned and walked back to the box office cottage.

What was he afraid of? He knew I couldn't mention the rumor about Nate withdrawing the money because I had no proof. His attitude toward me had changed at the rehearsal when Nate had pricked Julian with a real knife. He'd gone from cooperative and genial to aloof and cold. Why?

A real knife, a dead rat in a casket, a bloody chicken, and then there was the splattered nightgown planted in the Moyers' cabin. Now Nate Ryan was dead. Maybe Alex should be afraid.

CHAPTER SIXTEEN

"Jake wants to see you, ASAP," Marge said as I sauntered into the *Gazette* office, savoring the air conditioning. "Oh, and see me after. I've got some info on those dog tags. Very interesting."

I straightened my shoulders as I walked toward Jake's office, steeling myself for the inevitable chewing-out. I'd no doubt Barbara Henry had called Jake, complaining about my rumor-mongering. *They don't pay me enough for this grief,* I thought, gently massaging my aching bump.

His door was open, so I went in, plopped down in one of the green vinyl chairs laden with papers, and said, "Have at it." The papers crinkled in protest under my butt.

"Jeez, how'd you piss off Webber? He's one of the nicest guys around. Always cooperates with us. Knows the importance of keeping on the good side of the press. What the hell did you do?" He leaned back in his swivel chair as if he needed distance from me.

"Thanks for the support, boss. Last time I checked, journalists were supposed to ask penetrating questions. And don't give me that crap about the Door County villages and medieval hamlets." I held up my hand in protest. "I asked him about the rumor that Ryan was withdrawing his donation for the rebuilding of the theater."

"Whoa, hold up. Who told you this?" Jake's eyes narrowed.

"Lydia." I explained everything Lydia said about Ryan, including her sexual antics the night before his death.

"It doesn't matter now anyway," Jake concluded. "He's dead, and they're getting the money."

"Exactly," I agreed. "But don't you find it strange that he died before he could withdraw the donation? If he was going to withdraw it."

"Leigh, don't go there. Unless the tox screen shows something suspicious, according to the ME's initial autopsy, it looks like Nate Ryan had a massive heart attack. Though right now he's calling the cause of death undetermined. End of story."

"Why'd you call the ME? Don't you trust me?" My stomach was grumbling. I hadn't eaten since this morning, which was making me cranky.

"Chet just happened to stop by and I asked him. Why am I explaining myself to you? Who's the editor here?" He moved a few piles of paper around absentmindedly.

"Didn't want you to think I wasn't doing my job," I said petulantly.

"That's never been one of my worries about you." He stared at my face a little too long for comfort, then said, "What's going on with your house hunting?"

That reminded me that I needed to drop a check off at the realty office. "Found a cabin I can rent month-to-month."

"Where?" His long fingers were drumming nervously on the nearest paper pile.

"Gills Rock."

Jake tightened his lips, causing his goatee to jut out. "You sure you want to live that far up the peninsula? Heck of a drive to work, especially during tourist season, not to mention winter."

I knew what he was asking. He was aware that Joe lived there. Just as he was aware of our brief romantic dalliance. I'd yet to sort that out.

"It's only temporary until I decide what I'm going to do with my sudden windfall." Oops. Why'd I blurt that out?

"Someone die?" He rested his elbows on his desk and hunched forward.

"You might say that. Listen, I gotta run."

"Leigh." He dragged my name out, and I flashed on an intimate moment when he'd said my name in that same way as he'd brushed my hair from my forehead, then kissed me.

"Looks like I'm divorced." I studied the window behind him, the blue blend of bay and sky that seemed endless and without purpose.

He sat up straighter. "And when did this happen?"

I shrugged. "A few days ago."

"And you're telling me now?"

"If it's any consolation, you're the first to know." Okay, it was out and I didn't feel any better about verbalizing it. In fact, I felt worse, as if someone had punched me in the gut. Jake's stony expression only added to my misery.

We sat there for a moment, neither of us saying a word. What was I expecting? That he'd jump up, take me in his arms and tell me he loved me? Yeah, I was expecting that, and if he did, what would I do? I hadn't a clue.

Finally, I stood up, dislodging a few pieces of paper that were stuck to my derriere. "I gotta email the Ryan article to Webber, so if there's nothing else."

"No way. I told Barbara Henry that's not how this newspaper rolls." His eyes went to his computer screen. "When you're done with the piece, shoot it over to me. I'm the only one who makes changes around here. Got it?" He looked up for a moment, not waiting for my answer before he began typing.

"Uh-huh," I responded.

"I'm not even going to ask what you did now," Marge teased as she opened her middle desk drawer and pulled out the dog tags.

"So what's so interesting?" I said halfheartedly, my mind still on Jake's unemotional reaction to my divorce.

She rifled through a stack of papers and then eased one out from the middle. "Read this." She handed me an official-looking document with the seal of the U.S. Army on the top.

I started reading through the document and stopped at the address of the next of kin—Elsie and Lawrence Browning, Senior, Milwaukee, Wisconsin. "So Brownie's family isn't from around here," I said. "I wonder if they're still alive?"

"Did you read this part?" With her pen, she tapped the section that gave Brownie's physical stats: 6' 2″ and 185 pounds.

"This can't be Brownie," I said. "He was around five-nine at most. What was he doing with these dog tags?"

"Did you read this part?" Again she hit the paper with her pen.

"MIA June eighteenth, nineteen seventy." I digested the information. "He took this guy's identity, switching the name around."

"Looks that way," Marge answered, nodding her head.

"I wonder if Ken Albright knew."

"I'm sure you'll find out." Marge bent down, grabbed her purse and pushed back on her chair. "Have to run. The Busy Bees are coming to my house tonight. And I'm making my famous blue margaritas. The quilt patterns are always so much more creative after a few drinks."

After Marge left, I powered up her computer and did a quick search for Elsie and Lawrence Browning, Milwaukee, Wisconsin. Lawrence Senior was deceased, but Elsie still lived at the same address in Milwaukee. I jotted down the phone number.

Just as I shut down the computer, Jake appeared at my desk.

"Listen," he began, looking uncomfortable, a state he seldom was in. Cool and collected was the image he liked to portray.

"What's going on?" I said. "Change your mind about the article?" I didn't think that was the case. But something was up.

He was swaying from one foot to the other, his arms crossed over his chest.

"What are you doing tomorrow night?"

"Why?" I wasn't sure where he was going with this, but I decided not to make it easy for him.

"I got this gift certificate to the Camelot Inn, and I thought I'd better use it."

Wow, that was romantic. "Are you asking me out on a date?"

"Do you want it to be a date?" Now he looked annoyed.

"Yeah, I do." I didn't know if I wanted it to be a date. I'd only been divorced for a few days. But being cut loose unceremoniously made me want to start fresh, take back some control.

"You messing with me, Leigh?"

I pushed back on my chair, stood up and stepped into his personal space. "Would I do that?"

We were so close, I saw a few errant hairs he'd missed shaving. What was he seeing? The dark shadows under my eyes like bruises, the fine lines around my mouth, where insecurity and sleeplessness took root?

He didn't step back. Instead, he said, "I'll pick you up around seven."

He turned and started toward his office, then turned back. "Gills Rock or the mobile home?"

"Gills Rock," I answered, trying not to see the disappointment in his eyes.

CHAPTER SEVENTEEN

On my way home, I stopped by the real estate office in Egg Harbor to sign the rental agreement and pick up the keys to my "new" home. This would be my third move in two years. Though I didn't own much—books, a few art photographs, my clothes—the thought of uprooting Salinger and myself made me anxious. My plan was to start moving my stuff a truckload at a time, which probably wouldn't take very long—three to four trips at the most. My nomadic life was starting to feel old. Once the money from the divorce came through, I'd look for a more permanent home.

Avers Realty shared quarters with a coffee shop/bookstore and had an expansive view of Green Bay from the upstairs shops. Diane Avers owned both. She was a no-nonsense businesswoman who had the palest blue eyes I'd ever seen and a disconcerting habit of staring at you a little too long, as if she couldn't quite get you in focus.

When I walked in, she was putting folders into a leather briefcase. "I wondered when you were coming by." She sat back down, pulled a folder from the stack on her desk, took out the rental agreement and pushed it and a pen toward me.

Quickly I scanned the document, signed it and handed her the check for the first month's rent and the security deposit.

"He's looking to sell, you know." She lifted her outsized black-rimmed eyeglasses off her short nose as if they were too heavy. "You should think about it. With some TLC, that place could make you some money down the line."

I was about to say that I was in no position to buy a house when I reminded myself that I soon would be. "Let me see if I even like the place first." My hesitation had more to do with Joe Stillwater's close proximity than the house itself.

"I know Roy will consider any reasonable offer," she nudged me, ignoring my comment.

Okay, she'd piqued my interest. "What's he asking? And what's a reasonable offer?" When it came to business, I was hapless, mainly because I had no interest in it.

Diane handed me the listing sheet. "The place's been on the market for over two years. So he'd probably take eighty-five percent of the asking price." Those pale eyes were boring a hole into me.

"That's doable," I said, not sure if it was. Tom was buying out my share of the house in Illinois. But again, I had no idea what the Illinois house was worth. Was that in the divorce papers? I'd have to read them. I'd thrown them in my dresser drawer under my old sweaters.

"Then there's the land. That house sits on over ten acres, mostly forest." She was sensing blood in the water.

"I'll think about it. You going to Marge's tonight?" I asked, desperate to change the topic. Diane had started the quilter's group, cleverly named the Busy Bees, and several of her quilts were displayed around the upstairs bookstore. The quilts were in sharp contrast to the hardheaded businesswoman she presented—lush, vividly colored nature scenes.

"Have to. Margaritas and quilting." She tsked and shook her head disapprovingly. "Do I have to say more? Someone has to steer the ship."

After leaving Egg Harbor, I drove by the BT hoping to catch

Harper. Either she wasn't answering her door, or she wasn't there. Her phone rang to voice mail and I didn't leave a message.

It was almost ten o'clock by the time I'd moved my stuff into the cabin, which I'd discovered came with a field mouse living inside the dishwasher and more spiders than in a horror film. Except for needing a cleaning, the rest of the cabin seemed fine—a living room with a wood-burning fireplace, those massive built-in bookcases, kitchen, two bedrooms, one and a half baths, kitchen, window boxes. I opened all the windows to get the musty smell out and decided I'd start on the bathrooms tomorrow.

Salinger had worked herself into a frenzy, trying to herd the mouse around the kitchen. Finally, I'd opened the kitchen door and with a broom scooted the mouse outside, Salinger close behind—all my pleas to come back going unheeded. She'd return when she was good and ready.

Sitting on the kitchen step, I stared out into the dark, humid night. A sickle moon hung low over a stand of evergreens; a few stars punctured the sky like errant thoughts. I'd eaten half a sandwich earlier that I'd picked up at the market in Egg Harbor and was nursing my second glass of wine, a dry California chardonnay that fit my budget. My cell phone sat beside me like an accusation. I should call Lydia. By now she was probably back at her apartment above the studio. But that phone call would lead to her nagging me about not seeing the doctor as I'd promised. So nix to that. Then there was Joe. Shouldn't I at least thank him for directing me to this house? Let him know I was moved in? That would lead to his wanting to stop by. Not tonight.

Was it too late to call Elsie Browning? I picked up the cell phone. It was 9:50 p.m. I took the phone number from my pocket and punched in the numbers. The phone rang and rang and just as I was about to hang up, a woman answered in a thin, shaky voice.

"Is this Elsie Browning?" I asked.

"Yes, and who is this?"

"Sorry to call so late," I began. "I'm Leigh Girard, and I'm a reporter with the *Door County Gazette.*"

"Where did you say? Door County?"

Salinger took that moment to come bounding out of the woods, running toward me, barking frenetically.

"Is that a dog barking? I thought you said you were with a newspaper?"

"Salinger, hush." I pulled her close to me to quiet her.

"I'm not going to buy anything, if that's why you're calling."

"No, I'm not selling anything. In fact, I have something I think you might want." Okay, why was I sounding like a con artist?

"I can't imagine what that would be." Her voice hardened, all the shakiness gone. "So I'm going to hang up now."

"Wait, Mrs. Browning. I have your son, Lawrence's, dog tags."

"Who did you say you were?"

"Leigh Girard with the *Door County Gazette.* A man who was using your son's name had the dog tags. I was wondering if I could return them to you and maybe ask you a few questions about your son."

"My son went missing in action in Vietnam. We never knew what happened to him. How could you have his dog tags?" Now she was angry as well as suspicious. Good job, Leigh. Scare the elderly woman.

"If you're not too busy, I could return them tomorrow."

There was a long silence, then a deep intake of breath. "You know, I'm pretty sharp for an eighty-eight-year-old woman. So don't think you can pull the wool over my eyes, young lady. If you really do have my son's dog tags, I can meet you after mass tomorrow morning. St. Francis of Assisi Church, west side of Milwaukee, ten o'clock inside the vestibule."

"Can we meet later? I'm driving from Door County."

"Then you'd better get to bed, because you'll be getting up early."

Chapter Eighteen:
Friday, July 14

Rain had been falling steadily since Port Washington, where I'd picked up a fast-food breakfast sandwich and a supersize coffee, letting Salinger take a run in the field behind the restaurant before getting back on Highway 43. From all the physicality of the move, I'd slept like a teenager last night and been on the road by six o'clock. Well rested and well fed, I was ready to deal with Elsie Browning and this emotionally difficult situation. After all these years, to have a complete stranger contact her and say she had her MIA son's dog tags was beyond shocking. It was more like unbelievable. No wonder she was so leery.

Taking the Brown Deer exit north of the city, I spotted the golden dome of St. Francis of Assisi shimmering in the rainy morning. The church bells rang out as I pulled up across the street from the church. Leaving the windows sufficiently open, I gave Salinger a reassuring pat on the head and the remains of my breakfast sandwich as a treat.

"I'll be right back," I told her, exiting the truck and stepping out into the street.

Suddenly, a black sports car whisked by, sending up a wave of water that splattered my lime seersucker pantsuit and black flats.

"You jerk," I shouted after the driver, who was too far away to hear me. "Great, just great," I said aloud, looking at my wet shoes and water-stained pants' legs.

I'd chosen my wardrobe with care, wanting to give Mrs.

Browning the impression that I was a professional journalist she could trust. I'd even rubber-banded my unruly hair in a ponytail.

So much for best-laid plans, I thought, dashing across the street to avoid a red panel van coming from the opposite direction.

When I stepped inside the church's vestibule, a familiar, cool, dark silence enveloped me. The last time I'd been inside a church was for my mother's funeral. Thankfully, my thoughts were immediately interrupted by footfalls. An elderly woman entered the vestibule accompanied by a middle-aged priest. Though the woman was clearly quite elderly, frail and hunched with age, her hair was a dark teased halo, and she was dressed in a sporty pink pantsuit and white loafers with gold tassels.

"I think that's her," she said to the priest, pointing at me as if there were a roomful of people.

I stepped forward. "I'm Leigh Girard from the *Door County Gazette*. It was good of you to meet me on such short notice, Mrs. Browning." I held out my hand to her and instead of shaking my hand, she took it sideways and held it for a moment before letting go.

"The only reason I'm here, young lady, as I told Father Stan, who thought you might be up to something, is because of my son."

That seemed to be Father Stan's cue because he took in a deep breath and said, "May I see some proof that you work for the newspaper?"

In anticipation of that question, I'd brought a copy of my article on Brownie and Ken. A tiny photo of me was beside the headline. "This is the man who was using your son's identity, Brownie Lawrence." I handed Mrs. Browning the article.

As Mrs. Browning dug in her purse, searching for her glasses, Father Stan said, "You'd better let me look at that." He took the article from the woman's hand. I watched his eyes move from my face to my newspaper photo and back again. When he was sufficiently satisfied I was who I said I was, he handed the article back to me.

"Mrs. Browning, why don't you hold onto the article so you can read it later," I told her. She'd found her glasses, but didn't put them on.

"I'd like that," she said, folding the article and shoving it into her voluminous white vinyl purse along with her glasses.

"Let us see the dog tags," Father Stan demanded, his tone bordering on rudeness.

I was getting more and more annoyed by the priest's overbearing presence. My intention was to meet with Mrs. Browning alone so that I could ease into some questions about her son's service in Vietnam. Father Stan was acting as though I was a criminal after the woman's money and that she was incapable of taking care of herself. His judgmentally arched black eyebrows and pronounced widow's peak only added to my dislike of the man. Reluctantly, I took the dog tags from my bag and handed them to Mrs. Browning, ignoring Father Stan's outstretched hand.

She put one hand to her chest as she stared down at the dog tags. When she looked up, her eyes were glazed with pain and her mouth trembled.

"You'd better tell me how you got these." Father Stan's crow-like eyebrows arched even higher. If they were capable, they would have flown right off his face.

Clearly Mrs. Browning was too overcome with emotion to speak.

"Is there somewhere we can sit down?" I asked the priest. For all his hovering, he didn't see the woman was in distress or didn't care. "Mrs. Browning doesn't look too good."

"Are you all right, Elsie?" he asked, craning his neck toward the woman, specks of dandruff like snow on his cassock's shoulders.

She shook her head no, and then said, "It's like yesterday, losing him all over again."

"You know we talked about this, Elsie. God will see you through, just as He did before." He glanced at me. "Why don't we go into the rectory?"

Without waiting for a reply, he took Mrs. Browning by the arm and guided her back through the church and through two doors that led to the rectory, with me following behind like a recalcitrant child. Why was Father Stan so hostile toward me? Something more than protectiveness was going on.

The rectory was dark with heavy furniture from the 1950s and large stained-glass windows depicting various portraits of St. Francis of Assisi accompanied by animals. Mrs. Browning and I sat side-by-side on a brown leather sofa, and Father Stan pulled up a matching chair positioned equidistant between us.

Mrs. Browning was still holding the dog tags in her right hand, now running her finger over the embossed surface repeatedly, as if that could bring back her missing son. I'd explained how I'd gotten the dog tags and that Brownie had been using her son's name. When I'd finished, it was Father Stan who spoke first.

"So you're here because you think this person who called himself Brownie Lawrence knew Mrs. Browning's son in Vietnam? And that Mrs. Browning could help you find out who he was?" His words were for Mrs. Browning.

"That's what I'm hoping."

"I never met any of the boys Lawrence served with," Mrs. Browning said. "All I know is he was last seen during a night attack in the jungle. There was a lot of confusion because it was dark. After the attack, it was as if Lawrence had vanished into thin air. No one knew what happened to him. That's what we were told, anyway. Oh, if only Larry, my husband, were alive. He knew more about this. After we got the news that Lawrence was missing in action, I just shut down. All I did was pray and pray."

"Did your son write you letters? Send photographs?" Maybe Lawrence Browning had known Brownie, and he might have mentioned him in a letter.

"Yes, but I don't know if I want you to see them. They're personal."

As much as I needed to see the letters and photos, I didn't know if I wanted to see the pain revisiting them would cause Mrs. Browning. But then again, if I could find the connection between Brownie and Mrs. Browning's son Lawrence, maybe I could find out who Brownie really was and possibly what happened to Mrs. Browning's son.

"You don't have to show her anything," Father Stan piped in. "You know that."

Thanks, Stan. I closed my eyes for a moment and thought about how I could persuade this grieving woman to help me, especially with her spiritual guide protecting her from the likes of me.

"I understand your reluctance, Mrs. Browning. I really do. But think about this. The man who was using your son's name has a family, and they don't know what happened to him either. And maybe if I discover who he was, I might get more information about what happened to your son."

She turned her head and studied my face, then she looked at Father Stan. "What should I do, Father?" she pleaded.

"I think you should follow your heart."

That was a surprise. Maybe my words had swayed the hovering Father Stan as well.

"I live just around the corner," she said, easing herself up from the sofa.

The house was a modest brick bungalow, cream colored with a clipped lawn, one tree in the center like an island, and a statue of the Virgin Mary planted amid a foundation flowerbed surrounded by yellow and orange annuals.

"Everything is in the basement," Mrs. Browning explained as she flipped on the light switch and proceeded down one flight of stairs to the lower level. The house smelled stale and airless.

The room where she led me was covered in brown speckled carpet and paneled in knotty pine. Against one wall was a floral sofa. On the opposite side of the room was a built-in bar. There was an ancient exercise bike, a TV with rabbit ears, a table and two chairs and two homemade cabinets, painted yellow, next to the sofa.

Mrs. Browning went to one of the cabinets and pulled out a gray steel box. "My husband kept everything in here." She patted the box. "He would come down here and read Lawrence's letters over and over again. Or sometimes he'd just sit here holding them. There aren't many. Only ten. He went missing after only four months." She shook her head sadly. "I'll be upstairs. Just holler when you're done." She handed me the box and left the room. I could hear the slow shuffle of her feet on the stairs.

The letters told little about Lawrence Browning's experiences in Vietnam, except to repeatedly reassure his parents that he would come home safe and sound. Even his comments about the photos he'd sent were brief: *Me and some guys playing football; Charlie and me; Some guys in my unit.* Clearly he was shielding his parents from the realities of war. Though the last letter struggled to put a good face on what he was going through, the effort was almost as painful as the truth might have been. Disappointed, I put the letters back in the box and went through the faded colored photos. Since I didn't know what Lawrence looked like, I took the photos upstairs to ask Mrs. Browning.

She was sitting at her kitchen table, a mug held between her hands, staring out the window at her backyard. She was so lost in thought, she didn't hear me come into the room, and I cleared my throat, not wanting to startle her.

"Did you find anything useful?" she asked, turning around in her chair.

"Not in the letters." I sat down and spread the photos out on the table. "Could you point Lawrence out to me?"

"That's him, there." Her red-polished nail rested briefly on the photo. Lawrence Browning looked impossibly young with his blond hair and soft features. Even his attempt at a mustache made him look fragile. He had a broad, trusting grin and a pug nose.

"Do you know who this is?" I asked, indicating the photo where he had his arm around the shoulder of another man. "In a letter, he calls him Charlie."

She shook her head. I showed her a few more photos of Lawrence with other soldiers, and she couldn't identify any of them.

The photos told me nothing about the connection between Lawrence and Brownie. And it was impossible to decipher if Brownie was one of the men in the photos. One or two were about his height and coloring. But the photos were so blurry and discolored, they were indistinct.

"Thank you so much for your time," I said, gathering the photos into a pile and getting up from the table.

"So the letters and photos were no help?" she asked sadly.

"No," I said reluctantly. "And there's nothing else your son sent you?" Sometimes people had to be nudged, as if they needed permission to remember.

Her eyes looked away and when they returned to me, they were filled with anguish.

"This young man came to our house about five years after Lawrence went missing." She paused. "That would have been nineteen seventy-five."

"What did he want?"

"It was the strangest thing. I don't know. He asked me if I was Lawrence Browning's mother. When I said yes and asked him what he wanted, he said something about Lawrence being a good soldier who didn't deserve what happened to him. Then he left."

"And he never gave you a name?"

"Yes, he did. But I don't remember it. My husband tracked him down. Wait here a minute. I'll get it for you."

When she came back, she was holding a white leather address book stuffed with bits of paper and rubber-banded. She put on her large framed glasses and started searching through the loose papers. "I know it's in here. Just give me a minute."

Eventually, she found what she was looking for. "There it is. Anthony Rossi. And his address and telephone number are there too."

I flipped open my notebook and took down the name, address and phone number. Anthony Rossi lived in Cedarburg, Wisconsin, a few exits north of Milwaukee.

"Maybe you'll have better luck than my husband did."

"What do you mean?"

"He never would talk to Larry, and when he went to where this young man lived, no one answered the door."

Was it possible that Anthony Rossi was Brownie Lawrence? Had he come to tell Mrs. Browning what happened to her son and return his dog tags?

"Could I borrow one of these photographs of your son? It

might help me find out what happened to him. I'll give it back to you."

"Just don't lose it." She gazed off toward the window. "I have so little left of my son."

When I returned to the truck, all the windows had snoot marks on them, and Salinger was throwing her body against the door, barking and complaining. There was a note tucked under my wiper blade. "You should be ashamed of yourself leaving your dog in a car." Give me a break. All the windows were open at least six inches. I crumpled the note up and threw it on the floor. "See the trouble you get me into with your big mouth?" I scolded Salinger, who started licking my face in retribution.

"Okay, okay," I laughed. "You're forgiven."

I slipped her leash over her neck and took her for walk. While she sniffed the grass, then did her business, I called Anthony Rossi's number. A robotic voice told me the number was disconnected.

As I headed north on Highway 43, I debated taking the exit to Cedarburg, the last known address of Anthony Rossi. He probably wasn't at that address; he might not even be alive. But then again, what did I have to lose except time? I glanced at the car's clock: 12:35 p.m. Plenty of time to track down Harper Kennedy and show her the gold key and get ready for my "date" with Jake.

Cedarburg turned into a fool's errand. No Anthony Rossi at that address or listed in the area phone book. The woman who opened the door said she'd bought the house from a Sam Wetzel two years earlier. She had no idea who'd owned the property prior to Wetzel. Surprisingly, she still had Wetzel's phone number and forwarding address in Seattle, Washington.

I wrote Sam Wetzel's information in my notebook and left. Before getting back on the highway, I pulled over at a gas station and called Wetzel. He answered on the fourth ring. After explaining why I was calling, he said, "I bought the house in nineteen eighty from Jean Rossi. That would be Anthony's mother. I believe she moved to Florida to be with her daughter. Sweet lady. Her husband had recently died. That's why she was selling."

My heart did a flip-flop. "Did you ever meet Anthony Rossi?"

"Yup. He came to the closing with his mom. What happened to him after that, I don't know. I know he didn't go to Florida."

"How do you know that?" I asked.

"Because Jean told me so. I wanted to send him some of his personal stuff that he'd left in the house. Or maybe I should say he'd hidden in the house. See, I found this box shoved behind the hot water heater. Why he put it there, I have no idea. When I called Jean and asked her how to contact Tony, she told me to mail his things to her because she didn't know where he was. I thought that was odd. But I didn't say anything."

"Do you remember what was in the box?"

"His dog tags, insignias, purple heart, two photos, one of him in his uniform and another of him and his army buddies, a silver peace sign necklace and another necklace of different colored beads and—here's the shocker—a Silver Star for valor. When I thought about it later, I figured he was like so many of those guys who fought in Vietnam who didn't want any reminders. Too many bad memories. But why the heck didn't he just throw the stuff out? Why he'd leave them behind?"

"Maybe it was his way of starting over?" I surmised, wondering if this was an important piece of Brownie Lawrence's life story—or should I say, Anthony Rossi's life story. "How come after all these years you remember what was in that box?"

"Beats me. It just all came back to me when you asked about it. I mean, the guy was awarded a Silver Star. That's a big deal. I guess it just stuck in my mind."

For a moment neither of us said anything. Then Wetzel broke the silence. "Anyway, do you think Anthony is your guy? What was his name?"

"Brownie Lawrence. I don't know. Sam, do you have a fax machine?" It was a long shot. But what did I have to lose?

"Yeah, at my business. In retirement I'm running a coffee shop. What else in Seattle, huh?"

"I'm going to fax you a photo of Brownie Lawrence. Just let me know if you see any resemblance to Tony Rossi. Like height, body type, that kind of thing. And do you still have Jean Rossi's contact information?"

"Naw, sorry. Threw all that stuff out."

"Thanks for your help. I'll fax you that photo today."

"One more thing," Wetzel interjected. "I don't know if it's any help. But Anthony had been a medic. One of the insignias in that box was a medic insignia. If I remember anything else, I'll call you. I always enjoy a good mystery. Got a pile of them by my bed."

As I got back on the highway, my mind was spinning with possibilities. If Brownie was Anthony Rossi, and that was a big if, I'd have quite a cautionary tale. A Vietnam vet who'd been awarded the Silver Star, trained as a medic, whose fall from grace had been as dramatic as his recovery. Then to fall again.

"There's no way he'd drink sweet cherry wine, I'm telling you." Ken's words echoed in reply.

Had he fallen, or had someone given him a push? I wondered.

CHAPTER NINETEEN

After a brief stop at the *Gazette* to fax Brownie's photo to Sam Wetzel, I decided to go by the BT on my way home. Harper Kennedy was avoiding my calls. She had to be on the grounds because the evening's performance of *MOV* was at eight p.m.

Though it was nearly five p.m. on a Friday, traffic was light. So I eschewed my summer shortcut and took my chances on Highway 42. Near as I could tell, the media had cleared out, probably moving on to the next scandal, celebrity wedding or divorce. Nate Ryan was already old news. Of course, if his tox screen showed anything suspicious, the press would be back with a vengeance.

There was no answer at Harper's apartment. Where was she? I left her yet another voice message about needing a quote about Ryan. "Call me ASAP. It's urgent," I stressed dramatically. I was starting to sound like an actor. Flipping the phone shut, I wandered around the grounds. Maybe I'd run into her.

The late afternoon heat was so intense, even Salinger seemed unusually subdued, walking so sedately I let go of her leash. As I followed the path around the ticket office, Salinger suddenly let out a sharp bark and, before I could grab her lead, bolted to the beer garden where Rich was sitting outside under an umbrella, Dixie beside him.

I watched the two dogs greet each other with a few inappropriate sniffs, and then settled down, one on each side of Rich. I wasn't in the mood for Mr. Flirty Pants, but what choice did I have? Reluctantly, I joined the group.

"How's my favorite reporter?" Rich asked, slowly looking me up and down. I'd left my suit jacket in the truck and my ivory scoop-necked silk blouse clung to my chest. Rich probably thought I'd worn it just for him.

"Hanging in," I said, glancing off into the distance as if I were looking for someone else, which I was.

"I see you brought backup this time." He ruffled Salinger's fur. "Want a cold one? It's on the house." He gave me a wink that made me cringe.

"Thanks, but I'm still on the clock," I said. Though a cold one was exactly what I wanted, accepting a free beer from Rich came with strings attached.

"Kinda like a cop?" He tilted his head up at me, grinning. His dark mustache glistened with tiny sweat beads.

"Kinda." I winced at the comparison that hit a little too close to home. Like most of the county, he probably knew about my past interferences with police investigations.

"Hey," he said a little too enthusiastically. "I meant to tell you. I knew that guy who died."

Who was he talking about? "Nate Ryan?" I asked stupidly.

"No, the one you wrote about in the paper. Lived over on that nature land up by Marshalls Point."

"You mean Brownie Lawrence?" I stared down at him. Now he had my interest.

"Yeah, that guy. He and his buddy helped out with the landscaping here. In fact, they did most of those plantings for the Shakespeare garden I showed you. Shame about him dying like that. He was a real hard worker and did what he was told. But that other one, jeez. Talk about attitude. I couldn't tell him anything. Finally, I fired him."

"Why? What did he do?"

"Mouthed off to Nina. She criticized how they'd replanted

the hostas. He called her a bitch. And that was the end of him."

"When did this happen?"

"About two weeks ago. I told the other guy he could stay on. Then when he didn't show up last week, I just figured he didn't want the job anymore. I didn't know he was dead. It didn't say in your article, but do you know how he died?"

Not wanting to comment on Brownie's death or prolong our conversation, I shook my head and shrugged. "Have you seen Harper Kennedy around?"

"Try the cafeteria. Last I saw she was headed that way."

"Thanks. C'mon girl." I patted my thigh a few times to rouse Salinger who, instead of standing, burrowed her head into the sparse tufts of grass.

Rich chuckled. "I'll watch her for you till you get back." Though I could have picked up Salinger's leash and taken her with me, she looked too content.

"I won't be long," I said and started to leave.

"You heard Bob took off?" he called after me.

I turned around. "No. What happened?"

He shrugged. "Who knows? He must have left while everyone was at the after-party. 'Cause the next morning, all his stuff was cleared out and he was gone."

"Didn't anyone call him?" I stepped back under the shady oak tree.

"I left messages on his cell. But he never called me back."

"What about his family?"

"Alex talked to them. I guess Bob texted them that he needed some time to get his head straight and would be home in a few weeks."

Something about his story didn't ring true.

Rich slipped the red bandana from around his neck and swiped at his face and balding head, totally missing his damp mustache. "This heat is about to kill me."

"Bob told me he needed this internship to graduate. Why would he leave?" I asked. I couldn't believe Bob would take off like that.

"That's what I told Alex when he was ragging on about the kid and how he was going to write a letter to his college and really fix his ass. Sometimes Alex can be a real jerk." There was a sharp edge to Rich's words.

"Something must have happened for him to leave like that," I speculated.

"I think he screwed up one too many times and didn't want to face the music. Don't get me wrong. I like the kid, but he was kinda in a haze sometimes, if you know what I mean." He pretended to puff on an imaginary cigarette.

"Haze? You mean marijuana?" Bob hadn't struck me as a druggie. A nerdy college kid with an adolescent sense of humor, but not a druggie.

"He told me he saw some ghost-like figure hanging around the Moyers' cabin last week. I told him to lay off the weed."

"There was that weird nightgown in the closet. You saw it. Maybe that's what he meant."

"Like I said, in a haze." Again, he mimed inhaling and exhaling a joint.

For all his creepy flirtatiousness, I thought, as I walked toward the cafeteria, Rich had his finger on the pulse of the BT's comings and goings.

When I strode into the BT cafeteria, Harper Kennedy was sitting alone at a corner table gazing out toward the bay, clutching a sweating glass of ice tea.

"I know, I know. I forgot to call you," she said apologetically when I sat down across from her. "Sorry, but it's been crazy around here. You know, with Julian taking over Nate's part, and Nate dying and the media hounding me and everything else."

She'd yet to make eye contact or to let go of the glass.

"No problem. I had to come by here to take more photos anyway," I lied. "So what do you want to say about Nate?" I took out my notebook and pen. The gold key was practically throbbing in my pocket, but I was waiting for the right moment to show it to her.

"What can I say? It's not like I really knew him. We worked together like, what? A month? But, I guess, if I had to say something, I'd say he was amazingly talented . . . um, taught me a lot about acting, and that's it." She looked up and met my eyes as if checking my reaction to her comments.

"What about when he kissed you on stage during the curtain call? Were you upset?" Sometimes an unexpected question broke through the niceties.

She crinkled her pretty forehead. And I knew she was buying time.

"Oh that?" She dismissively flicked her hand at me. "He was playing to the audience. He was good at that. Wish I was."

"Anything else you want to add?" I wrote down a version of her words, which were generic at best. She'd deflected my attempt at getting a juicy quote from her about Ryan's lascivious kiss.

"Why? You don't think that's good enough?" Her voice went up an octave.

"It's really up to you." Why was she sounding so insecure? "Is everything okay? You seem upset." Her hair was pulled back in a severe ponytail that looked like a punishment.

She took in a deep breath and closed her eyes. "I'm just jittery about tonight's performance, that's all."

Aha, the right moment. "You always have your gold key charm to rely on," I said, smiling.

Her eyes went wide. "I can't find it. I've looked everywhere." Her hand went to her chest.

"When was the last time you saw it?" I was carefully leading her.

"After the performance when I was getting ready for the after-party. I remember distinctly taking it off and leaving it on my bedroom dresser in this little glass bowl I keep my jewelry in."

I didn't think she was lying, but with actors it was hard to tell. I slipped my hand into my pants pocket and pulled out the key, placing it on the table. "Is this it?"

"Oh, my God, you're a life-saver! Where did you find it?" Harper picked up the key charm and kissed it.

I certainly wasn't going to tell her the truth. "Over by the Shakespeare garden."

"What? How'd it get there? Someone must have taken it from my apartment. But why? Why would someone take it? Oh, I just don't understand people." Her words were flying out so fast, I thought her head might explode. "You didn't tell anyone about it, did you? Because no one else knows about it. No one." She gave me a searching look full of recrimination. "I knew I shouldn't have told you. Nina warned me about talking to reporters. I trusted you."

She stood up, nearly knocking over her chair.

"Harper, I swear, I didn't tell anyone."

"Yeah, right." There was disdain in her voice.

"Instead of lashing out at me, aren't you curious about who took it from your room?" Now I was feeling aggrieved.

That stopped her rant. She leaned forward, put both hands on the table, her hazel eyes boring into mine. "What? Do you think I'm stupid or something? It was Nate. Who else?"

"Why Nate?"

She rolled her eyes and shook her head. "He probably thought it was funny. Duh. I gotta go."

Rich was sitting where I'd left him with Salinger and Dixie

asleep beside him. "You find Harper?" he asked as I bent over to grab Salinger's leash. Too late, Rich's eyes dove for my gaping neckline.

My instinct was to put my hand over my open blouse, but I didn't want to give him the satisfaction of my discomfort. Little did he know that the left bra cup held a prosthesis. "I did. How about you?" I asked, deciding to call him out. Guys like him always depend on a woman's good nature. "You find what you were looking for?"

His face went deep red, but then he grinned. "Can't blame a guy for taking a peek."

"I've slapped guys for less," I said.

He raised both hands in surrender. "Didn't mean anything. You know, some gals consider that a compliment."

"Just so you know, I'm not some gals. But thanks for watching Salinger."

On my drive up the peninsula, I considered Harper's explanation about her missing gold key charm. It was plausible. Nate could have dropped the key when he went to Lydia's studio the morning he died and the police overlooked it. But Harper could have lost it when she attacked me. Or someone other than Nate could have stolen the key and planted it to throw suspicion on Harper.

But the bigger question that was plaguing me was, Why was I attacked? What had that person been looking for at Lydia's studio? Lydia's relationship with Nate had been carnal and brief. Did this person think Nate entrusted Lydia with something important? Like a signed statement withdrawing his donation to the BT? As far as I knew, there was no such document. And why would he even do that? He didn't know he'd die that morning.

As I pulled up in front of the cabin, I sat for a moment, savoring the green coolness of the trees, idly running my fingers through Salinger's fur as she continued to doze. Uneasiness crept through me as I thought about Bob. He never would have left his internship. No matter how much grief Alex gave him. Something else had sent him packing. Something had scared him. And it wasn't a ghost at the Moyers' cabin.

Chapter Twenty

The Camelot Inn, an upscale restaurant just north of Fish Creek on Highway 42, was a Door County incongruity. Armor-clad, life-sized knights astride horses guarded the entryway, which was surrounded by a moat. To enter the restaurant, you crossed the moat via a wooden bridge. A neon sign visible from the highway flashed *Immediate Seating.* As authentic-looking as the exterior décor was, it had little connection to the peninsula's Scandinavian history. The medieval theme was continued inside with wooden chandeliers, heavy furniture and medieval wallpaper festooned with unicorns, dragons, knights and comely maidens.

At the last minute, I'd decided to meet Jake at the restaurant, even though his stone cottage near Newport State Park was about fifteen minutes from my rental cabin. If the "date" didn't go well, I didn't want that awkward drive home together. My uneasiness about our relationship was still with me like a dull ache.

We were seated at the back of the restaurant next to a young couple who'd beamed loudly to the waiter that they were on their honeymoon, having been married in Egg Harbor at a resort lodge overlooking Green Bay. She was a very tanned blond with overdone makeup and a plunging neckline who laughed at everything her new husband said. He was equally tanned and blond and, from what I heard, not all that amusing.

Try as I might to stop them, my eyes kept straying toward the young couple with a tinge of envy. They were so obviously lost in each other. Had I ever felt that way about Tom—or any man, for that matter? Could I feel that way about Jake? I sipped at my wine, letting its coolness flood me with ease.

Just as the waitress served our salads, Jake's phone trilled, pulling my attention away from the couple. He squinted at the number and said, "Gotta take this, sorry."

He opened the phone. "Uh-huh. Yeah, when?" He nodded his head as he listened.

While he talked, the young couple at the table next to us was shooting daggers at him. Clearly Jake was ruining their romantic dinner. "Okay, thanks for the heads-up, Chet."

Jake hung up his cell and slipped it into his shirt pocket. "Ken Albright's been arrested for the murder of Brownie Lawrence." He picked up a slice of warm bread and slathered it with butter nonchalantly.

Though I wasn't totally surprised by the arrest, I didn't want to believe Ken had murdered Brownie. "Based on what?" I demanded a little too loudly, again drawing glares from the couple.

Jake's eyes glanced at the couple. "Keep it down, will ya?" He took a generous bite out of the bread. A few crumbs stuck to his goatee. I resisted the urge to pick them off and instead said, "Crumbs," pointing to the same place on my face.

He swiped the napkin across his chin and then leaned in. "We'll talk about this later."

I wasn't about to be shushed. "C'mon, you can't drop that bomb and not expect me to react." My crossed leg was bouncing up and down under the table in frustration.

He swiped at his chin again. "Based on the fact that his alibi didn't pan out."

"And?" I coaxed. I could tell there was more.

He knew it was useless to fight me. "And the cops found the

baseball bat used to cave in Brownie's skull. It had Albright's fingerprints on it. He'd stashed it in the woods. Dumb bastard."

The strolling minstrel picked that moment to start strumming his lute and singing "Greensleeves" as he wove his way slowly through the maze of tables.

Questions were swirling in my overactive brain. "Ken never mentioned that Brownie's skull was bashed in," I said, raising my voice to be heard above the strolling minstrel now headed our way. I recalled that stain where Brownie's body had lain, which had looked like blood.

Jake flinched at my loudness. "Why would he if he'd been the basher?" He speared a cherry tomato and popped it into his mouth. "How's your new place?"

"Fine, great," I answered, pushing my salad around my plate with my fork. "Don't try and change the subject. It doesn't make sense to me. Why would Ken bash in his skull?"

Jake put down his fork and leaned in again. "Maybe Albright was out of control. You have any experience with substance abusers?"

"Don't tell me you have."

He picked up his fork and loaded it with a slice of cucumber, lettuce, and several croutons. "One summer I interned at a social services agency in Chicago where drug-heads went for counseling. That's where I learned the real meaning of selfishness. Some of these abusers would kill their own mothers for their next fix."

In the year and a half Jake and I had been bedmates, he'd never said much about his past, which included a twenty-year-old daughter and an ex-wife. That had been the problem with our relationship: an inability to open up to each other. I'd been guilty of the same thing, keeping Tom in some dark corner. Maybe that was what had drawn us together, a self-protective need.

"But Ken's been clean." I stopped, remembering what he'd told me about his argument with Brownie and his bender in Green Bay.

"What?" Jake asked, knowing me too well.

"He did tell me that they'd had an argument and that he went on a bender in Green Bay and can't remember much."

The minstrel was now standing between our table and the honeymoon couple. Dressed in a puffy white shirt and black tights, with his long brown hair hanging over his ears, he looked more like a cast member of *Spamalot* than an Arthurian minstrel. His flounced shirt barely covered his backside. He was so close I could see the loose threads on his woven belt and the outline of his underwear beneath his tights.

"Could you play the most romantic song you know? It's our honeymoon," the woman gushed.

The minstrel, without saying a word, started strumming and singing a song about nymphs and shepherds. I could tell by the couple's perplexed expressions that they didn't find the song very romantic. When the minstrel finished, the man said, "That's the most romantic song? Shepherds and sheep and stuff."

The minstrel chuckled and tossed his head back. "In medieval times to 'barley-break' meant to have a roll in the hay." He walked away, strumming softly.

"Jeez, you think he could come up with something better than that," the man commented, then took a long swallow of his beer.

"I don't know. I sort of liked it. Especially that breaking barley stuff." The woman ran her tongue around her lips several times. "Want to break some barley later?"

Maybe those medieval troubadours were on to something with their hidden meanings and frolicking nymphs and shepherds.

"Did you tell the police about Albright's bender in Green

Bay and their argument?" Jake asked.

"I don't think Ken had anything to do with Brownie's murder," I answered defensively. "Besides I only know what Ken told me."

"Just tell them."

I shrugged my shoulders, mulling over Jake's explanation that Ken was so enraged he hit Brownie with a bat. I didn't buy it. Ken cared about Brownie. He'd never take his rage out on Brownie like that. Brownie was Ken's check on his temper. But if he'd been drinking before he left for Green Bay, who knew what he was capable of. Maybe the wine bottles he'd smashed were his, not Brownie's, as he told me.

"Were there other wounds on Brownie's body?"

Jake shook his head in disapproval. "How's the BT piece coming?"

"Jake, c'mon," I pushed. "You know I'm not going to let this go."

He tore off another piece of bread, buttered it and shoved it in his mouth, chewing it a little too aggressively. "Chet didn't say."

"What about the tox screen? Did he mention that? I'd be curious to know what Brownie's alcohol level was."

It was standard procedure to run a basic tox screen in any sudden death. The medical examiner had no doubt run one on Nate Ryan as well. I cut my cucumber slice into tiny pieces and popped a piece in my mouth, chewing slowly, mulling over what Jake had just told me.

"Enough already, Leigh." Jake held up his hand. "Your homeless stray dog Albright killed Brownie. They probably were doing drugs, got into a fight, and Ken bashed him one. Now can we talk about something else?"

"Addressless, not homeless," I corrected him. "Ken is addressless."

"Okay, addressless. Whatever," Jake conceded.

Jake was probably right. Why was I so certain Ken didn't kill Brownie? And if Ken didn't kill him, then who did?

"I've been following up on some things," I said wanting to throw some doubt on Jake's conviction that Ken had murdered Brownie in a drug-induced fit of rage.

"What things? And how come I don't know about these things?"

"It was on my own time." Lying was getting too easy. "And I don't know how it fits yet. As it turns out, Browning wasn't Brownie Lawrence. He had Lawrence Browning's dog tags. How he got the dog tags I don't know, especially since the real Lawrence Browning went MIA during the Vietnam War. I tracked down his mother in Milwaukee, and that's about as far as I've gotten. I have no clue who Brownie was." I held back the Anthony Rossi connection and my hunch that Brownie might be Rossi.

I glanced over at the honeymoon couple's table before I continued. The woman was feeding her new husband pieces of her chicken, having lost interest in our conversation.

"Maybe someone from Brownie's past found him and killed him," I suggested, knowing full well how far-fetched it sounded. "You know my piece on the two guys was picked up by the Milwaukee and Green Bay newspapers."

Just then the waitress appeared, took our salad plates and asked if we wanted refills on our drinks. I said no and Jake said yes.

I waited for Jake's inevitable lecture about him being the boss and how everything goes past him. Instead, that familiar ironic grin spread across his face, the one that always had the power to sway me. A man with a good sense of irony was hard for me to resist.

"What?" I fiddled with my spoon.

He put his hand over mine to stop my fiddling. "You find out anything, I'm the first to know. Okay? Anything at all, no matter how trivial. I trust your instincts."

Then he took his hand away, leaving me with a feeling that he was saying something else that had nothing to do with my journalistic instincts. I stared into his blue eyes, searching for what he meant to say. But it was like trying to read a perfectly blue sky, no hint of anything else but endless blue.

The waitress returned with our food and Jake's drink. As the warm, lemony scent of my whitefish dinner wafted toward me, I wondered if I should prod him. *Jake, how much do you really trust me? Enough to open up to me? Or were you asking about my ability to trust you?*

"Leigh," Jake said, bringing me back to reality. "Talk to Martin about his interview with Brownie and Ken." He cut into his steak, not bothering to look up. His prickly demand shoved aside all thoughts of hidden meanings and ironic grins.

"What? Why?" The very thought of talking to Martin about anything put my teeth on edge.

"Martin said something was off about Brownie," he said, chewing on his steak. "When he interviewed him, he'd asked him if he was related to an Edward Lawrence from Green Bay. Brownie stumbled around and said something about Lawrence being a common name or something like that. Then Ken got bent out of shape."

As I listened, I silently fumed. Jake and I had had an argument about Martin's interviewing Brownie and Ken, which I felt encroached on my article. Jake thought differently. Martin was to cover the environmental angle; I was to cover the human-interest angle. Now I learn that he'd stepped into my territory. Even as I fumed, I felt petty. Martin had made a passing comment about Brownie. If it had been anyone else, it wouldn't have bothered me. But it hadn't been anyone else.

"So what?" I tried not to sound as petty as I was feeling.

"Martin said Brownie was hiding something. And as it turns out, he was right."

"He should have pushed him harder. Or better yet, he should have told me. So I could have followed up."

"Leigh, look," Jake paused. Whatever he was going to say, he'd changed his mind. "Swallow your pride and talk to Martin about Edward Lawrence." He pushed his plate away. There was nothing left on it except a sprig of parsley and a faint pink river from his steak.

"Yeah, okay, whatever." I was sounding childish and didn't care. I took a last bite of my fish and left the rest.

The waitress saved me from spouting off a clever comeback. After we told her we didn't want dessert, she promptly cleared the plates and left.

"If anyone can nail down Brownie's real identity, you can," Jake offered.

Was he throwing me a bone, an olive branch, a white flag? Regardless of his intention, I softened.

"Why would someone hide his identity and steal someone else's?" I wanted his take on Brownie's deception.

"Lots of reasons, and most of them criminal."

That memory of Brownie strumming his guitar and singing "Take It Easy" came back as if in contradiction.

"Or maybe he just needed to reinvent himself, start his life over." Hadn't I done just that by casting off my old life in Chicago, leaving Tom and a failing teaching career and escaping to Door County? But I hadn't changed my identity. Brownie had been hiding from someone or something.

The waitress returned with the check and discreetly placed it on the table beside Jake.

"You heading home?" Jake asked.

Okay, what was he asking? "Yup," I answered. "You?"

Now it was his turn to fiddle with a spoon. "When did things get so weird between us?"

"It was always weird, Jake." That was such a un-Jake-like question I wasn't sure where this was going. Did he want to have sex, did he want to start over, have a real relationship? Or all of the above?

Jake paid the check as if this were a real date and walked me to my truck. The night was still warm with large clouds relieving the blackness. I unlocked the door and turned toward him to say goodnight. He pulled me close and kissed me as if it were a first kiss. All under the watchful gaze of the knights, their fiery torches guarding us both from whatever the night held.

CHAPTER TWENTY-ONE:
SATURDAY, JULY 15

In true Martin fashion, he insisted that we meet at Egg Harbor's new beachfront at seven a.m. When I called him last night, he mumbled something about his upcoming piece on beach flora, seven o'clock sharp, and then hung up.

Even though it was Saturday and the Egg Café was crammed with tourists, I'd treated myself to a designer coffee before heading up Route G to the beach. It was a few minutes after seven, and except for a heavyset man wading into the water with a snorkel, the beach was empty.

As I sipped the chocolaty coffee, I stared out at the horizon. There were still times when this place overtook me, erasing everything else like a sudden loss of memory. The sheen of the bay flat and glistening, the shimmer of dew on the slender beach grasses, the black-eyed Susans swayed by morning light, the blur of purple flowers, and the heat yet to rise.

"Waiting long?" Martin asked as he came up beside me.

I wasn't rising to the bait. "So what did Brownie tell you about Edward Lawrence?"

"Nothing?"

In a huff, I turned to walk back to my truck.

"Hold up," he called after me. "Why so touchy?"

"Look, I'm not in the mood to trade insults with you this morning. Either tell me what you know, or I'm outta here."

"Sarah got back yesterday." He smiled at me.

I rolled my eyes. So that accounted for his chipper mood. His ex-wife, Sarah Peck, had returned early from Chicago. Martin, who'd never gotten over the divorce, was hoping to rekindle their relationship.

"Yeah, so. I cleared my stuff out."

"Why are you like that?"

"I'm not going there."

"Leigh, Sarah wanted me to thank you for looking after her mobile home. That's first off. And"—he wiped his hand on his jeans and held it out to me—"I know I've been a real son of bitch to you from day one, but let's start over."

I stared at his hand and then at his chronically florid face. In the morning light, his red hair looked like it was about to catch fire. "You're serious?"

"Never been more so." He actually sounded sincere.

"Sarah put you up to this, didn't she?"

"Are you going to shake my hand or not?"

I shook his hand reluctantly, wondering what Sarah had said to him to account for this complete turnaround.

"They did a good job with the grasses. That is, if the tourists don't trample all over them," he commented as his eyes traveled over the plants.

I didn't trust Martin's sudden turnaround toward me. "Look, here's the thing. Jake said you found something out about Brownie when you interviewed him. What was it?"

His lips retracted, and he was biting down on whatever insult he was about to hurl at me. He actually sighed. "It was after the interview was over. I asked if he knew this guy Edward Lawrence from Green Bay. Ed Lawrence used to run the Sierra Club. He hemmed and hawed and finally said that Lawrence was a common name. I didn't think anything about it until Ken threatened me."

"Threatened you how?" Not another incident of Ken raging.

"Well, I was walking the path and suddenly he jumps out at

me holding that damn baseball bat. He kept hitting it against the palm of his hand, saying stuff like, Brownie doesn't like talking about his family. And what's that got to do with our cleaning up the land? That I should keep my nose outta people's business. He was really pissed. Then he blurts out that he caught some guy sneaking around their place a few nights ago and he was sick of all the attention."

"Did he know who the guy was?"

"It was too dark. He got away before Ken could catch him. Though he did say he had a beard."

This was a complete waste of my time. Some guy sneaking around in the woods whom Ken couldn't identify. Martin suspected Brownie wasn't who he said he was, which I already knew.

"Thanks anyway," I said, keeping the sarcasm out of my voice.

"Gotta help each other out. How's Lydia doing? I stopped by her shop yesterday, and Carrie told me Lydia hadn't moved back in yet." Lydia had a thing for Martin, which wasn't reciprocal.

My face went hot with guilt. I hadn't called her yet. Was she still at Joe's place? "Good as can be expected, I guess."

"Well, have a good one."

"You too." I walked up the short path to the parking lot, got into my truck and drove south to the *Gazette* office in Sturgeon Bay. Have a good one? How's Lydia? Gotta help each other out? What did Sarah do to Martin yesterday, lobotomize him? More like she did some barley breaking.

As I drove, I called the police station and asked for Chet.

"You can't see Albright, if that's why you're calling."

I was hoping to talk to him today. "Why can't I see him?"

" 'Cause he's on suicide watch. No visitors, no how."

"Did he make an attempt?"

"Can't say."

I thought about telling Chet about Ken's suspicions that someone gave Brownie cherry wine. But that proved nothing. "Can you at least tell him I called?"

"This ain't no answering service." He blew out an annoyed breath. "Yeah, I'll tell him."

"And one more thing, what was Brownie's alcohol level?"

"Still running tests. So stop fishing around there."

Getting answers from Chet was like cooking pasta. Throw it against the wall and see if it sticks. I decided to fling some pasta. "So the ME found something in the initial tox results and is sending the samples on to the state lab for further tests?"

"The ME's just being thorough, so don't make nothing out of it."

"Ken told me he suspects someone gave Brownie cherry wine. There were no bottles at the scene because he smashed them and threw them in the bay." I decided to fling some more pasta at the wall. "He claims that if Brownie started drinking again, he'd never drink cherry wine and that someone else gave him the wine."

This time Chet grunted. "Know that already. And what's cherry wine got to do with cause of death? Brownie died from a blow to the head with a baseball bat. So there's nothing else there."

"Have a good one," I said with more enthusiasm than I felt. Why was I nattering on about cherry wine?

"I intend to."

Just as I hung up, my cell rang. I glanced at the screen. Samuel Wetzel. I made an abrupt right turn off the highway and into a gas station, eliciting loud and prolonged honking from the driver behind me.

"You're up early," I answered. With the two-hour time difference, it was just after five a.m. in Seattle.

"Coffee waits for no man," he responded. "Listen, I can't be sure if your guy is Rossi. It's been a long time, and it's hard for me to imagine what Rossi would look like now. But I think your guy is about the same height as him. And Rossi did have a mustache. I know it's not much."

I was disappointed but not surprised. "Well, if you think of anything else—"

"Hold up. I'm not done," he said. "You know what I said about liking mysteries."

"Yes," I said expectantly.

"Last night I did some searches on the Internet and found a connection between Lawrence Browning, the MIA guy, and Anthony Rossi. As it turns out, Browning was in what we called a swing battalion. Basically, they were the guys who were flown into hot spots. It was like being flown into hell. So Browning's platoon went into this hot spot, were ambushed, and that's when he went missing. Guess who the medic was who treated the guys who made it out?"

"Anthony Rossi," I answered.

"Anthony Rossi," he confirmed. "Gotta pen and paper? Write down this site. Go to it and click on Tim Washington. He tells the story of that ambush. He doesn't mention Rossi, but you'll get an idea of what it was like, what we went through."

I took down the site. "If Rossi's not mentioned as the medic, how did you find out he treated the guys who made it out?"

"Rossi was the medic assigned to the platoon that needed help. That means he was there on the ground when they were ambushed."

"If you ever get bored with managing a coffee shop, you'd make a good investigator," I said jokingly. Sam had just given me a link between Browning and Rossi and moved me closer to finding out if Rossi was Brownie Lawrence and, if so, why he'd assumed Lawrence's identity.

"Yeah, right. That's all I need is another job. I'm supposed to be retired," he laughed. "Now you do something for me. Let me know how all this turns out, will ya?" He took in a deep breath and let it out.

"You were there, in Vietnam, right?"

"What gave me away?"

"You said, 'what we went through.' "

"Did I? Most times I don't want to think about it. Your call brought it all back. But, hey, I'm alive. A lot of guys can't say that."

CHAPTER TWENTY-TWO

"Leigh, where the hell are you?" Lydia shouted into the phone. "The tour's leaving in ten minutes. You'd better be on your way."

I'd just parked in front of the *Gazette* office with the intention of finishing the article on Nate Ryan and checking out the website Sam gave me.

Oh no, the wine tour was today. How had I forgotten? Especially since it had been my idea.

Two months ago I'd invited Lydia to join me on the Door County Premium Wine tour. Last fall, I'd pitched an article on the expanding Door County wineries to the Wisconsin magazine *Seasons*. And the winery tour was central to the piece. With more and more Door County wineries catering to wider and deeper varieties of wines, Door County wineries were no longer known just for cherry wine. In fact, there was now a whole range of Door County spirits from vodka to whiskey, as well as premium wines.

"I'm leaving the *Gazette* now." I screeched away from the curb and turned left at the first intersection.

"The *Gazette*? What are you doing at the *Gazette*?" She was shouting so loudly I held the phone away from my ear.

"Settle down. I can make it," I reassured her.

"There's not enough time to drive from Sturgeon Bay to Fish Creek, especially with Saturday tourist traffic. This is so like you," she said with disgust.

I was speeding up the street, praying the police were busy elsewhere. Lydia was right; I couldn't make it in ten minutes. "What's the first winery on the tour, just in case I don't make it? I'll meet you there."

"I can't believe you. I just can't believe you," she said, huffing and puffing into the phone. She was in full drama mode. As I impatiently waited for the first break in traffic on Highway 42, I heard Lydia call out to someone. "What's our first winery?"

She came back on the phone. "The Solemn Grape in Carlsville."

"I'll see you there," I said and hung up just as Lydia called me a selfish loser.

To divert myself from screaming at the enormous mobile home towing a compact car and going thirty-five miles per hour north on Highway 42, I listened to one of the nature tapes I'd bought at Earth's Bounty, a boutique nature shop in Sister Bay. As the soothing sound of waves hitting the shore flooded the truck, my breathing calmed, but my mind whirled with possibilities. If Brownie was Rossi, and if someone from his past had discovered his real identity, then at least there might be someone else who could have killed him. The suspicious bearded man Ken had seen sneaking around the woods near their shanty? The gentle background music swelled with the waves. I didn't want Ken to be guilty. I didn't want to believe that I had been so wrong about him and his capacity to rebuild his life. I didn't want to believe he'd hurt his friend.

Just like I didn't want to believe that I had been so wrong about Tom, I reminded myself bitterly. But I had been wrong. From the moment I told him I had cancer, he'd turned away from me. In his eyes, I was now damaged. And then to slap me with divorce papers because he wanted to start his life over with another woman, to start a family. Maybe I was wrong about Ken too. Maybe not.

In the distance I saw the forty-five miles per hour sign signaling I was nearing Carlsville. And like all perfect endings, there was the trolley waiting to turn left into the Solemn Grape parking lot.

"I don't want to know," Lydia barked at me, hanging back from the small tour group. "You're here. Let's enjoy the tour and the luncheon."

There was a brittleness about Lydia. Her normally curly hair was slicked back behind her ears, her navy cropped pants were bedazzled with rivets along the hemline, and her green top was festooned with sequins and cut on the bias. Her platform wedges were so high, she was taller than me. And she looked like she'd lost ten pounds, her body all jutting angles and hard surfaces.

I touched her arm. "Are you okay?"

She pulled her arm away and walked toward the tour group. I followed, deriding myself for not calling her. What kind of friend was I? Clearly she was miffed, and I didn't blame her.

I took out my notebook and joined her and the rest of the group, mostly middle-aged couples. For the first three wineries Lydia ignored me, ingratiating herself with an older man and his thirty-something son. I decided to concentrate on why I was here: to learn about Door County wines and wineries. But my attention kept drifting to Lydia. Her laugh was forced and her posture rigid, as if any moment she expected an assault.

By the time we reached the last winery, The Barn Winery in Fish Creek, where the luncheon was to be held, Lydia's posture had started to droop, but her beauty queen smile was still pasted on her face. Her jaw muscles must be aching.

The winery was a converted stone barn restored in a prairie style with tiled roof and low-slung horizontal windows along one side. I snapped a few photos of the exterior before I entered the winery, trailing behind the rest of the group. The cool stony interior of the tasting room was a balm from the unbearable heat of mid-day. As my eyes adjusted to the dim lighting I spotted Lydia standing at the far end of the tasting bar with the father/son duo. She caught my eye and waved me over. That was a surprise. Had she finally forgiven me?

Without hesitating, I walked past the other couples lining the bar and joined her, hoping this meant I was back in her good graces.

I was about to say something when the tour guide introduced the vintner, George, a robust-looking man with a generous belly who looked more like a brewmeister than a vintner. Unlike the first three vintners, who, though knowledgeable, weren't particularly good speakers, this vintner was a natural, who relished chatting about harvesting California grapes and driving them back at night to blend with Door County grapes in the tradition of one barrel at a time.

After touring the silver fermentation tanks and viewing the oaken barrels, he led us back to the tasting room where he chose a variety of wines from the winery's select series. Though I was past hungry and a little tipsy from tasting so much wine for the past three hours, I still could appreciate the fineness of these wines, deciding that I'd purchase a case of their Reserve Chardonnay, whose per bottle cost was what I normally paid for three bottles. After all, I was about to come into some money, thanks to my fortuitous and unexpected divorce.

George concluded the tour by asking if anyone had questions before we ate lunch on the outdoor patio. The older man with the thirty-something son who'd been annoyingly curious throughout the tour piped up, eliciting a communal murmured sigh from the group. He was a florid man with short-cropped white hair who I guessed had been either a professor or a politician, because his questions were more like opportunities to show off his knowledge about wine.

"What happened to your cherry wine?" he said, leaning back against the wine bar as if he were in a saloon. "I remember when you had that orchard in Sister Bay and sold nothing but cherry wine."

George chuckled good-naturedly and said, "Most people don't make that connection since we changed our name when we started this winery. I'll bet you even remember the old name."

The son was staring down into his wine glass and grinning. I couldn't tell if he was amused by his father or embarrassed.

"Sweet Cherry Winery," the man said, puffing up his chest proudly.

"Right," answered George. "Everyone hold on for a minute." George walked around the wine bar, reached down and brought out a bottle. Then he approached the man and handed him the wine. "I keep a few bottles around to show people. And as a reminder of how I got started in this business."

The bottle was red and the label white with a cluster of cherries below the name Sweet Cherry Winery. There was no mistaking that red color. It was the same color as the shard I'd found in the grass near where Brownie died.

"You're not making this wine anymore?" I blurted out, suddenly revved up.

"Someone's not been paying attention," George ribbed me.

I felt heat rush to my face. "Do you know if any other wineries use this color bottle for their cherry wine?"

George cocked his head quizzically. "Not that I know of. You into cherry wine or just the color of the bottles?" The group tittered.

I could feel Lydia's shooting me daggers. "I'm writing an article for *Seasons*. You know, the Wisconsin magazine. And I was curious about how the Door County wineries got started for the article. When did you stop making cherry wine?" Why was I explaining myself in front of a tour group who looked bored and hungry, waiting for me to shut up so they could eat?

"Seven years ago," George said. "If you want to know more about cherry wine, I highly recommend the Cherry Stone Winery. Their cherry wine is one of the best. They've been in the cherry wine business since it all began. But they don't use red bottles."

I was about to ask another question when Lydia poked me in my side and whispered, "Leigh, what are you doing?"

"My job," I whispered back. Though it wasn't the job I'd come to do, but another job altogether.

"So if there are no more questions, lunch is served. Head through that door to the outdoor patio." George pointed to a door on his right. "After lunch, if you're interested in any wines, there'll be staff here who can help you choose the right wine for you. Also, if there's a wine you'd like to sample, order it with lunch. Everyone gets a free glass."

A polite, brief applause ended the tour.

Lydia grabbed my arm a little too tightly as we walked toward the door to the outdoor patio, "Since when are you writing an article on cherry wine?"

"You know some tourists think cherry wine is Door County. I'm just covering all my bases."

"Yeah, right."

Even sitting under the green market umbrella, the heat was oppressive. I could feel sweat beading around my hairline, trickling down my chest and back. My dark jeans and black t-shirt were virtual heat-seeking devices. If I became any hotter, you could fry an egg on me.

To distract myself from the heat, I gazed out at the pastoral landscape. Past the grape vines were rolling umber fields that abutted a two-lane asphalt road. On the other side of the road stood a red barn, farmhouse and stable. The barn's tin roof reflected the intense sunlight. Everything seemed painterly.

"This is Leigh," Lydia began after we'd placed our wine order. Her face was flushed and strained as she fanned herself frantically with her tour program. "And this is Jeff and Steve."

Jeff was the younger version of Steve right down to the short-cropped haircut, except Jeff's hair was black and his nose a little sharper. As if they'd coordinated their clothes, they both wore pocket t-shirts, Steve's was red and Jeff's was blue, and khaki shorts and running shoes without socks.

"Leigh writes for the *Door County Gazette*," Lydia explained.

The two men smiled politely, nodding their heads. "I'll bet it's always a slow news day up here," Steve said. "Not like Detroit, where we're from."

"You'd be surprised," I answered. Apparently Steve hadn't heard about Nate Ryan's death. Or maybe he didn't consider a famous actor dying suddenly newsworthy.

"Leigh, don't go there. It's too hot for shop talk." Lydia nudged me under the table.

"What's the heat got to do with my job?" I snapped, miffed. She'd been ignoring me the entire tour, then she brings up my job and tells me not to talk about it. As guilty as I felt about not being there for her, I'd had enough. And the heat didn't help my mood.

Just then the waitress arrived with water, the antipasto appetizer and our wine. I gulped down half my water before taking a sip of my pinot grigio, then piled my plate with black olives, cheeses, pâté and crackers.

As we nibbled our appetizers, Lydia and Jeff drifted off into their own conversation, leaving Steve and me to fend for ourselves.

After learning that Steve was a retired Detroit car designer and wine aficionado who made his own wine, our conversation hit a lull. Steve seemed content to sip his wine and stare out over the burnt fields.

Lydia, on the other hand, was like a woman on fire, talking animatedly to Jeff about psychic healing. Jeff nodded, but he didn't look awfully interested. Lydia didn't seem to notice. She seemed charged, talking too fast about the mind–body connection, the soul and the afterlife. She kept saying, "Don't you think so?"

The one time Jeff disagreed, I thought Lydia was going to break in two. She placed her wine glass down on the table so hard, the wine sloshed over the rim and onto her hand.

At one point, Jeff took in a deep breath as if he were breathing for Lydia. Under the table her four-inch platform wedges tapped as if she were on speed.

To break our uncomfortable silence, I asked Steve, "If you live in Michigan, how do you get the grapes to make your wine?"

"I don't drive to California, pick the grapes at night and then drive them back in refrigerated trucks, like what's his name," he teased. "Believe it or not, I mail-order them. Saves on the gas money."

"I'll bet. So what kind of wine do you make?"

"I do a crisp chardonnay. Dry, full bodied, with a hint of apple." He went on to explain the machinery he used and how he fermented the wine. He was a vibrant older man, probably just like his wine.

"You seemed to know a lot about Door County's cherry wines," I coaxed, wanting to steer the conversation back to cherry wines and red bottles.

"Cherry wines, pinots, cabernets, zinfandels, merlots?" Jeff jumped in. He looked relieved to join our conversation. "My dad is like a walking wine encyclopedia."

Lydia popped an olive into her mouth and chewed impatiently while Steve beamed.

"Then maybe Steve, you could help me with something," I

encouraged. "It's about the cherry wine. George said they'd stopped making his cherry wine seven years ago. Would it be possible that a bottle of it would still be around?"

Before Steve could answer, the waitress brought our lunch: gourmet croissant sandwiches that were a blend of carved turkey, white Wisconsin cheddar cheese, and avocado, splattered with a creamy sauce and served with a side of sweet potato waffle chips.

"Looks delicious," Lydia said, taking a small bite.

"Any seconds on the wine?" the waitress asked.

"I'll try the cabernet sauvignon this time," Lydia said, putting her sandwich down and dabbing at the corners of her mouth primly.

I passed on the wine, but Steve and Jeff ordered second glasses. My head was starting to throb from the heat, and another glass of wine might push my throbbing headache into a migraine.

It took a moment before Steve answered my question, and I thought I'd have to repeat it. "About the cherry wine. I've got a few bottles of that sweet cherry wine you asked about stashed in my wine cellar. No longer drinkable, but I keep them as collectors' items. I imagine a lot of people do. Like a souvenir of their vacation in Door County."

"No longer drinkable though?" I pondered the implications of undrinkable wine that was no longer made. Where had Brownie gotten the wine?

"Not unless you like drinking vinegar."

When the luncheon ended, Steve and Jeff said their goodbyes and hightailed it to their cars, not even stopping in the wine-tasting room to purchase wine.

"Mind driving me back to Carlsville after I buy some wine?" I asked Lydia, who was staring after the two men.

"You get the impression they couldn't wait to leave?" Lydia asked.

"It's probably the heat."

"I don't think so." She slipped her card out from under Jeff's plate where he'd left it. She tore the card into four pieces and thrust it in his wine glass, the dregs of wine turning the pieces red. "I wasn't interested anyway. He's just getting over a divorce. Who wants to be the rebound person? Been there, done that. Sure, I'll drive you to Carlsville."

This was as good a time as any. "Speaking of divorce," I began.

Before I could finish, she said, "When?" resting her two arms on the black mesh patio table.

"Last week. And before you get on my case for not telling you, I wanted to wait a day or two to sort through my feelings, and then this whole thing with Nate Ryan happened. There just didn't seem like a good time to tell you."

At the mention of Ryan's name, Lydia shuddered, screeched back on her chair and stood up abruptly. "Didn't I tell you your life was headed in another direction? See, I was right. Now let's go buy some wine."

That was strangely upbeat, I thought as I stood up and followed Lydia. Where was the sisterly empathy? Was she still steamed at me?

The cool dimness of the tasting room was a welcome relief from the sweltering outdoor heat. Leaving the hot patio for the cellar-like atmosphere was like stepping from one season to the next instantly, in this case from raging summer to temperate fall. If only I could stay there.

We each bought a case of wine, Reserve Chardonnay for me and Petite Sirah for Lydia. The wines' descriptions came uncomfortably close to describing each of us. The chardonnay with its hint of acidity; the Sirah with its intensity. The only part of the description that was off was the well-balanced detail.

After our wine was loaded into the back hatch of Lydia's sporty red hybrid car, I climbed into the passenger seat and clicked my seat belt.

As Lydia pulled onto E heading west, she asked, "So what gives? Why all the questions about seven-year-old cherry wine?"

For a moment I considered not answering her, not sure where her sudden cheerful curiosity was coming from. Usually Lydia didn't encourage my investigative forays. Like Jake, she thought they were dangerous and better left to the police. I didn't want yet another motherly lecture. But she sounded truly interested, so I told her about Brownie's death, Ken's arrest and my research into Brownie's real identity, leaving the red bottle for last. She didn't say anything until I was finished.

"Jeez, I've seen some pretty nasty alcoholics, but drinking a seven-year-old bottle of wine that tastes like vinegar, especially after being on the wagon for so long? It doesn't make sense. And if he didn't drink the wine, why were the empty bottles there? And where did he get them?"

"That's what I can't figure out."

We sat in silence for a moment, each of us lost in our own thoughts. I kept waiting for the lecture, which didn't come. Maybe her brush with the police regarding Nate Ryan's death had changed something inside her psyche. Maybe she understood how helpless you felt. How you wanted to do something, anything, to take away that helpless feeling.

I turned and looked at Lydia. "I'm sorry I haven't called. How are you doing?"

Her mouth tightened, and she closed her eyes for a second. "I've had several offers from entertainment magazines for my story."

That wasn't what I'd asked, but it was what she wanted to tell me.

"Are you going to do the interviews?" If she was, I wanted to coach her, to tell her how to see through the reporters' questions. How she didn't need to answer them if she didn't want to. Above all, she needed to protect herself.

"Well . . ." She took in a long breath and let it out. "I already did it."

"When did this happen?" I felt my gut contract with worry.

"I don't know, a few days ago."

When Lydia was her most vulnerable, and I was nowhere around.

"A *PopQ* correspondent interviewed me. Flew out with a photographer, who took photos of where Nate died, me, my studio. Everything." Her voice trailed off.

"Why didn't you tell me? I could have come."

"And done what, Leigh? Held my hand, given the interviewer grief, told me it was a bad idea?" Her voice had ratcheted up a notch. "You wouldn't believe what they paid me. I could shut down the shop and spa for the rest of the summer and take a vacation. I really need a vacation."

"I wouldn't have done any of those things," I argued, wounded by her accusations.

She turned into the Solemn Grape winery and pulled up next to my truck. "Yes, you would have. At least be honest with yourself for once."

I sat staring at Lydia, who wouldn't look at me, her eyes straight ahead, riveted to the windshield. "Okay, maybe I would have done all of those things," I conceded. "But only because I care about you. I'm worried."

"You know what I keep wondering?" Her gaze still hadn't left the windshield. "I keep wondering if you hadn't left to go rescue that homeless guy, the one you're still so involved with, if any of this would have happened to me. I know it's not fair to think that. But I can't help but wonder."

I knew this had nothing to do with me. I was just a convenient target. "I don't understand why you can't forgive yourself. You did everything you could to save him."

"You don't get it." She turned to look to me. "I'm a nurse. I should have recognized the signs."

"What signs? What are you talking about? I thought he just collapsed." This was the first I'd heard of signs.

"When I thought back on it. There were signs. I didn't recognize them for what they were. I did see them, and if he had been anyone else, I wouldn't have ignored them. I was . . . I don't know what I was. In awe, afraid he'd leave, clinging to my good luck that he, Nate Ryan, big, big star, was in my crummy studio. So I kept going, ignoring his agitation, the flushing, his tiredness and confusion, and then it was too late. He was in full cardiac arrest."

"You did try to save him," I offered again. "What about him? Why didn't he say something about what was going on with him?" I tried to deflect some of the guilt away from her.

"He did. He said he was tired and his stomach was killing him. That he hadn't been feeling himself for days. I just thought it was the play, his drinking, his smoking marijuana. He was really drunk the night of the after-party."

"Was he smoking marijuana too?"

"He smoked a joint before we started. He said it would calm his nerves. And it did seem to at first. But then later, he went into cardiac arrest while in corpse pose. Maybe the joint masked his symptoms."

Now I understood. "And when you didn't object when he smoked a joint, you went against your better judgment?"

She nodded. "But I didn't know about him spiking his water bottle until after he collapsed. That guy was such a mess."

"He was drinking the morning he died?" I asked.

She stared at me, taking in a long deep breath, then letting it out slowly. "When I tried to resuscitate him I smelled alcohol on his breath. Before the police got there I sniffed his water bottle and it reeked of booze. Listen, you can't say anything about the joint, okay?"

"Sure," I said half-heartedly.

"No, I mean it, Leigh. Until the tox results are in, no one can know about this. Chet would have my head on a platter."

I raised my right hand. "I swear. But Lydia, it's going to come out in the tox screen."

"That he smoked a joint—yes. That I knew about it—no. He could have smoked it before he got to my studio. If it comes out I knew, I'll forever be the nurse who contributed to Nate Ryan's death."

"None of this is your fault," I reassured her. "So he smoked a joint. That didn't kill him. He died of a heart attack. And you didn't know about the alcohol. Like you said, he was a mess."

She shook her head sadly. "There's this phrase in medicine, 'the first golden hour.' If you can get a cardiac patient to the hospital in that first hour, sometimes he can be saved. That first hour I was moving Nate through yoga poses. And he was busy dying."

"You said *sometimes*," I reminded her. "*Sometimes* a person can be saved in that golden hour." Her guilt seemed beyond reason to me. But then, I'd never lost a patient. As Joe said, you never get used to it.

"Yeah, there's no way to know, is there? That's what I told the interviewer from *PopQ*."

"You told the interviewer Nate smoked a joint and was drinking?" I asked, incredulous.

"No, of course not. I told her about the signs and the golden hour."

"Look, Nate might not have died of a heart attack. The cause of death hasn't been determined yet. You've got to stop beating yourself up."

"You weren't there. I was. I know what I know."

There wasn't anything to say after that. Lydia had been her own judge and jury, and now everyone would know. I wondered if she'd feel better or worse. Guilt was a heavy burden not always relieved by atonement.

"Are you back home yet?"

"Can't. It's too soon. I'm still at Joe's."

I got out of the car, retrieved my case of wine and went to my truck. Before I could open the door, the dust of Lydia's departure filled the air.

CHAPTER TWENTY-THREE:
SUNDAY, JULY 16

My intention was to finish my article on Ryan at the *Gazette* office, basking in the air conditioning and the quietness of a Sunday. For all its charm, the cabin didn't have A/C and even the dense woods didn't provide enough coolness when the temps were hovering near a hundred degrees. By noon the cabin would be stifling.

But when I stepped inside the *Gazette* office, all the windows were open and a box fan whirled around hot air and grit to the tune of fluttering papers. The A/C must be out again.

Glancing down the hallway I saw Jake's door was closed and as I neared it, I could hear his muffled voice. I put my ear to the door and listened. He was muttering something about light, birds, hunting and she. He must be working on his poetry.

For some inexplicable reason his stone house near Newport State Park, which backed up to acres of savannahs and open fields, didn't inspire him. His creative work process reminded me of Nathaniel Hawthorne's. Tom and I had once toured Ralph Waldo Emerson's house in Concord, Massachusetts. The tour guide told us that Emerson worked in an upstairs room with his desk facing a window, overlooking the vibrant New England woods. While Hawthorne, who'd lived in the house with his wife Sophia, for a time worked in the same room, but his desk faced a blank wall. If I were writing poetry or a novel, I'd be gazing longingly out at the green vista, but then I probably wouldn't get any writing done. Maybe Jake had it right. No distractions.

Thinking about Tom made my stomach tighten. The divorce was like a rock lodged inside my gut—heavy, jagged and impossible to digest. I tiptoed back to my desk, flipped open my notebook, and started on Ryan's article. Work was the perfect antidote to self-pity.

The piece seemed to almost write itself. I briefly mentioned Ryan's sudden death at Lydia's studio, leaving out what Lydia had told me about the golden hour and her ignoring the signs of his impending heart attack. The *PopQ* article would hit the newsstands in four days and would probably delve into those suppositions. Lydia was my friend, and I couldn't betray her like that. At the most, Lydia was guilty of bad judgment.

The bulk of my article was devoted to Ryan's meteoric career. I described his film and stage credits, his struggle with drugs and his overcoming his addictions and turning his life around by coming back to where it all began—the Bayside Theater—to jump-start his career.

Though the part about his overcoming his addictions wasn't true, I'd made a promise to Lydia, which I intended to keep. If Nate was abusing drugs and alcohol at the time of his death, it'd come out in the tox results, and I could write about his sordid end then.

Throughout the article I interspersed glowing accolades from Nina, Alex and Harper to enhance my conclusions. Once done, I read over the piece and realized Harper's quote was weak. It said nothing. "He was amazingly talented, and I learned a lot about acting from him." She admitted she'd hardly known Ryan, and her words reflected that.

What I needed was a quote from Julian Finch, who'd known Ryan when he was a young and struggling actor. I glanced up at the office clock. It was only eleven a.m., and I had until Monday before noon to make the deadline. I paged through my notebook, rereading my interview with Julian. No usable quotes about Ryan.

Drumming my fingers on my desk, I considered how to contact Julian short of driving to the BT on the off chance he was there. Because of Barbara Henry's ridiculous protectiveness, I didn't have Finch's cell phone number. What did she think I was going to do, stalk the actors?

Feeling vengeful, I called her number, and her phone went to voice mail. Though I left her a message, I didn't hold out much hope of her calling me back before Monday's deadline. Maybe I should leave Harper's quote in and enjoy the rest of my day. No, there had to be someone who could help me.

Rich. He was like the BT's unofficial sentry/town crier. Though I didn't relish talking to him, he might know Finch's cell phone number. I dug Rich's number out of my bag.

"Hi, pretty reporter lady," he answered. "What can I do you for?"

Inside I groaned at his all too obvious and lame flirting. "Well, I'm trying to get a hold of Julian Finch. I'm on deadline and need to talk to him. To get a quote for my piece on Nate Ryan. Do you have his cell phone number?"

"Here I was thinking you were calling to talk to me." He tittered.

For an awkward few seconds neither of us said anything. Then he piped in, "Don't have his number. But I just saw him. He was headed out to White Fish Dunes. He goes there to unwind sometimes, is what he told me."

"When did he leave?"

"About ten, fifteen minutes ago."

"Thanks, Rich."

"Maybe we could catch dinner sometime?"

Oh, no. Okay, this was going to take some finesse. I didn't want to hurt his feelings, but I didn't want to encourage him either. And he wasn't taking my clear hints that I wasn't interested. So I decided on honesty. "I haven't told many people this, but I just got divorced, like, a few days ago, and I'm still trying to sort things out. But when I'm ready to get back up on the horse, I might take you up on dinner." Ugh! Did I really say get back up on the horse? For someone who made her living with words, that was pitiful.

"Got it. Enough said." Rich's tone had gone from flirty to sharp. I had hurt his feelings.

Rather than prolong both our miseries, I thanked him and hung up.

There was a long line of cars waiting to enter White Fish Dunes State Park. Maybe this wasn't such a great idea. After about fifteen minutes, which seemed like an hour, I entered the park and trolled up and down the parking lots looking for an open spot. Finally, I found one in the last lot adjacent to the gravel yard. I shoved my notebook in my tote bag, left the windows partially open and headed for the beach area. With the lot filled with nifty SUVs and sports cars, I doubted anyone would bother stealing my ten-year-old pickup truck.

When I reached the gray weathered nature center perched atop a rise that overlooked Lake Michigan and the dunes, I was stunned by what I saw. The beach was a circus of sunbathers splayed out on towels; swimmers bobbing in the lake, others dashing in and out, as well as hordes of colorful beach umbrellas, coolers, and volleyball nets. I'd never seen it so crowded or frenetic.

How was I going to find Julian if he was here? I almost turned around and left, but I'd already endured the long entrance wait, so I sat down on a bench, took off my sandals and crammed them into my bag. Then I started down the cement walkway that connected to the strip of thick brown meshing that protected the dunes. As I gingerly walked over the hot mesh path, I told myself that if I didn't find Julian, at least I'd enjoy the washed blue sky, gentle lake breeze and get some exercise.

Once the mesh path ended, I began weaving my way up and down the beach, peering under umbrellas and perusing the comatose sunbathers. No Julian. Suddenly, a toddler appeared in front of me, looking lost. "You're not my mommy," she accused me. "Where's my mommy?"

Before I could answer, a plump woman in a floppy straw beach hat and black one-piece bathing suit ran up to the toddler and grabbed her hand as if I were about to abduct the little girl. "Mommy's here, Ellie. Now don't run ahead of me again, okay?" Then she turned to me. "Sorry."

I didn't know what she was sorry about, but I could feel that rock in my gut again. "No problem," I answered, walking away quickly, squashing down the erupting emotions. Tom was going to have a family without me.

"Life sucks," I grumbled aloud, stomping my way down the beach, not adding the rest of the phrase: "and then you die."

When I reached the dog beach, the crowds thinned and there was no Julian in sight. My calves ached from all my bitter stomping. I stopped and watched two black labs chase each other in and out of the water, barking furiously. As I followed their mad play up the beach, I noticed a blue domed beach tent tucked high up on a dune. I'd come this far; I might as well check it out. Then I could stomp myself back to the parking lot and call it a full day.

As I trudged through the sand toward the tent, sweat rolled down my face, beading off my nose and going into my eyes. I pushed my sunglasses on top of my head, swiped at the sweat with the back of my hand and kept walking. Hot was becoming a permanent state with me.

Just as I neared the tent's opening, I spotted Julian Finch sitting inside on a beach chair, his head down, intently reading what looked like a playbook, looking cool and unruffled. Next to him was a matching beach chair. I wondered whom he was expecting.

His mind must have been elsewhere because it took him a minute to realize I was standing there.

When he looked up, his eyes seemed unfocused. "Leigh, what are you doing here?" he asked.

I was so exhausted by the walking and stomping in the heat, all I managed was, "Do you mind if I come inside? I'm about to burn up."

"Sit, sit, please." He placed the playbook on his lap and patted the other beach chair. The play was *The Importance of Being Earnest.*

I bent down, crawled inside and collapsed on the chair, then pulled my wet t-shirt away from my body in an effort to cool myself. As I fanned myself with my other hand, I glanced at Julian's unusual attire—white short-sleeved shirt, white cotton drawstring trousers and leather huaraches. He looked like a character from a PBS drama set in a nineteenth-century English manor. Only the greenish sports drink, which rested in his beach chair's cup holder, said otherwise. I stared at it longingly.

He must have seen me staring because he said, "Would you like a cold drink? I have water and sports drinks."

"Water would be great."

He opened a portable cooler next to him and took out a bottled water. Besides the sports drinks and water bottles, I caught a glimpse of a bottle of wine and a block of cheese, probably for whomever he was expecting.

I opened the bottle and took a long swallow. "I was hoping you could give me a quote about Nate Ryan for the article I'm writing on him."

"You tracked me here to get a quote about Nate?" he asked

incredulously. "Why didn't you call me or stop by the BT before the performance?"

Now I felt foolish. "Barbara Henry is pretty protective of the actors, so I didn't have your cell number. And the article is due before noon tomorrow. I suppose I could have come by before tonight's performance."

"Wouldn't you rather have a quote from Nina?"

"I have a quote from Nina." Why was he being so reluctant? "And you knew Nate when he first performed with the BT. Wasn't *Twelfth Night* his first professional acting job and *A Streetcar Named Desire* his first starring role?"

Julian's face was expressionless, as if I were describing someone he didn't know. "So maybe you could say something about him when you first saw him act, or maybe relate an anecdote about *Twelfth Night* or *Streetcar.*"

"That was twenty-some years ago," he stated flatly.

I'd tromped around this beach in the heat, and I wasn't leaving without my quote. "Nate told me you mentored him. His exact words were that you're a great guy, great stage actor, and he learned a lot from you." I took another swallow of water, rested the bottle in the cup holder, and slipped my notebook and pen from my bag.

"He said that?" Julian said, surprised and suddenly interested.

That did the trick—when all else fails, stoop to flattery. I hadn't pegged Julian as an actor with a big ego, but maybe all actors had big egos—goes with the territory.

"Okay, sure. What exactly are you looking for?"

A quote, I mused sarcastically. "Did you think he'd become such a big star?" Oops, irritation was making me sloppy. I'd broken the number one rule of interviewing—avoid yes/no questions.

"Not really," he answered, chuckling.

"Why's that?" It was like pulling teeth to get this guy to say something, anything, about Ryan.

"Nothing to do with Nate. It's just how this business works. Whether someone becomes a big star is next to impossible to predict. There are countless talented actors out there, and most of them won't become big stars." He paused. "It's all a matter of dumb luck. Being at the right place at the right time. But that applies to almost everything, don't you think?" There was a wistfulness to his words.

I nodded in agreement, wondering if Julian was talking about himself. Though talented, he'd never been a big star. By his own definition, he'd been unlucky.

"Do you feel that way about your own career? That you never got your lucky break?"

It was as if I'd shot him. He sat bolt upright in his chair, knocking the playbook off his lap. "Multiple appearances at the Globe Theater in London, three Broadway shows, an Academy Award nomination." He counted them off on his fingers. "If that's not success, then I don't know what is. Will you see my face plastered in a celebrity magazine? God forbid. I never wanted fame. I get paid to do what I love. How many people can say that?" He glared at me with such intensity, I looked away.

I'd hit a raw nerve. "I wasn't implying you weren't a successful actor, Julian. Like I said, I'm a big fan of yours." I could kiss that quote about Ryan goodbye. I'd offended him.

He bent over to pick up the playbook, shook it free of sand, then placed it on his lap. His hand trembled. "Dangerous. And magnetic," he stated. "You never knew what he'd do on stage. There was something unpredictable, maybe even primitive, about him. I don't think he understood it. It was just who he was." He crossed his arms and stretched out his long legs, digging his heels in the sand. "That's probably why he turned to drugs. He knew he was one lucky son of a bitch. Why would anyone want that fate?"

I looked up from my notebook. His rancor was gone. "Are you saying you didn't think he was talented?" I chose my words carefully. "That it was all charisma and danger?" Two seagulls landed in front of the tent, squawking loudly.

Julian kicked sand at them, sending them waddling down the beach complaining. "What do you think?" He waved his hand dismissively, whether at the seagulls or me I wasn't sure.

Why was he asking me? "I think he was a gifted actor. That's why it was such a waste when he seemed to . . ." I struggled for the right words. "To . . . I don't know, phone it in. Like in those ridiculous romantic comedies. He just lost sight of his own talent. He told me that it all came too fast and too easy."

"I didn't think he was that self-aware." He took a swallow of his drink. "Did I give you enough for your article?"

I scanned my notes. "I'll probably use what you said about Nate being dangerous. No one else said that about him."

He arched one eyebrow. "That's because they've never been pricked with a knife by him." His tone was so serious, at first I didn't catch the humor.

"No scar, I hope." I went along with the joke.

"Not that you'd notice." He patted his chest. "How's the BT article coming?"

"Interviews are over. Now all that's left is my weekend living with the BT. I want to experience what it's like being a member of a residential theater group." I still didn't know if I had the go-ahead, and after my run-in with Alex Webber, I wouldn't be surprised if he refused my request.

"You sure you're up for that treat? We're a pretty bizarre bunch, though harmless."

"It may not happen. I've been rubbing Alex the wrong way lately."

"What could you have possibly done to upset him? You're a

total professional. You tracked me down on a Sunday to get a quote. I call that dedication."

I couldn't tell if he was being ironic. "I asked him if the rumor was true that Nate was going to withdraw his half-million-dollar donation."

Julian went perfectly still, as if he was in shock. "Who told you that?"

"Can't say. But it was a reliable source. Of course, Nate died before he could withdraw the money."

"It's not Nina, is it?" I could see he was scrolling through possible sources in his mind.

"Why would you think the source is Nina?" Nina, who was overtly hostile to the press, would be the last person to tell me anything, especially something as critical to the theater's rebuilding project as the loss of Nate's donation.

"They acted like everything was fine between them. But the bad blood was still there, believe me."

"If there still was bad blood, why did Nate return to the BT or donate money?"

"I should have said that the bad blood is all on Nina's side. She never got over the way he treated her when they were married."

There might be something to what Julian said. Nina wasn't the least broken up over Nate's death. "Did Nina say something that makes you think she's still bitter?"

"Not to Nate's face, she didn't. She's too smart for that. But she was vehemently opposed to his returning to the BT. Eventually she gave in." Julian shrugged. "Nate Ryan was good for box office sales and fundraising. What could she do?" He crossed his legs and straightened the crease in his white cotton trousers. "So you didn't tell me how you found me here?"

I screwed the cap back on the water bottle. "Rich told me."

He nodded his magnificent head. "He doesn't miss much.

He's a sharp one. Always has been. Did you know he has a degree in engineering from Purdue?"

"He mentioned it."

"So are we good? Do you have what you came for?"

That was my cue to leave. I stowed my notebook and pen in my bag and struggled out of the low beach chair. "I think so. Thanks for the water."

"Always stay on the good side of the press, my drama coach once told me, even when they pan you." He saluted me. "So why don't you write down my cell number. Hang Barbara Henry. You can call me anytime."

I yanked out my notebook and jotted down his number, then left.

On my long walk back to my truck, I debated whether to drive back to the office and finish the article or call it a day. I was still undecided when I reached the cement walkway leading to the parking lot. Hurrying down the walkway wearing oversized sunglasses and a large-brimmed black straw hat that did nothing to hide her blond cotton-candy hair was Harper Kennedy. As she walked, her loosely tied sheer beach wrap swayed open, revealing a skimpy bikini and a very thin but toned body like a ballerina's.

I stepped off the walkway under the deep shadows of the large cedars. She was in such a hurry, she didn't notice me standing there watching her scurry past. Other than a small black straw clutch tucked under her arm, she wasn't carrying anything else—no towel, no umbrella, nothing. Why would she? Julian was waiting with everything she needed. Were they rehearsing lines? I knew she was playing Gwendolyn, Julian's love interest, in *The Importance of Being Earnest*. Then why meet at the Dunes? A tryst? Finch was old enough to be her father. Maybe they were just friends? Yeah, right. That bikini said it all.

The memory of Alex kissing Harper's hand at the Isle View

Bar flashed through my brain. This girl knew how to wield her assets to cast her spell on men. But what did she want from Finch? He knew a lot of people in the business. And now that Nate was dead, Finch was next in line to be enticed by her. Had she cast off Alex, or was she still working him?

As I stopped at the park's exit waiting for a car to pass, I debated whether I should go back to the office or go home. It was almost 2:30 p.m. Working at the office would allow me to check out the website Sam had found, but I was spent. The lure of Salinger's company and a cool glass of the Premium Reserve Chardonnay was too hard to resist. I turned right and headed north to Highway 57.

CHAPTER TWENTY-FOUR

As I neared the cabin's driveway, I noticed a dark car parked on the other side of the road. Anxious to get home, I sped past the car and turned into the driveway. When I pulled up in front of the cabin, I heard Salinger's frantic cries. She never cried like that unless something was wrong. Before exiting the truck, I located my pepper spray. I'd let my guard down once before, and it almost cost me my life. So I wasn't taking any chances. With the pepper spray in my right hand, I bounded up the porch steps, my heart beating wildly to the sounds of Salinger's mad scratching.

I'd barely opened the door when she squeezed through the opening, leapt off the stairs and dashed down the gravel driveway as if she were being chased.

"Salinger," I called out. "Get back here." For a moment I stood on the porch, wondering if I should just let her go. But her frenetic barking had me worried. Angry and a little panicked, I went after her, still gripping the pepper spray.

Just as I rounded the last curve, I saw the black car. It was now parked at the driveway's entrance, just sitting there. Salinger circled the car as if she was herding it. All the car windows were tinted, so I couldn't make out the driver.

"Salinger," I yelled, hurrying my pace. "Come here now."

Salinger stopped circling the car, looked back and started trotting toward me.

Then the car revved its engine and took off, squealing its tires.

I watched in dismay as Salinger tore after the car.

When I reached the edge of the driveway, I looked up and down the deserted road. No car, no Salinger. All that remained was the smell of exhaust filling the heavy afternoon air like a noxious vapor.

In a panic, I started running up the road north in the direction the car had gone, my sore leg muscles protesting. Though Salinger had a habit of running off into the woods chasing whatever took her fancy, she'd never chased a car before.

She'll come back, I told myself as I jogged. *She always comes back.*

When I saw the intersection of Timberline and Isle View in the distance, I stopped. Salinger was sitting under the intersecting road signs. I sped up, both relieved and worried. I had to reach her before a car whizzed by and she took off again. *Hurry, hurry,* I goaded myself.

But when I got closer, I let out a deep sigh. My fears were unfounded. She must have seen me because she started jumping up and down, lurching toward me, the rope taut. Someone had tied her with a rope to the road sign.

I knelt down in the weedy grass and ran my hands over her body, making sure she wasn't hurt while she licked my face. After finding no signs of injury, I untied the rope from the sign but left the other end tied to Salinger's collar.

"This is what you get for chasing after strange cars," I reprimanded her as we walked back toward Timberline. She had the good sense to hang her head in shame as she walked beside me contritely.

While we meandered home, I racked my brain for a logical explanation why someone had been sitting, idling their car at the end of my driveway. And even stranger, why they'd tied

Salinger to that street sign.

When we came to the cabin's driveway, the only explanation I could come up with was someone was interested in buying the house and was checking out the area.

Before going inside, I tied Salinger to one of the porch posts and walked around the periphery of the property, peering into the dense woods, seeing nothing. Finally, I circled around to the front porch to find Salinger dozing.

Leaving Salinger on the porch, I went inside and searched the cabin, going room to room, opening closets and looking under beds. There was no one inside and nothing looked disturbed.

After settling Salinger down with several dog treats, I called the realtor, Diane Avers, on her cell phone. She answered on the first ring. "So how's the cabin working out for you?"

"Other than no A/C and no Internet, it's great."

"Easily fixed."

"Has anyone shown any interest in the cabin?"

"Got a few calls, but no bites. Why, have you decided to put in an offer?"

"Still thinking about it."

"Don't think too long."

"I won't. Thanks." I hung up. An interested buyer might explain why a car was idling at the end of the driveway. But it didn't explain why someone had tied Salinger to a street sign.

Rather than sit around worrying, I refilled Salinger's water bowl, gave her another treat, locked the doors and jumped into the truck, driving away slowly as I scanned the woods. That scare had revitalized me.

CHAPTER TWENTY-FIVE

The ambush had happened at night, in the tangled jungle. Tim Washington described the torrential rain, the oozing, impossible mud and the heat over 120 degrees. Lawrence Browning was the only soldier who'd disappeared that night in the confusion of battle. Washington never named him. Toward the end of his two-minute recitation, he said that sometimes he thinks it was all a dream. But when he sees photos of himself in Vietnam, it all comes back. "I came home not quite the same person," were his concluding words.

Had Brownie come home the same way? Not quite the same person?

I studied Washington's photo, a nineteen-year-old kid with a baby face wearing army fatigues, the sleeves cut out of his shirt, a makeshift piece of cloth over his head, looking straight at the camera with a sad, knowing expression.

I powered down the computer and picked up the office phone, punching in the police station number hoping Chet was there. He was.

"Can I see Ken this afternoon?" I fingered the wine shard, its red glittery surface like a clotted blood drop.

"Be here before five." It was 4:35 p.m.

"Will you be there?"

"I don't need your interfering, Leigh. You got that?"

"But I have something to show you," I pleaded. I picked up the shard and watched the light flicker off it. "Something you're going to want to see."

"If you want to talk to Albright, you'd better stop yakking and get your behind here."

It wasn't like on TV crime dramas. There was no glass partition separating us, no in-house black phone, just Ken and me in a closed cinderblock room with an overhead light and two metal chairs. I'd been in this room more than once, and the memory made me queasy and lightheaded. I swallowed hard and tried not to shake, as the memory of a young woman's body rose up—how still and blue death had been.

"How are you doing, Ken?" I managed to keep my voice steady.

He looked wan and depressed, his massive shoulders slumped and his eyes red and puffy. "They're going to pin it on me." All the fight had left him, as if his rage had been siphoned off.

"Just be honest with me, Ken. There's only you and me in here. Did you hit Brownie with a baseball bat?" I needed to ask him that question. I needed to see what he looked like when he answered me.

He kept his head down as he shook it from side to side. "No," he whispered. I'd expected him to pound the table in anger or at least shout at me. This was worse.

"Tell me again what you saw when you got back from Green Bay. Everything. No detail is too small."

He cleared his throat before talking. "Brownie was under that tree I showed you, lying on his back. Next to him, like I said, were two empty wine bottles. The ones I smashed up then threw into the bay."

"Anything else?"

"Like what?"

"Was the baseball bat there?"

"No."

"What about the guy you saw sneaking around in the woods,

the one with the beard that you told Rob Martin about. Describe him."

He glanced up at me in surprise, and then looked down again. "I didn't see him that well. It was night, so I only saw an outline and the beard."

"Tall, short? Fat, thin? Anything."

"Medium height, maybe a little taller. It was hard to tell for sure. He had on baggy clothes and had a dark beard. He was wearing a hat too."

"What kind of a hat?"

"Like in them old black and white movies. Wide brim, turned down so I couldn't see his face. You think this guy killed Brownie?" He raised his head, making eye contact.

"That's what I'm trying to find out." Now was the question I'd been leading up to. "If I'm going to help you, Ken, you have to tell me everything."

"You calling me a liar?" The anger was back, and I was almost glad to see him show an emotion, even if it was anger.

"You haven't told me everything you know about Brownie, have you?" My instinct told me that from the moment Ken called me asking me to see where Brownie died, he'd made a decision to hold back the intimacies of Brownie's life out of some misguided sense of loyalty to his friend.

He slammed his fist down hard on the metal table, making me jump. "Don't push me and don't call me a liar."

Suddenly, the door opened and Chet jutted his head inside. "What's going on in here?"

"It was me. I slammed the table too hard to make a point."

"Uh-huh." Chet didn't buy it. "I'm right outside this door, Albright. So watch yourself."

After Chet closed the door, I continued. "Brownie's dead. He can't be hurt anymore. So if you're holding something back because of him, don't."

Ken's eyes shifted right. When they came back to me, sadness had replaced his anger. "He told me he'd been a medic in 'Nam. It was almost like being a priest, is what he said. The guys he treated confided in him. Too much sometimes. Things he didn't want to know. It was too much responsibility." He paused. "I don't know if I should be telling you this. It's got nothing to do with Brownie being killed."

"You don't know that, Ken. What if that person you saw sneaking around in the woods was from Brownie's past?"

"And hunts him down now after all these years?"

"Just trust me. What did Brownie tell you?"

The room went quiet as he struggled with his decision. I placed my hands flat on the cool metal table, waiting, praying I'd gotten through to him.

"Sorry, Brownie," Ken began, looking up. "But I gotta tell it. There was this young kid who was shot up pretty bad. Brownie was trying to save his life. But it didn't look good. He confessed to Brownie that he'd shot and killed one of his own guys during this ambush by mistake. He panicked, took the guy's tags and dragged his body into the jungle. Then he got shot. When he was being medivaced out, he confessed what he'd done to Brownie. The guy was pretty far gone, and Brownie said he didn't think he was going to make it. So Brownie took the tags and promised not to tell anyone. But afterward, he said he couldn't live with it. When he thought about this Lawrence Browning's family, it tore him up. He went to Browning's parents' house and almost told them, then chickened out. That's when he took on Browning's identity and started drinking."

"Did this guy who shot Lawrence Browning make it?" I asked.

"Yeah. Do you think he killed Brownie?"

"You mean Anthony Rossi, don't you?" I wanted to test my hunch that Ken had always known Brownie's true identity.

He didn't even try to deny it. "He wouldn't let me call him

that never. He said that person was dead."

"I don't know if that guy killed Brownie. Maybe."

It was a long shot. Brownie had kept his end of the bargain all these years. Why would this person seek him out now and kill him?

"Did Brownie tell you the name of the guy who shot Lawrence Browning?"

He jutted out his jaw as if in refusal. "Tim Washington."

I was so shocked, my mouth dropped.

"You know this guy or something?" Ken asked.

"You might say that." I'd just watched Tim Washington's account of that ambush online. I can't imagine what had possessed him to retell the horrors of that night to strangers and then let them put it online for everyone to see. Not once did he mention Lawrence Browning.

To his credit, Chet listened to the whole Lawrence Browning story without interruption, shaking his massive Viking head a few times, adjusting and readjusting the tiny American flag on his desk, and sipping from his coffee cup. When I was through, he asked for the website, logged on and watched Tim Washington tell the terror of that night ambush. Then he rocked back and forth in his swivel chair, hashing over what I'd told him.

"You know it's the story of a dead man told by the man accused of his murder."

"But worth looking into?" I encouraged.

"Maybe."

I was prepared for his skepticism. Opening my purse, I dug out the wine shard from an inner pocket and placed it on his desk.

"What's this?" He picked it up in his large hand and examined it.

"A shard from one of the wine bottles Ken smashed and

threw in the bay. The bottle is from the Sweet Cherry Winery. They stopped making this wine seven years ago. And no other winery on the peninsula uses this color bottle."

"So?"

"So why would Brownie drink a seven-year-old bottle of wine that most likely tasted like vinegar? And even more baffling, where did he get it from?"

Chet smiled broadly, putting the shard down and pushing it toward me. "Look, Leigh, there are things there about this case you don't know, and that's the way it's going to stay. I listened to what you had to say, and now you take that piece of glass and skedaddle. It's Sunday and there's a steak and a six-pack of beer waiting for me at home."

"Just tell me one thing and I'm gone. What was Brownie's blood alcohol level in the initial tox screen? You can at least tell me that." I needed to know if Brownie had been drunk when he died. If he hadn't been, then I wasn't sure why the wine bottles were there. Unless Ken had lied, and he'd procured the wine somehow and tried to drink it in alcoholic desperation, which I didn't buy.

Chet let out an exasperated sigh. "Let's put it this way, he could have driven home if he had a car and a home."

"Are you saying he was sober when he died?"

"That's not what I saying. So don't be putting words in my mouth there."

"So alcohol was in his system but he wasn't drunk. Then why is the ME running additional tox tests?"

"I hear you moved up by Gills Rock. How's that working out for ya?"

Okay, I'd squeezed what I could out of Chet. I stood up and swung my bag strap over my shoulder. "And Brownie did have a home. They both had a home together."

Before leaving Sturgeon Bay, I stopped by the *Gazette* office to use the computer again. If Brownie's story was true, and why would he lie, Tim Washington had killed Lawrence Browning in the confusion of battle and hid the killing. Washington had been nineteen years old when he was drafted. As he stated in his own words, "They called me Billy, like in Billy the Kid." A kid sent into a hellhole, where he mistakenly killed a fellow soldier. He'd been awarded a bronze star, was deemed a hero. After all this time, would he murder to keep his secret?

The place was eerily quiet and unreasonably hot. I went to Jake's office, pushed up all the windows to let in the breeze off the bay. Jake's desk, as always, was a mass of paper piles, magazines and books. Sticky notes ran across his computer top like a colorful border. I plopped down in his chair with trepidation, not sure I wanted to find Tim Washington, because that would mean confronting him with what he did years ago in the heat of battle as a scared kid. But what was the alternative? I booted up Jake's computer and leaned back in his chair. I was sweating, whether from the heat or my fears, I wasn't sure.

Though Timothy Washington was an annoyingly common name, I had enough information about him, such as age and military service, that it didn't take me very long to find him.

Timothy Washington, Green Bay, Wisconsin, deceased. He'd died two years ago.

I powered down the computer and sat listening to the sounds from the harbor, the low moan of a tugboat, the drone of a jet ski, the lapping of water. Though I didn't believe Ken murdered Brownie, there was nothing else I could do for him. Whatever Chet wasn't telling me about the murder would seal his fate one way or another. Sadness, like the coming twilight, filled the room.

Before I left the office, I phoned Elsie Browning and told her what I'd learned concerning her son's death in Vietnam, stressing that the information was secondhand and reminding her that the man who'd had Lawrence's dog tags was dead as well as the man who'd mistakenly killed him.

She didn't ask any questions, and when I was done, a terrible silence hung between us.

"Mrs. Browning, I'm so sorry," I offered.

She cleared her throat before she spoke. "Now at least I can stop hoping." She sounded so small and sad.

"Would you like me to mail you my research notes along with Lawrence's photo?" I didn't know what else to say.

"Yes, that would be nice. Thank you." Her voice was thick with emotion. "And Miss Girard, I'll light a candle for you tomorrow in church."

At least she has the solace of her faith, I thought, hanging up the phone.

Chapter Twenty-Six:
THURSDAY, JULY 20

"Could Nate Ryan Have Been Saved?" The headline blared across the front cover of *PopQ*. Below the headline was a full-page photo of Nate Ryan at the peak of his career: thick blondish hair, perfect bone structure and those blue eyes, dangerous and devilish. On the bottom right was a small photo of Lydia looking tense and harried.

"They've been flying off the shelf since we opened at six," said Jenny, the market's owner, as she rang up the magazine, a pink lemonade, a turkey sandwich and a bag of peanut butter–flavored doggie treats, Salinger's favorite. "Been selling a lot of the *Gazette* as well. Liked your article better, though. You tell Lydia when you see her, there's nothing she could have done."

After paying for my purchases, I went to the truck, where Salinger was waiting patiently for her well-deserved reward. She'd been my guinea pig for this morning's assignment—an article on the new doggie day care operation in Liberty Grove called Pet Adventures. Tag line: "Even your pet deserves a vacation." The facility catered to pet owners who wanted to travel with their pets. If the pet stayed overnight, you could choose a themed-adventure room from African Safari to Amazon Rainforest. Salinger was near exhaustion when I finished the interview after zooming—running around the enclosure with a pack of dogs—for two hours. Now maybe she'd sleep deeply tonight.

Since chasing the mysterious car, she'd been acting skittish all week, waking me up at night, growling and scratching at the window. Tuesday night she'd been so agitated, I threw on a robe, grabbed a flashlight and pepper spray and walked around the cabin, finding nothing. Last night I'd locked her in the kitchen and cranked my box fan to high in order to muffle her growls. After an uninterrupted sleep, I felt revitalized today.

It was another gloriously hot and clear blue-sky day so I decided to eat my lunch down by the Egg Harbor marina, where I could absorb the painterly view of the yachts and sailboats bobbing listlessly in the water. In the distance lay a lush green island like some promise of serenity, which I was craving.

I'd spent the week reporting on fluff stories that catered to the tourists, from the opening of a new gallery to a shop that sold only popcorn. I didn't see much future in the popcorn shop, but the gallery had promise, featuring oversized paintings, mostly vague dreamy scenes that could be Door County. It was hard to tell for sure.

So I'd had little time to work on the BT piece. Jake wanted me to report on the last performance of *The Importance of Being Earnest* on Sunday, celebrating the BT's sixty-fifth anniversary. After the performance, Nina was expected to announce that the fundraising goal for the rebuilding of the theater had been reached, thanks in large part to Nate Ryan's generous donation. Another celebratory after-party at Serenity House was planned for Sunday night's performance. Donors, cast and crew were invited.

When I complained to Jake about the endless stream of fluff assignments, he'd said, "When are you spending a weekend at the BT?"

"Still waiting to hear back from Barbara." I'd left a dozen phone messages, which had gone unanswered.

"I'll give Webber a call today."

"Knock yourself out." I was still miffed that Webber had told

Jake instead of me about Sunday's party celebrating their fund-raising success.

Neither of us said anything about our "date," the chaste kiss, or if we were ready for another date. Like drag-racing teenagers playing chicken, we were waiting for the other to blink, swerve off the road and say, "You win." I wasn't budging. This time I wanted to be courted and wooed. Or maybe I wanted a respite from men and the intricacies of what they called love.

There were no parking slots by the marina, so I parked in the small lot overlooking the harbor. I gave Salinger a peanut butter treat, took a sip of the lemonade and a bite of the turkey sandwich, then started reading Lydia's *PopQ* article. Before calling Lydia, I needed to assess the damage—and I was convinced there would be damage.

PopQ thrived on lurid gossip about celebrities. They had a weekly section called "What were they thinking!" where so-called experts rated celebs on their fashion *faux pas*, giving them percentage points: the worse the attire, the higher the percentage. Of all the magazines Lydia could have given an interview to, this was near the bottom of the proverbial barrel, often crossing the boundary between truth and reality in an effort to sell magazines. I shuddered just thinking what webs of fantasy they'd woven with Lydia's self-incriminating statements.

The article was positioned dead center, subtitled "Nate's Golden Hour." It was told from Lydia's point of view and full of self-blame. Lydia came across as incompetent at best and negligent at worse. "I knelt over him and didn't know what to do." Had she really said those words?

By her own admission, she didn't call 9-1-1 immediately. Instead, she'd given him CPR, even though she thought he was already dead—*thought*, not *knew*. Did it really happen that way? Lydia told me so many versions of that morning, changing the details with each telling, that I wondered if she even knew what happened.

As if the writer wanted to give legitimacy to the article, there was a sidebar titled "The Golden Hour," giving symptoms of cardiac arrest and, in a gesture either of momentary conscience or fear of a lawsuit, pointing out that Nate Ryan had exhibited only three of the signs. But the article added that even two signs should be taken seriously, according to Blaine Ving, MD.

The glossy colored photos made Lydia look hard, her yoga studio stark and her building shabby. Nate Ryan's photos showed him as a younger man full of promise and amazingly handsome and virile. The visual message was obvious: this hard woman had robbed the world of this beautiful man by not doing her job. There was no mention of Ryan's years of drug abuse. If Lydia's intention was to punish herself before the whole world, this article was her scarlet letter—there for everyone to see and to judge.

I read the article again, this time more slowly, jotting down what facts I could glean from the sensationalism and exaggerations. There weren't many, and most of them came from Dr. Ving's reported signs of a heart attack and the golden hour. Nate had complained of indigestion, tiredness and nausea. I flashed back on the vomit. The confusion Lydia had told me about wasn't one of the signs. But maybe when you're in the middle of a cardiac event, you're confused. Or maybe the joint he'd smoked had resulted in his confusion. Again, I speculated that Lydia might have joined him in that joint, which would account for her slow reaction time and spaciness. And that led me to question whether Lydia had even been capable of giving a yoga class. What had really gone on in Lydia's studio that morning?

I fished my phone out of my bag and speed-dialed Lydia's cell phone. After one ring it went to voice mail, telling me her mailbox was full.

Though I doubted Lydia was back at her living quarters above the studio, especially in light of the *PopQ* article, I called her shop anyway. Another voice message. It was Lydia explaining that the Crystal Door was closed until further notice. That meant Carrie was no longer holding down the fort.

There must be a stream of gawkers at her place, peering in the windows, taking photos and posing in front of the shop/ studio. I imagined the Facebook entries: "Wonderful time in Door County. Good beach weather. Here's where Nate Ryan died."

My last option was the Bay Hospital. Maybe she'd gone back to work to keep her mind off Nate's death. When I asked for Lydia Crane, the operator told me she wasn't on duty today.

"How about Joe Stillwater? Is he there?" Joe might know where Lydia was.

"I'll transfer you to the ER."

Before I could ask about Lydia, Joe launched into a tirade. "You seen that article on Lydia yet? Piece of crap, if you ask me. There's no way she could have saved that guy. I told her that. You know how many cardiac patients survive that golden hour? Not many. I suppose you're looking for her? She was at my place when I left around one o'clock for my shift. She said something about taking off. But she didn't say when. I think she was regretting giving that interview though. She looked real scared to me. And Lydia doesn't do scared."

"Did she say where she was going?"

"Nope. But she was on my computer most of the night. I only know that because I got up to go to the bathroom, and she was sitting at the kitchen table hunched over it. When I left for the hospital, she was back on the computer." He stopped. "Hey, she told me about your divorce. How you holding up?"

At the mention of the divorce, my chest tightened. "It's not like it was a surprise." I kept my tone casual and light—the gay divorcée, that was me.

"Don't take this the wrong way, Leigh, but your husband was a real asshole."

In a moment of weakness I'd confided in Joe about Tom's inability to cope with my breast cancer. "I gotta go."

"I guess you're not ready yet to talk?"

"I'm fine, really, Joe. There's nothing to talk about."

"Okay, water woman. Whatever you say." Calling me water woman brought back that night when I'd let Joe in; not just into my bed, but into the emotional side of me I'd let no one see, not even Jake.

"I'll be fine," I repeated. And if I said it enough, maybe I'd convince myself.

"When you're through being fine, I'm here for you," Joe offered.

After I hung up, I stared out at that island. In the shimmering heat, it looked like an oasis.

CHAPTER TWENTY-SEVEN

My relief at finding Lydia's sporty red car parked in Joe's driveway vanished as I peered inside. The passenger's side window was smashed in, her glove box hung open, and the contents were scattered across the floor and the passenger seat. Lying on the ground beside the car was the *PopQ* magazine, its pages fluttering in the breeze.

I glanced toward the blue house. The front screen door was ajar, tapping manically.

Driving up the peninsula, I'd phoned Joe's house repeatedly, getting a busy signal every time. Had Lydia taken the phone off the hook to escape the media? She might have. But would the media even know she was at Joe's? They did have their ways. And that *PopQ* article had been inflammatory enough to garner Lydia even more attention.

I went to the front door and called through the screen, "Lydia." No answer. Then I walked inside the tiny foyer and looked left into the living room. The room was a mess, sofa cushions tossed, books scattered and a blank space where the TV had been.

I froze and listened, afraid whoever had ransacked the living room was still there. But the only sounds were a clock ticking, the clattering of window blinds and a muted buzzing.

"Lydia!" I called again. Still no answer. *Maybe she's gone for a walk and someone broke in while she was away,* I told myself as I strode down the narrow hallway looking into the two bedrooms, which had also been searched, mattresses overturned, dresser drawers open.

My heart was thudding as I hurried toward the kitchen at the back of the house, praying that Lydia was not here, that she'd gone for a walk. But even before I reached the kitchen, I knew it was too late for prayers.

Lydia lay on the kitchen floor, an overturned chair behind her as if she'd merely fallen over in a deep sleep.

I knelt down beside her and touched her face. She was warm. "Lydia. Lydia." I tried to wake her, but there was no response. Then I spotted the small pool of blood by her head. I pressed my fingers to her neck and felt for a pulse; faint but there. Quickly I ran to the living room, tripping over cushions and books to find the phone, which was on the fireplace ledge under a pillow still off the hook. Frantically I dialed 9-1-1.

"I need an ambulance. My friend's been attacked. She's bleeding from her head. She's not waking up."

After giving Joe's address and my name, I called the police station. The dispatcher told me to stay put and someone would be there shortly. "And don't touch anything, ma'am," she warned me.

It took the ambulance too long to arrive. Thoughts of the golden hour kept whirling around in my brain as I sat on the floor next to Lydia.

"Hurry, hurry, please hurry," I kept repeating aloud. What? Did I think Lydia's eyes would flutter open at the sound of my voice? I wanted to cradle her, but I knew that would be a mistake. She'd been hit on the back of the head, and she shouldn't be moved. So instead I held her hand, as if I could keep her alive, as if my energy would save her. Suddenly, I heard Salinger whining and scratching at the back screen door, wanting to come in. I'd totally forgotten about her.

"No, Salinger," I commanded, "stay there."

She quieted, sat down and stood guard. "Good girl," I praised her.

As I waited, my eyes roamed the kitchen, thinking through what might have happened. If Lydia had been on the computer when she was attacked, the computer was gone. There was nothing on the table except an overturned coffee cup and spilled coffee. Strangely, this room hadn't been ransacked like the other rooms. Dishes were stacked by the sink, dishcloths hung over the stove handle, and the coffee pot was half full and still turned on, filling the room with a burnt coffee smell. A robbery gone bad? It looked that way. Or was it made to look that way? Joe had nothing worth stealing, as far as I knew. His missing TV was an old box model, his computer at least ten years old. The only logical conclusion was that Lydia had been the target.

The sound of the ambulance's siren broke into my musings. I let out a sigh of relief as the siren's wail grew louder and louder.

"Lydia, it's going to be okay. It's going to be okay," I said, gently squeezing her hand.

The siren suddenly went silent. Then Salinger started barking as doors slammed outside, followed by the crunch of gravel from footsteps hurrying toward the house.

"I'm back here in the kitchen," I shouted, glancing up at the kitchen clock. As two burly EMTs rushed into the room carrying medical cases, I calculated that the ambulance had taken thirty minutes to arrive. How long since she'd been attacked? I wondered. Was there time left in her golden hour?

"Ma'am, we'll take it from here," directed the EMT with the shaved head and bear tattoo on his forearm. The other EMT, a blond with dark eyebrows who was taking Lydia's pulse, smiled reassuringly at me.

My legs wobbled as I moved to a corner near the stove, watching in a daze as the EMTs worked on Lydia, trying to save her life. What horrified me were her stillness and the white lucidity of her skin.

As if I needed to explain, I said, "I found her like that."

Neither man looked up, just moved briskly, checking vital signs, starting fluids, prepping Lydia for transportation to the hospital. I tried to decipher what her stats meant, what her odds of survival were, but it was useless. External head injury was all I understood and something about the bleeding.

"Is she going to make it?" I asked, almost afraid of the answer.

The tattooed EMT didn't even look up from his work. "We're doing everything we can, ma'am."

Chet arrived just as the EMTs slid Lydia onto the gurney. He took me by the arm, gently leading me down the hall and outside, where he sat me down on Joe's porch swing. I didn't fight him. Salinger settled under the swing.

"Tell me what happened." he said, sitting beside me, causing the swing to creak in protest, his big black-shod feet planted firmly on the cement porch, as if he thought rocking the swing would send me reeling.

"I don't know. I found her like that." I tried to read his expression, but it had gone professional. He was protecting himself, just as I was protecting myself. "Chet, why would someone attack Lydia like that, even if it was a robbery? You saw her head and the overturned chair. Someone hit her from behind. Someone tried to kill her. Then the attacker went through the place. What was the person looking for? This wasn't a robbery."

Chet bit his lower lip. "I'm telling you this because we're friends. Nothing I tell you goes in that paper there. Lydia called me this morning. She's been getting death threats. You know, there's a lot of crazies out there."

"Because of Nate Ryan? Someone tried to kill her because she didn't save him, and then tried to cover it up by making her attack look like a robbery?" I didn't believe it. "That makes no sense. How did the person find her? No one except Joe knew she was at his house. I didn't even know where she was."

He leaned back on the swing, making it sway and my stomach lurch. "Tell me why you were here."

"Because I read that horrid article in *PopQ* and was worried about her. I kept calling her and couldn't reach her. Joe told me she was here. I was afraid."

"Afraid of what?"

"I don't know, Chet. Afraid for her mental stability, I guess. Ryan's death did something to her. You saw it."

Just then the two EMTs lifted the gurney over the front door threshold and carried it down the steps to the waiting ambulance. Neither of us said a word, just watched our friend being lifted, slid and tucked into the ambulance.

"Hold on a sec," Chet said to me. He shuffled down the front steps and approached the tattooed EMT. I couldn't hear what Chet said, but the EMT nodded in reply. Then the ambulance was gone, its awful siren fading into the distance, taking Lydia away.

When Chet came back to the porch, he didn't sit down. "Why don't you go on home now. There's nothing else you can do here."

"Are you going to check her cell phone messages? When I called her, her mailbox was full. Maybe whoever did this left a message." Though it was blisteringly hot, I was trembling.

"Like I said, go on home and leave the police work to us." He put his hands on his hips, letting me know he was done talking.

But I wasn't done. I stood up quickly and moved toward the door. I wanted to check the upstairs bedroom, the only room I hadn't searched. But Chet was quicker and blocked the doorway with his large frame. A desire to punch him, to push him aside, overcame my common sense. I raised my hand to hit him, but he caught it midair, holding my wrist tightly.

"Whattya doin' there, Leigh?"

"I have to go inside. I won't touch anything. I promise."

"You can't go in there now. It's a crime scene."

I pulled back on my arm, trying to free my wrist from his firm hold. "Let go of me," I demanded, blinking at the tears threatening my determination.

Instead of letting go, Chet tightened his grip. "I'm chalking this up to shock." He shook my wrist when he said it. "If you want to help Lydia, get yourself over to Bay Hospital. Lydia needs a friend." Then he lowered my arm and let go of my wrist.

"I was only trying to help. You didn't have to use police brutality on me." I rubbed at my sore wrist.

"You so much as interfere with this investigation in any way, shape or form, and I'll haul your ass in." His face was flushed, his mouth a taut line.

My wrist throbbed, and a surge of anger shot through me. Chet had gone too far. "You do what you need to do," I snapped. "And I'll do what I need to do."

He turned his back to me and strode into the house, shutting the door behind him. I stood on the porch, shaking, horrified by how close I'd come to hitting Chet. And how close he'd come to really hurting me.

Chapter Twenty-Eight:
FRIDAY, JULY 21

A cacophony of beeps filled the ICU room where Lydia lay sheeted and tethered, her chest rising and falling as a machine breathed for her. The breathing tube looked like a snake swallowing her.

"Open head injury," the surgeon had explained before he'd performed the surgery that might or might not save her life. Her skull had been fractured and now she was in a coma. No one could tell me if she'd ever wake again. I'd called her only close relative, a brother who lived in California. He told me to keep him posted. That explained a lot about Lydia.

Sometime in the night, her brain swelled dangerously, and I stood outside the glass room helplessly watching the doctor and two nurses work on my friend, relieving the pressure in her damaged brain. Now it was a matter of waiting, something I was lousy at.

I was about to get up to stretch my legs and check the time when Joe walked in the room carrying two coffees. He handed me one.

"I'll sit with her a while," Joe said. "Why don't you go home and rest? If anything changes, I'll let you know. Nothing you can do now. If you want, you can leave Salinger at my place again tonight."

"No, I'll drive by and get her after I leave the hospital." I sipped the coffee gratefully, not getting up from the hospital chair. "Tell me the truth. What are they saying? Is she going to make it?"

Joe pulled the other chair next to me and sat down, his dark eyes full of compassion and sorrow. "No way to know." His usual loquaciousness was gone, and that scared me.

"She coded last night," I said. "But they brought her back."

Joe pursed his lips, his chiseled profile somehow reassuring. "Yeah, I saw that on her chart."

"I've been sitting here all night thinking about who would want to hurt Lydia," I said, taking another sip of coffee. "And it all comes back to Nate Ryan. Chet seems to think it's some crazy who holds Lydia responsible for his death. I think he's just saying that to shut me up, and that he doesn't believe it. Lydia told me the day Ryan died he was going to withdraw his donation to the BT. Something Nina Cass did had made him furious."

"And you're going to find out what that was?" Joe added.

I glanced over at Lydia, then back at Joe. "What would you do?"

"I'd let the police handle it. But since it's you we're talking about, then I'd be careful."

"What I don't get is why attack Lydia now? For that matter, why attack Lydia at all? Unless her attacker thinks she knows something about Ryan's donation or—" I stopped.

"Or what?" Joe asked.

"Or Ryan's death. Maybe there was something in that *PopQ* article. Maybe Ryan didn't die of a heart attack."

Joe took in a big breath and let it out slowly, as if there wasn't enough air in the room. "He died of a heart attack, Leigh. That's what Lydia said. And didn't the ME confirm that?"

"Cause of death hasn't been determined yet," I countered.

"Look, there's nothing you can do right now." His eyes traveled my face. "You're tired. Go home and catch some shuteye.

228

You're not thinking straight." He squeezed my shoulder.

"Maybe you're right." I stood up and circled my head, loosening the cricks in my neck.

"Like I said, be careful."

Mired in weekend tourist traffic as I slowly inched up the peninsula, I listened to my voice messages.

"This is Barbara Henry, public relations director for the Bayside Theater." I moaned aloud at her unnecessary formality, which I suspected was a prelude to her rejecting my request to stay on the BT grounds for a weekend.

"When you arrive," she continued to my astonishment, "go to the box office to pick up the apartment key and your itinerary. You're in quad two, room four. Please follow the itinerary regarding mealtimes and seating at the plays. I assume you'll attend all three weekend performances and Saturday's after-party. Alex wanted me to tell you that you could use the dining lodge and go backstage when the actors are rehearsing in the rehearsal building—that's from one to four p.m. But you're not to bother the actors in any way." Click.

Bother the actors in any way? We'll see about that.

So Jake's magic touch—a combination of smarmy charm and tough love—had worked on Alex. Though if my article on Nate Ryan hadn't pleased Alex, Jake's magic touch would have fallen on deaf ears.

I must be back in Alex's good graces because he hadn't assigned me a room in the intern dormitory, that sprawling red and white clapboard building with a shared bathroom and no privacy. Though I wonder whose idea it had been to put me in Ryan's apartment. Most likely, it was the only one available.

Well, so much for going home and catching some shuteye.

The second voice message was from Jake. "Heading out to the hospital to see Lydia. Just found out the medical examiner sent specimens from Ryan's autopsy to a forensic toxicology expert in Madison. There were barbiturates in his system. Before you go all conspiracy theory, they haven't determined if that was the cause of death. So until the forensic toxicology results are in, cool it." He let out a deep breath. "We gotta talk. But it can wait till you wrap up your weekend at the BT." Click.

We gotta talk about what? About Ryan's death? About Lydia's attack? About us? That was so Jake. I just never knew where he was coming from or where he was going. Mystery can only take a gal so far.

CHAPTER TWENTY-NINE

Except for the lacy underwear and empty goblets and wine bottle, Nate Ryan's apartment looked exactly the same. Over a week ago I'd sat on this very sofa next to him, resisting his magnetic personality, and now he was dead. Maybe caused by barbiturates, maybe not.

If barbiturates had contributed to Ryan's death, that would relieve Lydia of her guilt, I speculated. Even though she'd said nothing when he'd smoked a joint, she didn't know about the alcohol in his sports bottle or the barbiturates.

After cranking up the A/C and depositing my small overnight bag in the bedroom, I searched the apartment—drawers, closets, under furniture, even the refrigerator. What was I expecting to find? A hidden letter from Ryan nixing his donation? A stash of narcotics? But it was as if he'd never been here. Most likely the police had gone through the place right after his death. If they'd found anything, I'd be the last to know.

It was nearly two o'clock, and I wanted to tour the backstage area while the actors rehearsed, so I quickly changed out of my sweaty clothes, savoring the chilly air on my bare skin. Just as I zipped up my white Capri pants, there was a determined knock on the front door. Maybe Barbara Henry wanted to make sure I was happy with my accommodations. Yeah, right.

When I flung open the door, Rich greeted me. "Hi, pretty lady." He was holding a bouquet of wildflowers whose stems were wrapped in tin foil and bound with a red ribbon. The flowers were a potpourri of yellows, reds, pinks, and whites. "Just thought I'd come by and give you a proper welcome."

He was as spruced up as I'd ever seen him, which admittedly wasn't saying much. His jeans were dark navy, creased, and clean. Instead of his usual t-shirt, he was sporting a white short-sleeved collared shirt. Though his running shoes were dusty, both shoes had laces. This was going to be trouble.

He held the flowers out to me. "Thought you might like them. They're from the BT gardens."

I took the flowers, gave them a few quick sniffs, inhaling an intensely sweet scent that bordered on unpleasant. "Thanks," I said, making no move to invite him inside.

He looked past me into the living room. "Mind if I come in?"

I did mind, but what could I do? The guy had brought me flowers like a smitten schoolboy. I didn't want to encourage him, but I realized that ship had sailed without me and was headed for rough seas.

"I was about to head out. But sure, I'll put these in water."

While I searched the cupboards for a vase, to my annoyance, he plopped down on the sofa, stretching his arms along the back and putting his rather small feet up on the coffee table.

The cupboards contained a collection of unmatched dishes and glasses, but no vase. I settled for a large shallow glass bowl and filled it with water. The flowers were too long and hung over the bowl as if they were suicidal.

When I placed the bowl on the coffee table, I said, "Best I could do."

"That's okay. They don't last long once they're cut. Just thought you'd like them. Did you know Shakespeare was an avid gardener?"

"No kidding." I remained standing, hoping he'd take the hint.

"You have anything to drink? I'm parched."

One of my expensive bottles of Chardonnay Reserve was chilling in the fridge, but I wasn't about to offer him that. I was still on the clock, and I needed him to leave.

"Water's all I've got."

"That'll do."

After I handed him the glass of water, which he promptly put on the table beside the flowers, he said, "Aren't you going to sit down?"

"Actually you caught me at a bad time. I need to check around backstage while the actors are rehearsing." I glanced at my wristwatch to make my point.

"Are you afraid of me?" He pushed back into the sofa and smiled.

Where had that come from? "Why would I be afraid of you?"

"I don't know. You seem different."

"Different how?" Now I was starting to feel afraid. The image of Lydia crumpled on the floor flooded my brain. I stared hard at him. Though tall, thin, and paunchy, his arms were knotted with muscles. He made his living using his body, lifting heavy cases of wine and beer, hauling plants, working in the gardens.

"I don't know. Jumpy, like you want me to leave. I'm harmless, you know. And I think you should give me a chance. We can take it slow. I'm okay with slow."

Here we go again. "Look, I'm sure you're a nice guy. But like I said, I'm newly divorced. I'm not ready to date anyone yet." Why couldn't he take no for an answer? He didn't seem to understand social cues. Something was tangled in his wiring.

He glared at me. "You didn't tell Ryan that when you two had your 'interview' in here." He put air quotes around the word *interview.*

"I don't know what Ryan told you, but nothing happened between us." Why was I explaining myself to this social misfit?

His smile turned to a smirk. "That so? Ryan said you were

ripe for the picking."

My face went hot with fury and embarrassment.

"You know why he didn't pick you? He felt sorry for you. How'd he put it? 'She's damaged.' That's what he called you. He said, 'Rich, those are the easiest ones to get. You just have to know how to play them. And once you get them, they'll do anything for you. So where's the challenge?' "

I was trembling with anger and shocked at his cruelty. "You'd better leave." I pointed to the door. "I mean it. Get outta here."

He didn't move. "Hey, sorry. I didn't mean to hurt your feelings," he said sarcastically. "I just thought you should know how men see you, that's all. Maybe then you wouldn't act so high and mighty."

It was like all the hurt and anger over Tom, my marriage and the divorce came gushing out. "Men? What men? Nate Ryan? Did it ever occur to you that he was lying? Even *you* have to admit he was a poor excuse for a human being. He took his talent and squandered it with drugs and meaningless sex. You know why Ryan said I was damaged? Because I resisted him. That's why. I resisted the famous Nate Ryan, and his ego couldn't handle it."

"I thought you'd say that." He took his time standing up, adjusting his jeans, straightening his shirt collar. Then he walked into my personal space. We were practically nose to chin, and I smelled a faint trace of beer on his breath. I didn't step back. I didn't flinch, but my heart was racing.

"Yeah, everyone knew Ryan was a liar, especially when it came to women. I just wanted to see for myself if anything he said was true. I guess I got my answer."

"What's that supposed to mean?" I spat at his face.

"He might have been lying about your wanting him, but I think he was right about you being damaged."

As he started for the door, I picked up the bowl of flowers, my hands shaking. "You can take these with you," I sniped, thrusting them toward him.

He looked at the bowl of flowers, then at me before he took the bowl. "We're not going to have a problem, are we, as far as that article goes?"

Now he was worried about the BT article? He insults and harasses me, and he's worried about the article. What a loser.

"You were never going to be in it anyway," I said dismissively, savoring my small triumph.

"Yeah, I kinda figured that." He started to leave then turned around. "You might want to rethink that decision. I'm the one who's been looking out for you."

I listened for his fading footsteps on the stairs before I inched open the door and made sure he was gone. There beside the door was the bowl of flowers. I picked up the bowl, yanked out the flowers and hurled them over the railing. Let the birds and insects feast on the pathetic bouquet.

CHAPTER THIRTY

Rather than take the flagstone path leading directly to the theater and chance running into Rich, I took a circuitous route through the cedar woods behind the quad. It would be impossible to totally avoid Rich this weekend, but I was going to try. I was still trembling from the encounter, my heart fluttering in my chest, his threatening words echoing in my head.

I hadn't eaten lunch, so I was starting to feel lightheaded. The woods closed in quickly. The towering cedars and deciduous trees loomed, their cool, restless shadows mirroring my uneasy thoughts.

My mind kept dissecting the bizarre interaction with Rich. What had been the purpose of his visit? Did he really think I'd respond positively to his aggressive, hurtful comments under the guise of helping me? And what did he mean, he'd been looking out for me? Had he been stalking me? Was it he who had tied Salinger to the road sign? And had he been lurking around the cabin at night? I had no proof, just my gut feeling, reinforced by our encounter that it was he.

The path veered right and, in the distance, I spotted the reddish-colored theater. When I reached the theater's backstage entrance, I was feeling sick, my head throbbing. I should have eaten lunch. Time for that later. It was already 3:15 p.m. I hurried up the red ramp, pulled open the heavy wood door, went inside and headed directly to the dressing room to scan the actors' quote wall.

Barbara Henry had given me a quick tour of the backstage area when I'd interviewed her, quick being the operative word. While she'd explained that most of the actors did their own makeup, I'd noticed a wood wall across from the makeup mirrors that was splattered with comments from the actors. I'd made a note to come back and read the comments.

The light was dim in the dressing room, so I flipped on the overheads and started reading, looking for viable quotes to use in the article.

"There's a magic here." Might be good.

"Two Shakes." Whatever that meant.

The most enigmatic: "Watch the actor behind the one in front of you."

As I stared at the last phrase, the words seemed to blur. I blinked my eyes several times, and then moved closer to the wall, which only made the letters blurrier. Suddenly, the entire room was fuzzier, my stomach roiling with nausea. I was going to be sick.

I dashed outside and threw up, breaking out in a cold sweat as I retched several times. Then I collapsed on the needle-covered ground, shutting my eyes and waiting for my stomach to settle. *Let this be a lesson,* Leigh. *Coffee isn't a meal.*

At the soft crunch of footsteps and the acrid smell of cigarette smoke, I opened my eyes. There was Nina Cass standing over me, lit cigarette in one hand, her other hand pulling at her tight curly hair. "You okay?" she asked.

She didn't move to help me, just stood there looking down at me as if I were contagious.

Cautiously, I inched myself up on my elbows, then slowly sat up, testing my stomach's stability. "Must have been something I ate—or didn't eat." I stood up and brushed at my white pants, which were now stained with dirt.

"You look positively green," she said, blowing smoke out of

the side of her mouth. "I was on break when I saw you run outside and heave, then collapse. When you didn't get up, I thought I'd better see what's up."

Gee, thanks for all the concern, I thought to myself.

"What were you doing in there, anyway?" She cocked her head toward the backstage door.

"Checking out the actors' quote wall."

She took a deep drag on her cigarette and spoke through the smoke. "Do us all a favor and only use the good quotes. Things have been pretty rough around here since Nate died. We don't need any negativity. We might be getting another large donation, and we need to keep everything on an up note."

I hadn't seen any negative quotes, but I'd gotten sick before I could read all of them. "Who's the other big donor?" I asked, intrigued, swallowing down the acidic taste in my mouth.

"Wouldn't you like to know?" With her tongue, she wet her index finger and thumb, then pinched the end of her cigarette methodically until the cigarette went out. "The donor remains anonymous until the ink is dry. So work with us here, would you? The BT is good for everyone on the peninsula."

She touched my arm as if we were great friends, and her look of sincerity was Oscar worthy. But I wasn't fooled. For whatever reason, Nina didn't like me. Maybe because she still believed I'd had sex with her ex-husband and was just another weak woman in a line of weak women, a reminder of her broken marriage.

"Nina," I began, striking the same syrupy tone, "my intention has always been to write an in-depth piece on the BT, highlighting its long history and its contributions to the fine arts. I don't know why everyone thinks I'm out to find dirt on the BT." Though my stomach was gurgling and my head pounding, I wanted to ask her what she'd done to make Nate so angry he wanted to withdraw his donation. But that would hardly convince her of my good intentions.

"No one believes you're out to screw us. We're just on edge until everything's finalized with this donation. When Nate died, the media was unbearable. So we're a little leery of the press right now."

"Understandable. But I'm the local press. I know what the new theater would mean to the peninsula's tourism business. I'm on your side."

She shook her head and smiled, a big warm grin I didn't trust. "Of course you are. Now that we're on the same page, I'm personally inviting you to the party after Saturday's performance when I'll make the announcement about the new theater. The party's at the house where we had the after-party for *MOV.*"

Barbara Henry had already invited me to that party, but I didn't say anything. Maybe Nina didn't know that. "So how's rehearsal going for *Twelfth Night?*" I asked. *Twelfth Night* was the next play after *The Importance of Being Earnest.*

"It's going to be the highlight of the season. Gotta go. See you later."

Before I could ask why it was going to be the highlight, she walked away. Wasn't *MOV* supposed to have been the highlight of the season? Probably that's what she said about every play.

I returned to the backstage area and searched the actors' quote wall, looking for the Two Shakes' quote. The mention of the two Shakespeare plays, *Twelfth Night* and *MOV,* might shed light on the quote.

There it was, written in faint ink on a slant. Underneath Two Shakes were the initials *NR.* When I returned to my apartment, I'd check the fifthieth anniversary book, but NR could stand for Nate Ryan.

But what was the significance of Two Shakes? Nate had never appeared in two Shakespeare plays in one season. If he'd lived, this would be the first time he'd have done so: *The Merchant of Venice* as Shylock and *Twelfth Night* as the Duke of Illyria. The famous opening lines spoken by the Duke came back to me: "If music be the food of love, play on;/Give me excess of it, that, surfeiting,/The appetite may sicken, and so die."

Was he saying he'd return to the BT to play in two Shakespeare plays? He couldn't have known that. Maybe it was a goal of his? He'd appeared in only one season of the BT, playing Sebastian in *Twelfth Night* and Stanley Kowalski in *A Streetcar Named Desire*. After that, his acting career skyrocketed. He'd been the overnight success most actors dream about being and only achieve after years of paying their dues. He was the exception that proved the rule.

Or was Two Shakes some private reference having nothing to do with Shakespeare?

Though I had a raging migraine, I went over the wall meticulously, reading every quote, even the ones written upside down and in the far corners. I didn't find one negative quote. There were quotes that were playful, bordering on cautionary, but clearly harmless, like the one about watching the actor behind the one in front of you. There were no quotes that would cast an aspersion on the BT. Nina was just looking for a way to tell me to be a team player and play nice.

I closed my notebook and kept staring at the wall, realizing that there were no quotes from Nina or Julian, veteran BT actors who had performed in numerous plays over many seasons. Maybe the wall was like a tourist guestbook: you had to be bored or inspired to write something.

Back in the apartment I popped two migraine tablets, then settled on the sofa with a bag of potato chips and the BT's fifthieth anniversary book. I read through the cast list for each season, year by year. In sixty-five years, the BT had performed only one Shakespeare play, *Twelfth Night*, which had starred Julian Finch as the Duke of Illyria, Danielle Moyer as Viola and in the minor role of Viola's brother Sebastian, Nate Ryan. This season was the first one to present two Shakespeare plays, bucking the BT's mission of bringing mostly contemporary drama to the BT stage. So I had no explanation for Two Shakes.

I had more luck with the initials NR. Only one other actor in the cast list had those initials, Natalie Rodgers, circa 1950, before the BT moved to their current theater and before there was an actors' wall. So the initials were Nate's. I felt the loosening effects of the migraine pills starting to overtake me. I closed the program and lay back on the sofa. It was 4:30. A short nap before the communal dinner at 5:00 p.m. couldn't hurt.

A buzzing sound woke me. I jolted upright in a panic, looking around, not sure where I was. The room was cast in twilight shadows, and the buzzing was coming from behind me. I stumbled up from the sofa to the kitchen counter. My cell phone was buzzing as if possessed. I flipped it open without even bothering to look at the number.

"Hello," I croaked, my throat scratchy from sleep.

"Leigh, it's Joe."

Suddenly I was wide awake and anxious. "Has something happened to Lydia?"

"No," he said quickly, then retreated. "Yes, but she's still alive. She's been medivaced to Green Bay. There's a neurosurgeon there who specializes in these types of traumatic brain injuries. She's in surgery now."

I walked over to the light switch and turned on the lights. The kitchen clock read 7:16. I'd slept for three hours. "Tell me the truth, Joe. How bad is it?"

He didn't hesitate. "It's bad."

I felt my stomach tighten. "Has her brother in California been notified?"

"Yeah, I read him the riot act. But that son of bitch isn't coming."

"She's alone?" I asked, horrified. "She can't be alone. I'm leaving now."

"Hold up. I'm with her. Soon as she went into surgery I called you."

"I should be there too," I argued.

"Nothing you can do now. So stay put. She'll be in surgery for a while."

I didn't want to stay put. But Joe was right. There was nothing I could do. "I don't care what time it is, you call me when she gets out of surgery."

"She's got a good chance," Joe reassured me. "This guy knows his stuff. If anyone can save her, he can. She's got a lot of things going for her. She's in good health." I heard his voice break.

"And she's got you there."

"Listen, I gotta get back. When I know more, I'll call."

I'd never heard Joe sound so low. "She's going to make it," I said with more conviction than I felt. "She has to."

Chapter Thirty-One

Just as the lights dimmed, I sat down in the canvas chair to the angry stare of Barbara Henry who'd greeted me at the tent's entrance with, "A minute later and I wouldn't have seated you," shoving the playbill at me.

As the curtain opened, I glanced at the cast list of *The Importance of Being Earnest,* noticing that two actors were playing two parts, and in the spirit of gender-bending that Oscar Wilde most likely would approve, Lady Bracknell was being played by Gary Westerly, a Chicago actor.

The play passed in a fog. I was beyond hungry, and all I could think about was Lydia, checking my cell phone from time to time. I'd put the phone on silent so if Joe called or texted, I'd see the message envelope.

Only two things broke through my fugue state: the marked diminishment of the bat population and Julian Finch's phenomenal performance. By the second act, you could feel the audience sharpen its awareness when he was on stage, savoring his every word and gesture, laughing in anticipation of his lines.

When he took his curtain call, the theater erupted into applause so thunderous, it was deafening. They cheered and shouted "Bravo!" standing in appreciation. Julian bowed modestly and gestured to the other actors to join him in the adulation. I couldn't help but think Ryan wouldn't have come close to Julian's performance.

As the applause died down, I quickly turned my cell phone

on and checked for messages again. There were none. After waiting for the audience to disperse and Barbara Henry to leave, I made my way backstage. How could Alex fault me for wanting to personally congratulate Julian and the cast?

The dressing room was a buzz with frantic activity, so no one noticed me standing in the shadowy doorway. I should have announced my presence, but I was mesmerized as I watched the actors transform from their onstage characters back to their real selves—caught between fantasy and reality—costumes half shed, pale faces emerging from the thick pancake makeup—as if they couldn't decide who they were.

"If it wasn't good for ticket sales, I'd almost hate you," Nina joked, catching Julian's eye in the wall-length dressing room mirror lit by glaring makeup lights. Her dark curly hair was held back by a tortoiseshell headband, which accentuated her sharp nose and chin and dark eyes. She rubbed cold cream over her face, neck, and chest in tight circles. The loose Oriental-style wrap she was wearing gaped in front, showing that she was braless.

Julian sat next to Nina, carefully removing his heavy stage makeup with cotton balls, working in upward strokes. "Just doing my part," Julian answered. But I saw a sly, self-satisfied smile play across his face. He was relishing the praise.

"And you do your part so well," quipped Harper, who was slipping out of her hoop skirt. She stood for a moment dressed in only a tight bodice, which precariously held her small breasts aloft, and black dancer trunks that showed off her slim legs and hips, the hoop skirt around her ankles. She seemed to be utterly oblivious to Matt Burke's leering gaze. He was ogling Harper in the mirror, appreciating her flagrant disarray.

"If I didn't know better, I'd swear you two are doing it," Matt said, continuing to leer at Harper.

"Still no luck, Burke?" Julian kidded.

"Summer's not over, old man," Burke responded. Shirtless, he stood up and stepped out of his pants, revealing his toned, muscled body, as if daring Julian to do the same.

"You know, I'm right here," Harper said hands on hips, chest thrust forward, still not moving to put on her street clothes. I half expected her to shed her bodice and stand topless to do Matt one better.

I saw Nina cast a fleeting glower at Harper. If looks could kill, Harper would be dead.

"On that note, I'm outta here," said Gary Westerly, aka Lady Bracknell.

"Good job tonight," Julian said. Gary saluted him and left.

Just as I was about to clear my throat and make my presence known, my cell phone rang. Everyone turned in my direction, a look of surprise on their faces.

Embarrassed, I held up one finger, saying, "Sorry. I have to take this," and walked out of the dressing room onto the stage.

"She made it through surgery," Joe said. "Now we wait. If she makes it through the next forty-eight hours, she's got a good chance for a recovery."

I let out a deep sigh. "That's wonderful news. Thanks Joe," I whispered.

"Where are you?" he asked. "Why are you whispering?"

"Backstage at the theater."

"Go do your job. And call me later."

I hung up and held the phone to my heart, letting my breathing settle. Lydia had made it through surgery. Then I walked backstage ready to be reamed out by Nina.

"Okay if I come in?" I said sheepishly.

"A little late for that," sniped Nina, who was standing at the far end of the room, hanging up her costume and throwing me daggers.

"Hey, Leigh," Burke began, ignoring Nina's remark. "You

want some?" He held up a half-empty whiskey bottle. "We're celebrating."

"No, thanks," I said glancing around the dressing room.

Harper had slipped into a summery spaghetti-strap dress and was perched on the edge of the dressing table, sipping at her drink. Julian was still working on his makeup, his cup almost empty.

"Not to speak ill of the dead, but I'm gonna anyway," Burke blathered. "No way Ryan coulda done better than Julian."

Burke walked over and tapped Julian's shoulder. "You are one talented dude. I only hope I'm half as good as you one day." He raised his cup to Julian and then gulped down the rest of his drink.

At the mention of Ryan's name, I felt the room go tense. "You're well on your way," Julian said to Burke. I wasn't sure if Julian meant well on his way to being a better actor or a drunker actor. "Anyone want to head over to The Port for a nightcap? You're invited, too, Leigh."

Nina stared at me as if daring me to accept Julian's invitation as she said, "Another time. I'm beat."

"Aw, c'mon Nina," teased Burke.

In spite of herself, Nina laughed. Other than onstage, that was the first time I'd seen her laugh. It changed her whole appearance, softening her sharp features and making her more attractive, almost beautiful. This must have been the woman Nate had fallen in love with.

"If I change my mind, I'll catch up with you later."

"Who's driving?" Harper asked. "Not you," she cautioned Matt. "You're already past designated-driver status."

Matt put his hand to his heart. "I'm mortally wounded by your cruel words."

Harper snapped her fingers in Matt's face. "Play's over. Back to reality."

"Didn't you know all the world's a stage to Matt?" Julian joked.

"Okay, I know when I'm outnumbered," Harper conceded.

"If you don't mind squeezing into my truck, I'll drive," I offered, smiling at Nina in defiance.

"Let's take my car. Plenty of room," Julian piped up. "How about you drive it, Leigh?"

"My pleasure," I answered, not believing my good luck. A night out with the tipsy cast members was a journalist's dream.

Chapter Thirty-Two

From the way the hostess merely nodded to us as we entered The Port's dining room, I figured the cast must be regulars. Only a few tables were occupied, so we practically had the room to ourselves. Julian guided us to a table with a view of Lake Michigan and the marina. Here and there the lights from boats glittered on the water, making the dark less absolute.

"The usual?" the waitress asked, handing only me a menu.

Everyone nodded their heads. "How about you, honey?" she asked me.

Though I'd have loved a glass of white wine, if only to catch up with the group's festive spirit, I'd promised to drive. Besides, I wanted my wits about me. Maybe I could tease out info about the anonymous donor and, more importantly, what Nina had done to so enrage Ryan that he'd considered withdrawing his donation. Living cheek by jowl with each other, one of them might know something.

"An iced tea and a cheeseburger?" For some reason I was craving a cheeseburger.

"Sure thing. Anything else?"

"And an order of fries, and a salad with blue cheese dressing." I couldn't drink, but at least I could stuff my face.

"Be right back with the drinks and your salad," she said. Then she tapped Matt on his head with her pencil. "And you, Mr. Burke, better behave yourself. No more monkey business. Nobody wants to hear you sing."

248

Matt put his hand to heart again and said, "I'm mortally wounded by your cruel words, lovely lady."

"Uh-huh," she answered, and then sashayed her hips as she walked away.

"I think she wants me," Matt joked, resting his head on Harper's shoulder playfully.

"You think everybody wants you," Harper said, pushing his head off.

"So, Leigh, how was Ryan?" Burke rested his elbows on the table and leaned in as if we were BFs sharing secrets.

"Honestly, Matt." Harper play-slapped his arm.

"You've got a dirty mind, Harper. I meant acting-wise. How was Ryan, acting-wise?"

I didn't think that was what he'd meant, but I went along with it anyway. "I'm no critic. I only know what I like. He was surprisingly good as Shylock."

"Yeah, but our guy Julian here was better, right?" He kept his focus on me. Though I knew he was drunk, his intense gaze was unnerving.

"You don't have to answer that," Julian said to me. "Matt's on the verge of making a complete fool of himself, and it's best to ignore him when he's like this."

Matt was about to put his hand over his heart again and protest when the waitress came with our drinks and my salad. "That burger will be right up, sweetie," she said to me before leaving.

"As I was saying," Matt slurred, putting his hand back over his heart. "I am mortally wounded."

Harper cut him off before he could finish his sentence. "By your drunkenness." She took his hand and put it over her heart.

They all burst into a fit of giggles, even Julian. I might have to order a drink. Harper held Matt's hand over her heart a beat too long before pushing it away.

"I was reading your actors' wall today," I began, trying to change the tenor of the conversation. "I was surprised that you never wrote anything on it, Julian." I glanced sideways at him. "How come?"

"What would I say? Having a great time, wish you were here?" Julian popped an olive into his mouth and chewed vigorously.

"Didn't Nate Ryan write something on it? At least I think it was him. The initials were NR." I was purposely playing dumb in order to tease out information from the group.

"Jeez, back to him again?" Matt said. "I thought we were off him."

"Oh, you mean Two Shakes," Harper said. "Yeah, that's an inside joke. I saw it too and asked him about it."

"And what did he say?"

"Something about how long it takes him to seduce a woman. You know that saying about two shakes of a dog's tail, meaning really fast?" She snapped her fingers. "That's how long it takes him, and if you think about it, he was pretty much a dog." She sipped at her beer, all eyes on her. "What? Why's everyone looking at me like that? I'm not saying anything that wasn't true."

"So he was bragging about his sexual exploits?" I asked. Even factoring in her intoxication, there was something off in her explanation. Was Ryan that egotistical? When he'd written the quote, he was a nobody; not even an up and comer, but just another struggling actor looking for his big break.

She shrugged her shoulders, causing one of her dress's spaghetti straps to slip down her arm. "Hey, that's what he told me."

"What do you think, Julian?" I asked. He'd been quiet throughout Harper's comments, nervously twisting the stem of his empty martini glass in his fingers.

"If that's what he said, then that's what it is."

"Here's your burger and fries, honey." The waitress put the

plate down in front of me and I almost swooned with the aroma. "Another round?"

No one objected.

I took a generous bite out of my burger, relishing the charred meat and gooey cheese before continuing. "I thought he might be referring to two Shakespeare plays." I took another savory bite, chewing in a state of near rapture.

"As far as I know, the BT has never performed two Shake-speare plays in one season," Julian said.

"Except this season," I said.

"What difference does it make what it means?" Julian said, annoyed.

"What difference does what mean?" Everyone was so engrossed in the conversation, no one noticed Nina enter the dining area. She was standing beside our table, holding a glass of red wine. She must have stopped in the bar first. Dressed in skintight black jeans and a lacy red camisole that clung to her like a wet t-shirt, she was oozing sexuality.

"Oh, Nina," Julian said. "You decided to join us after all. Let me get you a chair." He popped up, grabbed a chair from a nearby table and placed it at the end of the table.

When Nina sat down, she repeated her question.

Matt jumped in. "That weird thing Ryan wrote on the actors' wall about Two Shakes. Leigh wanted to know what it meant. I guess he told Harper about it."

"And what did he say?" Nina looked to Harper for an answer, her eyes wide with interest.

As Harper repeated the inside joke, Nina rolled her eyes. "Nate could be such an ass sometimes," she said fondly.

Her response was all too rehearsed—the eye-rolling, the wistful tone. I felt as though I was the understudy in a play I hadn't learned yet. And Nina was both actor and director. My plan to probe the actors about the unknown donor was dashed by

Nina's arrival.

"Speaking of Nate," began Matt, who was now slurring his words. "You guys see that article in *PopQ*? I mean, do you really think Nate could have lived if that chick hadn't panicked? And that was weird, too. She was a nurse. Shouldn't she know what to do?"

"You can't believe anything that trashy magazine says," Harper said.

"Yeah, but you gotta wonder why she didn't call 9-1-1 right away," Matt answered. "What kind of a nurse doesn't call 9-1-1? I mean *I* even know to call 9-1-1."

"That chick is my friend, Lydia Crane," I said tightly, struggling with my rising temper. I could feel my self-control slip away. I wasn't letting drunken Matt slander Lydia. "And right now she's in a Green Bay hospital, fighting for her life because somebody bashed her head in." I had the good sense not to blurt out anything about the barbiturates found in Ryan's initial autopsy.

"What happened?" Harper asked, shocked.

"The police are calling it a robbery gone wrong, but . . ." I hesitated. How much did I want to tell them? My hunch that Lydia's attack had something to do with Ryan's threat to withdraw his donation made me cautious. I glanced around the table, wondering if one of these actors had tried to silence Lydia. If so, my bet was on Nina, who had the most to lose.

"But what?" Julian asked. "You don't think it was a robbery?"

"No, I don't. I'm the one who found her. And the robbery looked staged to me."

"Then why was she attacked?" Harper asked.

"Maybe some crazy person read the article and wanted to avenge Nate's death. Like you said, Matt. The chick panicked," I said angrily.

"I didn't know someone attacked her, or I wouldn't have said that," Matt responded, his head down.

That was amazingly lame, but then, what do you expect from a drunk? "I guess that makes it all right then."

"Leigh," Julian began. "Matt doesn't know what he's saying. Please let us know if there's anything we can do."

"There's something you could do, Nina," I said.

She looked surprised, putting down her glass carefully as if afraid she'd spill it. "Like what?"

"Tell me what you did that made Nate want to withdraw his donation?"

Everyone stared at Nina, waiting for her answer. She wrinkled her forehead in confusion. "I already told you Nate never said anything about withdrawing the money. I don't know why you keep asking me that."

I didn't need to protect Lydia anymore. The damage had already been done. "Because it's true. Lydia Crane was with Nate before he died. He told her he was withdrawing the money because of something you did."

Nina squirmed in her chair. "Well, she's wrong." She pushed her chair back slowly and stood. "Look, I'm tired and it's getting late. I'll see everyone tomorrow."

Then she addressed me. "I'm sorry about your friend. But nothing happened between Nate and me. Nothing. The last time I saw him, he was leaving the party arm-in-arm with your friend Lydia." She emphasized *arm-in-arm*. I knew what she was implying. Lydia had been another of Ryan's conquests, and she was right.

With Nina's departure, the festive mood was shattered. We paid our tab and left. On the drive back to the BT, Matt fell asleep in the back seat, his head resting on Harper's shoulder. This time she let it stay there, falling asleep as well. Julian kept up a polite banter for about ten minutes, and then he fell silent, playing a classical music CD in lieu of conversation.

As I drove west across the peninsula through the star-punched night, I thought about the abruptness of Nina's departure and her overreaction to my question about the purported falling-out between her and Nate.

"Julian," I whispered. "Do you know anything about a disagreement between Nina and Nate before he died?"

"Like I told you. Nina was still bitter about the way Nate treated her when they were married." He spoke softly. "But I never saw Nate show any animosity toward Nina. So no, I never witnessed any disagreement."

When I unlocked the apartment door, the fragrant aroma of flowers assaulted me. *You gotta be kidding me,* I thought as I stood on the threshold, a rush of fear rising up in me. I fished the pepper spray from my bag and went inside, leaving the door open in case I had to make a quick exit. This time Rich had gone too far.

I flipped on the lights, my eyes drawn to the coffee table where a cut glass vase held a bouquet of red wild roses interspersed with fir twigs. I stepped closer. No note, just the message of the red wild roses—flowers of deep romantic love.

The apartment felt empty, but I searched it anyway, finding nothing and no one. Then I went to the door and rechecked the lock. It only worked if I used the key. I closed the door and re-locked it. The flowers had to be from Rich. And as the grounds-keeper, he might have access to all the apartment keys.

The roses' scent was cloying and I felt sick by Rich's intrusion. But there was nothing I could do tonight. I dragged the tweedy blue club chair across the living room and crammed it under the front doorknob. If he tried to get in here tonight, at least I'd hear him coming.

Once in bed, sleep eluded me. After tossing and turning for a while, I got up, made myself a cup of coffee and watched the morning light slowly fill the apartment. Rather than think about creepy Rich, I mulled over who had assaulted Lydia. There was no doubt in my mind that that person had also attacked me at Lydia's studio. And though the gold key charm had proven to be Harper's, I was far from convinced that Harper had been the attacker.

Whoever attacked me had been looking for something at Lydia's studio. Had this person found it? Or was that the reason for Lydia's attack? The person was still looking for it. Or maybe Lydia's attacker thought Lydia knew something and needed to be silenced. What did she know?

It all came back to money—the donation to rebuild the new theater. Who stood to lose the most if the new theater wasn't rebuilt? Not the actors, but the theater's owners—Nina and Alex.

I'd only done cursory research for the BT article on Alex and Nina's roles as owners. Now, in light of what Lydia had told me regarding Nate's threat to withdraw his donation, their roles bore more scrutiny.

And if Julian was right, Nina was still bitter about her failed marriage to Ryan. The prospective loss of Nate's donation could have pushed Nina over the edge.

The apartment didn't have wireless, so I threw on a pair of khakis, a t-shirt and flip-flops before heading out to the Egg Harbor Library, the quietest, nearest wireless venue.

CHAPTER THIRTY-THREE:
SATURDAY, JULY 22

The library didn't open until ten a.m. on Saturdays, so I sat parked directly in front of the building that jointly housed the Egg Harbor Library and the village hall and booted up my computer. The sky was a thin layer of blue, like a stretched balloon, a very stretched, very hot balloon that looked about to burst.

On the east side of the parking lot, a few tourists milled around the open Visitor's Center, pointing and turning as if they were lost, which they probably were.

I Googled Bayside Theater, Door County, owners, and started scanning down page one. About halfway down the first page, I stopped. The heading read: Bayside Theater newest owner. The entry was dated June of this year. I clicked on the entry and a Beverly Hills Hospital newsletter popped up. Under the newsletter's section titled *Doctor News* was a short blurb about Theo Sinclair, M.D., a Beverly Hills plastic surgeon, who was now part owner of the Bayside Theater. There was no other information given about the partnership or Dr. Sinclair.

I fumbled around the hospital site looking for the doctor specialty section, then clicked on the plastic surgery section and found Theo Sinclair's biography, credentials and photo. He'd graduated from Johns Hopkins Medical School, completed his plastic surgery residency at UCLA, and was as handsome as the movie stars he listed as clients, according to his bio. He had dark hair and eyes, perfect features, and resembled an older

Keanu Reeves.

Then I exited the hospital site, typed in Sinclair's name and searched again. There was another short blurb about him when he'd invested in a minor league baseball team approximately ten years ago. Except for Sinclair being single and living in Malibu, I found nothing else of importance.

What did being a part owner mean? Were Nina and Alex still owners and, if so, how much of the theater did they own? Other than this newsletter announcement, I couldn't find any other information about this partnership, Theo Sinclair, or this new financial arrangement. The middle of June had been the start of the new season. Why hadn't the BT put out a press release about the new partner/owner? Why keep it a secret?

Questions were whirling in my mind. Maybe there was no announcement because there were conditions to this new partnership. Maybe Alex and Nina had to raise enough money to rebuild the theater before the partnership took effect. But then there'd been the announcement in *Doctor News* declaring Sinclair a partner. Was he also the anonymous donor Nina had mentioned?

Staring at the fading screen I mulled over who might know about the new partner and would give me a straight answer. Nix Barbara Henry, as well as Nina and Alex.

Quickly, before the screen went blank, I clicked on the hospital site again and jotted down Sinclair's office and home phone number. Was there no privacy left in the world? I asked myself as I backed out of the library/village parking lot. Apparently not, and what was I complaining about?

It was still too early to call the West Coast, so I drove back to the BT grounds intending to soak up more theatrical ambiance for the article. As I turned left into the parking lot, I spotted the BT white cargo van behind me with Rich at the wheel. I pulled into a slot near the dining lodge and he pulled in beside me.

For a few minutes I sat, considering my options, listening to the ticking of my truck's engine. My first instinct was to jump out, stomp over to Rich and accuse him of breaking into my apartment and leaving the flowers. But I had no proof. That left me with running off into the woods or onto the beach, which gave him too much power. Or I could act like a professional. I opted to act like a pro. I got out of my truck, gave him a curt nod and started for the white stone path that led past the dining lodge.

"Buy you a cup of coffee," Rich called after me.

I hadn't slept and was in no mood for his slimy flirtations, or worse, his insults. But I needed to put an end to his stalking me. And the dining lodge offered me the safety of a public place to do that. "You promise not to hit on me if I say yes?" I answered tartly.

For a minute he didn't say anything, deciding if he was going to zing me back. "I think I can resist."

I followed him into the dining lodge and sat by the window overlooking the bay while he went to the ubiquitous coffee urn, filled two coffee cups, and then carried them over to the table.

Every table had powdered cream and an assortment of sweetener packets. Rich dumped three packets of real sugar into his coffee and took a sip, not bothering to stir it. Satisfied, he said, "I was out of line the other day."

It was too hot for coffee, but I slowly stirred in two packets of artificial sweetener and some powdered cream. It gave me something to do other than look at Rich, who was wearing a sleeveless undershirt and thready cutoff jean shorts and exuding a strong musky scent. Tufts of underarm hair completed his rustic look. "So Ryan didn't say those things about me?"

"Not those exact words," he hedged.

"Uh-huh."

"You're not going to make this easy, are you?"

"Listen, Rich, you and I are not going to happen."

"Yeah, I kinda got that."

I wasn't convinced that he did get that. "Then what do you want from me?"

"First off, to square things with you." He looked down at his hands. "Did you like the roses I left you?"

"Breaking into someone's apartment is a criminal offense," I lashed out, not able to hold back any longer.

"I didn't break in," he responded defensively. "I had a key."

"It's still breaking in, key or not." He just didn't get it. "And another thing," I was on a roll. "Have you been stalking me?"

He leaned back in his chair looking hurt. "Man, you really got it out for me. Anything else you want to accuse me of?"

"So that's a no?"

"Yeah, it's a no. Geez, you aren't all that."

I looked hard at him, wondering if he was telling me the truth. If he was, then someone else was stalking me, which scared me. Better the devil I know than the devil I don't know.

"You said first off. Was there something else?"

"You heard from Bob?" he asked out of the blue.

"Why would I hear from him?" The way his eyes traveled over my head to the door, I knew he had talked to Bob. "Where is he?"

"I didn't say I heard from him."

"You didn't have to. Your eyes gave you away."

"Okay, I heard from him. But I don't know where he is." He put his hand up a little too close to my face to make his point. "All he said was to tell you something. That's why I asked you for coffee. Not to get it on with you."

"Tell me what?"

"It's about Danielle Moyer's disappearance. He found something at the old cabin."

"Danielle Moyer? She disappeared years ago. What are you

trying to pull?"

"You don't believe me, see for yourself. I saved his text."

He wrestled his phone from his shorts pocket and scrolled to the text, then slid the phone across the table.

"Lost Lee's cell #. Tell her evidence at cabin. Danielle Moyer w/s ghost. Bob" The text was sent today, the sender was Robert Davidson.

"Did you call or text him back?" I asked, rereading the text.

"He didn't answer, so I left a voice message with your cell phone number."

"What about the cabin? Did you check it out?" I slid the phone back to him.

"I haven't had time."

I studied him trying to decipher if he was telling me the truth. It was like staring down a deep well.

"Do me a favor, will you? Tell Bob that Leigh, L-e-i-g-h, is onto him. And one more thing. My apartment is off limits. You got that? And stop following me around," I added for good measure.

It was as if he hadn't heard me. He grabbed two sugar packets and inched them across the table until their edges touched my arm. I didn't move, just stared at his dirt-clogged fingernails. "When you change the water in the vase, throw out those yew branches and add a packet of sugar. It'll make the roses last longer." Then he took his hand away.

Rather than answer him, I got up, leaving the sugar packets on the table, and walked toward the dining lodge exit.

Before I reached the door, he yelled, "You got me all wrong."

As I followed the path toward the apartment quad, I considered Bob's text. Contrary to what I told Rich, a part of me believed Bob had found something at the cabin, but I didn't want Rich to know that. There was no way Rich could have faked that text. Maybe I should check out the cabin again.

But the bigger part of me was starting to worry that Rich was seriously unbalanced. The sooner I was finished with this article and back home, the better. Hurrying up the limestone steps, I started formulating how I would handle Theo Sinclair, M.D., plastic surgeon to the stars.

"Nate talked me into becoming a part owner," Theo Sinclair explained. He had a flat Midwestern accent and an openness I hadn't expected.

I'd told him I was writing an article on the BT, which was sure to go national because of Nate's death, and that Nina was announcing the partnership tonight after the performance, along with the identity of the anonymous donor. It wasn't a complete lie; Nina was announcing the anonymous donor.

Sinclair had expressed no knowledge about an anonymous donor. Though he seemed enthusiastic about the possibility, calling it "Just what the doctor ordered."

"Nate came to me last year for a consult. Can't say more than that. Anyway, we got to talking, and that's when he made his pitch. His ex-wife Nina Cass was desperate to rebuild the theater, and Nate wanted to help her out. He admitted that I'd be helping him as well, since he was trying to make a comeback via the BT."

"As a partner are you involved with the production end of things?" I was leading him ever so gently to what I really wanted to know. Were there conditions on this partnership?

"I leave that up to Nina and Alex. My involvement is purely financial. My tax accountant thought it was a good investment. Didn't Nina or Alex explain this to you?" Suddenly, he sounded suspicious.

"Nina was a little fuzzy on the details and said I should talk to you about it. Like I said, Nina intends to announce the new partnership tonight. I just wanted your side of things."

"Well, you've got it." He was definitely on guard.

"Are there any conditions to your partnership?"

"Like what?"

"Like do you have the option to end the partnership if not enough money is raised to rebuild the theater?"

"Listen, any partnership can be dissolved depending on the terms. You should know that."

"Right, but you didn't answer my question. Is there a condition in your partnership contract that if not enough money is raised to rebuild the theater, your partnership is null and void?" He was already suspicious, so what did I have to lose by asking again?

"Look lady, I don't know what you're fishing around for, but the terms of the partnership are none of your business. Now I'm due in surgery, so if you have any more questions, you can call my lawyer." He hung up abruptly, without giving me his lawyer's name or phone number. I'd bet my meager salary his next phone call would be to Nina.

CHAPTER THIRTY-FOUR

After a quick lunch of peanut butter, saltine crackers and diet soda, reminiscent of my college days, I decided now was the ideal time to check out the cabin. It was almost two o'clock, which meant everyone would be occupied elsewhere: the actors and crew in rehearsal, and Rich busy setting up the beer garden for this evening's performance.

After locking my apartment door, I shuffled down the steps and around the back of the building, avoiding the main theater grounds.

Traveling light, I'd taken the essentials—pepper spray, maglight, notebook, pen, cell phone and baseball hat. Though the heat was like a wet blanket, I'd worn jeans, running shoes and a long-sleeved cotton shirt, anticipating the array of insects after my blood. All exposed areas were doused in bug juice.

It was a short jaunt through the BT woods to the shoreline trail. When I reached the trail, ominous clouds were moving in, blotting out the sun and turning the sky smoky gray. Maybe it would finally rain and end the drought. Ignoring the heat, I quickened my pace, wanting to get on the path to the cabin before anyone saw me.

As I rounded the curve, I saw the bench, the unofficial marker, and starting jogging toward it. When I reached the bench, I stopped to catch my breath while I looked up and down the trail. Satisfied no one was following me, I donned my baseball hat and walked left into the woods. The dense tree cover and heavy clouds made the narrow rocky path barely visible. Afraid I might trip over a fallen tree branch or hummock, I slipped my maglight from my pocket and shone it in front of me as I walked.

Every few minutes I stopped and glanced back, making sure no one was behind me. The skittering of squirrels and the fluttering of birds added to my paranoia.

Finally, I spotted the green painted cabin through the thick clustered trees. Seeing the lonely isolated cabin made me want to turn around. Instead, I increased my pace, keeping the light focused on the path. If Bob had found something in the cabin that explained Danielle Moyer's disappearance, I wanted to see it.

When I reached the cabin, I switched off the maglight and moved toward the kitchen window I'd pried open. But as I walked past the front door, I noticed the piece of wood nailed across the door was no longer there.

Someone's been here recently, I thought, looking around. A few feet away, I spotted the wood slat resting against a cedar tree. Whoever had removed it intended to put it back. Staring at the now unfettered front door, I debated whether I should go inside the cabin.

"Hello," I called, my voice echoing through the woods. "Anyone here?"

A crow cawed loudly in answer, then something scurried through the underbrush. My first instinct was to run back to the shoreline trail and return to the safety of my apartment. But after a few deep breaths, my hammering heart calmed. My rational side told me that other than animals, no one was here. The door was open. I might as well take a look.

I put my fingers through the splintery hole that once held the doorknob, opened the door and walked across the rutted threshold into the cabin. Even with the windows unboarded, it was dark inside, the overhanging trees and gloomy day added to the darkness. I turned on my maglight and made my way down the short hallway to the kitchen. A rank smell I hadn't noticed before now permeated the air. Probably a dead field mouse, I reassured myself.

On the kitchen table there were three white stoneware plates and glasses instead of two place settings. The candle was still there, only it had burnt down to almost a nub. Matches were also on the table. I struck one on the table and lit the candle. It was so dark inside that my shadow grew and ebbed around the room as I searched through the cabinets and drawers, finding a few odd pieces of silverware, a chipped cup and a faded, water-stained photograph caught in the back of a drawer. Even in the intense halo of the maglight, I couldn't make out the faces of the three people. I put the photo back in the drawer.

All that was left to explore was the pine cupboard, which I was purposely avoiding, saving it for last, afraid whatever I found inside would send me running from the house before I finished my exploration.

I left the kitchen and checked out the west-facing bedroom. Other than cobwebs and dust almost as thick as a carpet, the room was empty. As I entered the second bedroom, I stopped. Pushed against the wall was what looked like a sleeping bag, which hadn't been there before. It was rolled up and tied with a piece of rope, and something stuck out of the top. Resting the maglight on the floor, I squatted by the sleeping bag, untied the rope and unrolled the bag. A faint smell of body odor wafted up. Tucked inside was a pair of men's jeans and a plain white t-shirt. The t-shirt was what had been sticking out of the bag. I picked up the maglight and examined the jeans, which were torn at the knees, frayed at the bottoms and mud-splattered. The tag had been torn out of the waistband; the same for the t-shirt. If I had to guess, I'd say the clothes were a large. What were they doing inside the abandoned cabin rolled up in a sleeping bag? Was someone living here?

I put the clothes back inside the sleeping bag just as I'd found them, rolled up the bag and tied it with the rope. As I stood up, a wave of dizziness came over me. The cabin's rank smell, mingled with the stink of body odor, filled my nostrils. It felt like I couldn't get enough air. I still hadn't found anything relating to Danielle Moyer's disappearance. There was only the kitchen cupboard left to explore.

When I returned to the kitchen, the candle had sputtered down to a puddle of wax, its light all but gone.

As I reached for the cupboard's wooden knob, I told myself there was nothing in there but a tattered nightgown with a brownish stain. But still I hesitated, my hand on the knob, a clammy sweat breaking out all over me. I touched my forehead with the back of my hand as if checking for a fever. Okay, get a grip.

Instead of flinging the door open and ending the mounting suspense, I directed the maglight's concentrated circle on the middle of the door as I ever so slowly eased it open, keeping my eyes focused on the light. A white filmy object came into view— the nightgown I'd seen before. I let out a deep breath and flung the door open. What was I expecting, a dead body?

Then I let out a yelp and fell backward against the table, knocking the dishes to the floor in a resounding crash. Still holding the maglight, I shined it at the horror inside while I listened to the scuttling of animals overhead.

A woman had been shoved in the closet, her long dark hair covering her face, wearing a nightgown splattered with blood. As I moved the maglight up and down her crumpled body, I put my left hand to my chest in relief. The woman was a mannequin. Someone had put this horrific thing in the closet after I'd last been here. Was this what Bob wanted me to see?

Even though I knew it was a mannequin, it still gave me the creeps. The grotesqueness of the bloodied nightgown, the mannequin's head bent over, the hair covering the face, created a scene out of a horror film meant to terrify whoever found it. I stepped closer and pushed the hair from the face, letting out another yelp in spite of myself. Her eyes were open and looking right at me, glassy blue with black irises, so real I wanted to shut them as if she were dead and needed to be put to rest.

Bob's text message played in my mind. "Danielle Moyer w/s ghost." The part of me that thought Bob had sent the text was all but gone, replaced by my belief that Rich was the culprit. I didn't know how he could send that text to himself. Unless he had Bob's phone. And if he'd sent the text, then he'd planted this mannequin with the blood-splattered gown for me to find.

For what reason? Payback for not wanting to date him? Was he that sick? Suddenly, I was shaking. I had to get out of there and fast. I dug my cell phone out of my purse and quickly took a photo of the mannequin, as if even I wouldn't believe it if I didn't have proof.

Then I ran down the short hallway and into the woods, the maglight guiding me like a glow of safety, lighting the stony narrow path through the dense woods back to the trail, back to the real world. My imagination was in full gear, every sound loud and menacing as I crashed through the woods, making too much noise. If Rich was hiding somewhere, he had only to listen to find me.

I shined the flashlight up ahead and saw that the shoreline trail was just a little farther. Why had I fallen for his sick joke? Because I couldn't believe he was that demented. I prided myself on reading people, using my gut to get a sense of who they were, studying their gestures as if they were moving pictographs, listening for the meanings behind their words. I knew Rich was a social misfit when it came to women, but I didn't think he was vindictive enough to do this. Even his inappropriate flowers weren't malicious; misguided yes, but not malicious.

Just a few more feet and I'd be back on the trail. I slowed my pace and took off my hat, fanning my face with it. Suddenly, I was yanked backward by my hair. I grabbed at my hair, trying to free it, dropping the maglight and my hat in the process, then turned and slapped at my assailant.

"Hey, quit it," Bob said, letting go of my hair and putting up his arms in front of his face to ward off my slaps. "It's me, Bob."

My adrenaline was running so hard, I slapped at him again. "You scared the hell out of me!" I shouted.

"You came. I didn't think you'd show up." He was grinning sheepishly.

"Listen, you idiot." I was still pumping with nervous anxiety and fright. "You could have given me a heart attack. What are you doing here, anyway? I thought you were staying with some college buddies or something." I was starting to calm down. He looked as scared as I felt.

"Shush," he said. "Not so loud." He pulled me by my arm deeper into the woods.

"Let go of me," I jerked my arm away. "This better not be one of your and Rich's practical jokes because it isn't funny. It's demented."

"It's not a joke, okay. Something bad is going on here. Really bad."

"What are you talking about?"

"Come back to the cabin and I'll tell you."

I crossed my arms firmly across my chest. "I'm not going anywhere with you. You tell me now, or I'm going to report you to Alex. You've been living in the cabin all this time, haven't you? I saw your clothes rolled up in the sleeping bag." I stared up at his pudgy face, taking in his sickly smell of body odor and dampness. "I'll bet he'd like to know that. You know he called your parents and complained to your school."

"Yeah, well, he's a dick. I tried to tell him what was going on. But he wouldn't listen. And now Nate Ryan's dead. And your friend got attacked. I saw the photo of you and her on the Internet."

"What do you know about any of that?"

"I heard something I shouldn't have. Only after Ryan died and your friend ended up in the hospital did I realize something wasn't right. That's when I sent that text to Rich and asked him to show it to you."

"What did you hear?" I wasn't convinced, but he had my attention.

"The night of the after-party, I saw that friend of yours leave with Ryan. Then he comes back all smiles and high on something. He even patted me on the back as if I was his BFF. He was like bragging to me about how he was going to save the BT, then his cell phone goes off. It must have been a text because he's, like, reading it. And he turns kinda pale and then bolts like he's got some big appointment at three-something in the morning. By then the party's winding down, so I decide to bolt too. As I'm walking, I see Ryan on the trail up ahead. He's not running, but he's walking fast and muttering to himself, angry like. Just as the trail curves right, he disappears into the woods. He doesn't even see me, he's so upset. I know he's heading for the Moyer cabin, so I follow him. When he gets there, I hide near enough to watch. Someone's pried open the front door and he goes in. That's when all hell breaks loose."

"What do you mean? Was someone else there?"

"I couldn't make out most of what they were saying, but yeah, someone else was there. They were shouting. Well, mostly Ryan was shouting. At one point, he shouts, 'I could kill you,

you bitch.' Then she screams back, 'Like you killed her.' "

"Who screamed back?"

"Hold up, let me finish. Then Ryan really flips. 'You can kiss the new theater goodbye. If you think you can threaten me.' Stuff like that. Then she screams, 'I didn't do this!' "

"And then what?" His erratic storytelling was starting to irritate me.

Bob shrugged his shoulders. "Then Ryan storms out."

"And the woman?"

"Guess." Was this some kind of game to him? He certainly wasn't acting like someone who was frightened enough to disappear.

I thought I knew who the woman was, but I wanted Bob to tell me. "I'm not going to guess."

"It was Nina. She left about five minutes after Ryan, looking around like she knew someone else was there hiding in the woods. But she didn't see me."

"Did you hear the name of the woman Nina accused Ryan of killing?"

"Nope. But after they left, I went inside the cabin. I nearly puked when I saw what was there. Hanging from the kitchen rafter was this dummy wearing a bloodstained dress. And get this. Pinned to her gross dress was a cast list for *Twelfth Night*. A red circle was around the name Danielle Moyer. So I'm thinking Nina meant Danielle Moyer."

"That's what someone wants it to look like," I answered, concluding the same thing, but still not sure if Bob was behind the whole prank, although he had nothing to gain by it.

"I tried to tell Alex about it the next morning, but he told me he was done with my crap and he fired me. So I cleared out. Hitchhiked to Madison. But when I heard about Ryan and that lady, I came back."

"Why should I believe any of this?" It all sounded so fantastical. But then Bob reached into his pocket and pulled out a piece of paper.

"Check this out. It was pinned to bloody Mary," he chuckled. "I kept it to show Alex."

It was the second page of the original playbill from the BT's production of *Twelfth Night* 1988. And just as he'd said, Danielle Moyer's name was circled in red ink. As far as I knew the BT didn't keep old playbills, so it was looking like Bob wasn't the culprit, though Rich could have kept an old playbill. "And you're sure you found this pinned to the mannequin."

"I'm not making this up, okay? Alex didn't believe me, and there's no way the police are going to take me seriously. But you could do something. Rich told me how you were involved in those murders along the Mink River and ended up solving them. How the police had arrested the wrong guy."

I cringed at the memory of how close to death I'd come, solving the murders.

"Maybe you could find out what happened to Danielle Moyer. That's why I came back. I knew you wouldn't believe me unless I showed you."

"Nobody knows what happened to Danielle Moyer. I've already looked into that." But maybe I hadn't looked hard enough.

"Then what about Ryan dying all of a sudden like that. And that lady who tried to save him, why was she almost killed?"

"I'm leaving that to the police." It was a big fat lie but I didn't want Bob to be in danger. I had to convince him to go home.

"Yeah, right," he scoffed. "Rich told me you've been asking a lot of questions that are making the actors squirrelly."

"Go home, Bob. I'm just doing my job. Nothing else. If Alex finds out you're living in the cabin, he could contact your college and really get you in trouble."

"Don't you find it strange that Ryan dies after I hear Nina accuse him of killing Danielle Moyer?" He wasn't going to let it go.

"There's no evidence that Ryan was murdered. Just like there's no evidence Danielle Moyer was murdered. Nobody knows what happened to her."

"What about the lady who was attacked? What about her?"

I had no good answer for that. "There's probably no connection between the attack and Ryan's death. And that lady's name is Lydia. Go home and enjoy the rest of your summer."

"You don't have to look out for me, you know, Leigh. I can take care of myself." He straightened his shoulders and sucked in his stomach.

"That's what I tell everyone too. And sometimes I'm wrong."

"I'm not leaving," he said belligerently.

Suddenly, voices came from the direction of the trail. Like criminals, we crouched down and waited for the voices to fade away.

"Listen, I'll make a deal with you," I whispered, getting up slowly. "I'll do some more digging into Danielle Moyer's disappearance, but you have to promise me you'll go home."

"Yeah, okay." He answered too quickly to convince me.

"What do you think you can do hanging around here and living at the cabin? If what you say is true, if someone murdered Ryan, then it's too dangerous for you to be here. Can't you see that?"

"I have to prove Alex wrong. He has to take me back so I can graduate."

I felt sorry for Bob. I doubted Alex would take him back. Through no fault of his own, his future had been jeopardized. "Here's the deal," I said. "Once it's dark, get your stuff from the cabin and go to quad two apartment four, that's where I'm staying this weekend. I won't be back until after the party. I'll leave the door unlocked, but lock it after you get in. Take a shower and get some rest. Okay?"

"Okay," he agreed reluctantly.

Not persuaded by his feeble okay, I added, "You can't tell anyone, and I mean *anyone,* even Rich, that you're staying at my apartment."

"He didn't even know about me crashing at the cabin."

I looked at him skeptically. "And don't take the shoreline trail back to the apartment," I cautioned.

"Duh," he answered. "What do you take me for, a rookie?"

CHAPTER THIRTY-FIVE

The audience quieted as Nina walked to the edge of the stage still in costume, her emerald green satin dress at odds with her determined, almost frantic expression. She managed a faint smile, then her face settled into that perfect blank canvas that gave nothing away. But sitting front row center, I could see her foot tapping under her long crinoline skirt, as if she were keeping time to polka music. She was nervous.

As she stood there, her smile flickering on and off, her foot tapping away, Alex emerged from the wings pushing a large sheeted easel. By the way he was grinning and practically skipping across the stage, I was sure the BT's campaign had achieved its goal. I slipped my pen from my bag and clicked it, poised for the news.

"Ladies and Gentlemen, as you may or may not know, the Bayside Theater launched a capital fund-raising campaign last year to rebuild the theater," Nina began, her strong, steady voice projecting. "I'm pleased to announce that through the generosity of patrons such as yourselves and business and corporate donors, we've been able to reach eighty-five percent of our goal."

A rumbling of disappointment went through the audience. "But wait. There's more." Nina stepped back to the sheeted easel. Now she stood on one side of the easel and Alex on the other. "Before his untimely death, Nate Ryan pledged a half-million dollars, putting us within ninety percent of our goal.

And the good news is"—she gestured to Alex—"Alex, will you do the honors?"

Alex threw back the sheet and revealed a graph showing that the BT had exceeded their goal by one percent. At the top of the graph was the bold headline: The Nate Ryan Theater. The audience burst into enthusiastic applause, some cheering, others shouting, "Bravo!"

Nina and Alex were beaming, basking in the audience's adulation, making no effort to quiet the crowd. When the applause finally died down, Nina continued. "By next season, if all goes well, and I'm confident it will, you'll be sitting in an indoor theater on comfortable seats enjoying state-of-the art stage craft. Seating will increase from five hundred to seven hundred. Patrons like you will experience theater as good as in Chicago, and maybe even as good as in New York."

Another burst of applause and cheering erupted. Again, Nina waited for the audience to quiet before resuming.

"My heartfelt thanks to all of you who have supported the theater by attending our performances and to those of you who have donated to this campaign. And my very special thanks to Nate Ryan, whose generosity made this possible." She looked up and threw a kiss toward the rafters.

"Are there any questions?" Alex asked.

I raised my hand. Not waiting to be acknowledged, I said, "Who's the anonymous donor who put you over the top?"

Alex grinned and gestured toward Nina. "She's standing right here."

Nina took a deep bow to the thunderous applause, and then quickly left through the wings. She didn't even glance at me.

Alex said, "Enjoy your evening and drive safely," before exiting as well.

How could Nina be the anonymous donor? I pondered as I sat and waited for the audience to shuffle out of the theater before walking over to Serenity House for the party. As far as I knew, Nina didn't have that kind of money. She made her living doing regional theater, which probably didn't leave much for a nest egg. And her brief stint in film when she was married to Nate couldn't have given her that kind of money. Of course, the money could have come from their divorce settlement.

I did the math on the playbook. Her donation was roughly a quarter-million dollars. Would Nate have agreed to such a hefty sum to be rid of Nina? And if the money hadn't come from the divorce settlement, where had she gotten it? Well, nothing like a celebration party to ask the hard questions.

As I exited the tent, a few theatergoers were milling around the grounds. The sun had set an hour ago, and the colored fairy lights strung overhead cast a festive glow. Instead of heading immediately over to Serenity House, I decided to stop by my apartment and see if Bob was there yet. Since I wasn't able to convince him to go home, I felt responsible for his safety. Bob had overheard the argument between Nate and Nina and had connected the bloody mannequin with Danielle Moyer's disappearance. He might be in danger, and he was too young and impulsive to understand that.

When I reached my apartment door, I looked around, making sure I was alone. Then I put the key in the lock and realized as I started to turn the key that the door wasn't locked.

Slowly I eased the door open, not sure what to expect. The apartment was dark. I flipped on the lights and checked the bedroom and bath. No Bob. Where was he? I plopped down on the bed and called his cell phone. On the first ring, it went to voice mail.

"This is Leigh. I'm at the apartment. It's after ten-thirty. Where are you? Call me." I hung up, that queasy feeling back in my stomach.

Uneasily I shut off the lights, closed the front door and left it unlocked.

There was no need to hurry, since the actors were probably still taking off their makeup and changing into their street clothes. I meandered down the shoreline trail, listening to the melodic rhythm of the bay rushing the shore, back and forth, back and forth, mirroring my thoughts. *Should I make a detour to the cabin to see if Bob is there or go on to the party?* The avenue of trees darkening, looming over me, their coolness offering little comfort, every sound magnified by the stillness, only added to my apprehension. *What if he's been attacked and is lying unconscious in the cabin, near death like Lydia?* I shook my head as if that would dislodge the image.

As I neared the bench marking the path to the Moyer cabin, the trill of my cell phone broke through my speculations. Holding my breath I answered, "How is she?"

"Better than expected," Joe said. "She's still in an induced coma, but her vitals are good and the swelling in her brain is going down. Now she just has to make it through the next twenty-four hours."

"You're not holding anything back from me, are you, Joe?" I wanted to believe him, yet I was afraid to. Until Lydia was out of the coma, I wasn't celebrating.

"Let's just get through the next twenty-four, okay? Then we can worry about what comes next."

"What comes next?" I asked as I reached the bench and sat down. "You mean her recovery."

"I mean we'll worry about that when she's out of the woods. Okay, water woman?"

"Okay," I answered reluctantly, aware that Joe was protecting me.

"You know you saved her life," he said. "If you hadn't found her when you did, she wouldn't have made it."

His kind words made me uncomfortable. "The surgeon saved her life. I just happened to show up and find her."

"You're lousy at taking compliments, you know that?"

"I'll work on it. Thanks for the update. If anything happens—" I began.

Joe interrupted. "I know, I know. I'll call you, no matter what time it is. But nothing's going to happen. Just watch out for yourself. I don't need two friends in the hospital."

"I can take care of myself," I said, hearing the hollowness in my boast. Joe had the grace not to contradict me.

I flipped my phone shut and sat savoring the lingering afterglow, tingeing the bay fuchsia. Lydia was going to make it. I could hear the cautious confidence in Joe's voice. But the mystery of her attack remained, like the dark that was now extinguishing threads of twilight into nothingness, all brilliance gone.

I glanced over my shoulder, then at my watch. It was almost eleven. *I'll be quick*, I told myself as I jumped up and dashed into the woods, turning on the maglight and hurrying down the rocky narrow path. I had to know if Bob was at the cabin and if he was all right.

When I reached the cabin, I didn't hesitate, but opened the front door, the maglight guiding me as I went inside. The bedroom where Bob had stowed his sleeping bag was empty, as was the other bedroom. Okay, he'd taken his stuff. So where was he?

In the kitchen, I tripped over something and went flying head first across the floor, somehow managing to hold onto the maglight. Splayed face first on the floor, I choked on the dust and dirt, pain radiating from my left ankle. I sat up and flashed the maglight on the floor. I'd tripped over a piece of wood. I felt around my ankle cautiously. It wasn't broken, but it hurt. Swearing, I tossed the slat into a far corner, stood up, and flung open the cabinet door. Bloody Mary was gone.

Once outside I moved the maglight to where the wood door slat had rested. It wasn't there. No Bob, no Bloody Mary, and my spiffy black linen trousers were ragged at the knees. As I hobbled down the path to the shoreline trail, I was angry and worried.

CHAPTER THIRTY-SIX

The party was in full swing when I arrived. Loud music punctuated by laughter drifted from the open windows of the prairie-style house. I grabbed a glass of white wine from the impromptu bar set up in the kitchen before stepping down very gingerly into the massive open living room that was clogged with people. My ankle felt like it was beating to its own rhythm.

Perusing the room for Nina, I took in the frenzied activity among the dancing couples and groups of chattering and laughing people. Matt Burke and Harper Kennedy were locked in a version of dirty dancing. Her slender figure seemed engulfed by Matt's gyrating body. Another couple I didn't recognize were also doing their version of dirty dancing, only dirtier. Alex was holding court with the lighting and tech crew, gesturing dramatically. Beside him Barbara Henry nodded her head like a performing myna bird. We'd made eye contact when I entered the room, but she'd immediately looked away as if she hadn't seen me. It baffled me how she kept her job as PR director.

Trying not to limp, I skirted around the room to avoid the frantic dancing and made my way toward the French doors leading out to the patio, thinking Nina might be outside smoking. Sure enough, she was standing next to Julian, plumes of smoke rising into the night. Both held crystal highball glasses. When she saw me approach, she called out to me, "Leigh," a broad grin on her nervous face.

Her warm greeting threw me. I'd expected her defenses to be

up. Mine were most definitely in full-alert mode.

She was wearing a long, flowing florid peasant dress a la 1960s hippy era, a daisy tucked in her curly dark hair. Julian was playfully dressed in white linen trousers and shirt, a silky teal ascot tied round his neck. They both seemed blurry with drink.

"Before you ask," Nina said, her husky voice full of humor, "Nate left me the money in his will. I couldn't say anything until it was all confirmed. So there. Now you know."

Another surprise. If my math was right, that meant Nate had left Nina about a quarter-million dollars. You didn't have to be a genius to conclude that if he'd withdrawn his donation, he'd also change his will.

Julian chuckled. "I think she's speechless."

"Though I don't appreciate your bothering Dr. Sinclair, I hope you're through snooping around now."

Instead of rising to the bait, I said, "Nina, could I talk to you for a moment in private?" I glanced at Julian, who was staring at me as if I had something on my face.

"What now?" She flung her cigarette over the patio ledge. Its red tip swirled out over the ravine and down into the woods.

"Do you want me to leave?" Julian asked.

"I've got nothing to hide," she said defiantly.

"It's about Danielle Moyer." I saw her dark eyes widen in surprise.

"Nobody knows what happened to her," Julian said, putting his arm around Nina's shoulder as if he was protecting her from me.

"That's not true, is it Nina?" I needed to push her, to show her I wasn't going to be disarmed by her this time.

"Give us a minute, would you, Julian?" she said, looking up into his face.

Julian took his arm away, shrugged and ambled slowly toward

the French doors and into the living room.

"Look," she said angrily. "I don't know what you think you know or don't know, but I have no idea what happened to Danielle Moyer. And I've about had it with your ridiculous questions and accusations." She bumped me as she started to walk away.

"That's not what you said to Nate the night of the after-party."

She turned back and hissed in my face, "You weren't even at that party."

"Why did you accuse Nate of killing her?"

I watched the play of emotions on her face—shock, fear, anxiety—waiting for her denial. "How did you . . . ?" She stopped talking, but it was too late. She'd confirmed what I already knew. A few people had come out on the patio and were looking out over the ravine.

She leaned close to my ear and whispered, "I can't talk to you about this here. You understand? Meet me later."

Was she stalling for time to come up with some plausible story, to figure out how I knew what she'd said? Or was she sincere in wanting to tell me her side of things? I didn't know. But I wanted to hear what she had to say, and I didn't want to give her too much time to change her mind. "Hal's Tap in an hour."

"I can't be there so soon. Make it two hours?"

"I'll be waiting for you."

Hal's Tap wasn't listed in any of the Door County tour books, and unless you'd mistakenly turned down Maple Grove, you'd never find it. It was in the middle of the peninsula, in the middle of nowhere, surrounded by woods. The tavern was a local hangout. Hal Pinski, owner and barkeep, had moved to Door County from Chicago in his thirties. Now nearing seventy, he was still an imposing man, with a shock of white hair. He still carried himself like the wrestler he once was.

The only clue that the peeling clapboard building was a bar and not an abandoned farmhouse, which it once was, were the neon beer sign in the window and the assortment of aging pickup trucks and cars parked in the grassy lot out front. The first time I went there, Jake had to vouch for me before Hal would serve me. One night I'd witnessed Hal refuse to serve some rowdy tourists who'd stumbled upon his place, claiming the locals in the bar were having a private meeting. He was probably breaking some law, but since the police frequented the tavern, everyone turned a blind eye.

It was past one in the morning, most of the tables were full, and the jukebox was playing "I Go to Pieces" by Patsy Kline. I went to the bar and was waiting for my white wine when I spotted Nina sitting in the last booth near the restrooms, her back to me.

"I told your friend there to take the back booth," Hal said as he put the wine glass down on the bar. "Want me to start you a tab?"

In answer I gave him a ten, told him to keep the change and hobbled to the back booth. "I wasn't sure you'd come," I said, sliding into the booth.

"I almost didn't," Nina answered. On the table were an empty tumbler of what smelled like whiskey, another full one in front of her, and a shredded napkin. Gone were her lighthearted hippy clothes. She wore a black hoodie, white t-shirt and jeans. I waited for her to continue. "Before I say anything, you have to tell me something first."

"Depends on what it is."

"How did you know I accused Nate of killing Danielle?"

There were two ways I could play this: tell her the truth and expose Bob, or lie. I opted to lie. "I heard you. I was there that night in the woods."

She thought about that for a minute, her fingers pulling at her curls. Then she said, "What else did you hear?"

"I answered your question. Now answer mine. What do you know about Danielle Moyer's death?" I soft-balled the question, omitting the Nate-killed-her part, so she could tell me in her own way.

"Aren't you even a little curious why I agreed to meet you? After all, it's your word against mine."

I had wondered. It *was* her word against mine. "Damage control?" I suggested. "You're going to tell me that you didn't say that. That I misheard. That your words were taken out of context. Or, as you said, you might deny the whole thing."

"I thought about saying all of those things. But—and it's a big but—I'm not going to do that. I'm going to tell you the truth. Here's the deal." She looked over both shoulders, which seemed a bit dramatic, since no one was paying the least attention to us. And the jukebox was blaring a Johnny Cash melody that drowned out our conversation. "Nothing goes in that article, get it?"

"I can't promise that."

She started to get up.

"Okay, nothing goes in the article," I agreed, not promising it wouldn't go in a different article. "Now what about Danielle Moyer?"

She laughed and shook her head. "Poor deluded Danielle. That naive girl honestly believed Nate would leave me for her. She was just the first in a long line of girls who fell for his crap. But then, I don't have to tell you about him, do I?"

I let that pass. I wasn't going to be sidetracked. "But you weren't married to Nate when Danielle disappeared. In fact, you hadn't even met him yet."

"She didn't disappear. I mean, sure, she didn't tell anyone

when she left here. Not anyone but Nate, that is. But she didn't disappear. She went to Hollywood, thinking she'd break into the movies."

"Then why all the secrecy? Why didn't she tell her parents?"

"Beats me. She was always an odd one. It pains me to say this, but she really was talented and beautiful. But some insecurity held her back."

"And Nate?"

"He finished his season with the BT, went to Hollywood, resumed his relationship with her and became a big movie star."

"Then why did you say he killed her?"

"Because he did, indirectly. After he married me, he didn't end it with her. I didn't find out about it until later when the shit hit the fan, that he'd set her up in an apartment, their own private love shack." Her words were bitter and angry.

"So she was his mistress and you knew nothing about it?"

"Stupid, right? I was so in love with him then. I never suspected a thing, and I probably would never have found out if it hadn't been for what she did."

She was breathing hard and turning her glass around and around, the whiskey sloshing out, making wet circles on the table.

"What did she do?" I asked, sensing a shift in her. That hard edge was gone, and in its place was a crushing vulnerability. She seemed to shrink into herself.

She stopped turning her glass and looked up at me. "Have you ever been hurt, really hurt, by someone you loved and trusted? Someone you'd given your whole self to?" Her protective wall was down. The question was sincere.

"Yes," was all I said, forcing myself not to think about Tom and all the promise I'd poured into our marriage, and how I'd failed miserably.

She shook her head knowingly. "It sucks, doesn't it? Makes

you do crazy things you'd never normally do. But you want to know about her." She bit her lower lip. "Here's the short version. She got fed up with waiting for Nate to leave me, took off in the middle of the night, just like before. She left no note, didn't take any belongings, she just disappeared. But she made one mistake, and it cost her." She was talking fast, as if she needed to be done with it. "Where she was headed, no idea. But she decided to hitchhike, got into some lowlife's car. He raped her and left her for dead by the side of the road in the California desert."

"How do you know all this?" The story was too awful to have been concocted.

"She called me and asked for my help. Told me everything. She begged me not to tell Nate. Why, I don't know. Maybe she was ashamed." Her voice faltered. "I helped, all right. I paid all her hospital bills, wired her some money and told her to never call me again."

"So she, what? Disappeared again?"

Nina let out a loud sigh. "She disappeared, all right. About a week after she left the hospital, she slashed her wrists in some seedy desert motel in Darwin, California. The only reason the police called me was they found my phone number in her things." She swiped at her tears with the back of her hand. "And you know what I did to protect Nate?"

"What did you do, Nina?" I was almost afraid to hear the rest of her story.

"You have to understand. Nate had just starred in his first major feature film. Things were happening for him. We—I—couldn't afford for any of this to come out. And really, what would be gained by telling her family how she'd ended her life?"

"They'd at least have closure," I answered.

"Closure is highly overrated. Believe me, I know. So I told

the cops she was a distant cousin with no family except me. She'd been using an alias, Olivia Williams. So no problem there. I paid for her burial, and I got on with my life."

"Did you tell Nate?"

"Not until the next girl. The news stopped him in his tracks. Of course, it all but ended our marriage. But not before he knocked me around a few times. But hey, I had it coming. According to Nate, I'd helped destroy the love of his life." Her mouth was a tight, bitter line.

"Then why did he marry you if Danielle was the love of his life?"

"How fleeting is fame," she said sarcastically. "I guess you don't remember that Nate and I were the 'it' couple that year?" She put air quotes around *it*. "I'd managed to take my success with the TV sitcom *Girl Town* and land a string of mediocre light comedy parts. Nate was the hot new star. Danielle's sad end would have been a scandal we wouldn't have recovered from. At least not easily."

"Celebrities have overcome worse things," I countered. "It was because you couldn't bear the embarrassment and the guilt."

She downed the rest of her drink and reached for her purse. "We're done here."

"So that's why you lured Nate to the cabin that night and planted the mannequin. You wanted to punish him." I wasn't finished.

She laughed hysterically. "Do you think I care anymore about him or Danielle or the other women? Besides, why would I jeopardize his donation by pissing him off? Nate was a means to an end for me. I wanted a new theater, and the least he could do was help me get it. In return, I'd convinced Alex to feature him in a few plays, so Nate could jump-start his career."

"Then why were you there?" I wanted to hear her explanation and judge whether what I suspected was true. That someone had lured both Nate and Nina to the cabin.

"Because I got a text asking me to meet him at the cabin. It was signed Nate and the ID read Private Caller."

I wasn't sure I believed her. Though in light of everything she'd told me about Danielle's death, why would she lie about this? "Do you think Nate sent the text?"

"No. He was as shocked as I was when he saw that grotesque thing hanging there."

If it wasn't Nate or Nina, then who'd sent those texts? "Did you ever tell anyone else besides Nate about Danielle's suicide?"

"No, of course not. I told you, I was protecting Nate."

"What about Nate? Do you think he might have told someone about Danielle's suicide?"

Her eyes shifted right, then left. "I don't know why he would. But he might have, maybe when he was out of his mind on drugs."

She rubbed at her forehead. "Listen, I'm tired and it's late." She grabbed her purse and slid out of the booth. "Remember, we have a deal. This goes no further." Her nervous wall was back up.

I stood up as well, wanting to be eye to eye with her, wincing as I put weight on my ankle. "Someone else already knows. Think about it. If you really didn't lure Nate to the cabin, and he didn't lure you, then whoever did it knows about Danielle's death and is seeking some kind of revenge. Why else plant the mannequin and the playbill?"

She leaned in close and whispered into my ear. "That's why I came here. I'm scared." Then she turned and walked out.

After she left, I went to the bar, ordered another white wine and sat in the booth nursing my drink.

If I believed Nina, the mystery of what happened to Danielle Moyer was solved. Tomorrow I'd follow up her story with a call to the Darwin police to verify. What I couldn't verify was whether Nina hadn't lured Nate to the cabin. Contrary to what she said, was she still seething with anger and hurt after all these years? Julian thought so.

Maybe she'd seen Nate leave with Lydia. After all, Bob had seen them leave together. Maybe that sent Nina over the edge and she wanted her pound of flesh. But there hadn't been enough time for her to arrange that horrid mannequin. And, as she said, why would she jeopardize Nate's donation as well as her inheritance?

And if it hadn't been Nina, then who? Other than Nate, the only person here who'd been a cast member the summer Danielle disappeared was Julian Finch. What had been his relationship with Danielle, a young, beautiful, talented actress who'd disappeared, only to reappear in Hollywood as Nate's girlfriend, then later his mistress? Did Julian know about Danielle's suicide? I'd have to recheck the dates, but I was pretty sure Julian's and Nate's paths had crossed early in Nate's film career, which would mean Julian might have been in Tinsel Town the same time as Danielle.

But something else I couldn't remember was buzzing around in the back of my brain like an illusive fly. I closed my eyes, as if that could make me remember. Nothing. Then I opened them and gazed down at my watch. It was almost two o'clock, and I was finally tired.

Chapter Thirty-Seven: SUNDAY, JULY 23

When I stumbled into the kitchen to make coffee, Bob was still curled up on the sofa under a brown faux fur throw, his bare feet sticking out. To my relief, I'd found him asleep on the sofa when I got home in the wee hours.

Oh, the untroubled sleep of the young, I thought, trying not to wake him as I ran water into the coffee pot. As exhausted as I'd been, my sleep had been sketchy and filled with disturbing dreams of the Moyer cabin in which the hanging mannequin came alive, her icy blue eyes staring, her finger pointing at me in accusation.

Bob's head popped up and he mumbled, "What's going on?"

I shut off the tap and asked, "How'd you sleep?"

He scratched at his head. "Sofa beats sleeping bag any day. It's nine o clock already," he said, staring at the kitchen clock. "Man, I must have been racked out. I didn't even hear you come in."

I wasn't used to chitchat before coffee, but I shook off my usual grumpiness. The sight of Bob's soft doughy face and unruly hair was just too puppy-like, and I was missing Salinger, who was enjoying her African Safari room at the Pet Adventure Hotel where I'd boarded her for the weekend.

"When did you get here? I came by after the play, and you weren't in the apartment."

"I don't know. It was dark. But nobody saw me. If that's what you're worried about," he answered petulantly.

"And you didn't go anywhere else?"

"Geez, what's with the third degree?" He wrapped the throw around his shoulders, looking hurt.

"When I didn't find you here, I went by the cabin. And you weren't there either." I rested the heavy coffee pot in the sink, standing on my right foot to take the pressure off my aching ankle.

"Why are you up in my grill this morning?"

"You have to be careful," I said sternly.

"Yeah, I get it."

I doubted that he got it. "Did you take the mannequin from the cabin?"

He put his head down. "She was creeping me out. After you left, I dragged her into the woods and sat her under a tree." He grinned up at me.

As I poured the water into the coffee maker, I wondered if Bob's impulsive, goofy nature would plague him his entire life. Would he become another Rich, whose sway he'd fallen under? Would he, too, turn his back on his potential and eventually morph into a social misfit? Alex had to take him back. After the weekend was over, I'll go to Alex and vouch for Bob, plead his case. Or better yet, I'll have Jake work his magic on Alex.

"Did you find anything out about Danielle Moyer?" he asked.

I put the pot on the heating element, flipped the on switch, and turned around, taking in his open, earnest expression. Should I tell him? I did promise him I'd look into it. "I know what happened to her," I began.

He jumped up from the sofa as if I'd doused him with cold water and came into the kitchen area. "No way." He'd slept in the same t-shirt and jeans he'd been wearing yesterday. And from the musky odor he was emitting, he hadn't taken a shower, but had just collapsed on the sofa and fallen asleep.

"Way." I couldn't help myself.

I'd only agreed not to print anything in the BT article, so I gave Bob the factual version of Danielle's sad and tragic life, leaving out Nina's attempts to absolve herself of blame. When I finished, his mouth hung open and the coffee was ready.

"So," he said enthusiastically, "whoever planted that mannequin knew all this stuff about Danielle Moyer. That's why her name was circled on the cast list. But what I don't get is why? It's like what, thirty years ago she disappeared?"

I opened the cupboard looking for coffee cups. "Actually more like twenty-five years. You want coffee? Got some donuts too." I picked up the box to show him.

"Sure. Black's good. And I never say no to donuts."

I took out two cups, poured the coffee, and handed Bob a cup. Then I grabbed the package of donuts and my cup and hobbled over to the sofa.

"What's up with your foot?" Bob asked as he sat down beside me.

"Ankle," I responded. "I fell over a piece of wood inside the Moyer cabin last night when I was looking for you."

"I didn't leave it there," Bob said defensively.

"Have a donut," I said, opening the box and offering it to him. "Relax. I wasn't accusing you."

We sat silently sipping our coffee and munching on our donuts.

Suddenly, Bob burst out, "Ryan was murdered. It all makes sense. And it was because of Danielle Moyer."

I cocked my head at him quizzically. Not because the thought hadn't occurred to me, but because now I knew how I looked when I was making what the police and my friends considered wild accusations based on nothing but a gut feeling—dilated pupils, raised voice, a slight flushing of the face and a little spittle at the corner of the mouth. Not a pretty sight.

"What?" he asked. "You don't find it suspicious that he died after Nina and him had it out in the cabin? I mean, like the very next morning." He bit into another powdery donut.

"Coincidental—yes. Suspicious—maybe. We have to go by the facts." Did I really say that? I should be jumping at Bob's idea wholeheartedly. Here was a kindred spirit. What was holding me back?

"The medical examiner hasn't signed off on the cause of death yet. He's still waiting on the tox results." I wasn't going to tell him about the barbiturates in Ryan's system. "And until he does, the cause of death is undetermined. Lydia's convinced he had a heart attack. And she should know. She's a nurse."

"She was like in the middle of a life-and-death thing. She couldn't know for sure what was going on with him," he countered, sounding more and more reasonable. Maybe there was hope for Bob after all. Just point him in the right direction.

The nagging feeling that Lydia hadn't told me everything returned. I shifted uncomfortably, resting my left foot on the table to ease the throbbing in my ankle. "She's trained to deal with crises." I was purposely playing devil's advocate, wanting to see where Bob's leaps of imagination would take him.

"I give you that. But did you know that certain poisons can cause a heart attack and they're really hard to detect?"

"Now you're scaring me," I joked half-heartedly, thinking back to Nate's vomit. Poison might cause a person to vomit, but so might a heart attack. "How do you know that?"

"Rich and I were talking about that woman who killed her two husbands with antifreeze and how she almost got away with it."

"Antifreeze? How'd she get them to drink antifreeze?"

"Put it in their Gatorade and Jell-O, which masked the sweet taste of the antifreeze. But it couldn't have been antifreeze, because Ryan dropped dead suddenly and these dudes lingered, big time." He nodded his head, raising his eyebrows.

"Why were you and Rich talking about some woman killing her husbands with antifreeze?" I asked.

"Rich warned me not to let Dixie go near the theater garden because some of the plants are poisonous. Then he kids me about how I should poison Alex with one of the plants. He says no one would know, 'cause it would look like a heart attack. After that he starts telling me about this woman who almost got away with murder."

"I'll look into it," I said to appease him. The last person I wanted to talk to was Rich. Even if Rich was joking, his bragging about heart-attack-mimicking plants was downright disturbing. "Right now we have to go with what we know, which isn't much." I sounded like the university instructor I used to be.

Bob looked crestfallen. "Yeah, you're probably right."

I didn't want to encourage Bob. But I'd research poisons that mimic heart attacks, then see if any of those plants were in the theater garden. "I still have to call California today to verify Nina's story. I also need to recheck the dates Julian was in Hollywood."

"What's Julian got to do with this?" Bob was blowing on his coffee and then taking loud slurps. Powdered sugar ringed his upper lip from the two donuts he'd inhaled.

"Maybe nothing. How about I drive you to Green Bay this morning, and you can catch a bus home to Milwaukee?"

"Aw c'mon, Leigh," he begged, his brown puppy eyes full of youthful petition. "What's one more day? You're taking off tomorrow, right? You can drive me to Green Bay then."

Driving Bob round trip to Green Bay would take four hours out of my last day with the BT, four hours I could use soaking up BT ambiance. On the other hand, I didn't trust Bob to stay in the apartment unless I was around, and I didn't have time to babysit him.

"Enough with the droopy eyes. Here's the deal. You can't leave the apartment. Promise me."

"What am I going to do here all day?" He pouted like a petulant two-year-old.

I picked up the TV remote from the coffee table and clicked the power button. MTV blared a rap song. "There's TV. Or here's a novel idea: read a book." I leaned over and grabbed a mystery novel, P. D. James's *Devices and Desires,* from my backpack and shoved it at him.

He turned the book in his hand as if it were contaminated. "Where are you going to be?"

"Doing my job, and in case you get any crazy ideas about taking off, I'll be coming by every so often, and you'd better be here."

"You're not my mom, you know." He scowled at me.

"Wouldn't wish that on my worst enemy," I retorted.

He pushed his glasses up his nose. "Yeah, well, whatever."

CHAPTER THIRTY-EIGHT

After I showered and made Bob swear again that he wouldn't leave the apartment, I drove to the Egg Harbor Library and searched the Internet for information about Julian Finch's brief sojourn in Hollywood. As I suspected, he'd been in Hollywood the same time as Danielle. Proving nothing except that their paths could have crossed. Would Danielle Moyer have reached out to him when her life spiraled out of control, or would she have been too humiliated? I didn't even know the tenor of their relationship, which could have been strictly professional.

Before logging off, I Googled poisons that mimic a heart attack. Though I had no concrete evidence Ryan had been murdered, I was intrigued by Bob's idea. There was a healthy list of poisons, some of which I could summarily dismiss either because the poison took too long for symptoms to appear or the symptoms didn't match Ryan's or the poison was so exotic, like a puffer fish extract, it was too difficult to obtain.

There were several poisons that fit the bill, mostly plant-based poisons. I jotted down their names. Even though the medical examiner was running more sophisticated tox tests that would most likely detect the presence of poison, I'd have to cross-check the theater's garden plants against the plant-based contenders later, if for nothing else than to satisfy my curiosity.

A drop of sweat rolled off my nose and plopped on my notebook. I rubbed at it, smearing the word *moonflowers*, one of the poisonous plants. What was I doing?

Other than learning the fate of Danielle Moyer, I was no closer to finding Lydia's attacker or knowing whether Ryan had been murdered. Poisonous plants, a celebrity's sudden death—this wasn't a Shakespearian tragedy.

I grabbed a tissue from my bag and wiped my forehead before phoning Darwin, California. After being shuttled around, I finally reached someone who was able to confirm the details of Danielle Moyer's, aka Olivia Williams's, death. Nina had told the truth.

As I went over my notes about Danielle's suicide, it hit me, what had been buzzing around at the back of my brain last night. Harper Kennedy. She'd told me during our interview that Danielle had committed suicide. And when I'd questioned her about the suicide, she'd said something like "What else could have happened?"

I bounced my pen on my chin, lost in speculation. Had Harper made a lucky guess about Danielle's suicide, or did she know about it?

Paging through my notebook, I located the interview with Harper Kennedy. She'd grown up in Peru, Illinois. I Googled the Peru County Sheriff's Office phone number and called it.

I explained to Officer Boden that I was doing fact-checking for an article on the BT actors, and that Harper told me she'd been arrested protesting the incinerator. I'd also assured him that whatever he said wouldn't go in the article.

To my surprise, Officer Boden was more than happy to help a small-town journalist, giving me the details of Harper's arrest. She hadn't been arrested protesting the building of an incinerator as she'd said. Harper had been arrested for selling drugs on the street. She'd pled guilty, and because it was her first offense did community service in lieu of jail time. She was eighteen years old at the time.

"I remember her," Officer Boden said. "Nice enough girl.

Just got messed up with a bunch of dirt bags. Glad to hear that she's turned her life around."

"And what was her community service?"

"Volunteering with the local Boys and Girls Club."

It would have been the last place I'd send a young drug-dealing offender.

CHAPTER THIRTY-NINE

The musky scent of perfume hit me as Harper opened her apartment door. I'd bought an elastic wrap for my ankle and two turkey sandwiches at the Egg Harbor Market, gave one sandwich to Bob, stowed the other in the fridge, and dashed over to Harper's apartment, trying to catch her before rehearsal started.

"I was just on my way out," she said, not moving to let me in. "Rehearsal's in ten minutes." She was wearing a skimpy pink V-neck t-shirt, bare midriff, skinny black bra straps showing, and white shorts, also tight and skimpy.

"This'll only take a minute. Can I come in?"

She let out a deep sigh and gestured me inside. "Can't this wait until after rehearsal? You know how Alex is."

"Just two questions, and I'm gone."

I opened my notebook to her interview just in case she challenged me on what she'd said. "Harper, why did you lie about your arrest? You weren't arrested for a protest. You were arrested for selling drugs."

Instead of being embarrassed, she rolled her eyes and shook her head. "What's the big whoop? That's all in the past. I did my community service. I didn't tell you because I was afraid you'd make a big deal out of it. And look, you're here, making a big deal out it." She stood in the middle of the room, her hands on her tiny hips, her perky breasts thrust out. "I suppose now you'll put that in your article. Well, go ahead. I was a dumb kid.

I'm not that person anymore. Is that all you want, 'cause I have to go."

"Just one more thing. Why did you say that Danielle Moyer committed suicide?"

"What's with you, anyway? Danielle Moyer? I don't get why you're harping on about her. Again, old news. She disappeared, she committed suicide, who knows?"

"Did someone tell you she committed suicide?" I pressured.

She rolled her eyes again. "Julian might have mentioned it. Now I really have to go."

Not waiting for me to leave, she whipped past me, leaving a musky trail behind her. The door was open, and I should have followed her out. Instead, I thought about what she'd told me. If she was telling the truth, Julian knew about the suicide. But she'd already proven herself a liar.

I glanced around the messy apartment, clothes over chairs, shoes on the floor, an ashtray loaded with cigarette butts (Nina's?), dirty glasses and dishes piled up in the sink and on the counter top. She wouldn't even notice my rummaging around. And she hadn't asked me to leave.

I went to the door and shut it. I don't know what I expected to find, but I didn't trust Harper, and this was too opportune to pass up.

Gwen's warning came back to me. "Don't be fooled by her innocent act. She's a barracuda." And a liar and a former drug dealer.

As I searched the apartment, it was obvious Harper never hung anything up or put anything away, and only cleaned when she ran out of things. On the coffee table under a stack of playbooks was the *PopQ* issue featuring Nate Ryan's death. There was a glass ring stain over Lydia's photo. The bedroom and bathroom were just as messy. I'm no Susie homemaker, but Harper's apartment made me look like a domestic goddess.

Though she was spending the entire summer/fall season with the BT, her two suitcases were still open on the bedroom floor, shoved against the wall as if she was ready to bolt at any moment.

When I returned to the kitchen, I started going through the cupboards, finding the usual dishware sets and glasses, a box of gourmet crackers, assorted cereal boxes.

The cupboard over the fridge required a chair. I grabbed the desk chair from the living room, stood on it and peeked inside the cupboard. Something was shoved near the back. I reached inside and grabbed what felt like the neck of a bottle. As I pulled it out, I swallowed hard, staring in amazement—distinctive red bottle, white label with a cluster of cherries below the name Sweet Cherry Winery. I'd found a bottle of sweet cherry wine stashed in Harper's cupboard. What was that doing here?

Don't jump to conclusions, I cautioned myself. So there's a bottle of sweet cherry wine shoved in the back of a cupboard. It could have been there for years, maybe forgotten or left behind for the next actor. And over the years no one had claimed it. Didn't Steve, the retired car designer from the winery tour, say people liked to keep a bottle around as a souvenir? Those old bottles turned up everywhere.

But as I studied the bottle, I wondered about the coincidence, Ken's words playing back to me. "Brownie would have never drunk cherry wine." And yet, there had been two spent bottles of cherry wine beside Brownie's dead body.

"What the hell are you doing?"

I jumped, nearly dropping the bottle of wine as I turned toward the angry, accusatory voice. I'd been so engrossed in my thoughts I hadn't heard the door open.

Barbara Henry was glaring up at me. Her ample bosom puffed out in indignation. She wore one of her voluminous sundresses. This one was splattered with large blue and yellow flowers.

"Getting a bottle of wine," I said, concealing the wine's label as I stepped down from the chair. Maybe I'd look less guilty if I stated the obvious.

"Does Harper know you're in here?"

"How else would I know where the wine was?" I answered nonchalantly, though my heart was racing.

For a minute she mulled over my explanation. Then she said, "I don't know what you're doing in here. But I'm telling Alex." She paused. "And Harper."

"Why are you making such a big deal out of this? Harper knows I'm here." I started for the door, cradling the bottle to my chest.

"And leave the bottle." She held out her hand.

"It's not even drinkable," I said, reluctantly giving her the bottle.

"Then why do you want it?"

When I opened my apartment door, Bob was munching on his sandwich, engrossed in *Devices and Desires*. He looked up. "What? I'm here, haven't moved since you left thirty minutes ago."

Ignoring his taunt, I went to the desk and picked up the fiftieth anniversary booklet. There was nothing I could do about tattletale Barbara. If Alex asked me to leave, I'd leave. But until he did, I was going to continue my investigation.

"Scrunch over," I said, sitting down next to him. I opened to the page containing the photo of Julian and Danielle from *Twelfth Night* 1988. "Take a look at this."

He put the book down on the side table and peered over at the photo. "So, they were in the play together."

"Look at it closely. What do you see in their body language?"

Something about the photo had stuck with me, and I wanted another opinion to see if I was right.

Bob studied the photo. "You mean the way Finch has his arms around her like he's doing her? I'd definitely hit that."

"Yes," I said, exasperated. "And what about her?"

"What? She's smiling. She looks happy."

"Right. Now look at this." I pointed to the cast list for *A Streetcar Named Desire*. "Nate, Julian and Danielle appeared in *Streetcar*." Then I pointed back at the cast list for *Twelfth Night*. "Nate had a minor role in that play. *Twelfth Night* ran mid-season. And *Streetcar* was the last play of the season. Nate must have joined the BT mid-season. And Danielle disappeared after *Streetcar*, at the end of the season."

I waited to see if Bob would come to the same conclusion I had. "So you're thinking Julian and Danielle had hooked up, then Nate comes along and she drops Julian and hooks up with Nate."

"It's a definite possibility."

"I wouldn't go by that picture. They're actors. Someone probably told them to look like they're doing it to sell tickets."

Bob made a good point. I closed the book and got up, though not ready to concede my supposition. "But Julian knew about Danielle's suicide if I believe Harper. And he was in Hollywood the same time as Danielle and Nate. Maybe Danielle reached out to Julian for help. And maybe he still had feelings for her. And . . ." I paused, not sure where I was going with this.

"Julian knew about Danielle's suicide? How'd you find that out?" Bob questioned, taking another bite of his sandwich.

"Harper told me. But she's already lied to me once. So I'm not sure I believe her."

He munched on his sandwich, considering what I'd proposed. "I don't get where you're going with this," Bob said.

Where was I going? "Still putting the pieces together."

"Aw, c'mon Leigh, I'm not going to do anything. You can tell me."

I shook my head. "Nothing to tell yet, just a lot of speculation. But you'll be the first to know." I went into the kitchen, opened the fridge and took out my sandwich. "Gotta run. And remember, stay put."

I didn't wait for his reply, but limped down the walkway and the stairs and over to the rehearsal building area. Sequestered under a shady cedar, I found one of the green canvas chairs, sat and ate my sandwich.

"Hey, Leigh."

Did this guy have a GPS device set on me? I wondered as I took another bite and accidentally bit the inside of my cheek as well.

"Mind if I join you?" Rich asked. Dixie was with him. She jumped up and sniffed my sandwich.

I tore off a small piece of turkey and gave it to Dixie. "Free country," I retorted.

"Still mad, huh?"

I didn't answer, just kept chewing and looking out toward the water. I could ask him the names of the poisonous plants in the BT garden. But the question might lead back to Bob, so I didn't.

He stood there, running his fingers over his balding head as if searching for his missing hair. I could feel his intense stare.

"You're wrong about me. You'll see." And then he was gone, Dixie trailing behind him.

I didn't like his "You'll see." The words were harmless, but his tone threatening. But I wasn't going to hide from him anymore. Tomorrow I'd be outta here. Hopefully that would put an end to his unwanted attention. If not, that's what restraining orders were for.

After about an hour, the cast and crew emerged from the rehearsal building. Julian was out the door first, walking fast in the direction of the quad apartments. I didn't see Alex or his henchwoman Barbara.

"Julian," I called after him, running to catch up, my ankle protesting in pain.

He stopped and turned around, smiling. "Leigh. I've been meaning to come by and see how you are settling in. Anything you need from me, just ask."

Julian should be the PR director, I thought, gazing up into his warm and inviting face.

"There is something."

"Walk with me. I've only fifteen minutes."

He was practically trotting. I quickened my pace, trying not to put too much weight on my ankle.

"You're limping. What happened?"

"Nothing, just clumsy."

"I'll slow down. So what do you need?"

"You remember Danielle Moyer?" My intention was to start easy, earn trust, then go in for the kill.

"Of course. I acted with her in several plays. But that was a long time ago."

"Right, I saw that in the fiftieth anniversary booklet. It seems she disappeared after the production of *A Streetcar Named Desire*. Do you have any idea why she did that?"

We'd reached the flagstone steps leading up to the apartments. He stopped. "I always wondered. One day she was there and the next, it was like she vanished into thin air. Her parents were never the same after that. It killed them."

Was he lying? He seemed so sincere. "Well, here's the thing. Harper told me Danielle committed suicide in California. Danielle went there to be with Nate. But it didn't work out." I paused, letting that information sink in, studying his reaction— head tilted in surprise, a quizzical look. "And Harper said you told her about Danielle's suicide."

He smiled, then chuckled, shaking his handsome head. "Dear sweet Harper. I don't know where she got her information, but it wasn't from me. I never knew what happened to Danielle."

"But you were in love with her?" It was an outrageous question to ask him, but I had to ask it. I had to see if there was any validity in my interpretation of that 1988 photograph.

Unexpectedly he put his hands on my shoulders as if he had to steady me. "Actors fall in and out of love from play to play. We had a brief fling, and then it was over. So are we good?"

"Sure." There was nothing else to ask him.

He started up the flagstone steps, then turned back. "Everyone's heading over to Serenity House after the play tonight. Why don't you join us? It's your last night with us, and Matt's threatening to sing show tunes."

"Wouldn't miss it."

CHAPTER FORTY

"Julian denied knowing anything about Danielle's disappearance," I complained to Bob, who was throwing a ball against the back wall, clearly bored out of his mind. "And stop that. Someone might hear."

"They'll think it's you."

"Where did you get that ball?"

He stopped throwing and gave the ball a few quick squeezes. "Stress ball. I take it with me everywhere. College students get stressed too, you know."

He cocked back his arm, but before he released the ball, I grabbed it from his hand and shoved it in my pocket. "I should have your stress."

"Hey," Bob protested, staring at my bulging pocket. "Anyway, I've been thinking about Julian and this Danielle babe, and you're dead wrong. If anyone's lying, it's Harper. She's a real player, if you know what I mean." His pale eyebrows went up and down luridly. "Julian, he's an old-timer and, well, he's kinda like been a regular for the past four seasons. And I gotta tell you, of all the actors, he's the best. Always asks me how I'm doing, stuff like that. He even went to bat for me with Alex. Rich thinks he's a good guy too. And Rich ought to know."

I cringed at the mention of Rich's name. "You put way too much faith in Rich's opinion."

"I don't see why you're so down on Rich," Bob continued. "He's been looking out for you."

"Looking out, how?" I didn't like the sound of that.

Bob shrugged. "I don't know. It's just something Rich would do." He picked up the mystery book and started reading it, dodging my question.

He was lying, and not just about Rich's so-called "looking out for me." From the onset, when Rich showed me Bob's text message, I'd been suspicious. I stared at Bob as he read. He didn't look up from the book, but he must have felt my stare, because a slow flush traveled up his neck to his face.

"Rich contacted you, didn't he? That's how you found out about Lydia's attack. He asked you to come back here." It was all starting to make sense.

Bob tossed the book on the coffee table, got up from the sofa and moved to the door.

"He was bringing you food to the cabin, wasn't he? I wondered how you were eating. But why involve me?"

Bob had his back to the door, one hand in his pocket, the other on the doorknob, looking like he was ready to run. "I never left," he whispered the words. "It was only after your friend Lydia was attacked that we decided to involve you. It was Rich's idea. He said you solved two murders last year."

Rather than scream at Bob for not telling me the truth from day one and push him into silence, I clamped down my temper. "There's no proof Nate Ryan was murdered, unless you know otherwise. And the only reason I got involved in the murders of those two young women was because I found the first victim." I was pacing back and forth, as if I could walk away that horrid memory.

I finally stopped pacing and stood in front of Bob. "Your friend Rich is using you to get to me. He's been stalking me."

His eyes shifted right. "He wouldn't do that."

"Oh, wouldn't he?" I challenged, striding over to my tote bag and yanking out my notebook. I had to prove to Bob that Rich was dangerous. I leafed through the notebook until I located my interview with Rich. Bingo! Moonflowers were in the BT garden, just as I thought. Then I flipped forward to my notes on poisonous plants and read the toxic effects of moonflowers. I couldn't prove it but maybe the reason I'd gotten sick that day backstage wasn't because I hadn't eaten. Maybe it was because I'd inhaled Rich's bouquet of flowers. I distinctly remember the white flowers that looked like morning glories and their unpleasant sweet scent.

I went to Bob. "See this list of poisonous plants?" I rapped the paper. He was looking at me like I'd gone crazy. "Now look what it says about moonflowers. Even inhaling them may cause nausea and dizziness. Moonflowers are grown in the BT garden." Bob had the good sense not to say anything.

"And your friend Rich gave me a bouquet of flowers with moonflowers in it. And guess what? I got sick."

He sidestepped away from me. "He probably didn't know they'd make you sick."

"Then why did he warn you about not letting Dixie near the garden because some of the plants were poisonous? Oh, he knew."

Bob looked down. "Man, that doesn't sound like him."

"He knows you're here in my apartment, doesn't he?" Guilt was written all over Bob's face.

"Yeah, but I didn't know about the flowers. He shouldn't have done that."

I'd played right into Rich's hand. My reputation for rescuing strays had bitten me in the ass. "And the mannequin, did you do that?"

"No," he protested loudly. "I found it in the cabin, just like I said, after Nate and Nina left. You don't think it was Rich, do you?"

That was exactly what I was thinking. What I still didn't

understand was, why have Bob lure me to the cabin?

"What were Rich's exact words when he told you to send that text to him about Danielle Moyer and the ghost?"

"He said he knew for a fact that Ryan was murdered and that you could get to the bottom of it."

"He doesn't know anything. If he did, he'd go to the cops. He used you, and he used me. He's playing some psychotic game."

Bob was shaking his head. "He's not like that. He isn't. You got him all wrong."

I'd failed to convince him, and I was hopping mad. "Look, if he shows up here tonight while I'm gone, do not tell him I'm on to him. If you do, I'm personally calling your parents and telling them where you've been all this time."

"I'm not that good a liar."

"You've been pretty good so far."

CHAPTER FORTY-ONE

Maybe it was the maximum-strength analgesics or maybe it was the nearly three hours of sitting and watching *The Importance of Being Earnest*, but my ankle was pain free, so I decided to take the shoreline trail to Serenity House rather than drive. I needed the time to think. My conversation with Bob was weighing on my mind.

Before leaving the grounds, I strolled by the beer garden to check on Rich's whereabouts. I didn't need him "looking out for me" by following me down the trail.

He was busy serving customers and didn't even notice when I walked past. The picnic area was crowded with playgoers, some standing, some sitting on the green canvas chairs, drinking and chatting. Their voices sounded disembodied under the twinkling fairy lights, which cast shadows, as if this was all a dream no one wanted to wake from. I found a chair and sat for a moment, savoring the enchantment. This was no *Midsummer's Night Dream*, but if I closed my eyes, it could be. Then I spotted Nina and Julian emerge from the back of the theater, and the enchantment was broken. I stood up and started toward the shoreline trail.

As I walked, I gazed out over the water and watched the scuttling clouds move fast across the night sky. The wind was picking up, and waves were rolling and crashing against the rocky shore in a loud crescendo. Everything was in flux.

Had Nate been murdered? And if so, by whom? The bloody

mannequin with the playbill around its neck was meant as a warning. Whether to Nate or Nina, I wasn't sure. But the message was clear—the past had come back to haunt them. Danielle Moyer's bitter end would be avenged. But had revenge led to murder? Rich thought so, if Bob was to be believed—if Rich was to be believed.

My ankle was starting to ache again. I should have worn the elastic ankle wrap instead of stowing it in my bag. The walking had agitated it.

Rounding the trail, I spotted the bench marking the path to the Moyer cabin, a welcome sight. When I reached the bench, I plopped down, retrieved the elastic wrap from my bag, slipped off my sandal and pulled the wrap over my ankle. It was so swollen, I had a hard time getting my sandal back on. But after some maneuvering and moaning, I got my foot in the sandal. Then I unzipped the bag's inner compartment and retrieved two more analgesics from my pillbox and dry-swallowed them one at a time.

Carefully I stood, a swirl of warm wind lifting my hair, and tested my ankle. Even with the wrap, it throbbed painfully. Okay, change of plans. I'd hobble back to the theater grounds, retrieve my truck from the back lot and drive to Serenity House. I'd only come about a quarter of the way, so I had ample time.

I stepped back on the trail and started walking cautiously, trying not to put too much weight on my left foot. Then I stopped. Had I heard something? The waves were thundering on the rocks so loudly, it was hard to tell. I started to turn around, but never made it.

An arm clamped tight around my neck, my left arm pinned, rendering it useless, as I was dragged into the woods.

Screaming, I clawed frantically at his arm, but the more I clawed, the tighter his hold got. I could feel myself slipping away. *If you lose consciousness, you'll die. Fight.* I dug my heels into the hard ground as the woods closed in above me like some final curtain. He shook me and pressed harder against my throat. I looked up at the trees as they started to blur, as if pleading with them for help. I realized, as I slipped into blackness, that I'd made a fatal mistake. One I wouldn't live to regret.

The darkness was absolute and cold. I blinked my eyes several times, afraid that death was black and endless, a place of both darkness and awareness—the worst kind of afterlife. But then I heard pounding, loud, hurried, insistent. I wasn't dead. I was alive. As I lay on my back in the dark, three things reached into my consciousness. There was a wood floor under me. I was inside the Moyer cabin. And I knew my attacker. The scent of anise, sandalwood soap and faint BO lingered on my skin.

Then the pounding stopped. I took in a deep breath, as if I hadn't been breathing for a long time. My throat hurt, my ankle was beyond pain and I heard footfalls, followed by branches being shoved against the house.

Though it would probably be useless to plead for my life, I had to try. I rolled over on my side, propped myself up, got to my feet and limped to the back door barefoot. During the attack as he'd pulled me into the woods, my sandals must have come off.

"Julian," I rasped, swallowing down the pain. "Julian," I called out again, this time louder.

All noise stopped, except his footsteps coming to the back door.

"Don't do this," I begged.

"How did you know it was me?" he asked, too calmly, as if we were discussing the weather and not my imminent death.

"I didn't. Not until now, when you attacked me." He must have leaned in to hear me because the tree branches he was holding scratched against the wood door like fingernails.

"You couldn't see my face. I was wearing a mask." Even whispering, his imperial voice boomed through the wood door, sending waves of dread through me. He sounded so reasonable, and that scared me.

"Not your face, your smell. Anise and sandalwood." I didn't add the faint BO. I was dealing with a psychotic narcissist who'd waited twenty-four years to avenge the suicide death of Danielle Moyer, the woman he'd believed belonged to him.

His laughter was so loud and deep, it startled me, and I pulled my head back from the door. "I really do like you, Leigh. You're always so . . . so surprising. That's why this pains me so much. But as Will Shakes says, 'The die is cast.' "

I had to get through to him. "You don't want to kill me. Think about it. You were justified in killing Nate Ryan. A jury would understand your motivation. If you kill me, there's no justification."

"Jury?" He chuckled sarcastically. "There's not going to be jury. I've been too careful. And once I get rid of you, I'm free. You have no idea how satisfying it was to kill Ryan. How I seethed with hatred over the years as I watched his career soar, knowing what he did to my beloved Danny. Then, when he crashed in flames, oh, what joy I felt. But he had to come back here, to my theater, to where he ruined Danny. He had to die."

"My death will haunt you," I said, aware of how fruitless my pleas were, but I wasn't giving up.

"I haven't lost any sleep over that homeless guy, so why should your death bother me? Ryan had to be punished. You two got in the way. Just like your friend the slut."

"You killed Brownie?" I asked, shocked. "Why?"

"He saw something he shouldn't have. Now I'm done with you and your questions."

"What did he see?"

"Have you prayed tonight, Leigh?" he asked menacingly. "I

promise it'll be quick. Just breathe in deeply, surrender and let the smoke work its magic."

"Julian, no! Please!" I cried. Then I heard the striking of a match, the crackling of burning wood, and his footsteps running away. Already smoke was seeping into every chink and cranny, the flames devouring the weathered log cabin. All that would be left when the fire was put out would be the stone chimney and my ashes.

Don't panic, I told myself. *You don't have much time before the smoke overcomes you.* All the exits were barred. But there had to be a way out. There just had to be. Then I heard the frantic scuttling of animals overhead. Was there an attic? I remembered a small window tucked under the roof's overhang. And if there was an attic, there should be a trap door to access it.

I grabbed a kitchen chair, dragged it to the hallway, and stood on it. I felt around the ceiling, running my hands up and down the bumpy plaster, the smoke rising around me. I tried not to inhale, but it was impossible. The air was thickening with smoke and heat, and trickles of sweat ran down my face and arms. Then I felt a knob. Without hesitation, I pulled hard on it and the door crashed down with a loud creaking, knocking me sideways off the chair and onto the floor. Choking, I put my hand over my mouth, jumped up, kicked the chair away and climbed the crude ladder into the attic, pulling up the door by the rope and shutting it behind me.

In the dark attic, I couldn't see the animals, only hear and smell them. Something brushed against my leg and scurried away. Then a loud fluttering of wings started, back and forth, hitting the attic walls over and over. The smell of ammonia assaulted me. Bats, wild with panic, were everywhere.

Stifling a scream, I took off my blouse and tied it over my head. I had to find a way out. The tiny attic window was still boarded, but it was outlined in light. I made my way toward its feeble glimmer, crawling on my hands and knees, searching as I went for anything that could pry the window free. Nothing. When I reached the window, I pushed on it, but it wouldn't budge. I kept pushing and pounding and finally gave up.

In my fury, I hadn't noticed that the fluttering had stopped. The bats were gone. Where did they go? My eyes roved the attic and there, high up in a corner, was a smoky oval of light I hadn't notice in my panic. I crawled to it. The bats must have flown in and out of the attic through this hole under the eave. It wasn't easily visible from the outside; it was barely visible on the inside. I pushed with all my force on the jagged hole, and it started to crumble away. I pushed again, enlarging it. Quickly I untied my blouse and put it back on, then I wedged myself through the opening and out onto the narrow ledge under the overhanging eave. I could see the flames were now up to the windows. The heat was intense.

I had only one option. Jump. *It's only one story,* I told myself. Not that high. But I'd have to jump out to avoid the encroaching fire. Quixotically, I flashed on my years of dance training, the brilliant height of grand jetés across a dance floor. The ledge wasn't long enough to get a running start, but the scissoring dance move might get me out and over the flames and ease my landing. "Remember to plié." The warning words came back to me.

I moved to the very end of the eave, took in a deep breath, swung my arms back and forth a few times and went for it. Run, run, leap and off. For a moment I was airborne, my legs scissoring in the air, and then I came down, landing in an awkward plié, my ankle erupting in a sharp pain as I rolled over onto my side. I was free of the burning cabin. I was alive.

Flames were licking up the sides of the cabin, sending smoke and embers into the night sky. I had to get out of here before the entire woods went up in flames.

I eased myself up on one foot, holding onto the nearest tree. Tentatively I put weight on my injured ankle. A burning pain shot through it, but the ankle held. I didn't think it was broken. I tested it again, then grabbed a nearby branch as a makeshift crutch and limped barefoot toward the rocky path.

Try as I might, it was impossible to hurry. The jagged rocks cut into my feet, and my makeshift crutch made for slow going. A million thoughts flew through my brain. My bag. I had to find it and call 9-1-1. I remember dropping it as Julian dragged me into the woods. Julian. Where was he? Still lurking in the woods to make sure I was dead? Or had he gone on to the party at Serenity House, his cool charm assumed, like all the roles he'd played, confident that the last loose end—me—was taken care of?

Just as I neared the shoreline trail, sirens cut through the night. I let out a deep sigh. It was going to be okay. The fire-fighters would douse the fire in time. I just had a few more steps. Suddenly, I saw a dark figure start down the path carrying something under his arm. I froze. As the figure came closer, I realized it wasn't Julian. The figure was too gangly and too bald. It was Rich and he had my bag tucked under his arm like a football.

"Leigh, are you hurt?" he asked.

"I've got to call the police." I took my bag from him, then moved around him and continued toward the shoreline trail.

"Wait." He was behind me. "Don't you want your sandals?"

I stopped. "Where are they?"

He took the bag from me and retrieved the sandals. Leaning against a tree, I struggled into the sandals, wincing in pain. "We've got to stop Julian," I demanded in a whispery voice as I continued down the path.

"Julian? What's Julian got to do with anything?"

As soon as we emerged onto the shoreline trail, I hurried to the bench, all thoughts of my throbbing ankle and cut feet gone. I flipped open my cell phone and dialed 9-1-1. When the dispatcher answered, barely taking a breath, I explained how Julian Finch had tried to kill me, his involvement in the deaths of Nate Ryan and Brownie Lawrence, emphasizing the importance of arresting Finch. Then I asked her to contact Deputy Chet Jorgensen. "And make sure you tell Chet to check Julian Finch's arm for scratch marks. I scratched him when I was fighting for my life."

"I'll see what I can do, ma'am." She was professional enough not to comment on my involvement in yet another murder case.

I closed the phone and shoved it in my bag, grabbed the branch and stood up shakily, nearing falling backward onto the bench. I waited a moment, then started down the trail.

"I knew you'd solve it," Rich said, walking slowly beside me. "How'd you figure out it was Julian? Why don't you lean on me?"

I could feel the adrenaline fading, a profound exhaustion overtaking me as the pain ratcheted up. Reluctantly, I let him put his arm around my waist and threw the branch away. I had no fight left in me.

"I didn't suspect him, not really. My focus was on Harper and Nina. Julian panicked. And if he'd killed me, he would have gotten away with it."

"And me," Rich added, stopping a moment.

"And you what?" Then I realized what he was saying. "Well, you were acting strangely."

His arm tightened around my waist, pulling me in too close.

"Listen, Romeo, don't push your luck," I said sharply.

He eased up on his grip. "I didn't want you to fall, that's all."

"Too late for that," I said, suddenly laughing hysterically in spite of myself.

"You okay?" he asked as I continued laughing.

"My ankle's messed up, I jumped off a one-story house, my windpipe was almost crushed and I was almost burned alive. Oh, I almost forgot the best part. My rescuer tries to cop a feel."

He started to say something, then stopped. I could feel his body stiffen. Then he began to shake with laughter. "Guilty as charged."

After that, the only sounds were the sirens growing louder, punctuated by the waves pounding the rocks as if they were beating them into submission.

When we reached the grounds, the fairy lights were out and the patio area was empty.

"You want me to drive you to the hospital to have someone look at your ankle?" he asked. "I promise, no monkey business." He put his hands up in mock surrender.

"That's what interns are for," I joked. "Bob can take me."

I started toward the apartment quad and stopped. "Did you tie Salinger up to the road sign?"

He nodded.

"And sneaking around my cabin at night, was that you too?"

"Someone had to look out for you," he said, crossing his arms defensively. "In my gut I knew Nate was murdered. And that it had something to do with Danielle Moyer."

"Because of the mannequin and the playbill," I said.

"Yeah, and what Bob told me about Nina accusing Nate of killing someone. That someone being Danielle. By then you were involved, and I felt responsible."

"You should have said something instead of sneaking around scaring me half to death," I chided him.

He chuckled. "C'mon. No way you would have let me keep an eye on you."

He was right. "Thanks anyway."

"Sure thing," he answered.

Getting up the apartment stairs drained the last of my energy.

As I opened the apartment door, I was surprised to see Bob slouched on the sofa, his feet on the coffee table, engrossed in a TV program. Hadn't he heard the sirens? I thought for sure he would have left to see what was going on.

"Didn't you hear the sirens?" I asked him, hopping to the sofa, then plopping down ungracefully.

He dragged his eyes away from the TV. "Yeah, I heard them. Watch this crazy dude on this reality show about exterminators. He's going into the barn. Biggest wasp nest I ever saw. And all he has is bug spray. Cool." He continued watching. Then suddenly he took a few quick sniffs. "Hey, you smell like smoke. Were you in a fire or something?"

"You could say that. How come you didn't go see what was going on outside?"

"Wow, there's no pleasing you. You said stay put, no matter what. So I stayed put."

I took the remote from the coffee table, turned off the TV and said, "We're going for a ride. Make sure you bring your driver's license."

"Where we going?"

"The hospital."

CHAPTER FORTY-TWO:
MONDAY, JULY 24

From behind the blue and pink striped curtain I heard raised voices and running feet.

"Possible overdose," a nurse said as she ran past my bay, where I was sequestered on a hospital bed in the ER. I was waiting for transport to radiology for an MRI to see if the tendon in my ankle was torn. The x-ray they'd taken showed no broken bones.

It was past one a.m. and after a cursory exam I'd been given a sedative, easing the chronic pain and allowing me to doze in a fitful sleep. Every so often, I jolted awake, flinging my arms around at imaginary bats, gasping for air. Relief flooded through me as I opened my eyes to the bright overhead fluorescents. I wasn't inside the darkness, dying. Smoke wasn't rising around me, filling my lungs. And bats weren't flying at me. I was in Bay Hospital. Safe.

I heard wheels traveling fast toward me. "I've got a pulse," someone said, "but it's weak." Then the commotion moved away and, down the hall, a door opened and shut, then the flickering quiet of the ER returned.

Suddenly, the curtain was pulled back and I let out a yelp.

"Sorry." Chet clutched his police hat in his hands, looking decidedly uncomfortable. "That was Finch they're working on. Overdose." He cocked his head toward the ER station. "How you doing there?"

"Nothing's broken, but the tendon in my ankle might be

torn. Finch overdosed?"

"Yeah. I should have seen that comin', when he started talking all crazy. Saying stuff like 'Don't let me be mad.' Then he runs off to the bathroom and locks the door."

"O, let me not be mad," I said.

"Something like that." He stared at me in confusion.

"It's from *King Lear*. You know. Shakespeare." I giggled. The sedative was making me wacky. "Is he gonna make it?" I asked, trying to control the hysteria bubbling up inside me.

He shook his head. "Don't know. He downed that there oxycontin before I could bust open the bathroom door. Dumb bastard."

"Where did this happen?" Maybe it was the sedative, but I was having trouble following Chet's story.

"Arrogant scumbag was at that cast party at that whatchamacallit house. I asked him to push up his shirtsleeve and just like you said, his arm was scratched up pretty good. That's when he hightails it to the bathroom, locks himself in and swallows them pills. He must have had them on him."

A sick thought came to me. With me out of the way, was he going to finish avenging Danielle's death by killing Nina?

"I showed the ER doc here the bottle. There were about twenty-one pills left. I counted them before I handed the bottle over. Now, here's the thing. Finch had a scrip for them pills all right. But it was for twenty pills. Considering he'd taken enough to cause him to black out, it's pretty clear-cut he was stockpiling them oxycontins. Soon as the final tox results on Ryan come in, we got our murderer. These killers always make a mistake."

Through my drugged haze, I realized what Chet was saying. "You knew all along Ryan died from an overdose of oxycontin, didn't you?"

Chet shrugged his massive shoulders. "Not for sure. And it might have been an accidental overdose. Not murder. We weren't sticking our necks out on this one. And I didn't need you"—he pointed his finger at my face—"mucking everything up. What with Ryan being this celebrity and all."

"Did Lydia know? Is that why she was so stressed out and wouldn't tell me anything? She told that *PopQ* guy Ryan died of a heart attack. She was so guilt-ridden."

"She suspected drugs were involved. I told her she couldn't say anything until we had the tox results. She understood."

"Finch must have thought she knew something, though. Why else would he try to kill her?"

Chet looked away.

"What aren't you telling me?" I pressed.

"No clue why that scumbag attacked Lydia. Now what's this about Finch and Brownie Lawrence?"

After I told him that Finch had confessed to killing Brownie, Chet scratched his head, perplexed. "You're gonna have to testify to that unless we can get a confession out of Finch. That is, if he lives."

"No problem. Now are you going to tell me what you're holding back? C'mon, Chet. I was almost killed. Don't you think I deserve to know the whole story? Lydia is my friend too."

He leaned down by my ear. "You didn't hear this from me." I felt the warmth of his breath oddly comforting. "Lydia admitted she and Ryan smoked a joint before that there class."

He stood up and arched his back. Now Lydia's guilt made sense. When Ryan collapsed, she was probably too out of it to react as she'd been trained. She blamed herself for his death.

"He would have died anyway. She couldn't have saved him," I said.

The ER doc came up behind Chet. "Can I see you a minute, Officer?"

Chet and the doctor stepped away. All I could hear was mumbling.

When Chet returned he said, "Looks like you're testifying."

"Finch died?"

"Yup. Doc couldn't resuscitate him. At least he saved the state the cost of a trial." Chet squeezed my shoulder reassuringly. "Need a ride home?"

"Thanks, no. My ride's out in the waiting room. What about Ken?"

"Soon as you're up to it, come by the station and give a formal statement. That'll get the ball rolling."

"I'll be by tomorrow."

"Now why did I know you'd say that?"

CHAPTER FORTY-THREE:
THREE MONTHS LATER

It was a windless sunny day, the October air crisp and clean. Bundled in sweaters, Lydia and I sat on the cabin's wood deck and listened to the crows cawing to each other. With every caw, Salinger growled but didn't run off. Attentive and loyal, she sat between us, giving what comfort she could. I was doing the same thing. I'd invited Lydia to stay with me until she was strong enough to resume her old life. When that would be was hard to tell.

"It's so . . . so . . . so . . . What's the word I want?" She stared off into the woods, her voice wistful.

I waited for her to remember. I'd been waiting a lot since she moved in here two weeks ago. "Don't rush her, don't finish her sentences," the physical therapist had advised me. "Let her find her own words in her own time."

"Peaceful, that's it. Peaceful."

Despite myself, I let out a sigh. "More wine?" I offered, raising the bottle. She was finally off the steroids and narcotics, and we were celebrating.

"Why not?"

I refreshed her glass and then mine.

"Is this the Reserve you bought from the winery?"

"Pretty good, huh?"

She tilted the glass back and forth several times, watching the wine coat the glass before she took a sip. "Yummy."

Yummy was something the old Lydia would have said. But I

knew the old Lydia was all but gone. I had only to look at the slight indentation in her skull, hear the hesitation in her speech.

"Chet told me Ken Albright's been cleared of all charges."

"Yeah, and he's decided to stay on at Marshalls Point after all."

"And Brownie's family? I can't remember. Did you find them?"

Over the months of her recovery, we'd avoided talking about the murders and her assault. I was waiting for her to bring it up when she was ready.

"Not his mother. She died about ten years ago. But I located Brownie's sister and told her everything. I wanted her to know that before he was murdered, he'd turned his life around."

The bitter irony of Brownie's death still haunted me. He'd survived Vietnam, a lifetime of substance abuse, had finally gotten his life back on track, and was murdered because he saw something he shouldn't have. Brownie had been collateral damage, and he didn't deserve that fate.

A blue jay let out a loud squawk as it landed in a nearby birch tree. We watched it hop from limb to limb, complaining, then finally settle on a high branch that shuddered under the jay's weight.

"And you didn't forget," I assured Lydia.

"You're a good friend," she said.

"Hardly," I scoffed.

"No, don't say that. That madman almost killed you too. I should have told you everything."

I waited.

"I did a bad thing," she continued. "No one knows about it. But I have to tell someone. It's been weighing on me."

"I can keep a secret," I assured her.

"I know you can. Well, here it is. After Nate and I had that joint—it's like yesterday. I can see him so clearly that morning.

Anyway, I thought the joint would calm him down. But it didn't. He asked me for a piece of paper and a pen. Then he made me witness what he wrote. I didn't want to. But I was high and not thinking straight. So I signed it."

"What did you sign?" She seemed to have lost her train of thought.

She turned toward me. Her eyes looked beseechingly into mine. "Nate revoked the donation to the Bayside Theater. I didn't want to sign it. But he was so insistent." Again, she trailed off.

"What happened to that paper?" I asked, thinking probably that's what Julian had been looking for in her studio the night he hit me over the head.

"I tore it up and flushed it down the toilet."

"When did you do that?"

"At Sarah's place. After I called 9-1-1, I took the paper and stuffed it in my yoga top. I knew Nate was already dead. And the BT needed a new theater. What difference did it make?"

Had Nate confided in Julian that he was going to withdraw the money? Was that why Julian had to kill him that morning? I'd never know. Just as I'd never know whether Julian's revenge included murdering Nina. Had Julian suspected Nate had written his wishes down and possibly told Lydia? Another unanswered question.

Lydia's hand was shaking so badly, she put her wine glass on the table. "Then later, I thought I might have done the wrong thing. But then it was too late to fix it."

"You did what you thought was right. Julian was bent on revenge. You were an innocent bystander."

"As were you," she said, touching the side of her head briefly.

"Ken Albright's been freed. You're getting stronger every day. There's no point in telling Chet about this."

Lydia smiled and touched my hand. "You're a good friend, Leigh."

"I'm working on it."

"So what did you decide? Are you buying the cabin?"

My settlement from the divorce was safely tucked away in my bank account, so I could afford to buy the cabin. But I was aching for something new, something that was mine alone, something I could build from the ground up.

"Still weighing my options."

Just then the blue jay darted low over our heads. I watched its brilliant blue body disappear like the last note of music echoing into silence.

ABOUT THE AUTHOR

Gail Lukasik was born in Cleveland, Ohio, and was a ballerina with the Cleveland Civic Ballet Company. Lisel Mueller described her book of poems, *Landscape Toward a Proper Silence,* as a "splendid collection." In 2002 she was awarded an Illinois Arts Council award for her work. She received her M.A. and Ph.D. from the University of Illinois at Chicago, where she taught writing and literature. She writes the Leigh Girard mystery series. *Kirkus Reviews* described her second Leigh Girard mystery, *Death's Door,* as "fast-paced and literate, with a strong protagonist and a puzzle that keeps you guessing." *Kirkus Reviews* called *The Lost Artist,* her first stand-alone mystery, "a highly intriguing tale loaded with suspense and historical interest."

DATE DUE